Praise for The Sewing Machine

'An extraordinarily accomplished and beautiful debut novel woven with historical detail.'
—Rachael Lucas, author of *Wildflower Bay*

'*The Sewing Machine* tenderly evokes the true value of the personal heritage we pass down, through generations and beyond families, with the objects that we love. Illuminating our shared history through the private histories of four remarkable women, this is a hopeful and poignant debut that lingers long after the final page.'
—Helen Sedgwick, author of *The Comet Seekers*

'Reflects the social attitudes of each generation she focuses on, and this venerable warhorse of a sewing machine witnesses the struggles that, from the factory worker of 1911 to the blogger of 2016, are essentially the same: work, bereavement, identity and the uncovering of family secrets. In a way that befits the subject matter, Fergie adroitly weaves it all together in a tapestry of strong characters and accomplished writing.'
Alastair Mabbot, *The Herald*

About the Author

Natalie Fergie is a textile enthusiast, and has spent the last ten years running a one-woman dyeing business, sending parcels of unique yarn and thread all over the world. Before this she had a career in nursing. She lives near Edinburgh.

The Singer 99K, which was the inspiration for this novel, has had at least four previous owners. It was bought for £20 from someone who lived in Clydebank, just a stone's throw from the site of the factory where it was made a hundred years earlier.

It's quite possible that there are another eight sewing machines in her house.

She blogs at www.nataliefergie.com and can be found on Twitter as @NatalieSFergie.

THE SEWING MACHINE

THE SEWING MACHINE

NATALIE FERGIE

This edition first published in 2017

Unbound

6th Floor Mutual House, 70 Conduit Street, London W1S 2GF

www.unbound.com

ISBN (eBook): 978-1-911586-24-1

ISBN (Paperback): 978-1-911586-04-3

Design by Mecob

Cover image:

©Shutterstock
©Textures.com

For Gavin

Super Patrons

Maureen Adam
Claire Askew
Sally Atkinson
Katrina Balmer
Susan Bromiley
Jenni Buhr
Rupert Bumfrey
Lucy Burns
Yvette Campbell
Hilary Campbell
Marianne Cant
Jay Carlyle
Andrea Carr
Ann Carrier
Lyndis Clarke
Heather Corbishley
Susan Crawford
Ingrid Curl
Yvonne Davies
Cinzia Discolo
Arianne Donoghue
Sheila Dunn
Moira Dunworth
Jan Eaton
James & Moira Fergie
Adam Fergie
Gavin Fergie
Patty Foggo
Janet Freeman
Sarah Gee
Kathleen Gibb
Katherine Grant
Mairead Hardy
Stefanie Hillen
Amelia Hodsdon
Duncan Hothersall
Wendy Hough

Nikola Howard
Karen Howlett
Fiona Hunter
Ruth Huskisson
Louiz Hutchings
Melinda Jackson
Rachel Jonat
Fran Kennedy
Dan Kieran
Ann Kingstone
Rachel Knight
Riki Kongtong
Mit Lahiri
Ann Leadbetter
Michelle Lincoln
Jane Lithgow
Susan Livingstone
Veronica Martin
Simon Mather
Julie Matthews
Clair McCowlen
Heather McDaid
Caroline Mersey
Deborah Metters
John Mitchinson
Charlotte Monckton
Marina Moskowitz
Shirley Muir
Fergus Muir
David Munday
Isobel Murdock
Nickerjac
Sakthi Norton
Mary Paulson-Ellis
Gillian Philip
Justin Pollard
Erica Preston
Nicky Prys-Jones
Fiona Pullen
Nurhanne Reckweg
Jennifer Romero

Robyn Roscoe
Helena Russell
Yuenwah San
Sarah Sandow
Margaret Scott
Susan Sharpe
Jill Shepherd
Madeleine Shepherd
Siobhan Shields
Suzie Shinnie
Deborah Skelton
Bekki Slowley
Ella Smith
Åsa Söderman
Annette Squire
Elizabeth Streeter
Elaine Sundstrem
Amy Taylor
Debbie Tomkies
Anna Trimmings
Caroline Turner
Maggie Vaughan
Karen Vernon-Parry
Julie Wade
Margaret Walker
Susan Walker
Christine Walton
Paula Waters
Helen Wherrett
Mary Whitehouse
Helen S Yewdall

With grateful thanks to Sarah Sandow

Dear Reader,

The book you are holding came about in a rather different way to most others. It was funded directly by readers through a new website: Unbound.

Unbound is the creation of three writers. We started the company because we believed there had to be a better deal for both writers and readers. On the Unbound website, authors share the ideas for the books they want to write directly with readers. If enough of you support the book by pledging for it in advance, we produce a beautifully bound special subscribers' edition and distribute a regular edition and e-book wherever books are sold, in shops and online.

This new way of publishing is actually a very old idea (Samuel Johnson funded his dictionary this way). We're just using the internet to build each writer a network of patrons. Here, at the back of this book, you'll find the names of all the people who made it happen.

Publishing in this way means readers are no longer just passive consumers of the books they buy, and authors are free to write the books they really want. They get a much fairer return too – half the profits their books generate, rather than a tiny percentage of the cover price.

If you're not yet a subscriber, we hope that you'll want to join our publishing revolution and have your name listed in one of our books in the future. To get you started, here is a £5 discount on your first pledge. Just visit unbound.com, make your pledge and type BOBBIN17 in the promo code box when you check out.

Thank you for your support,

Dan, Justin and John
Founders, Unbound

Apprentice

Summer 2010

Edinburgh

Secrets are hidden in the fabric and creases of the old hospital. They turn up on a daily basis, but their importance is not always recognised by those who discover them.

The joinery apprentice is tired and hungry. It's been hours since he ate his packed lunch – provided by his mother every day without fail – and he just wants to get home. Unfortunately, the foreman has other ideas and has been on his case all afternoon, giving him irritating bits and pieces of work to complete which amount to very little. The last task of the day is a perfect example of this and once again it means he is working on his own. When he thinks about all the people who died in this place it makes his skin wrinkle. He was born a stone's throw away in the Maternity Pavilion, one of the first buildings to be torn down, but feels no loyalty to it. The rest of the site is being repurposed, transforming it from a grand Victorian infirmary into an upmarket lifestyle location stuffed with photogenic cafés and shops, and with apartments he will never be able to afford without a serious win on the lottery.

The long medical wards overlooking the Meadows are being converted into flats, and glass-walled towers infill the spaces where once there were closely-mown lawns or, more recently, semi-permanent Portakabins for Clinical Chemistry and Medical Physics.

On Lauriston Place the stone buildings of the Surgical Hospital are empty. The blind-windowed turrets, which used to be home to bedpan washers and baths, are still infested with silverfish. Here, the planned renovations have barely started and the black-and-white chequered corridors are almost silent, no longer trafficked by trolleys and wheelchairs and the occasional high-tech bed with bleeping alarms and flurries of anxiety. The aromatic blend of morning porridge, disinfectant and visitors' flowers has been replaced by plaster dust, and essence of decaying pigeon.

In the former Orthopaedic ward, the smell is of old timber as the fittings are removed. The apprentice has been told to dismantle the small walk-in cupboard which once housed the ward telephone. It doesn't seem like a joinery job to him – it's more like demolition – but he doesn't question the instruction. One of the first things he learned in this trade, before anyone even showed him how to use a chisel, is that there is no merit in being a troublemaker.

On the soundproofed wall of the booth is a printed card, barely held in place by amber Sellotape.

FIRE 3333

CARDIAC ARREST 2222

He shivers at this brutal reminder of mortality.

Just below chest height is an empty shelf, strung with disconnected telecoms cabling. He bashes the wood from below with his fist. More dust. He should be wearing a regulation face mask but it's nearly knocking-off time and he can't be bothered to go and get a fresh one. He puts the curved claws of his hammer into a gap in the simple frame, which has held the shelf up for fifty years, and holds his breath as he levers it downwards.

The tongue-and-groove panelling creaks under his effort and then comes away suddenly, forcing him to take a step backward to evade the swords of splintering timber. He waits for any small, furry creatures to scurry away in search of a fresh hiding place. Goodness knows how the mice survive here now, he thinks. It's not as though there's any food for them.

He nudges the pile of debris with a steel toe-capped boot. Nothing. Mummified rodents are almost worse than live ones, but he wants to be sure and gives the mess one last scattering kick before he bends over to investigate properly.

At the bottom of the heap is a Manila envelope. He picks it up and tries to read the address but the strip lights in the poorly lit corridor are broken and it's impossible to make the words out. He abandons his half-completed task and opens the door opposite, marked Doctor's Office.

Like the rest of the hospital, the room seems to be inhabited by new life and there is a rustle from the corner as he walks in. The tall windows are festooned with cobwebs and one of the blackout blinds is falling off its roller. He holds the envelope up to the compromised sunlight and wipes the green stamp carefully with his thumb. Twelve pence. He wonders how long ago the postage for a letter was twelve pence, and peers again at the address, trying to decipher the handwriting.

As he stands there he hears the main ward door open, and he stiffens as the foreman shouts to ask if he is finished yet. He instinctively puts his hand in front of his mouth to muffle his reply and conceal his rule-breaking, but decides not to respond. The last thing he needs is a health and safety lecture.

He listens until he's sure he is alone, and then pulls out a chair and sits down at one of the desks. He sets the envelope on the surface in front of him and starts to go through the drawers, but they yield nothing more than blank sheets of paper and dried-up ballpoint pens. Disappointed, he lifts the handset of a push-button telephone and sits up straight.

'Yes, this is the doctor speaking.'

And then he remembers his meeting with the careers advisor at school. He replaces the receiver carefully. 'In your dreams, pal. No chance of that,' he says.

He gets up from his seat to have a closer look at the cabinetry and the abandoned equipment. The X-ray viewer is a familiar feature of TV dramas and he walks over to investigate, flipping the switch beside it. There is a loud buzz and it flickers into life. He cannot turn it off fast enough.

On the blackboard beside the door, someone has written

GOODBYE 1st MAY 2003

in white chalk. He pulls out his phone and takes a photograph of the message to show to his mum.

The envelope is still lying on the desk and he picks it up and shakes the dust off it before stashing it in one of the many pockets in his work trousers. After a final look around the room, he heads out of the ward, back along the chessboard corridor to the exit, and out into fresh air. He leaves his hammer behind, certain that he'll be back on Monday to finish the job.

It's not until he is sitting on the top deck of the bus that he remembers his find. It had been drummed into everyone on their first day at the hospital that all such items must be handed in at the Site Office. As he gets off the bus near his girlfriend's flat, he sees her and shouts her name. She looks up and smiles. The red pillar box is six paces away and with barely a pause he pulls the letter out of his pocket and posts it, before running to meet her and wrapping her in his arms.

It's Friday night and the weekend is already looking good.

Jean

21 March 1911

Singer Factory, Clydebank

'There is going to be a strike!'

Jean heard the words as they flowed around her, nudging at the edges of her attention. She tried to put them aside. From across the workroom, the foreman watched her. Every so often he took the pencil stub from behind his ear – an action out of kilter with his recent promotion – and made a mark in his new notebook. Until a few weeks ago he had been one of them, and she wondered if he had realised how much things would change when he took on the new job.

The long workspace resembled a schoolroom for a hundred and twenty pupils with individual tables arranged in groups of eight or ten. No one knew why it was called the Testing Flat, any more than they knew the reason why the needle-making room was called the Needle Flat. It had always been that way.

To many of the women in the workshop, the foreman was still the little boy with the sticking-out ears who once lived at the poorest end of town. He was the child to whom they had given thick slices of bread when they saw him playing with their sons in the street, the lad who always smelled of stale pee. They weren't bothered in the slightest about his new position, but he wasn't part of their group anymore.

He cleared his throat and spoke decisively and formally, as he had been instructed. 'Can you not test this machine, Miss Ferrier? Is there a problem?'

Jean resisted the need to push her shoulder blades down and together, to stretch her neck and ease the stiffness of four hours sitting at the bench. She knew, because she had been counting, that this was the seventh machine that morning that had needed more than a twist of the tension screw to the right or left by way of final adjustment, and she speculated whether they were being given to her on purpose.

She didn't waste time looking up but kept her eyes on the machine. 'It's the needle; I just need another one.'

He tapped his important new watch. 'You need to work more

quickly, this is unacceptable.' Satisfied with his instruction, he walked away in search of a different victim.

The whispers continued to ruffle past her but she remained purposefully deaf to them and reached across to the toolbox she shared with the seven other women at her table. To her left, the windows reached upwards to the high ceiling. The plainness of the walls was broken only by a peripheral blast of colour from the collection of outdoor coats and bright scarves that hung in the gaps between each tall glazed rectangle.

'Definitely the needle,' she muttered to herself, and with the screwdriver in one hand and the faulty steel gripped tightly, she removed it. She closed her eyes and ran the fine metal shaft between her fingers. The steel was smooth, like a piece of spring grass just before it's chewed for the sweet sap. A tiny burr at the tip confirmed her diagnosis. She replaced it with a fresh one and checked that the bobbin had enough thread for the test. Not too much, not too little. Finally, she made the required number of stitches on the white cloth with more deliberation than usual, watching closely as the needle punched down through warp and weft, one stitch after another. She checked the stitch length and the under-seam, and when she was happy with the results, she wound the snapped-off thread around the spool pin on the top of the machine to signify the test complete.

Only then did she allow herself to listen.

The current of words was now an unruly torrent.

Frances, her neighbour at the big table for the last three years, and at eighteen years of age, her senior by just a couple of months, gave Jean a forceful nudge and nodded towards the end of the long room where a young man had appeared at the open doorway. He seemed to be looking for someone in particular as he searched the candlewick of hair braids and tightly-pinned buns before him. And then he found her.

His heavy boots drummed on the wooden boards as he strode without fear of consequence past racks of machines on the left and seated women on the right.

Everyone in the room knew Donald Cameron. At twenty-five years old he had the presence of a man of forty. He ignored the protesting foreman and strode onwards, making far more noise than was strictly necessary, until he arrived at Jean's table and leaned towards her, close enough to kiss.

'You're visiting then?' she said.

The smell of him was in every breath. The heat of his skin.

The leather apron. The freshly-burned ginger hair on his arms where smelting sparks contributed daily to the snowscape of tiny scars.

'Not for long,' he replied.

She looked at him along with the eyes of the women who worked alongside her.

Rough blue canvas trousers held up with a thick leather belt, and granite-heavy boots. A sweat-stained collarless shirt covering broad shoulders, the sleeves rolled tightly to the inside for safety, twisted into a knot and tucked securely in place at the bicep. What her friends were unable to see was the penny-brown triangle on the tail of his shirt, which had been there since that day last December when he had taken her in his arms in the one-room tenement flat he rented and asked her to marry him and she had said yes, and they had spun around together so quickly she had become giddy, leaving the flat iron to scorch.

He grasped his heavy gauntlets together in one hand and she noticed again the firm, rounded muscle between forefinger and thumb, enlarged from wielding a three-pound hammer day in, day out. It was her favourite part of him.

She strained to hear his voice above the noise of a trolley going past, delivering the next batch of machines.

He repeated the words the others had spoken. 'There is going to be a strike.' His confidence gave them life and purpose.

'Why?'

'Three women in the Polishing Flat have been moved, and the dozen who are left have been told they must complete that work as well as their own.'

'Piece-rate workers suffer again.'

'Aye.'

'How did you hear about it?'

'Two of them came to see me. Walked up to the foundry as bold as you like.'

This was not strictly true: the women had stood at the door and hesitated at the blast and ferocity of the place, but he thought them courageous and it would do no harm to let people know of their determination, especially with that foreman lip-reading his words from across the room.

Jean was aware that those close to her were listening to every word. 'What happens next?'

He pointed at the windows. 'Look outside.'

She scraped her chair backward, not caring about the noise or the scrutiny, and looked down into the yard below. A few dozen women were already gathered and as she watched, they were joined by a ribbon of figures emerging from the stairwell. 'It's started already?'

He was close beside her. 'It has. There's a meeting after we finish. Tell your friends. Tell everyone.'

And then he marched back along the room, and was gone.

She went back to her place and took her seat in silence, feeling as though the eyes of the whole room were upon her. The department supervisor, a salaried, slicked-down man with clean fingernails who reeked of cologne and knew Jean only by the works number on her brass tally disc, came out of his glass-windowed domain and made it obvious he was watching her. It was a regular occurrence these days. She allowed him this, but when he returned to his office she finally freed Donald's instruction and sat with her hands stilled in her lap, as the words pleated around the room.

'There is a meeting tonight when we finish. Wages are being cut and the union have called a strike. Be there.'

There was a danger that the words might become unravelled and rewoven into something new after so many softly spoken passes, but anger had bred an engineered precision into the swell of vowels and consonants, and there was no confusion at all in the message. Within minutes Jean could inhale the energy around her.

The factory horn signalled the end of the day. Workers gushed down the wide stone stairs and the sounds of lathes and saws were replaced with chatter about football and children and new dresses and rent due. Jean wanted to bottle the conversations, tighten the lid, and take them home with her to feed upon later.

Outside the huge gates, they mingled in the street as the afternoon light faded, heads still thrumming from the noise of the machinery. Jean and Frances forged ahead, arm in arm, with three generations of joiners, printers, needle-makers and painters. The saltiness of graft filled the cool evening air.

Behind them the main building resembled a cake in a bakery shop window with two layers of pale stone frosting recently added to the top. The vast industrial campus was spread over more than a hundred acres. Jean had school friends and neighbours in every department and between them they turned pig iron and timber into ten thousand sewing machines every single week.

They waited.

'What do you think will happen?' Frances asked.

'Who knows?'

'What will your father say about it?'

Jean pushed a few loose strands of dark brown hair behind her ears.

'He will be for the company. He always thinks they know best.'

'And Donald?'

'My Donald thinks that every single one of us should be in the union.' There was pride in her voice.

'Must be hard, that.'

'Not for me, but it makes for an interesting Sunday. I'm surprised you can't hear them at your front door two streets away.'

They felt the crowd begin to shift and move as a group of men made their way through, tapping shoulders and parting the sea of workers. At the front a wooden crate was pushed into position and Donald vaulted onto it; he was surprisingly light-footed for a big man. He raised his arms and gathered the crowd, all talk of dinner and home silenced.

'This morning, comrades,' he began, speaking slowly and with deliberation, allowing his words to carry. 'This morning, the company acted against a small group of workers. Three women in the Polishing Flat have been moved to other departments.'

Irritation rumbled across the crowd and he paused before continuing. 'The work of fifteen is now to be done by the twelve who remain.'

The mutterings grew until he could barely be heard. He waited, skilful in managing the discontent, and granting time for complaints to be voiced and anger to build.

'Comrades, we must remember that an injury to one, is an injury to all.' He opened his arms as though to embrace them. 'We are calling a strike in support of these fellow workers and we ask you to join us. It is a time to stand together and send a message that we will not be treated like this. There must be fairness. This is the first of many changes the company is planning that will affect all of us. Our brothers and sisters. Our mothers and fathers. Our friends and comrades. It is time to act.'

Jean looked back once more at the huge clock tower, visible for miles. She caught the flash of late sunlight on glass as an office window closed and wondered if someone was pointlessly attempting to eavesdrop from hundreds of yards away.

As the meeting drew to a close, the two young women set off for home, inspired by the speeches and the plans.

'This has been a long time coming,' said Jean. 'They have pushed us around for years and this is just too much.'

Frances agreed. 'Those women have bairns to feed and rent to pay. How can they possibly do more work in the same amount of time?'

'And if they do it to three of us, and nothing is said, who will be next?'

'Exactly. My cousin worked in that department before she had the twins. The defect work is very particular. You have to look for the wee dents in those cases and put filler into the scratches that are too deep to polish out. It's not a job that can be rushed.'

'Which only makes it worse.' Jean sidestepped a large puddle on the path. 'Now we know why they were all over the workshops in January, writing everything down.'

'So, will you strike?' Frances was suddenly uncertain. 'It's a big step.'

'We'll show them. You can't produce sewing machines if there's nobody in the factory.' Jean swung her leg and took a sharp kick at a stone, launching it into the grass ahead. A rabbit sprinted out of the undergrowth and escaped the missile. 'Look, that's what they think we are: rabbits, scared rabbits. And they are wrong.'

After her friend peeled off to her own flat, Jean increased her pace. She pounded along the streets, which were panelled with row after row of rust-coloured sandstone tenements. The smell of white oatmeal pudding and griddled pork sausage wafted from open windows. News of the strike had travelled quickly and she tried to ignore the increasing nausea as anxiety burrowed into her stomach.

Jean pushed open the heavy door of the tenement stair and paused to draw breath before treading up to the top floor. Discontented male voices flooded towards her as she approached the open door to the flat.

Her father stood with his back to her, holding forth to six workmates. 'They are a bunch of hot heads who have no idea how these things are done. Those of us who have worked our way up have the respect of the company. I will not be striking for the sake of three women.'

The room was filled with their power.

Her father's oldest friend was next to speak. 'Nor me, George, nor me. Folks should listen to those of us who are time-served. Our own union negotiates with the company on our behalf and if there are new and bigger unions I fail to see how it will be of benefit to any of us here in this room.'

It was obvious from the way they stood, square on, arms folded, utterly confident, that they saw themselves as a cut above the majority in the factory.

The words were out of her mouth before Jean could stop them. 'It's not only three women.'

Her father turned to face her. 'And what would you know about it?' There was scorn in every word.

They were all looking at her now, these men who had known her since she was a baby. She stared at the floor.

'Nothing, clearly.' Her father was unimpressed.

She felt a sudden flash of anger and found her voice again. 'Yes, there are the three who have been moved, but this affects all of us. Who can say what they will do next?'

He raised his voice, squashing her words. 'That's not the point. The company knows best what is needed to run the factory, far better than a dozen women.'

'Because they are just women?' She knew very well his views on this.

'Because the supervisors have been doing studies.'

It was her turn to laugh. 'Aaaah. The famous Scientific Management, you mean?'

'That's the one. All calculated to make every department more efficient, and that means higher profit and better wages for everyone.' He stepped forward. He wouldn't be spoken to like this, especially not in front of his friends.

Jean wondered what her mother would have said. Would she have been able to talk him around? Probably not, and it was just as well she wasn't here to see him put her daughter down in this way. Jean tried to backtrack, but knew it was pointless. 'We'll see. At the moment it's still being discussed. There are meetings tonight.'

'No doubt your Donald is up to his oxters in all this?' The question was rhetorical – he knew fine and well that his future son-in-law was involved. 'You can tell him that he is wasting his time. He'll get no support from me.' He swept his arm around the room. 'And not from any of us. You are going to be wed, lass, in three months. If you go on strike, who will pay your rent?'

Her voice faltered. 'Hopefully it will be over by then and the company will see sense and reinstate the women.'

He paused for just long enough to make her feel undermined. 'I wouldn't bet on it.'

The men began to shuffle, their resolve wearing a little. None of them wanted to be witness to a family argument and they began to reach for their coats in readiness for leaving.

'I must go. See you tomorrow, George,' said one, and then another.

'You will indeed,' he replied. 'I'll come down the stair with you and get a breath of air before my food is ready.'

Jean hugged herself in the sudden emptiness of the room. Her thoughts were interrupted by the sound of a different factory horn booming out further along the Clyde. She added a shovel of coal to the fire in the belly of the range. It was her job to get a meal on the table and she knew that standing doing nothing would only make matters worse. The arrangement was never spoken of, but it had always been this way ever since it had become just the two of them. She hung the soup pot on the hook above the sooty flames and stirred it as it started to bubble. Her father was gone for forty minutes and she could smell the beer on him when he returned but it was clear he had no intention of sitting opposite her to eat and he left her alone in the kitchen. She took her usual place at the table and spooned the broth from side to side in the bowl, allowing it to cool. She knew better than to waste food.

After Jean had cleared up the dishes and refilled the coal scuttle, she headed out to escape the atmosphere and walked the familiar route along darkening streets to the working men's hall. It was obvious that she had missed the main part of the meeting and she began to search for Donald in the huddles that had formed. She didn't have the confidence to launch herself into the body of the kirk to find him and it wasn't until the hall was emptying and she had almost given up that she heard a soft voice in her ear and felt a strength beside her.

'I'm glad you came.' Their fingers linked as he spoke.

'Why would I not?'

'I thought you might not be able to get away.'

'Don't worry about that. His bark is worse than his bite.'

'How was he?'

She felt the tension, which she had kept twisted up inside her, begin to ease and she paused for a moment before she replied. 'As you'd expect. He's a master in the foundry with apprentices to think about.'

He frowned. 'That sounds like an excuse to me.'

'You might not want to hear it, but it's true. He didn't actually say the words, but I know the lads are in his mind. He wants to do his best for them, as he did for you once, remember?'

'Aye, well, after this I doubt I'll ever be more than a journeyman.' He straightened his back. 'The strike is going ahead. Two thousand already and many, many more tomorrow. Perhaps everyone.'

'Except the skilled trades; you'll not get them out. Not yet, anyway. You should have heard them, Donald. They are just as determined as you are.' She corrected herself. 'As we are.'

'Jean, this is wrong, what the company are doing. They are making a whole section suffer for the sake of a few paper minutes on a chart. The saving they will make is tiny; in fact, by moving those women they will save a few shillings on wages, but it will slow up the production. It's called cutting off your nose to spite your face.'

'My mother used to say that when I was small.' Jean looked up at him. 'I know, and I'm with you.'

'You are? It doesn't sound much like it.'

'Oh, I will strike, you can be sure of that.'

He smiled at her. 'I shouldn't have doubted you. I'm sorry.'

They were the last to leave and as Jean looked around at the empty seats she thought that it was as though the meeting had never happened. 'Are you worried about tomorrow?'

'Worried? No. We are in the right. They will soon see that.'

'Yes, but convincing men like my father to walk through the gates won't be easy.'

'Nothing easy is ever worth having.' He opened the door for her. 'Come on. We can walk back the long way. It's not too cold tonight.'

She took his hand again. 'Do you ever wonder about them?'

'The managers?'

'No, I mean the machines. Do you ever wonder where they go?'

He shook his head. 'When they leave the foundry they're just lumps of metal. It's too hot and noisy and fast to stand about and think about things like that.'

'I suppose.'

They walked slowly, falling naturally into step.

'Do you?' he asked.

'When I first started in the Testing Flat, I counted every

machine.' She half laughed at the astonishment on his face. 'Now you think I'm silly.'

'Jean, I promise you, I will never think that. You have more than enough brains in your head for both of us.'

'That's not true at all,' she protested.

'We'll have to agree to disagree about that.'

She squeezed his hand before continuing. 'I gave up counting when I got to five hundred because it only took a few weeks to get there.'

It was his turn to laugh. 'You must have done thousands of them by now.'

'I don't think about every single machine – that would be ridiculous – but I can tell from looking at the clock when I'm doing the last one of the day.'

'And then what?'

'I slow down and make it last until the siren sounds. We have to wind thread onto the bobbin to do the testing, and we're only supposed to put a few yards on, but when it's the last machine, I fill it right up so the new owner has plenty to get her started. And then I try to imagine who that person might be. Will it be a lady in a grand house who will use the machine to make silk dresses?'

'I don't think that's very likely,' he interrupted. 'People like that have servants to do those jobs.'

She ignored him. 'Or will it be bought by someone in a faraway land, like the places on the big map on our classroom wall at school? I won't ever know.'

'Enough of your dreaming,' he teased. 'I want to celebrate.'

'It's a bit soon for celebrating, isn't it?'

'I want to celebrate *us*, Jean. You and me. And I think that means ice cream.'

He let go of her hand and lifted her up by the waist in the street and birled her around. And then he kissed her and she didn't care who saw him do it.

Connie

September 1954

Edinburgh

As Connie approached the flat she could see her mother working at her sewing machine in the bay window, making the most of the last of the afternoon light. She waved as she walked up the short path and into the tenement close, but Kathleen remained bent over her work, oblivious to what was happening outside in the street – once she made a start on a task, she kept going until it was completed.

Connie turned her key in the lock and pushed the door open. 'Hello. I'm back,' she called.

'You're home just in time to give me a help with something,' came the reply.

'Two minutes.' Connie slipped her coat onto the waiting wooden hanger in the deep hall cupboard and did the buttons up to keep it nice. As she walked into the sitting room the sewing machine stilled for a moment. 'Right, what is it you want me to do?'

'I've almost finished this bit of work, and I just need to get things swept up and tidied, so I was wondering if you would fetch the dustpan and brush from the scullery for me.'

'Is that all?' Connie picked up the hem of her pale-green work-dress and, as though she was six years old, spun around twice. 'I thought you wanted me to be a model for your latest ballgown.'

Kathleen smiled. 'Unfortunately not. I think my ballgown stitching days are long gone.' She adjusted her spectacles. 'I'm almost finished, just one more seam and I'll be done.'

The machine came to life again and the needle pounded up and down through the cloth. The fact that she was sewing so quickly meant only one thing: the bobbin was almost empty. She spun the handle faster and faster, in the hope of outrunning the last few inches of thread and somehow making it stretch for half a yard, but sure enough, a hand's length from the end of the fabric, the needle began to punch a row of useless holes without catching the thread underneath.

Connie laughed. 'You never win, you know.'

'That's not true.' Kathleen was indignant. 'There have been times when I've managed it.' She examined the unfinished seam. 'Not many, I'll grant you that, but there have been a few.'

'You should have kept a record of the winning occasions in one of your notebooks, and then we would have evidence.'

'Don't make fun of those books, my girl,' came the reply, and then, more softly, 'They are very important. You wouldn't understand.'

'Well, I won't know about that particular secret unless you spill the beans about them. You keep saying you'll tell me and then you don't, so until you do, I'll keep teasing you.'

Kathleen sat herself more upright in the chair and raised one shoulder and then the other to ease out the stiffness in her neck. 'I'll explain all about it when I hand the machine on to you.' She sighed. 'But you're right about one thing. After more than forty years of using this workhorse, I should probably know by now that I can't beat it.'

'What is it you've been making?'

'It's just a new petticoat for a wee girl along the road. I'm putting some growing-tucks at the bottom, near the hem. Hopefully that will make it last a bit longer.' She slid back the shiny chrome-plated cover to reveal the bobbin race and extracted the bobbin, which was one-third full of scarlet thread. 'Oh,' she said. 'That's a pity, I could have sworn there was more white on this.' She hunted in the box beside her for a new bobbin and smiled triumphantly when she found one that was already wound with white cotton. 'Did I tell you that your father put his foot through a sheet last week when he turned over in bed? When I've finished this, that's the next job on my list.'

'Goodness.'

'Oh, he denied it, of course, but the noise of it ripping woke us up and it was definitely his foot that was tangled up in it and not mine.'

'So you're going to put it sides to middle?'

'Not this time – I've already done that once. I'm afraid its bed-covering days are numbered. I'm just going to salvage what I can for pillowcases and the rest can go for cleaning rags.' She dropped the bobbin back into the race. Her thrift was ingrained, and she could no more discard useable cloth than she could catch an unnecessary bus.

'Right, Mother, while you're finishing up, I'll get that dustpan and I'll boil the kettle for tea.'

'Before you go, just thread the needle for me, would you? It's so difficult once the light starts to go.' Kathleen leaned out of the way to let her daughter get nearer to the machine.

'Of course.' Connie flattened the end of the cotton between her lips and aimed it at the eye of the needle. It went through, from left to right, on the first attempt.

'Thank you. Your dad's already left for the library, so it's just us. I made the sandwiches this afternoon. They're in greaseproof, on the cold shelf.' Kathleen peered out of the window. 'They said on the wireless that it was going to rain this evening and I do think it's just about to pour.'

'I wonder which unlucky opponent in the Edinburgh chess world will be his victim tonight?'

'He didn't say.'

The first few drops clattered against the glass pane and Connie anticipated her mother's next request. 'Has he got his umbrella with him?'

'I don't think so. And his scarf is still on the coat stand. I noticed it after he left.'

'Don't worry about it.' She ignored her aching feet. 'I could do with stretching my legs after tea. I'll take them along to him. It's not far.'

When she was alone with the sewing machine once more, Kathleen took a small notebook from the drawer of her desk and opened it. She put the edge of the next unused page under the needle, lowered the needle bar, and gripped the two tails of thread firmly with her left hand. The needle pierced the paper abruptly, one stitch at a time, as she made a seam along the length of the page. An inch from the top she paused and slipped a small square of white cloth under the foot, made two more stitches, and then added a piece of *broderie anglaise* edging below it before trapping the scraps between the stitches and the paper.

Finally, in her practised teacher's copperplate hand, she made a note.

Petticoat, for Betty Smart's daughter – no charge (K)

The worst of the sudden rain had been and gone by the time Connie left the flat, but she honoured her promise and made her way to the library. She arrived at the Art Deco building before the meeting had come to an end and listened at the door of the Nelson Hall where the chess tournaments took place, before opening it and slipping quietly inside. It was an impressive space. Banks of windows at each end of the room took up half the wall from waist height all the way up to the ceiling. In the summer evenings it was especially lovely because there was then barely a need for electric light, and the scent of beeswax rose from the sun-warmed floor. Tonight the lights were on and the long tables, each inlaid with four chessboards, were already in use. Every place was taken. In spite of the numbers the hall was surprisingly quiet, the silence broken only by the tap of rook and pawn as they battled for victory in the hands of men.

As the last few games drew to a close, she stayed near the door. It was unusual for her father to still be playing at this time; normally he would have won in the first quarter hour. As the chairman of the Chess Committee, he should by now be getting ready to go on to the stage and announce the results, but instead he was engrossed in what appeared to be an extended struggle for dominance. She knew most of the members by name but this man was unfamiliar. From her position at the entrance of the room she saw her father mouth 'checkmate'. His opponent leaned forward across the marquetry squares to study the remaining pieces and then he nodded. They stood up, or rather her father stood, and the younger man unfolded himself from the chair.

Even though he had his back to her, Connie couldn't take her eyes off him. His wavy hair was the colour of caramel toffee and there was something about how he held himself. He had a presence which seemed to come from far more than simply being at least a head taller than anyone else in the room.

She was still looking at him when the announcements began.

'Good evening, everyone. For those who missed the introductions at the start of the meeting, my name is Bruce Baxter, and as Chairman of the Fountainbridge Chess Club, I would like to thank you for coming along tonight, especially in such inclement weather.'

The intimations and results progressed and Connie found herself listening more closely than usual to try to catch the stranger's name, but at the critical moment a bout of coughing from an elderly man in front of her obliterated the information she was hoping for. She shook her head in irritation and took a seat at one of the vacated tables.

'Finally, I would like to apologise to the ratepayer from Stockbridge who requested, in a letter to the press almost sixteen years ago, that we purchase India-rubber chessmen to alleviate the constant clatter of our meetings in the city libraries.' A round of applause broke out across the room at this announcement, which Bruce made at every meeting. He waited until it died down. 'I'm afraid that, as yet, our parcel containing these items still seems to be lost in the post.' It was an old joke now, but it never failed to raise a smile. The mostly male membership, who hadn't wanted to disturb their fellow players' concentration before, put the much-used wooden chessmen back into the boxes without now caring about the noise and began to leave, pulling their collars up against the late summer rain which was again battering the windows.

Connie gathered up a stack of boxes and took them to the cupboard. She might as well make herself useful, she reasoned, while she waited for her father. This was nothing at all to do with the fact that the subject of her earlier interest was still in the room.

Bruce was now deep in conversation with three members of the committee, and their table was strewn with correspondence and an open accounts book.

'Excuse me.' She tried to make herself heard, but the pelting rain on the glass drowned her out. 'Excuse me.' She spoke more loudly, just as there was a lull in the clattering. Her words came out as a shout, and they all turned around, including the visitor. She felt a blush spread up from her chest and bloom across her face. 'I'm sorry.'

'My goodness, Connie, I didn't know you were here.' Her father frowned at her. 'Is everything alright? Has something happened to your mother?'

She shook her head. 'No, nothing. But she sent me with your umbrella and scarf. You went out without them and…' She pointed at the windows.

'Ah yes, it's a foul night. That was a kind thought, but I'll be here for a while longer. We have some business we need to discuss, so I'm afraid you'll have a bit of a wait.'

The tall newcomer stepped forward and addressed Bruce. 'Perhaps I can help with that, sir? I stayed back to say thank you for the game, but I do have my umbrella with me.'

Connie didn't want to look at him and found herself studying her feet and wishing, for no good reason, that she had polished her shoes before she had set off for the library. She chided herself; it was quite ridiculous to be blushing like an adolescent at thirty-three years old.

The two men shook hands. 'Bruce Baxter, and this is my daughter, Constance.' He looked up at the stranger. 'I don't think I saw your name on my list tonight.'

'Morrison, Alfred Morrison. People call me Alf.'

'You had me on the ropes for a while there, Mr Morrison. Where did you learn to play chess?'

'Merchant Navy, just after the war. There were a lot of slow hours to be filled at sea. I got plenty of practice.' He glanced at Connie, but couldn't meet her eye. 'I'd be happy to loan you my umbrella.'

She was polite but firm. 'That won't be necessary, I'll wait for my father, but thank you.'

'No, Connie, I want you to take up the offer. Your mother will worry if we aren't home by nine, you know that.' Bruce nodded his thanks. 'That's very kind, Mr Morrison. I appreciate it.'

She knew when she was beaten. 'Very well, I'll say goodnight then.' She waved a goodbye to her father's friends and headed towards the door, leaving her unwanted escort to scrabble for his coat.

It was dark by the time they went outside. The rain had worsened and was slicking off the pavement and into the already full gutter.

'This really isn't necessary,' she said, as the umbrella-wielding figure appeared beside her. 'I'm not made of sugar, so I'll not melt.'

'Nonetheless...' he replied.

She stepped forward, and relying only on her ears, she didn't look for traffic in the thundering downpour. Seconds later she had the breath squeezed from her as a firm arm wrapped around her waist and she was dragged back from the road in a screech of horns.

Red coat – repair to lining (Connie) – be more careful crossing the road!

Green gingham apron (Connie).

Fred

Blog: Late June 2016

Edinburgh

Run, 4.2K. Along the old railway.

I've been trying to clear my head before Granda's funeral tomorrow, and preparing myself for the onslaught of people afterwards at the wake – or what the old folk call a Purvey – when everyone is invited back here to the flat for a cup of tea, something to eat and a whisky. I seem to have spent the whole weekend cleaning windows, and washing everything from the floors to the plates, cups and spoons. My hands look like prunes.

In honour of Granda's sweet tooth there will be no dried-out, curly-edged cheese sandwiches, just cake. And millionaire's shortbread, of course.

There are cakes from the neighbours, cakes from the old guys at the allotment, cake from Eva in the corner shop and some rather wonky-looking muffins from the kids next door. Lemon drizzle, chocolate, coffee, cherry. You name it and we have it – I could open a cake emporium.

The next big thing is that I have to decide what to do about the cat. Mum and I didn't even know he had a cat until last week – he hadn't mentioned it to either of us. The next-door neighbours (the ones with the kids) were looking after it but they are off on holiday next week and I'll be here for another fortnight sorting stuff out so I have no good reason not to take it back really. It's a complication I don't need though, and I think a visit to the dog and cat home may be on the horizon.

With perfect timing, Mum is having double glazing fitted at her house, which means there are boxes everywhere and there's no space for me. It feels a bit weird to be staying here but it's either that or a hotel, so I'm just going to use the sofa bed for now.

I made pasta for lunch (carb loading before my run) and then I managed to trip over that old sewing machine, which I've been using to prop the kitchen door open – and of course I went my length across the room, olives and spaghetti flying all over the place. If the cat had been a dog it might actually have been useful in the clearing up department, but now I have to wash the floor AGAIN because Mum is coming round later.

His neatly formatted words appear on the screen. He double-checks the admin dashboard for the blog to make sure the settings are still set at 'Private, Password Protected' and clicks 'Publish'.

'Coffee time, I think.' He stands up and goes over to the sink to fill the kettle. As he turns on the cold tap the unwanted cat makes its presence known by jumping onto the draining board and nuzzling his arm.

'I suppose you are after some food?'

He knows without looking that the shelf in the larder where the last tin of cat food had been that morning is now empty.

'If you think I'm buying you that canned muck, you can think again. Not a chance, pal. It stinks, and I have better things to spend money on than feline designer dinners.' They both look out of the window. The earlier rain has slowed to a drizzle and he reconsiders his priorities. 'I'll have coffee later – I think it's time for an expedition to the shop.' He lifts his training jacket from the back of the chair and puts it on, zipping it up slowly so that the breathable fabric doesn't get snagged on the teeth. The only footwear he has brought with him on this unexpected trip north are his expensive running shoes, now sopping wet, and a pair of black brogues which, he discovered yesterday, have sprung a leak. He reluctantly eases his stockinged feet into the damp leather and opens the front door to leave, pausing only to grab a carrier bag from the drawer in the hall table, where they have lived all his life.

He is completely unaware that in the space of just a couple of days he has somehow become a man who talks to his cat.

The shop on the corner is familiar and yet different. Fred knows there is something new about the place, but can't put his finger on what it is that has changed. He half waves to Eva as he enters. She sits on her stool behind the glass-topped counter, below which is an ever-changing array of pocket money sweets. Flying saucers, fizzy frogs and liquorice bootlaces nestle beside fat white chocolate buttons studded with hundreds and thousands in rainbow colours. As a child he had spent hours in front of the selection every Saturday morning as he made the very important decision about what Eva would put into the pink candy-striped paper bag for him. She knows everyone's buying habits, and has owned the shop for long enough to comment freely on their purchases.

He picks up a basket. That's it: the baskets are different. Gone are the scratchy wire-covered handles; they have been replaced by smooth yellow-and-purple plastic. He walks around the aisles, noticing how new excitements have crept onto the shelves. Balsamic vinegar now stands next to malt, and expensive gluten-free coconut whirls are beside the iced shortbread. He takes his time, and eavesdrops on the commentary coming from the front of the shop. If someone had a mind to, they could discover the ins and outs of every family for half a mile, he thinks.

Eventually he takes advantage of a lull in the stream of customers and puts his basket on the counter.

'Nice new baskets, Eva.'

She smiles and picks up the box of dry cat food.

'Is that for your Granda's cat?'

'It's a temporary arrangement.' He pulls the bag from his pocket. 'The cat, I mean.'

'I see.'

The electronic till beeps with every item. Cat food. Bread. Fish fingers. Salad cream. *Evening News*. Milk.

Eva holds on to the milk carton.

'They can't have milk, Fred.' She is an expert in cats, as in everything.

'The milk isn't for the cat.'

'It upsets their tummies.' She refuses to hand it over until she is sure he is listening.

'It's for my coffee.'

'I read it in a magazine.' She releases her grip on it and he grasps the carton quickly before she can change her mind.

'Thanks, I'll be sure to remember that.'

'What's it called?'

'Mmmm?' He is preoccupied with packing the bag in the correct order.

'The cat. What's it called?'

'I have no idea. Granda never told us about it.'

The woman behind him in the queue sighs with impatience. Eva points at the green digital total on the till. He pulls out a handful of change and extracts the correct amount, one coin at a time. 'I think that should be right.'

'Remember about the milk.'

'I will.'

'I'll be there tomorrow, for the funeral.'

He crumbles a little. 'Thank you,' he says, so quietly that she sees the words instead of hearing them.

Back in the flat, Fred pours chicken-flavoured Nibble Munch into a bowl and addresses the cat. 'I'm not having cat litter or a cat tray, or a poop scoop or cat deodorant. I absolutely refuse.'

He sluices his hands with washing-up liquid, working the foamy bubbles into his fingernails, hearing Nana's voice in his head – 'Clean hands, Fred, before you have your supper' – and then dries them carefully on the roller towel that hangs on the back of the door. Back at the computer he begins to type, saying the words out loud as they form in the search bar.

'How often do cats…'

The dropdown menu appears:

How often do cats poop

How often do cats pee

How often do cats need worming…

He stares at the screen. 'Worming,' he says, out loud.

The cat looks up from its bowl and blinks at him.

'Maybe it's better not to look.'

But he does.

'Good grief. There are cats that are trained to use the toilet. I am *not* teaching you to do that. You can go outside like any other self-respecting moggy.'

Jean

March 1911

Clydebank

Jean had been lying awake for an hour, and more than anything else, she wanted to stay under the woollen blankets and pretend to be ill. Unfortunately, the position of her bed in the recess in the kitchen meant that any minute now her father was likely to be through to eat his porridge and drink his tea, both of which he would expect to be ready. She stretched one last time, touching the cool plaster at the foot of the mattress with her toes and reaching her arms over her head to feel the wall behind the pillow. It was a daily source of satisfaction that she could do both at the same time, even if she had to wriggle to make it possible to reach. Her mother had been a tiny woman and Jean had assumed for most of her childhood that she would be the same, but she was definitely taller.

She heard her father coughing hard in the next room and rushed to be decent before he knocked on the door. Yesterday's clothes hung beside the bed-space and she braced herself before putting her feet onto the cold boards. She must get on; there was not a minute more to be wasted. She lifted the blue dress off the hook and slipped it over her head, feeling the well-worn cloth slide across her still warm-from-the-bed skin. The buttons up the front defied her speeding fingers and she turned away from the door as her father knocked a warning and then walked straight in without waiting for her reply.

With any luck he would eat and leave, she thought. The tidying up would be left for her alone, as always. So be it. She added more coal to the embers in the grate in the hope that the fire would tickle on until she could get home at the end of the day.

She felt like a deserter as she walked to work. The crowds were thinner than usual, but there was still a steady stream of folk passing through the gates and getting off the trains at the Singer station. She marvelled every day at the clout of a manufacturer of domestic sewing machines having not just its own railway station, but its own trains, with engines that didn't stop at all the usual places but streaked past platforms of annoyed travellers to bring workers directly to the factory. As a sign of influence it was unassailable.

Frances was not at the gate. Jean walked past their customary meeting point with her head down and her scarf wrapped around her face in the hope of not being recognised. She had been the most vocal of any of them but it was as though her father had injected glue into her veins as she slept. She felt powerless to oppose him.

As she entered the workroom she looked around in disbelief. Instead of the hundred who normally took their places at the tables, fewer than a dozen women had arrived. There was a strange atmosphere, as though they were ashamed.

The foreman seemed determined to be at his most pernickety, which didn't bode well for the rest of the day. The women were unwilling to have their conversations listened to, and they worked in silence until the factory siren sounded the signal for lunchtime.

Jean forced down her potted-meat sandwich and then walked down the echoing stairs and headed for the gate. She could see from a distance that Donald was waiting for her, hands in his pockets, feet apart.

'What happened?' he asked when she reached him.

'Are you cross?'

'Cross? No, I was just worried about you.'

He put his arms around her, and she snuggled up against him, breathing in his familiar smell. They began to walk.

'I didn't have the strength for a battle this morning. Father was so angry last night. He told me before I went to bed that if I didn't go to work this morning he would throw me onto the street.' She paused. 'And he said that no daughter of his is a slacker.' She felt the rough callouses at the base of his fingers graze her skin as he squeezed her hand.

'Do you think he would do that?'

'I don't know. I didn't want to find out.'

'Come and live with me.'

He had said this many times before and she had always laughed at the idea and teased him about wanting her to be his housekeeper. But not this time. 'I can't. It's another three months to the wedding.'

'I'll let you have the bed. I can sleep in the chair.'

'I couldn't let you do that.'

'Well, we can put the bolster down the middle of the mattress if that's what's stopping you.'

She laughed in spite of herself. 'I'm not worried about that sort of thing.'

'What, then?'

'I don't want it to be like this.' She sighed. 'I want to have a proper wedding, with our friends there to celebrate with us.'

'I know you do. I want that too.' He turned to face her. 'But things are different now, Jean. We didn't know this would happen.'

She shrugged. 'I expect he will calm down.' It was a lie; she didn't believe it for a minute.

'Are you going to work this afternoon?'

Their route had taken them back to where they had started.

'Should I?'

'You have to do what's in your heart, not what a man tells you to do.'

'Not even you?'

'Particularly not me. That's not how we do things, is it?'

For more than a minute she didn't speak.

At last she squared her shoulders and looked up at him. 'Right, then. I'll get my coat. Wait for me.'

She climbed up the deserted staircase. In her absence, the foreman had taken a place at one of the benches, and was sitting there with his head in his hands. He heard her footsteps and turned around. 'You too?'

'Yes.' She felt she should apologise but the words wouldn't come.

He glanced over at the supervisor's glass-fronted office. 'He's gone to a meeting.' The assertive tone was gone and he was almost whispering. 'I wish...'

She felt sorry for him. 'It's hard.'

'I can't. I just can't. My wife would never forgive me.'

Jean could see how it was. There was no point in making this man, heavy with family expectations and fresh worries, feel worse. 'It will be over soon. They – no, we – will be back in a day or two.' She lifted her coat and her scarf from the hook on the wall and looked around at the long room with its solitary, beaten occupant. And then she hurried down the stairs, each flight taking her to Donald.

He had waited, as she knew he would. She wrapped the cobalt-blue wool around her neck against the wind, walking with her head up this time, and demanded to know about all the union's latest plans.

The most exciting news was that a march was being organised, with a brass band and huge banners. No one would be able to ignore them.

As they reached her street, she felt the familiar knot in her stomach, and somehow found the strength to ignore it. She wasn't looking forward to going home, but it had to be done. Donald had an important meeting to go to in Glasgow, and it wasn't reasonable to expect him to be by her side all the time, fighting her battles for her.

After she waved him off, she thought about how she was going to explain herself, but she wasn't any further forward by the time she was standing outside her door. She listened for voices, alert to the tiniest of sounds, and only relaxed when she was sure the flat was empty. Her goal was to avoid any conflict. The best way to achieve this was to try to make things as ordinary as possible, she decided, so she started on the chores. She cleared the dead cinders from beneath the grate and added waxed butcher paper to the barely warm coals from the morning, hoping to tease the fire back into life. Perhaps if dinner was ready when her father got home, it would take his mind off the strike for a while. She filled a pot with water and began to peel the potatoes, her sharp knife paring away the thinnest possible ribbon of skin.

Her respite was short-lived.

The sound of heavy nailed boots thudding up from the ground floor filled her with dread. Her father burst through the door and blazed straight into the kitchen. 'Why are you not at work?'

Jean stepped back towards the sink in the window space. She didn't dare to reply.

'Answer me, girl? They are chaining the gates shut tonight and those of us who want to work will be locked out. This is your fault.' He took four enormous strides towards her. 'You and that good-for-nothing man of yours.'

She had no time to escape and was forced to lean backward over the sink to avoid the onslaught. A cold strip of stoneware dug into her back and she felt its dampness seep into her dress.

'Nothing to say? Cat got your tongue?' He came closer. 'I've seen that Donald Cameron, standing on platforms, spouting his revolution. This is his doing and I've had enough of it.' Still further, he leaned.

By now she was bent so far back her head was touching the window pane.

He took an enormous breath and emptied his lungs into one word. 'Enough!'

She was pinned there, unable to move, too scared to even take a breath. She began to feel lightheaded.

Just as she thought she couldn't stay on her feet any longer, he retreated. She gasped and drank in a lungful of air.

He wasn't finished.

'I know you are involved in this. I told you last night that if you are foolish enough to go on strike then you have to leave.' His words were laden with a calm malevolence. 'I've made my decision and I don't want you here. I'm not feeding you or putting a roof over your head when you show me such disrespect. Take your things and go.'

'Leave?' There was no doubt that he meant it.

'I want you out of here by the time I return from my meeting. You and your like are not the only folk who can organise themselves. We are going to make representation to the management.'

He was gone as suddenly as he had arrived and her ears buzzed in the abrupt silence.

Jean felt sick, her stomach seemed to hit the floor and bounce back up again and her mouth filled with acid. She retched and up came her lunchtime sandwich, all over the dishes in the sink. The dizziness returned and she gripped the hard edge as sweat formed across her brow. Somehow she managed to turn the tap, flooding the bowls and plates with cold water and scurrying the half-digested bread down the waste pipe.

How long did she have? Even if there was the vaguest chance that he might calm down, she wasn't sure it was safe for her to be in the flat with him. Not anymore.

Donald would be in the city centre by now, planning the rally. She would have to do this by herself. There wasn't much to collect. Three dresses, her work pinafore and sleeves, her underthings, shoes and coat. Her nightgown. She pushed everything into the carpet bag once owned by her mother and looked around the room. Was there anything else?

Yes.

She walked into her father's bedroom with its high wooden bed and stood in front of the small dresser. She knew that somewhere inside it, wrapped in a plain cotton handkerchief with a pink flower embroidered in the corner, was her mother's brass wedding band. There were no other daughters or sons now; she was the only survivor and she was going to claim it, by right. With any luck he wouldn't notice it was gone, not for months. She opened the bottom drawer, and searched every garment until she found what she was looking for, tucked into the folds of a too-small shirt he would likely never fit into again. She slipped the ring onto her right hand for safekeeping, and tucked the handkerchief up her sleeve. A few minutes later she was outside, carpetbag in hand and the door key in her pocket. The neighbours would talk, but she didn't care. There were more important matters to worry about.

Connie

Early October 1954

Edinburgh

Kathleen listened to her husband as he told the doctor that the indigestion had started in the morning when he got up. She knew this wasn't true. The curtains were drawn around his hospital bed, and from her seat in the corridor she could hear his precise, head teacher voice booming out across the ward. He was clearly feeling a lot better now than he had a few hours earlier when he had struggled to put on a fresh pyjama jacket for the GP's visit. As soon as she had the opportunity to speak to this young man, she thought, she would make sure he had all the facts.

She knew Bruce had been up several times in the night, which was most unlike him. He was normally a sound sleeper, never stirring until the morning light began to slant through the gap between the shutters and onto the dark-blue Axminster rug beside their bed. By the time she had woken up, he was already sitting in the chair at her dressing table, rubbing his jaw – but wasn't like any sort of toothache she had ever seen, and who had toothache and dyspepsia at the same time anyway? She had wanted to go to the telephone box opposite the flat and ring for the doctor right away, but he had insisted that she must wait until Connie had left for work, and she had done as he asked.

And now here he was in the Royal Infirmary, in a long medical ward overlooking the Meadows, with a lot of other grey-faced men who were sitting bolt upright in bed as though they were ready for a military inspection. The nurses walked up and down, each carrying a tray covered with a cloth, and from the sounds emitting from the occupants of the screened beds, Kathleen decided it wasn't tea and toast that were being transported around the ward.

The wooden chair was hard beneath her thighs, and she was sure one of her stockings was laddered after catching on a splinter, but she was grateful to have somewhere to rest after rushing all the way to the hospital. The ambulance-men had apologised but it hadn't been possible for her to travel with them and she had set off on foot with-

31

out having as much as a piece of bread for breakfast. It was now late morning and the unmistakeable aroma of mashed turnip was curling out of the ward kitchen and heading in her direction.

At last the screens were wheeled back and the house officer appeared, holding a file of case notes. He looked as though he had been up all night, a hint of flaxen stubble evident on his chin.

'Mrs Baxter?'

'Yes, that's me.'

'I've just been taking a history from your husband and I'm going to run a few tests.'

Kathleen was taken aback. 'So he can't come home?'

'I'm afraid not.' He rubbed at the black ink stain on his middle finger and pushed the cap onto his fountain pen more firmly. 'You can expect him to be with us for a few days.'

'But he said it was indigestion.' She floundered at the unexpectedness of the announcement, and forgot to relay anything about what had happened before the ambulance had arrived.

'It might well be his tummy that's the problem, but we need to be sure.' He glanced up the ward towards the double doors, which had swung open to admit a posse of white coats. It was headed by a balding man, who marched towards them with his shoulders set square, as though he was on a parade ground. 'I need to go now. It's time for the second ward round. I'm sure Sister will explain about visiting times.' He stiffened his back and took a step sideways, out of the way of the procession, before falling into line at the back.

'Dad's in hospital?' Connie was just home from work and still had her coat and hat on. She couldn't believe what she was hearing, but judging by the state her mother was in, it had to be true.

'Yes, he's in the Infirmary.' Kathleen gave up trying to put butter on the piece of bread she had hacked off the loaf in a great lump. She didn't have any appetite anyway, she thought, so what was the point? 'We can visit this evening.'

'I want you to stop doing that and come over here and sit down.' Connie pulled a kitchen chair out from the table and steered the shaking figure onto it. 'He was alright this morning. You need to tell me everything.'

Kathleen slumped as she sat down. She seemed almost broken. 'He said he had heartburn and I tried giving him bicarb and warm water but it didn't do any good so I had to telephone for the doctor to do a house call.'

'Anything else?'

'I don't think so. They came with an ambulance.'

'An ambulance? You didn't say that before.'

'Didn't I?' She remembered again about the pain Bruce had in his chest for a few minutes before the GP arrived and she fretted about forgetting to mention it at the hospital. 'We are so lucky, you know. So lucky to have the National Health. It isn't like it used to be.'

'You'll forgive me if I don't feel very fortunate at the moment, Mother.'

'There's no need to be sharp. Your father is in good hands.'

Connie lifted the kettle, which was squeaking on the gas, and flooded the tea leaves in the pot with boiling water. 'I'm sorry, I know you're worried.' She gave the steaming liquid a stir with the long spoon kept beside the stove specifically for the task, and put the lid on the teapot. 'It's such a shock, that's all. Are you sure we can't visit any sooner?'

'We can't. The Ward Sister was very precise.' Kathleen stood up. 'I don't feel like having tea. I think I'll go and put his shaving things in a bag for him, and I need to get his book and his hairbrush and his...' Her voice trailed off into nothing.

'He will be fine.'

Kathleen stood in the middle of the kitchen as though marooned and looked around her, unable to focus on anything. 'We don't know that. We really don't.' She sounded quite desperate.

'Would you like to leave for the hospital right away?'

'I think so.'

'Even if we have to wait outside the ward?'

'Yes. I want to go now. I need to be there.'

'Right. You put your coat on and we'll be out of the door before you know it.'

'He'll need his things.'

'I'll get them. You just worry about yourself.'

'His new pyjamas are laid out on my bed. I hemmed them this afternoon.'

'With all this happening, you got the machine out and sewed?'

'I know.' Kathleen shrugged. 'I had to do something to occupy myself while I was waiting for you to get home. It was either that or wear a channel into the carpet runner in the hall.'

As they arrived at the doors of the ward, they heard the bell being rung for the beginning of visiting hour.

'We are here just in time,' said Kathleen. She took her hat off and patted her hair into shape. 'Come on, let's see if he's had any of those tests they told me about this morning.'

It was Connie who saw the Ward Sister's face as they made their way along the corridor, and she knew immediately that the bag of clean pyjamas wouldn't be needed. She slipped her arm into her mother's and readied herself for the news.

'Mrs Baxter.'

'Yes, Sister?'

'Is this your daughter you've brought with you this evening?' She didn't wait for an answer. 'I wonder if you would step into my office for a couple of minutes. I think the doctor would like to have a word with you.'

'Is Bruce coming home already?' Kathleen looked hopefully at Connie. 'We didn't bring his clothes or his overcoat, but I'm sure we could go home and collect them.'

'We need to be patient and wait for the doctor, Mother.'

'He was wearing his nightclothes when he was admitted, you see.' Kathleen pressed on, beginning to catch the edge of the truth now, but not wanting to acknowledge it. 'It was because of the ambulance.'

'One of the nurses will make you a cup of tea,' said the Sister, 'and I'll find the doctor for you. My office is just here on the left.' She showed them into a small room with a view across the treetops. 'I'll be back as soon as I can.'

'He doesn't have his shoes either,' Kathleen said quietly as she sat down. 'Or his socks.'

'I'm sure the doctor will be here soon.'

They sat and waited, and after a while a nurse in a grey dress and a starched apron arrived with a pot of tea on a tray, and a small jug of milk and a bowl of sugar made lumpy by wet teaspoons. She took bone-china cups and saucers with tiny rosebuds on them from the glass-fronted dresser next to the fireplace and arranged everything on the table. She didn't say anything and didn't look at either of them properly before hurrying away. Connie almost expected the girl to curtsey, she was so nervous.

Eventually, they poured the tea for themselves. And then the doctor came, the same tired young man who had admitted Bruce that morning, and he told them the news they didn't want to hear.

'I'm very sorry,' he began. 'Mr Baxter had a heart attack half an hour ago. We did our best to help him but I'm afraid he passed away.'

'Oh,' said Kathleen quietly. She twisted her handkerchief in her hands. 'I forgot to tell you about the pain in his chest. Does that mean this is my fault?'

'Definitely not,' said the doctor. 'I think I explained this morning that we wanted to do some tests? Well, that was because of the medical history he gave me, and the note from his GP.'

'So he told you?'

'He did.' He paused. 'Sometimes a heart attack is very sudden, and there is almost no warning. And this is what happened to your husband.'

'I see.' She twisted her wedding ring around on her finger. It was loose now. Her hands had shrunk like the rest of her as the years had passed. 'Did he...?'

'He didn't feel anything. There was no pain.'

Kathleen didn't know if he was telling the truth or not, but she chose to believe him because it was the only thing to be done.

At home, after she had held Kathleen and let her cry and keen until there was nothing left, Connie went to the larder and returned with an almost full bottle of whisky.

'Come outside with me, Mother, and we'll raise a toast.'

'It's dark.'

'It doesn't matter.' Connie poured two measures into the antique crystal tumblers and added a splash of water to each.

With lights from the tenements above showing their way, they walked slowly onto the square of grass in the centre of the back green, and lifted their glasses.

'To Dad.'

'To Bruce, the best husband in the world, and certainly a better man than that charlatan Philip Wright.' Kathleen drained her glass and went back into the flat without saying another word, leaving Connie behind her in the darkness, with a thousand questions.

Pyjama trousers, shorten two inches. (K)

Grey dress, dyed black. Take in two sizes. New zip. (K)

Fred

Blog: Early July 2016

Edinburgh

Run: 5K. Cramond. Windy. 25 minutes.

The funeral went well.

As well as any funeral can go, that is.

He was ninety.

Ninety! I'm thirty-five. I cannot BEGIN to imagine what it's like to live that long.

Mum asked me to speak so I did my best.

I told them that his name was Alfred (they knew that already, obviously) – and I'm Fred, so I carry a little bit of him around with me all the time. He was a grounds-man and he was a few years younger than Nana. Every year he grew snapdragons for her on his allotment and he stopped growing them when she died. I was still at primary school when that happened.

He was on his own for nearly thirty years. That's almost as long as I've been alive. There were so many people there. I'm rubbish with names but I did recognise some people from his allotment, even though I haven't been there for years.

I haven't really got my head around it yet – it was so sudden. One day he was fine – he actually rang me to remind me about Mum's birthday – and then the next he was gone. He was found by the grass-cutting men from the council, sitting in the park opposite the flat in the sun-

shine. The man driving the lawnmower said he'd been talking to him just an hour earlier.

I'm glad the funeral is over. I hate standing up and talking in public, but I did it for Mum.

She is coming round later. Apparently, she has 'news'. I expect it's about her big holiday. I wonder if she'll still go.

Ordering takeaway pizza had been a bad idea. They sit at the kitchen table with half-eaten slices in front of them as the melted cheese congeals into a rubbery mess.

'What's the news then, Mum?' he asks, eventually, when all the other subjects they could conceivably talk about have been exhausted.

She picks up a piece of cold crust and dunks it into the little pot of garlic and herb dip, before abandoning it uneaten. 'I was going to tell you once the paperwork was all sorted out, but the sooner you know the better, really.'

'Tell me what? Have you cancelled your trip?'

'Oh no, I'm still going. Granda would have been very cross if he thought I was reneging on that plan, not after all the time it took to make the arrangements and everything.' She stops scratching at the patch of eczema on her arm, which flares when she is stressed, and puts her hands on the table, fingers interlaced. 'Four months travelling around Europe with a rail pass is exactly what I need to take my mind off all this.'

'So if it's not that, what is it then?'

'He has left you the flat.'

'This flat?'

'Come on, Fred. What other flat do you think he owned?' She reaches into her bag, takes out a large tube of emollient and squeezes a white dob of it onto her arm.

'He left it to me?'

'Yes.' She smooths the whiteness out and makes small, methodical circles in the cream with her fingertips. 'To you.'

'But why not to you? You're his daughter.'

'Are you saying you don't want it?'

He replies a little too quickly for decency. 'No, I'm not saying that at all.'

'He knew my mortgage was finally paid off, I told him at Christmas. And he knew I didn't want another property to be worrying about. We talked about everything a few months ago and he said that he would see his solicitor and change his will. He was very definite about it – he wanted you to have a foot on the property ladder.'

Fred thinks quickly. 'Did he put any conditions on it?'

She sighs. 'You mean, can you sell it?'

'I suppose.'

'Well, it probably wasn't what he intended, but he would have wanted you to do whatever you think is best.'

'I wonder how much it's worth?'

'Fred!'

'What?'

'Do you really think you would do that? Sell it, I mean?'

'I would have to get it valued and work it out from there.'

'So you might come back here?'

'Home?' He manages to be dismissive and superior in a single word. 'I left home a long time ago, Mum. It's unlikely, but I suppose anything's possible. I'm still doing contracting at the bank so it's a bit complicated at the moment.'

She is almost lost for words.

He looks around the kitchen at the cream mock-tiled wallpaper, which is embossed with brown salt and pepper pots. 'This place could provide a hefty deposit on somewhere in the south.'

'Yes, but you probably won't be making hasty decisions if your job isn't secure, will you?'

'Oh, I'll always get work,' he states with the assured confidence of someone who has never been unemployed. 'It's just a matter of how things are structured. They've as good as said they'll be keeping me on for at least a year, and there's always project work in banking.'

She swirls the last of the cold coffee around in the bottom of her mug and watches as the grounds re-blend after the sediment is disturbed. 'We need to wait for the will to be officially read and then for probate. It can take several months. I'm his executor and I know what's in the rest of it. There's nothing complicated; just a couple of small charitable bequests, and this flat.' Her phone vibrates on the table beside her and she answers it.

'Hello? You're almost finished? Right, thanks for letting me know, I'll be back in about twenty minutes.'

'The double glazing company?'

'Yes, I thought it was best to stay out of the way.'

'You're far more trusting than I would be.'

She picks up her bag and hugs her son close. 'You worry too much.'

After she has gone – and the cat has installed herself on the warmth of the just-abandoned chair – Fred makes more coffee and stands motionless in this childhood-familiar place, listening to the whine of the washing machine in the flat above as it reaches peak-spin.

He is about to be a homeowner.

'So, you're still going on this trip then?' Fred walks alongside his mother as they head into the city centre along busy pavements, weaving in and out of laden shoppers and slow-moving pensioners with walking sticks.

'I am.'

'And the solicitor is happy with that?'

She pulls the leaf-green walking jacket – bought in anticipation of her holiday – closer around her. The ever-present Edinburgh wind seems to chill, even on a sunny day. 'We'll find out for sure in about half an hour when we meet them, but it's my decision, it's nothing to do with them.'

'Yes, but...'

'They've looked at the will – they drew it up after all. As I understand it from talking to them on the phone, even though they did the legal work, it's still going to take ages to get things sorted out.'

'I thought it was quite straightforward. That's what you said before.'

'It takes as long as it takes, apparently, and even with an uncontested, uncomplicated estate, there isn't much that can be done to speed it up.' She glances across at him. 'But once I've signed the papers this morning they can be getting on with it all while I'm away, so there's no reason to put off the trip.'

'I suppose I just thought, you know, with everything' – he dodges a woman with a pram – 'you might have decided to stay here until it was all settled.' She is ahead of him now and he takes a few longer strides to catch up. She is changing, he observes. All his life she has been blonde, and her hair has got lighter and lighter as the years have passed. He had assumed she was getting it highlighted, but he can see now, as the breeze catches it, that the pale straw colour is fading and she is simply going grey.

'What's the problem?'

'No problem at all.' He is unable to voice what he's thinking – that she is getting old, and that means she will be next.

'Then I'm going. I've had this trip planned in my head for years, since before you were born, if I'm entirely honest.'

He refocuses and makes one last attempt to dissuade her. 'And the hospital don't mind?'

'Well, my manager isn't ecstatic, but I'm taking a break in service and I'll decide what to do when I come back.'

'Hold on a minute. You'll decide what to do?' This is worse than he thought. 'Are you planning to stop work altogether?'

'I don't know. I don't need much to live on, so I might take early retirement, or go part time and have some adventures.'

'This trip is quite adventurous enough already,' he mutters under his breath.

She hears him. 'I suppose it is. But as I told you, the mortgage is paid off, and there's nothing keeping me here, so I'm going to grab the chance. Even Granda told me to go – he didn't want me hanging around to look after him. He helped me to plan it with a pile of guidebooks he got from the library.'

'You never told me he was involved in the nuts and bolts of the planning!'

'You didn't ask.'

'Ouch.'

'I didn't mean it like that. Why do you have to take everything as a criticism?' She jumps over a particularly large puddle with a lightness of step many twenty-year-olds would envy. 'You were always busy with your life in the south. I used to go and see him every Friday evening.'

'Just like we always did…'

'Yes, just like we always did. He made my tea, and we would spread the maps out on the table and make plans. I wanted to take him with me actually, but he said it was my journey, not his.'

'That would have been quite a trip.'

'Carpe diem, Fred. Carpe diem.'

'OK, I get the message.' He smiles at her. 'You are a bit…' He hunts for the word. '… A bit unusual. I can't think of anyone else I know whose almost sixty-year-old mother is about to swan off for several months with just a rucksack and a rail ticket.' This is true, but his uncertainty about it all is mostly to do with the fact that his small group of acquaintances is now four hundred miles away from where he lives, and their number is shrinking by the week. It's the sort of conversation you have over the water cooler with your workmates, and that life feels as though it's another world at the moment.

'Less of the "almost sixty", please! I've got a couple more years before I collect my bus pass.'

He doesn't answer, using the excuse of crossing the road to avoid replying.

She carries on. 'I'll stay in touch. I'm not vanishing altogether. I'll have my phone so you can ring me if there's a real emergency that can't wait, and I'll have email, although I can't promise I'll be terribly prompt at replying. I am going to try to have a break from the electronic world for a bit.'

He feels as though he is being cut adrift, and realises with discomfort that this is exactly how he behaves towards her most of the time. An occasional text when he needs something. A phone call every couple of weeks. That's completely normal, he thinks. It's how his friends stay in touch with their parents. He searches his memory. Isn't it? This whole thing feels strange. It's he, and his contemporaries, who should be going off travelling and having adventures, not their responsible parents. This is all the wrong way round.

He changes the subject. 'I was hoping you might meet Samantha before you go, but you leave on Wednesday so it won't be possible.'

'When will she be here?'

'Next month. She's coming up for a visit.'

'That's a pity. You haven't talked about her much.'

The truth is that there isn't much to say. Fred had rushed back to Edinburgh when he got the phone call about his grandfather and had assumed she would follow him north, but it hadn't happened. She had said she was desperately busy and she didn't want the project they were both working on to get behind schedule. He had explained it away at the time, to himself and to everyone else, by saying that work wouldn't give her the time off and his mother had frowned a little. The excuse had been a lie, and he knew it. The truth is that there are rumours of a promotion and he is sure that this is behind her reluctance to be away from the Head Office. He simply hadn't felt strong enough to argue.

'It's early days. She's nice. Professional.' This is hardly a ringing endorsement, but he can't think what else to say.

'Maybe when I come back? You can bring her round to the house for tea.'

Fred can't imagine Sam sitting in his childhood home with its squishy sofas and over-stuffed bookshelves, higgledy-piggledy with colour. Her flat is all steel and glass and white leather.

'Yes, I'll do that.'

'Good.' His mother stops outside the imposing entrance of the solicitor's office. He can see his misshapen reflection in the gleaming brass plate on the wall and steps forward to open the door and allow her to step into the thickly carpeted hall ahead of him. Granda taught him to do that for a lady when he was a very small boy, and he has never forgotten it.

Fred sits in the flat which will soon belong to him. On the kitchen table in front of him lies an envelope; his grandfather's familiar hand-writing has scored a pattern of deep trenches into the paper.

My dear Fred,

I don't know if the fact that I have skipped a genera-tion and passed the flat to you will have come as a surprise or not. I suspect you probably thought it would have gone to your mother, but she has her own home now, and I think that Nana would have wanted this place to be yours. It has been in the family for a long time, since it was built in 1890, to be exact. Your great-grandma owned it and it passed to Nana after that, and now it's your turn.

It's the place I have lived in for more than sixty years. It's the place your mother called home and that has always been very important to me. I remember her telling us about you before you were born, and I hoped then that it would one day be your home too. It's where she brought you when you came back from the hospital as a tiny babe, and it's also where you spent a lot of time as a toddler, hiding under the table. Do you remember?

When you started at primary school, it was where you came at the end of the day when Mum was working. This place has our history in the walls and in the floors, Fred.

I don't know the circumstances of how it changed hands from me to you, or what sort of state it's in. I have tried to keep it tidy and clean, but climbing on stepladders is a bit much when you are my age and your mother would have had plenty to say about that!

This is your home now, not mine and not Nana's, so make

sure you go through the cupboards and get rid of anything you don't want. Or perhaps I should put that differently and request that you keep only what you DO want. There is nothing worse than having to live with someone else's knick-knacks. There are a few things which have been here for a very long time and which you might want to look at carefully before you decide what to do with them. My gardening tools are under the stairs – they may be of some use. Next to my bed there is a photograph of you when you were four years old, holding up a carrot next to my shed. I know you haven't had much time since you moved away but spades and forks are always useful. The other thing to look at is your Nana's sewing machine. Not the electric one, which is temperamental and a cursed thing in my opinion – probably only fit for the dump – but the old one with the bentwood cover which is next to my wardrobe. It belonged to your great-grandma. You might want to check if it still works before you decide what to do with it.

There is nothing special about any of the other furniture, no secret antiques of great value or importance. I gave a box of things to your mum last year for safekeeping.

I have no idea what you will do, and I understand that you may want to sell up and move to somewhere more exciting and suitable for your job. I don't want you to be tied to this place. Do not stay here because of a sense of obligation. Believe me, if I was your age I would have the paintbrushes out within a week of being handed the keys. It's only my wish not to worry your mother that has prevented me from doing some of the work for you.

This has always been a home for friends. My pals from the allotment used to come here every Christmas Eve and bring their families – twenty or more folk squeezed into the kitchen for mince pies and carols. Your friends came to play here too, and maybe one day there will be other young voices, or maybe not. Nothing in this life is guaranteed, as we all know.

One last thing. The kitchen window sticks when you raise the sash, so be sure to do it with care – you don't want to have it landing on the daffodils outside.

With all my love,
Granda

Jean

April 1911

Clydebank

The meeting room was packed, and from his position behind the speaker's table on the stage Donald looked out across the rows of faces. Not a chair was unfilled and the gangway spaces were crammed too. He was desperate not to let them down but he knew they wouldn't be happy about the news he was about to reveal. He walked out to the edge of the platform, his boots thudding on the boards, and waited for them to stop talking to one another. It was important to him – and to the movement – that they heard it officially from the union and not by means of the whispers that sneaked up alleys and along shop queues. He owed them that, at least.

When they fell silent, he began. 'My friends, thank you for coming here this morning.' He stopped and waited as a few more stragglers entered the hall at the back. 'Comrades, there has been a meeting with management, and I have news for you.'

He paused, and the seconds ticked by. How was he to say this?

'Unfortunately it's not the news we wanted to hear.' He watched heads shake and shoulders sink as their mood deflated with a resigned moan.

A deep voice shouted from the middle of the hall. 'Come on, Donald. Don't keep us waiting – what is it?'

The simplest way to tell them was to be honest and straightforward. 'There is going to be a ballot on the strike. The management have sent out postcards to each and every one of us asking if we will return to work.' He waved a piece of paper in the air. 'In fact, they are being delivered as I speak to you this morning and many of you will find them lying behind the door when you get home.'

Feet shuffled. 'How do you know this?' A woman's voice this time.

'I have my sources; best not to say who.' The worst part was to come. 'And there is more. If they get six thousand replies stating an intention to return to work, then the company will open the gates and restart the machinery.' He stood up straight and looked from face to face along the rows. 'It is important that we are not cowed by this.' There was an undercurrent of muttering and he didn't want there to be any doubt so he waited until he had their attention again. 'They do not, and they will not, accept our demand for collective bargaining.'

Jean, sitting in the front row, felt the crowd crumple around her. She looked down at her shoes. The soles were thin and she could feel every stone through them.

Donald raised his voice. Although untrained, the activist passion in him began to take over. He started to walk to the left-hand side of the stage. 'This means there is NO CHANGE.'

She followed him with her eyes as he moved across to the right-hand side, as did everyone else.

'EACH DEPARTMENT will have to negotiate on their OWN account for wages.' He pointed at figures in the audience. 'They want YOU, and YOU, and YOU to think this is progress.' He walked back to the centre and banged his fist on the table, one thump for each word. 'NOTHING. HAS. CHANGED.'

'But it's money in our pockets, and I have rent to pay,' someone called out from the back of the room.

He was sympathetic, but firm. 'We ALL have rent to pay. We have come far. Do NOT be scared into this.'

It was impossible to know if he was making any impression.

He made one final appeal. 'I urge you, if you decide to return the ballot, write these words across it – "Refer to Strike Committee". They must listen to us.' There was some applause and cheering, and more than a little anger, but he sensed an almost overwhelming resignation. As the hall emptied, there was a flatness of spirit which worried him.

Jean headed slowly back to her childhood home after the meeting. As she walked, she tried to glean some insight into the future by eavesdropping on the conversations taking place at stair doorways as she passed. There was little to feel positive about. She didn't want to go to the flat to face her father again; it had been exhausting dealing with his animosity – albeit from a distance – and he was sure to be delighted with this development. The relief at being away from his anger and rules was beyond words. But needs must. Her ballot postcard would be at the flat so that was where she had to go.

The mortice was unlocked so there was no need for the key in her pocket. In spite of the early spring sunshine, the flat was cool and the fire almost out. The embers on the range would barely give enough heat to boil a kettle, she thought, and she had to remind herself that it wasn't her place to bank the coals up, not anymore. Her envelope was propped up on the heavy wooden shelf above the range. Jean couldn't remember the last time she had received mail. She lifted it down. Behind it there was another, addressed to her father in an identical hand. And there was one for her mother, too.

She heard the footsteps behind her and twisted around.

'You have come back. About time,' her father said, standing between her and the door. 'The postman brought that.'

'I see,' she replied. She picked it up again and ran her finger along the raw edge where a knife had been used on the flap. 'When did it arrive?'

'It came with the second delivery.'

'And you opened it.' She looked him straight in the eye, newly confident.

'I did.' He was unmoved. 'Is there a reason I shouldn't open letters delivered to my own address?'

She could not believe that he thought this was acceptable, but on brief reflection realised that it was not surprising at all. 'But it has my name on the envelope.'

'It's my home. My name on the door. My name on the tenancy. My rules.'

There was no point in arguing about this; she wouldn't win no matter how outraged she felt.

'So what is it, then?' she asked, pretending she didn't know. She was resigned to being unable to change the attitude of a man who felt he owned the place and everything in it, including his daughter.

'A card from the company managers. Everyone has one.'

'Everyone?' She feigned surprise.

'It's about returning to work.' He was matter of fact.

'I'm not going back until they reinstate the women and change their practices.'

He walked past her to the sink to get a cup of water. 'You'll be waiting a long time then. This is as good as things are ever going to be.'

She removed the card from the envelope and read it. And it was then that she realised that not only was the envelope open, but the ballot had been tampered with. 'There's a part missing.'

He drained the cup and left it in the sink with the rest of the unwashed dishes. 'No.'

'There is.'

'No.'

'Where is the part they want me to return? There is supposed to be a section I write on and then return… not that I am going to, but it should be there anyway.'

'I've already dealt with it.'

She shook her head. 'But it was addressed to me.'

'It's for the best.'

'The best?' Her throat was so tight she had difficulty getting the words out.

'You live under my roof and I'm your father.'

'I don't. You threw me out, remember?'

'You chose to go. You could have stayed.'

'I can't believe you actually sent it back when it has my name on it.'

'It's my decision; you don't know what's best for you. It takes a man to understand business.'

She wanted to be completely sure. 'So you have returned it in my stead?'

'I have.'

'And what did you write on it?' This was futile, she knew the answer before the question was out of her mouth.

'I said that you want to return to work.'

'But I don't.'

'You are a fool.' The old anger resurfaced. 'Your head has been turned by that Donald Cameron and you don't know what's best for you. There are bigger considerations. People have rent to pay and mouths to feed. This is not about your ridiculous ideology. It's about real life and real people going to bed hungry.'

'I know it's hard, I understand that. Don't you think I realise?' She looked at him standing there, so sure of his opinion, and in that moment she knew she wasn't going to back down. 'But as for the union, there *is* a need. They should be for everyone, not just you and your friends.'

'This is company business. The master trades have reconsidered our position and we are going back to work.' He raised his voice still further and glared at her. 'This is my decision. And you will abide by it.'

'What about Mother's card?'

'I have returned that too. She would have agreed with me.'

'You really think so?'

'I do.'

'She is in the cemetery, Father.' She folded her arms and stared back at him. 'Without even a headstone.'

He seemed to grow before her, fury written all over his face.

'You think I don't know that? How dare you! You have no idea how hard things were.'

Jean knew immediately that she had gone too far. He would never forgive her for this.

She gripped her envelope and moved towards the doorway while there was still time, and then she was in the stairwell and racing down the stone steps and out into the street, heart pounding, pelting along the cobbles to find Donald. He must know surely, where she could get a new card to replace this useless one. There had to be a way of recording that it had been returned in error. But as she ran she got a stitch in her side and she slowed to a lumpy stop with tears in her eyes. There was no point now. No point in any of it.

'They won't win,' Jean insisted when she met Frances on the corner of the street, but there was doubt in her voice for the first time, an uncertainty creeping in at the edge.

'I'm not sure anymore,' replied her friend. 'My aunt knows one of the secretaries and she was told that yesterday there were great piles of postcards on the boardroom table. Three or four thousand of them.'

'Let's go to the factory. If there is news it will be there that we'll hear it.'

They continued in silence, not a companionable walk, but a fretted, lip-bitten absence.

A crowd had formed at the factory, pushing and straining forward to read the notice which had been tied to the still-chained gates.

'What does it say, Frances? See if you can get to the front.'

Frances was taller and able to see over the heads of others, so she pushed herself forward into the crowd while Jean waited for her to return. Jean could see from the look on her friend's face when she reappeared that it wasn't what they wanted to hear.

'It says that more than six thousand people have said they will go back to work,' said Frances.

'An interesting number.' Jean was scornful.

'I don't believe it either. It's far too convenient.'

'I must go back and tell Donald. He was going into Glasgow today and if I'm quick I can catch him before he sets off.'

'I'd better go home too. My mother will want to know what's happened.'

'See you later then.' They hugged goodbye and Jean turned to elbow her way through the growing crowd of men and women who were still arriving to discover the result of the count. She began to run through the streets, racing home to the flat where their bed was divided, as promised, with a long bolster. Up the stairs to the top floor, three flights, sixty-six steps. Her heart felt as though it might jump out of her chest. She was just in time; he had his coat on and was counting coins for the fare to the city.

'It's over!'

'We won?'

And then she had to tell him.

'No.'

He seemed to shrink before her eyes. 'Are you certain?'

'More than six thousand said they will go back, so that's it. We lost.'

'You are sure? Absolutely sure?'

'If you don't believe me you can go and read it for yourself. There is a notice on the gates.' This was unkind and she knew it, but her disappointment got the better of her. He should know that she wasn't in the habit of lying.

'If you say that's the case then it must be, but it's not what people were telling us.'

'They all have empty cupboards, I suppose.'

'Just another week and we'd have done it. One week.'

'Do you really think that?'

'Who knows? Everyone told us they had voted to stay out. But we already know that some cards were sent out in error.'

'Like the one which was sent to my mother. She's been dead for ten years.'

'Very true.' He rubbed his forehead as though he had been struck by a sudden pain. 'And we weren't in the grand offices when the secretaries were doing the counting, either.'

'So what happens now?'

'We abide by the wishes of the majority.' He straightened his back and stood tall. 'But it won't be the same. The company must realise that we are organised now and that they can't make changes without expecting a fight. They may have won the battle but the unions will win the war.'

Connie

Early December 1954

Edinburgh

Connie waited for days after her mother's whisky-tinged outburst for more information about the mysterious Philip Wright to come out, but the window for any revelations seemed to have been only briefly opened and then firmly closed again and she felt unable to ask questions when there was so much else to deal with. Their initial hospital stoicism had melted away and left them alternately in rivers of tears or unexpected drought, with occasional bubbles of uncontrollable laughter as they shared memories of a man who could always be relied on to find the humour in any situation.

As the weeks went by and still Kathleen kept her past life to herself, Connie stopped waiting for answers and left the subject alone. The presence, at his funeral, of Bruce's colleagues from the Education Department along with so many of his former pupils, some of them now teachers themselves, had prompted her to re-examine her reliable but tedious office job, and she had begun to scour the Situations Vacant column in the newspaper on Thursdays to see if there was anything more interesting. She wasn't a natural risk-taker, and while it was repetitive, her job wasn't unpleasant, so she was in no hurry. In the weeks after her father's death, she had at first felt as though her confidence had gone with him. He had always told her that she could do anything if she worked hard to get it, but for a long time it seemed that all the spark had gone out of her and sometimes just getting out of bed on the dark mornings was a struggle. A few speculative letters, neatly typed out in her lunch break hadn't resulted in any interviews and she was beginning to think that employers were seeing her as middle-aged, and too inflexible to learn anything new.

She was scrubbing the morning's porridge pan when she heard their firmly-sprung letter box snap closed. The starches slithered between her fingers and she tried not to get the gloop stuck under her nails. She briefly considered shaking the suds from her pink hands, and collecting the post immediately, but that wouldn't get the job done. The enamel pot was the last item to be washed, so she renewed her efforts with the washing-up brush and applied a little more pressure to the bristles in an attempt to remove the sooty residue left behind by the gas jets. There was no point, she thought, in rushing to get the job finished if she had to come back and do it all again later.

The thin roller towel which hung on a piece of dowelling on the back of the door was soft against her skin. She dried her hands carefully; she didn't want chilblains again. Her feet were cold on the never-warm flagstone floor in the scullery, despite the sheepskin slippers Mother had given her for her birthday, and she wiggled her toes to get the circulation going before stepping back onto the durable kitchen linoleum. The shiny yellow surface squeaked beneath her feet as she walked across to the hall where a scattering of envelopes lay on the carpet runner. She bent down and scooped them up against her chest. Dampness from her apron crinkled the soft paper.

Four of the five were Christmas cards and she set them down on the hall table and examined the official-looking one with her name on it first. The typewritten address was evenly spaced and correctly spelled. She closed her eyes and felt the depression of each individual letter to assess the evenness of the hands on the keys. There were no clues about the contents; it was thin, perhaps just a single sheet of paper, and she observed that the bright-red stamp had been stuck on not quite straight, as though the secretary had been in a rush.

Did this mean another application had been rejected or that she had been asked to come for an interview? She suspected that it was the former because an invitation might also have included a map or other instructions, and this was really quite an insubstantial letter.

'Mother!' she called out, looking along the hallway to the bedroom. There was no reply and, after waiting for a moment, she shouted more loudly, 'Mother, are you there? The postman has been.'

Kathleen, slightly hard of hearing – although she refused to admit it – was in the bedroom at the back of the flat. Saturday was the day for changing the bedsheets and airing the mattresses. When Bruce had been alive, she had always done it on a Monday, but she didn't have the energy for it on her own anymore, so the task had migrated to Saturday mornings when she could get some help with the blankets. At her age, her doctor told her, a certain stiffness in her back was to be expected, but her spine now ached all the time and she was thankful that she didn't live alone. She gathered the laundry up in her arms and headed out into the hall where she was met by Connie, hurrying towards her.

'Heavens, girl. At your age, is it not about time you learned to be more ladylike?'

'Did you not hear me calling? I think you are going deaf, Mother. Look, I have a letter.'

Kathleen, her arms full of sheets and blankets, gave her only daughter that look; the exasperated expression that mothers have been inflicting on their offspring for thousands of years. 'Are you not going to open it then?'

Connie turned the envelope over in her hands, running her fingers around the edges of it, trying to divine what might be inside. 'I'm a bit nervous, to tell the truth. I rather want this particular job and it might be another rejection.'

'Alright, we'll do it together, but I need my spectacles. Let's take it to the kitchen and we can see what it says. It might be from somewhere really exciting like the Electricity Board for all you know.'

'True.' Connie tucked the envelope in her apron pocket and held out her arms. 'Give me those sheets.'

Once the laundry had been put into the scullery there was no excuse to delay further. Connie sat down at the kitchen table and looked at the still-sealed envelope one final time before sliding the blade of the breadknife under the flap.

Dear Miss Baxter,

Thank you for your application for the position in the Sewing Room at the Royal Infirmary.

Please attend for an interview on Tuesday 11th January at 10am.

The department is on the top floor of the Jubilee Pavilion. Please do not use the lift.

Yours sincerely

H. Archer

Connie looked across at her mother. 'I have an interview.'

'Well, that is good news. When is it?'

'The eleventh of next month.'

'After the turn of the year then.'

'Is that going to be enough time?'

'Enough time for what?'

'To make myself something new to wear. It's so long since I had to impress a stranger.'

Kathleen leaned forward, trying to read the upside-down text. 'Which job is this?'

'It's for something completely different from bashing away at a typewriter in a noisy office. The Sewing Room in the Royal are looking for a seamstress.'

'You want to sew for a living?' Memories crowded into Kathleen's mind from a time before Connie was born, before Bruce, when all she had was this flat and her Singer sewing machine. Hundreds of hours spent stitching new dresses and repairs and curtains and bedding, most of it for other people: customers who didn't always pay on time. She could feel the desperation as though it were yesterday.

Connie, unaware of how her mother was feeling, folded the single sheet of paper back up and returned it to the envelope. 'Sewing seems no worse than typing all day. It's at the Infirmary, and I think it would be nice to do my bit to help, you know?' She sniffed hard and rummaged for her handkerchief. The grief came upon them still, when they least expected it. 'I'm too old to be a nurse, but I want to do something which matters.'

'I understand.' Kathleen waited until the tears had been wiped away before continuing. 'And you think this is it?'

'I don't know, but it might be.' Connie's mind was starting to race ahead. 'You'll help me, won't you?'

'I will, of course, but I'm sure you're more than capable of making yourself a nice skirt.'

'If this freezing weather keeps up, I might need a winter coat as well.'

Kathleen went over to the stove and struck a match. The gas burner under the kettle roared into life. 'We just need to make sure you have the best chance, that's all.' Her long hair had been pinned into a tight bun that morning, but it was starting to come loose with the effort of the bed-changing. She reached up and pulled out the hairpins which were barely holding it all in place and combed the silver-grey strands down to her waist with her fingers. With the practice of decades, she gathered it into a bunch at the nape of her neck and twisted and twisted until it curled onto itself like a rope. 'Leave it with me, I have an idea,' she said as she stabbed the pins securely back into place.

2 roller towels for the kitchen. (K)

6 face flannels, edged with bias binding from scrap box. (K)

Fred

Mid-August 2016

Edinburgh

The heavy rain of the previous few days has passed and a summery warmth has returned. Fred's morning runs have become less muddy affairs and that means less laundry, for which he is grateful, but he has developed an annoying pain in his knee which won't go away.

The old sewing-machine case is acting as an excellent doorstop in the passageway between the front and the back of the flat. Dried-out varnish on the domed lid has split lengthwise along the grain of the veneer, giving the appearance of peeling tree-bark. A sixth sense seems to guide his feet around the lump of timber and iron as he ferries ancient pieces of carpet out to the skip. He has added several new strata to the layers of floral tablecloths and well-worn towels, but he is unimpressed that a plastic curtain track and a grotty shower curtain have appeared overnight from someone else's clear-out. He heaves the more modern sewing machine, which he has established is broken, onto the top of someone else's stained duvet as a statement of skip-ownership.

He walks from room to room with his phone in dictation mode and scrutinises the decor with the eye of a property developer.

'Delightful tenement flat. Kitchen. Bathroom with sink, bath and WC. Two bedrooms. Box room. Sunny aspect.'

He pauses.

'It needs to be rewired, probably a new kitchen, new bathroom – who calls it a WC anyway? Every wall needs to have the old paper stripped and the plaster repaired so complete redecoration is essential. And it needs new windows, and decent central heating.'

He blushes with sudden disloyalty.

Through the kitchen window he can see out across the back green where his neighbour is removing the clothes pegs from the long row of small-child socks and T-shirts that have been hanging on the washing line for most of the day. He turns on the taps and runs the hot water, squeezing in a generous burst of green washing-up liquid and remembering how he used to stand at this same sink on a chair, elbow deep in the white froth, as Nana handed him the crockery from their after-school snack, one cup or bowl at a time.

The solitary mug and toast-crumbed plate washed, he sits down again and goes back to his secret blog, which is hidden from the world by technology and acts as his confidante and confessor.

The words, neatly formatted, appear on the screen.

Blog: Mid-August

Edinburgh

With perfect timing, Mum has left to go on her trip and now everything is falling apart.

Got back from London two weeks ago and I'm not feeling half as positive as I did.

It seems that the project I was working on has been reorganised and I am superfluous to requirements. I had to clear my room in the flat (not that I had much worth keeping), hire a van and drive it to Edinburgh. Most of the stuff is still in boxes.

Granda would tell me, if he were here, to treat this experience like a new allotment. He translated most advice into something horticultural, come to think of it. It was all a variation on the 'Dig hard, prepare the soil, plant the seeds and watch them grow' mantra. I remember most of life's troubles being given that treatment, from making friends at school to taking exams. He was consistent, I'll give him that.

I'm not sure I have the patience for waiting, though. In fact, I'm furious.

I signed up online with a recruitment agency in town last week and I went to see them this morning. The twenty-something who interviewed me said that it's important to have an online presence. Apparently employers routinely search the internet for the names and social media profiles of applicants. This is a bit of a problem – having spent the last ten years trying not to be visible online because it's such a minefield, it now looks as though I am going to have to pretend to be a gregarious bloke with a positive outlook on life, when all I want to do is hide away from the world and eat industrial quantities of crisps and cheese in a vain attempt to cheer myself up.

I'll be the size of a bus in a month.

I'm sitting here at Granda's kitchen table hoping he will arrive back from the allotment any minute now with some radishes or maybe some carrots. He'll put his boots on the kitchen windowsill (and wait for Nana to shout at him for it) and then he'll start to wash the dirt off his hands by tipping a teaspoonful of sugar into his palm and adding a squirt of washing-up liquid. And then, while the hot water pours into the runnels and crevices, he'll ask me how things are and he will really, REALLY want to know.

But it's not going to happen and I am completely gummed up with tears and snot and ache and utter fed-upness.

Dusk has fallen without him being aware of the time passing, and the glow of the laptop screen is now the only light in the room. Next to the computer, a dull skin forms on his mug of forgotten hour-old tea. He takes a mouthful without thinking and the cold tannins make his tongue pucker. Between the horrible taste and the tear-salt crusting on his cheek, he realises he's in a sorry state and is just about to go and wash his face when he becomes aware of something moving around his ankles.

'What the…?' He freezes. 'Oh. It's you. Could you not make a noise to warn me? Miaow or something?'

He glances at the clock in the corner of the screen. 'Food. You want food again, don't you? Perhaps I should call you Pavlov.'

The cat starts to purr as though on cue and he stands up like a good owner to do her bidding. 'Alright, alright, I'll come back to this in a minute when you give me some peace. I may as well put something in the oven for myself as well, while I'm on my feet.'

As he prepares his dinner, he reviews the current situation. There is no spare money for men in white painters' overalls, and with the exception of his interview at the agency, he has spent every minute over the last fortnight attacking the flat with a cleansing fury. The worn carpets in his old bedroom have gone, revealing flower-sprigged sage-green linoleum. He had expected floorboards and instead been met by this additional layer of hard, slightly shiny stuff, cold against his feet and lethal when wet. It has taken two days with Granda's claw hammer to get the nails out of the floorboards, followed by several hours with a Stanley knife to hack the lino into small sections, but he has finally reduced it to manageable portions and dumped it into the skip outside.

Once his meal is safely in the oven, he goes back to the blog.

Today I started to get to grips with the kitchen. If I'm going to live here, even for a wee while, I want to be able to use one room properly without tripping over things that need to have Important Decisions Made about them.

Sam will be up at the weekend and I want to make sure at least one room is habitable and nice to be in. Her place is always immaculate.

I've moved the furniture around a bit, pulled the kitchen table out of the alcove and into the middle of the room, and I asked my neighbour to help me move the new sofa bed from the sitting room into the kitchen for now so I can live in one room and keep the other doors closed until I'm ready to deal with the rest of it.

I had assumed that I'd be getting rid of the entire con-tents of this place and having it all taken to the dump but things are different now and I might as well go through everything properly. There isn't any rush – it looks as though I'm going to be here for a while.

I thought I would be fine with the clearing out but it's been hard. I did the pots and pans on the lower shelves of the larder, washed them out and put it all back in afterwards. I don't suppose I'll ever have cause to make a tray of jam tarts or a Christmas cake but you never know. After that I did the domestic stuff under the sink. Sponge scourers, Brillo pads, fabric conditioner, all organised neatly and with three of everything. It's funny how much of the food here resembles what I used to have in my old place, right down to the same brand of tomato ketchup. The first thing I saw in the larder was the Marmite. Granda always had a jar of it (three jars, actually) and he used to have it every morning on his toast. Two slices, cut diagonally, no butter, and when he had finished spreading it he would poke the knife into the slice, between the two toasted surfaces, to wipe off the last of it and make sure none was wasted. I used to watch him lick the knife surreptitiously so Nana wouldn't see, and then he'd give me this enormous theatrical wink.

When I looked around the flat in June I realised that there were brown glass Marmite jars all over the place; there were cuttings sprouting in them on the kitchen windowsill for a start, and they must have been there for a few weeks because they had a good network of roots. I topped them up with fresh water and a sprinkling of sugar, just as he would have done. I haven't killed them yet – I think they are geraniums.

It's these small personal things that remind me that he really has gone. There's another jar on the sideboard next to the phone with pens in it. And I was looking at his bedroom and there's one with cufflinks and collar stiffeners on the tallboy.

There was even a jar beside the sink in the bathroom with his razor in it and another one next to it with his toothbrush, so of course I've thrown those out – and I'll save my own jars to use from now on. I hope someone has put the ones I left behind at the old flat into the recycling.

In the larder I found jam jars with labels written by Nana – herbs, mostly, and things she used to call dry goods like stock cubes and pearl barley. It's as though Granda couldn't bring himself to wash away her handwriting. Come to think of it, I'm not sure I can throw them away either, so I have kept the jars and thrown away the contents. It's the same writing that is on my birthday cards –

I still have all of them. I kept them in a shoebox that lived on the top of their wardrobe and it's still there, I checked.

And then I found the old tin of cocoa. It must be ancient, at least forty years old; the price is in shillings and pennies. Nana, and then Granda, must have refilled it over and over again. I opened it up and it's almost empty but the smell is so familiar and comforting. It's the taste of going to bed and of bedtime stories and being wrapped up in a quilt when I was poorly. I can't abide the cloying sweetness of milky hot chocolate and all the trimmings that get added in coffee shops: the whipped cream and marshmallows and syrups. It's like having a pudding in a cup. Give me proper cocoa any day. I washed the tin out and it's drying on the rack beside the sink. Tomorrow I'm going to go to the shop and buy a fresh supply so I can refill it again.

The timer on his phone pings to remind him about his food. The smell of melted strong cheddar and mustard escapes from the hot oven as he opens it to reveal his favourite meal. Across the bubbling surface of the cauliflower cheese, flashes of green brassica foliage stud the toasted breadcrumb topping. He serves himself a huge plateful and carries it over to the table. At least I can cook, he thinks.

Jean

They went back to work on the tenth of April and it was less than a week later that Donald was called to the office. He wasn't alone in finding that his services were no longer required; a slew of strike organisers found themselves in the same position. He had worked at the factory every day since leaving school at fourteen but an impeccable attendance record hadn't protected him from being sacked. They hadn't called it that, of course. He was told that new processes meant there were too many foundrymen and he was welcome to apply for another job when they started hiring again.

When Jean got home from her shift, he was already back in the flat after spending another day on a fruitless search for work. He shook his head before she had a chance to ask the question. She laid her wage packet on the table beside him and knelt on the washed floorboards. 'There is a job for you somewhere. We just have to find it.'

There was enough money for the rent, but little for fuel or food. A woman's wage couldn't make up for what he had been paid for working in the foundry.

'I have tried.' There were tears of defeat in his eyes. 'I went as far as Greenock with the fish porter, but there is no work there for me.'

'There's nothing else?'

'I'm told the insurance men are hiring – they have jobs for salesmen – but I'm a practical person, not a bean-counter.' He hit the table hard in frustration. 'We need to leave this place.'

'I don't want you to feel bad, but I think you are probably right.' She placed her hand over his and felt the smarting heat of it.

She eased herself wearily to her feet and walked over to the cold range. On the shelf next to it, tucked behind the box of fire-spills, was the letter from Donald's cousin that had arrived three weeks earlier. They read it every night and it gave them some hope. A response was now overdue and she noticed that the address was smudged with fresh tears since she had held it that morning. Inside was one possible future.

Dear Donald,

We are unhappy to hear that there is no improvement in your circumstances.

I have asked at the docks and the owner has sympathies with your situation. He will make a place for you. It won't be skilled work, but it's something. You can stay here with me and Hannah until you have rent saved for your own place. We will manage together.

Write when you have decided.

Your cousin,

Tom

'Edinburgh it is, then,' she said, more brightly than she felt.

He half smiled. 'It looks like it.'

'I'll write back to them this evening.'

'Jean, I have to say this to you now, before I lose my nerve.' He took a deep breath. 'This isn't how I thought things would be for us. You turned eighteen last week, and there are plenty of men who could give you a better life than me. If you want to stop all this, and find someone else, then I understand.'

She knew what it had cost him to say this. 'Well, since we are speaking plainly, you must listen to me as well. I am with you because I want to be, never doubt it. We will get through this together.'

'I hope so,' he whispered under his breath.

'I am sure of it.'

He got to his feet and held her tightly before breaking away.

She washed her hands and face in the chill water at the kitchen sink. From the second-floor window she looked down on children playing peevers on the pavement below. In every tenement along the street there were families she had known all her life. Leaving would not be an easy thing to do.

Donald set the table with plates and a knife at each place, and cut fat slices of bread from the loaf, making sure she had the softer fresh edge and giving himself the rough, dry end from the day before. And then he pulled out her chair with a flourish and seated her as though it were the finest of establishments. There was no brew of tea with the range unlit, but it didn't matter.

'So, Jean, tell me about your day?'

This was his last connection with the place where he had worked for eleven years. She did her best.

'Well, there is a new manager in the Pay Office. Very smart. Smells of cologne and coconut, which don't go well together, I can tell you. His hair is loaded with Macassar oil and it looks as though it's been painted on with a brush – completely flat, it is, with a parting down the middle. He wears a suit with thin stripes and a white shirt that has so much starch in the collar, you can see the rash on his neck. He looks very uncomfortable.'

'Is he from Glasgow?'

'Oh no. American, but from a different place to the old one. He talks so slowly; it's like watching treacle drool off a spoon. He watches over the wages being collected and looks as worried as if it's his own money he's handing over.'

'It's a wonder the place doesn't have its own bank. It would make sense, and if they can build a damn power station…'

She moved on quickly, not allowing the idea to fester. Filtering the news had become a nightly task. Nothing too good or exciting, and especially nothing from the foundry, not that she knew much, but still. 'There is talk of stopping the long bobbin machines again. Can't see it myself, but you know how that rumour never goes away. And they are designing new decals. Rococo, they call them.'

He smiled for the first time since she had arrived home. 'Too much ice cream being eaten on a Saturday afternoon, if you ask me.'

'You're right. Now, I'd best get on with that letter, before the light fails.' She swept the breadcrumbs from the table with her hand and screwed them up tightly in a piece of paper before putting a match to it in the empty grate. She didn't want more mice, even if they were going to be leaving this place soon.

Jean

Jean dragged the table over to the kitchen window beside the sink in an attempt to avoid lighting a candle or worse, burning gas. The tap dripped cold water onto the crazed stoneware but she barely noticed; it had been like that for months.

Her father was on the warpath, and after his accusation that Donald was 'only after one thing' it had taken every ounce of cunning she possessed to keep the two men from meeting in the street by chance. Tonight, she had managed to persuade Donald to meet his friends in the bar on the corner; they had promised him a pint of beer.

'This is how it must feel to be a spy,' she said to the empty room, as she surveyed her tools.

Two bobbins. Dip pen. Ink. Scissors (borrowed from Frances). Bags saved from their minimal food shopping. A wooden reel of white cotton. A Bible.

She had told no one of her plan. This was in part because she didn't feel the need to hear their opinions about risk and recklessness, but also because she wanted to protect them. If they knew nothing, and she was found out, they could deny all knowledge with a clear conscience. She sat down on the hard chair and pulled forward a paper bag, smoothing it, feeling the gritty detail of a few grains of sugar beneath her fingertips. She measured the length of the paper she needed and marked it, using the straight edge of the bread board as a guide. The words had been inscribed across her mind for weeks. She lifted the pen, loaded the nib with black ink as she was once taught, and wrote, slowly and neatly. If her old class teacher had been looking over her shoulder he would have been pleased with her penmanship. Pleased, but incredulous.

The words came to the edge of the bag and spilled over onto a second line. A wasp of irritation rose up inside her and she swatted it back. She needed to make her lettering even smaller or this would not work.

As she pondered, she turned the discarded paper bag diagonally.

She rolled it into a tight tube and tied it into a knot so that her words were hidden inside. And then she threw it with some force into the empty coal scuttle.

Three more bags were similarly despatched until she was happy with her prose.

She opened the Bible. Years of Sunday School attendance helped her to find what she was looking for with ease. She breathed the familiar words of Ecclesiastes chapter three, savouring the seventh verse:

'A time to rend, and a time to sew; a time to keep silence,
 and a time to speak.'

She raised her eyes upwards briefly, lined up the scissors and swiftly sliced off the edge of the page before she could change her mind, leaving the printed verses untouched. In tiny copperplate script, she wrote her message along the strip of thefted paper, forming each letter slowly with feather-light upstrokes and firm downstrokes. As soon as the ink was dry, she lifted one of the bobbins between finger and thumb and lined up the paper strip against the central spindle. One rotation at a time, her words disappeared until the paper was wound into position. She unwound a long length of thread from the wooden cotton reel and fastened it around the centre of the bobbin. A quickly made slip-knot, a tug, and it was safely held. Finally, she spooled the cotton into place, forming a perfect spiral of white, which hid the secret message completely.

She was finished.

The bobbin sat in her palm, one third full, securely knotted with a half hitch.

It was indeed time to speak.

At ten minutes to the final hour, Jean picked up an empty bobbin from the box in the centre of the worktable and loaded it with white thread in the usual way. Anyone in the department who was watching her might have noticed her trembling fingers and sympathetically assumed it was down to nerves on her last day at work.

'Behave, girl,' her inner voice scolded.

She rested her fingers on the glossy black surface of the machine to steady them and deliberately allowed the bobbin to slip from her fingers onto the wooden floor. Making no fuss, but at the same time assuming that the whole world was scrutinising her every move, she bent down to pick it up, and substituted it for the paper-wrapped bobbin that was hidden in her deep skirt pocket. She had practised this small act at home, over and over, making sure it was a smooth process and that she didn't fumble in the folds of the fabric.

'Test as normal. Test as normal.' Her mind raced. She sat back on her chair, undid the half hitch and dropped the new bobbin neatly into the race.

Seven minutes.

Her hands were clammy with guilty perspiration. She began to thread the machine from the spool on top of the machine but it was impossible. Her hands shook and she was unable the pass the cotton through the eye of the needle.

'Calm down. Take a breath. And another one.' She breathed the instruction without a sound.

At the fifth attempt the white fibre slipped through the tiny hole and she tightened the clutch to lower and raise the needlebar, allowing the mechanism to collect the bobbin loop from below.

Five minutes.

There was still time to change her mind.

The workshop clock on the wall ticked loudly above her and she asked herself for the hundredth time why anyone would be interested in the words of a factory girl from Clydebank. She hadn't told anyone about her plan, not even Donald. Little by little his spark was fading in front of her eyes. His job had always defined him but now he seemed to have lost all confidence, so she had taken over. She had written letters, dealt with the rent man, and finally, given her notice at the factory. Hiding the message was more than an act of defiance. It was necessary.

She silently whispered her way through the steps, lips barely moving.

'Cloth. Fold. Under the needle. Lower the foot. Hold the ends. Wind the handcrank. Stitch forward. Raise bar. Pivot. Lower bar. Twenty stitches. Raise bar. Pivot. Lower bar. Adjust the big screw for the stitch length. Stitch. Raise the lever. Pull. Be careful now. Cut the thread from sample. Inspect. Please, PLEASE, let it be good.' She checked the stitches from above and below, and was satisfied. 'Put the cloth back ready for shipping.'

She looked up to check the time.

One minute.

'Remove the reel. Run off a length of thread, twice fingertip to wrist. Don't waste any.' She almost laughed out loud; who would care? 'Keep machine threaded. Wrap thread around spool pin. One turn. Two. Three. Four. Five. Six. Half hitch. And another one. Pass machine forward.'

Except that she couldn't pass it forward.

The loud factory siren was booming out across the site, signalling the end of the working day. The machine would now sit on her table until Monday morning, awaiting a new worker, and its protective brown paper wrapping.

Jean was lightheaded from the strain. At the same time, she knew that it didn't matter anymore. If the supervisor or anyone else discovered her deed it would be too late for them to do anything to hurt her.

She knew that her message would probably be read once – if at all – and then discarded without a second thought, but she didn't care. It was enough for her to have made the statement.

The factory exhaled, coughing out hordes of workers who bumped and cajoled her down the wide stone staircase and into the beckoning roundness of evening sunshine. The brightness made her screw up her eyes after the flat electric light of the factory and she paused on the final step, gripping the painted iron railing so firmly that her knuckles went white. She couldn't afford to have any regrets; there was no work for Donald in Clydebank. It was time for a fresh start.

At the gate she turned to look back at the stone building, still growing with new floors and yet more development planned. Progress seemed unstoppable and it was odd not to feel a part of it now, but their decision was the right one, she was sure of that.

Jean took her time walking back to the tenement, hugging friends as they peeled off up their own streets and waving to less well-known faces. The next few days would be taken up with preparations for leaving. There wasn't much to pack. So little wage for so many weeks had meant selling everything they didn't need. She had already given away the cooking pots and sold their chinaware. What the pawnbroker wouldn't take had gone for pennies to anyone who offered.

Donald's tools and indenture papers were packed into his canvas work bag; he had to have them with him if he was to stand any chance of foundry work. They had just two small cases for everything else – all they would be able to manage on the train.

It would be an adventure, she told herself. And if it wasn't, she would just have to make it so.

Connie

Boxing Day 1954

Edinburgh

'I think it's time.' Kathleen stood at the door of Connie's small bedroom. Outside, the church bells pealed across the park calling her neighbours to the Sunday morning service. She hadn't set foot in the place since the funeral.

'Time? Time for what?'

'It's time we went through your father's things.'

'You mean his clothes?' Connie put down her magazine and gave her mother her full attention.

'There is plenty of good cloth in those things; some of them were hardly worn.'

'I'm not sure I want to…'

'Waste not, want not.'

'You want to cut his clothes up?' This was taking thrift a little far. 'Dress fabric isn't on the ration anymore, you know.'

'Don't be cheeky.'

'I'm sorry.' She meant it. This was a big step; Kathleen had refused to give away Bruce's old suits and shirts, or even move them from their place on his side of the wardrobe to somewhere else in the flat.

'He's been gone for almost three months now and I know he would want to help.' Her voice softened as she remembered the milestones father and daughter had shared; the school nativity play, the first length of the swimming pool, the secretly baked cake they had made her for Mothering Sunday, just last year. 'He was always so proud of you.'

'Are you sure about this?' Connie got up off the bed and smoothed the counterpane. 'I mean, you haven't set eyes on any of it since…' She couldn't say the words.

'I can't bring myself to give them away. I don't like the idea of some other man walking about in his suits or wearing his ties.' She shuddered. 'It doesn't bear thinking about.'

'That's OK. I understand.' She put her arm around Kathleen's shoulder and steered her out of the room and towards the kitchen. 'Let's have something to eat first and then we'll get started. No time like the present.'

'That was my thought too.'

And then Connie was embarrassed to hear her mother say exactly what she had been thinking herself. 'If there isn't anything suitable for your interview, there will still be time for you to buy yardage instead.'

Kathleen turned the small key in the wardrobe lock. Despite her offer, she wasn't at all sure how she would feel about seeing Bruce's clothes again. The unmistakeable aroma of mothballs flooded into the room as she slid the bolt on the second door and opened them both up to the late morning sunshine which was pouring through the windows. So many memories.

She stood back and looked at the left-hand sleeves of shirts, jackets and coats. It was like the rail in a men's tailor shop. Bruce had been a meticulous man and all the coat hangers faced in the same direction, the shirts organised by age and wear. Below the hanging space were his shoes, polished to a gleaming shine and held in shape by shoe trees.

'I don't mind about these,' she said. 'I'm sure there is a charity that will make sure they go to someone who needs them.' She started to remove one of the laces.

Connie reached out quickly and snatched the shoe. 'What are you doing?'

'Shoelaces are always useful.'

'People who need shoes, Mother, will also be needing something to keep them on their feet.' She held out her hand for the lace.

Kathleen sat down on the bed and put her head in her hands. 'Oh my goodness. What was I thinking?'

Connie patiently rethreaded the eight holes and adjusted the lace so it lay evenly. She fetched a cardboard box from the scullery and loaded all the shoes, well-polished and garden-only, into the box. 'What about his slippers?'

'Under the bed, exactly where he left them.'

'You stay there. I'll do it.' She bent down to retrieve them. 'Do you remember me cursing when I knitted these?' She stroked the rough carpet wool. 'My fingers were raw by the time I was finished.'

'I do. And I remember you standing in the snow waiting for the shop to open so you could be sure of getting the soles for them too.'

'They are so' – she searched for the right word – 'so robust. They must be ten years old, at least.' She turned them over to examine the stitching. 'I don't know why he kept them all this time, I can't imagine they were ever very comfortable, and he had those nice tweedy ones you gave him at Christmas anyway.'

'He kept them because you made them for him, of course.'

Connie nodded and put the slippers into the box. 'Maybe they'll do someone else a turn, you never know.'

They tackled the clothes rail next. Connie took the wooden hangers out one at a time and started to make a pile on the bed. Two grey wool suits came out first, with a waistcoat for each, a tweed jacket, another suit in dark blue, an even darker blue overcoat, a mackintosh and, finally, the shirts.

'Right then, let's get to it.' Kathleen paused for a moment as she looked at the lifetime of school meetings and theatre visits and afternoon tea with scones, and then she waved her hand over the heap like a magician. 'You can have anything you want.'

'Anything at all?'

'Yes. If we put our thinking caps on we should be able to make some dresses at the very least, and maybe even that winter coat you need as well.'

They opened out every garment and checked all the pockets. The pre-war suits had numerous useful buttons on the front and on the cuffs. To Connie's surprise, the trousers had buttons for the fly; she had expected zips. Kathleen stroked the suiting thoughtfully. 'Father chose this at the tailor's in Leith just after he was appointed to the Education Board.'

'I remember.'

'You know, until he had that dark-navy suit, he had worn the same plain grey to school for years, even when he was a head teacher. He used to wear a long black gown over the top and he kept his chalk in the wings. He always said there was no point in buying anything different because he wasn't there to be fashionable.' She paused for a moment, remembering, and then turned her attention to the overcoat. 'It's a pity about this coat; the cuffs are a little threadbare.'

'It's good wool. I'm sure we can use it for something.' Connie took it from her mother and turned it inside out. 'The lining too.'

Kathleen turned back to the almost empty hanging rail. 'We're almost finished; there's only the shirts left. One, two…' She counted the hangers. 'Eleven, if we count the ones he wore to cut the grass in the back green. He liked a nice shirt, did your father.'

'Let me see.' Connie lifted them up one after another and inspected them.

'They aren't very interesting – just plain white cotton – but some of the buttons are mother-of-pearl and could be very pretty on a blouse, and the cloth could perhaps be dyed.'

'Maybe we could dye the buttons as well?'

'We could try, but I think they are nice enough as they are.'

There were other things in the internal drawers of the wardrobe; pyjamas and underwear and socks, and these were put into the same box as the shoes without being examined too closely.

'I think that's everything apart from his ties and his dressing gown.' Connie held up a spruce-green silk robe, which had a small paisley print in red and gold and a twisted cord piping around the collar. 'I never saw him wear this.'

'I don't think he ever did. I made it for him before the war and he said it was far too good to use around the house, so it just stayed in the wardrobe. Such a waste, really.' Kathleen lifted the ties off their hanger. 'Come over here for a minute and hold your arm out for me.'

'Alright.'

Kathleen counted the occasions off, one tie at a time. 'New school, your twenty-first, promotion, Christmas, election to the Board, birthday—' She stopped suddenly and sat down on the padded stool next to her dressing table, holding a piece of crimson silk. 'Our wedding.'

'That's Dad's tie from your wedding?'

'He wore it once a year, every single year, just for me.'

'You've never mentioned it.'

'It was a secret. Well, not a *secret*, secret. Just a private thing between us.'

'Have you still got your wedding dress?'

'No, it was cut up to make things for you when you were a baby.' She was wistful. 'I think I might have the lace trim somewhere.'

Connie didn't want to miss an opportunity to hear all the details. 'Tell me about the wedding. I need to know everything about it.'

'It was lovely. One day you'll find out what it feels like, I hope.'

'Maybe, but I'm not holding my breath.'

'It will be when you least expect it. That's how it was for us.'

And just as Connie was hoping for more revelations, Kathleen seemed to bring the shutters down on the past and she changed the subject. 'We'll take these through to the kitchen where it's warmer and we can start making some proper plans. I'd like to get on with the sewing as soon as possible. We can begin by taking all the buttons off these shirts this evening while we listen to the Home Service.'

Blouse, blue dyed cotton with red piping and red covered buttons (C)

Blue cotton skirt (C)

Blue handkerchief, red hem (K)

Fred

Blog: Early September

Edinburgh

Sam is coming up for the weekend. It feels like ages since I saw her. Texts just aren't the same. I'm picking her up from the station this evening. She's travelled all over the world – Florida, Spain, New York, even Dubai – so I want to make an effort. I'm looking forward to showing her around. It's a pity the Festival is over, but she couldn't make it away from work until now.

I've ventured into the sitting room and started making piles of stuff for the charity shop and a separate heap for the bin. I might sell some things on eBay, if I can work out how it operates. Taking good photos isn't as easy as it looks; thank goodness it's pixels I'm burning, not film.

The clear-out continues. The charity shop pile is where I've put the mismatched glasses and china and I think that's where Granda's clothes will go, once I've put them all through the washing machine, of course. It was an odd feeling to be putting shirts and trousers on the pulley in the kitchen today. I must have seen Nana do it hundreds of times and all of a sudden it's me standing there instead of her.

The auction pile is a lot less definite: there's the sewing machine, which I seem to trip over a dozen times a day. But, to be honest, I really don't know what I'm doing. The decision-making all feels very complicated and not at all as straightforward as I thought it would be.

Better get going. I don't want to be late.

The train is an hour and twenty minutes behind schedule and it's dark when Samantha eventually steps onto the platform. She is clearly tired. Fred sees immediately that the prospect of a bus journey across the city is not going to be well received and he decides to splash out on a taxi he can ill afford instead.

After the cab pulls away, she looks up and down the street, following the line of tenements. 'When you said it was a flat, I thought you were talking about an apartment, not an ancient monument.'

'Sorry.' He wonders why he is apologising – it's not as though he can do anything to shave a century off the deeds.

'I was kidding. I'm too used to my own place, that's all.'

He opens the front door and the familiar smell of lavender furniture wax warms the air; the flat smells of his childhood. He shows her through to the kitchen.

'I'd kill for chilled Pinot.' She hooks one finger around the door handle of the fridge as though it might be contaminated, but brightens when she sees the familiar green glass bottle. 'Where are the glasses? I am completely parched.'

'Let me show you round first.'

She sighs and puts the bottle down. 'Will it take long? I really want a drink after that train journey from hell.'

'I want you to see it, that's all. This is the kitchen, obviously.'

'It looks like something from the 1950s, and not in a good way.'

'Well, I don't think it's been updated for a while, that's for sure. Granda was at his allotment more than he was here.'

'I thought you said he was quite elderly?' She speaks as though this is a thoroughly undesirable state. 'I'm sorry about the funeral – work was impossible and I really couldn't get away.'

He isn't sure he completely believes her, but it's pointless to ask for details. 'Granda was ninety. I suppose that's older than average.' He pauses. His grandfather wasn't some actuarial statistic. He was the man who taught him to draw cars, and helped him remember the names of the constellations in the night sky. Before Fred can find the words to explain, she has set off along the hall.

'It's not very big, is it?' she calls from the sitting room. Then she opens and closes all the other doors, giving each room a cursory look.

'I haven't finished clearing out,' he apologises.

'I can see that – there is stuff all over the bed. So where am I sleeping, then?'

'We can use the sofa bed. I bought it a few weeks ago and it's quite comfortable.'

'Hmmmm.'

Fred has never seen her behave like this before. He tries again. 'So, what do you think? I reckon it has great potential.' He is defensive without realising it. 'And I suppose I could change a few things.'

She looks around. 'If you aren't going to buy a place brand new, like I did, then you need to look at a property with the eyes of a developer.'

'I would, if I was going to sell it, but I'm not sure about that yet. There's legal stuff that needs to happen first. We're still waiting for probate so I can't do anything major until that's been completed.'

She continues as though he hasn't spoken. 'You need to knock out the internal walls, open it up a bit.'

'Not sure I can do that; it would affect the flats above me.'

'Not even with structural support?' She doesn't seem to believe him. 'It would make it a lot more spacious, that's for sure.'

'I like it how it is. It's traditional. There's nothing wrong with the layout.'

She is unimpressed. 'Well, yes, if you want a coal range taking up half the wall and a utility room that has a gale blowing through it from outside.'

'That's from before there were fridges; my Nana managed without one until the 1960s. I suppose your grandmother did too.' He is increasingly irritated.

'Yes, but we *have* fridges now, so that gap could have been blocked up a long time ago.' Her voice softens. 'I'm sorry, Fred, I'm shattered and I can see it's not what you want to hear, but it's like a time warp.'

He can feel himself getting annoyed. 'It's a home, not a designer apartment.'

'I know, but...'

'It's nothing a coat of paint won't fix.'

She sits down at the table and pours her own wine since Fred clearly isn't going to do it for her. 'Let's see how far you've got. For example, have you done anything about choosing a new kitchen yet? I'm really good at that sort of thing.'

'I thought I'd move the furniture around and take measurements, maybe go for something in keeping with the old black range. Free standing, you know?' He has been looking at vintage websites, trying to find the right look and has realised, to his surprise, that a fitted kitchen isn't a compulsory purchase. The larder is well provided with shelves, there is a big table and a good-sized sink. He needs to buy new appliances, and install a modern cooker, but most of what's in the room has a certain charm. It just needs elbow grease and a good scrub.

She drains her glass. 'All those nooks and crannies; not my style at all.'

'Well, you aren't going to be living in it, so that's not important.' The words are out of his mouth before his brain catches up.

'My opinion doesn't matter?' Sam pours a second glass of wine.

'Of course it does.' Fred realises too late that this is all going terribly wrong, and tries desperately to back-track. 'But until things are sorted out legally, the less I spend the better.'

'I'm not sure you understand. It needs to be done properly. Have money spent on it so that you get the best return.'

'Nope. It doesn't.'

'What about the bathroom? There isn't even a proper shower.'

This is true; since he's been living in the flat he has been forced to have baths, something he hasn't done for years, quite possibly since he lived here as a child. The surface of the enamel on the bath is rough from years of scrubbing and cleaning and this, rather than the perfectly serviceable kitchen, will probably be his first priority. 'It will need a new suite,' he concedes.

'No kidding. You think? I can't believe you haven't thought about all this already. When does the skip arrive?'

'The skip?'

'You said you were ordering a skip.'

'Oh that. I've had one already, and the next is booked for two weeks' time when you are back up so we can do some of the work then.'

'We?'

'I thought we could do it together.'

She splays out her hands and examines her manicure. 'What makes you think I would want to do that?'

'I thought you would be interested? You know, peeling back the layers of the place, finding the history.'

She shakes her head. 'If I come all this way for a weekend, Fred, I want to go out and have coffee with you, not spend it wearing a hazmat suit.'

Right on cue, Crabbie appears outside the kitchen window and stares in through the glass, mewling to be let in.

'Tell me you haven't gone and got yourself a cat,' says Sam, and she starts to fumble in her bag for something.

'She was my Granda's cat. Her name is Crabbie.' He reaches

across the draining board to open the sash window. 'She's quite friendly.'

'Don't you dare open that window.'

Fred stops. 'You don't like cats?'

'I'm allergic.' She pulls a blue inhaler from her bag. 'They make me wheeze. I wondered why my chest was getting tight.'

'Ah. I see.' He sits back down and shrugs an apology to the cat. 'I didn't realise.'

Sam takes her phone from her pocket and switches it on. She opens up a browser. 'Shall we look for a hotel, unless you can tell me where the nearest one is?'

'A hotel?'

'Well, I can't stay here and inhale cat fumes, and unless you want me to spend the night by myself, you won't either.'

Blog – phone-blogged in the middle of the night

Well, that didn't go as well as I thought it might. People can be very unexpected when you see them out of context.

I'm not sure what to do.

I could take Crabbie to the Cat and Dog Home next week – that would be one way of sorting the problem out. Maybe Sam will change her mind when she sees how nice the flat's going to be when it's finished. And if she really doesn't want to live here with me then I suppose I could put it on the market and move back down south.

She got an email last night just after we booked in at the hotel. Apparently she's been called back to the office to sort out some major problem so that's our romantic weekend over before it's started. She's getting the eleven o'clock train.

Sam is more relaxed on the way to the station. Their differences seem to have been resolved, and she is back to being her usual bright and chatty self. Fred buys her a latte from the coffee seller on the concourse – it might be ages before the refreshment trolley arrives. He stands on the platform and watches as she works her way along the carriage, looking for an unallocated seat, and then, as the train starts to move, he blows her a kiss and waves.

His phone pings five minutes after the train leaves the station and he looks at the screen.

```
I'm really sorry, Fred, but this is not
going to work. I wasn't sure, but I am
now. It's been nice, but things are dif-
ferent with us living so far apart. Hope
you find someone else soon.
```

There isn't even an x at the end of the message.

He stops walking and reads it again.

'Did you even wait for them to announce the destination?' he says out loud, and shoves the phone deep into his coat pocket.

The rest of the day stretches ahead of him. There is food for two in the fridge, chocolate dessert, double cream and, although it's well hidden behind a family-sized box of cornflakes, there is a bottle of champagne in the back of the larder. He won't be needing that today.

Five minutes later his phone pings again and he scrabbles for it, hoping she has changed her mind, but it's just the message repeating on the screen. Technology is once again his enemy.

He doesn't go straight back to the flat but takes a detour westwards along the canal path, a place he was forbidden to explore when he was a child. The warehouses are closed now and some have been converted into upmarket flats with a waterside view of the narrowboats that are berthed in the sweep of the basin. He looks at the towpath with fresh eyes. The surface underfoot is even and not covered in puddles. Perhaps it might be a place to go for a run? With this thought in his head, drowning out all the others he doesn't want, he heads back to the flat, to his cat and the sound of next door's children squabbling as they race around the washing poles in the back green.

Blog – update.

That went spectacularly well.

I wasn't even halfway home before I got a 'Thanks but no thanks' text. I consoled myself by going to the fish and chip shop on the end of the street and bought a big portion doused in salt.

Cholesterol?

I LAUGH in the face of your lipids and plaques.

Sorting out boxes in his grandmother's bedroom in the company of her dressing table with its three mirrors has made Fred acutely aware of his receding hairline. It's been a couple of months since he had a haircut. His last visit to a salon was in London at that place in Islington with the Italian coffee and tiny biscuits, served as the shears snipped.

He goes into the bathroom and studies his reflection. Before he has time to change his mind, he lifts the nail scissors from the shelf, and leans over the bath.

Snip.

A clump of blond hair falls from his fingers. As the first clipping lands he knows it's too late to change his mind. He works from the back of his neck, upwards. The snippets of hair get more and more sparse as he moves across the top of his head, and it's all the evidence he needs that this is a good decision. He doesn't tidy up as he goes along; the asthmatic vacuum cleaner will deal with the mess in the bath later.

He fills the sink with hot water. The mirror is covered in condensation but he doesn't bother wiping it; this is a task to be done by feel. He skooshes cold shaving gel into his hand and smears it all over his head, where it blooms into puffy foam on his scalp.

With each stroke of the razor he gets rid of Samantha and banking contracts and wine bars. It takes longer than he expects. Eventually, he rinses the remains of the gel off, and watches with interest as a mixture of hair, dust and froth washes down the plughole. He repeats the gel/fluff/shave/rinse combination a second time, feeling every centimetre of skin carefully.

'That's better.'

In the wiped clean mirror, his reflection nods agreement.

Jean

Early July 1911

Leith

The train drew into Waverley station in the early July evening. They waited until everyone had disembarked, clinging to the idea that, for as long as they stayed in the carriage, none of this was really happening. Jean had never travelled beyond Glasgow, and this new stage in their lives was both essential and terrifying. There was nothing in the west for them now. No work for Donald, and as her father had made clear, no family ties for Jean.

George's fury had been mountainous. He had been angry with her, of course, but most of his rage had been directed at Donald. Despite their every attempt to explain, he would not be calmed and had made it clear that they did not have his blessing.

They left without any fuss on a day when the factory was working at full capacity. There was nobody to wave them off.

It had been a long journey. Glasgow Central Station was smoky and yet oddly uplifting with its high roof and imposing ranks of ticket booths. It was clearly a place of business. In contrast, Waverley seemed smaller and more contained. This was in keeping with what Jean had learned at school; that the capital was a more genteel place with few of the powerhouse factories of its sister city in the west.

They were the last to disembark, and as she stepped off the train, Jean had a sudden rush of hope. It came from nowhere, and she couldn't have explained it if she had tried, but the weight of the last month seemed to ease. The metallic smell of the brakes and the soot from the engine clung to them like a cloak, and as they walked off the platform and onto the concourse, a man approached them; Tom was as good as his word and had come to meet the train. He shook Donald's hand and clapped him on the shoulder and nodded in the way that men do in public when they think someone might be watching.

'This is my Jean,' said Donald, putting his arm around her shoulder and pulling her close. He seemed more at ease than she had seen him for weeks.

Tom lifted his cap. 'Pleased to meet you at last.'

Jean smiled back at him, all at once shy and lost for something to say.

'We are glad to be here,' said Donald.

The two men shared the luggage between them, leaving her empty-handed.

'Hannah said right away that you had to come to Leith.' Tom looked at his cousin. 'You have grown some, since we last met. How old were we? Nine?'

'Something like that.'

As they walked up the steps beside the thick stone walls of the North British Hotel, they were enveloped by the smell of roasting meats from the kitchens and Jean realised that, after days of feeling nauseous, with a rock-like lump in her stomach, she was suddenly hungry. At the top they turned right, past the top-hatted doorman, and crossed Princes Street. It was a good half-hour walk, down Leith Street and onto Leith Walk, and then further into the side streets, thankfully downhill all the way. Who knew travelling, and sitting down at that, could be so wearisome?

The tenements were not dissimilar to those Jean was used to. Familiar smells and sounds of families going about their evening routine surrounded her, as mothers called on children from the windows above. They arrived at a heavy black door, and Tom fumbled in his pocket for the key before he gave up and tugged the brass bell pull that connected to the flat above. Three rounds of stairs to the top landing brought them to their destination.

Tom pushed open the unlocked door. 'Hannah?' he called out.

'Here,' came the reply, and a small woman with the beginning of wrinkles around her eyes appeared in the hallway. 'You are here at last. We have been looking forward to today very much.'

It was a room and kitchen flat, bigger than the one Donald had been renting. Jean looked around her. To the right as she entered was a doorway into a small bathroom. The tenements had been recently built, at the turn of the century, and there was a bath and toilet for each flat. No sharing among families, and no chanty pot under the bed at night. Next to the bathroom, which was festooned with laundry hanging over the bath, a second door led to the kitchen. The range, almost the same as the one she had grown up with, was lit, and the smell of broth warmed her heart. Under the window was a sink and at the other end of the room was a bed recess, with the bed made up. Beneath that was a truckle bed – this was already pulled out, and two excited children aged perhaps six or seven were in residence. A table was set in the middle of the room, laid with bowls and spoons and cups. There was a loaf, and a bread knife and four chairs that didn't match. Above the range was the pulley, hanging with working overalls, shirts, school uniforms, socks and underwear.

Jean realised quickly that Hannah and Tom had given up their own bedroom and intended to sleep in the kitchen with the children. This could not be. It was completely wrong; she never, ever, intended to be a burden and she wondered how to protest without causing offence. Even beginning to say the words might seem rude and unkind, and she reluctantly concluded that, for now at least, it was necessary to simply be gracious. These things could be sorted out at a later date. She hoped that soon, maybe even in a couple of weeks, they would be in a position to gain their own tenancy and she could then find a way to repay this kindness.

'Let me take your coat,' said Hannah. 'You look as though you are about to fall.'

And indeed, now that she was finally here, Jean did feel quite shaky. The last week had been hard. Donald was completely guilt-ridden and could not stop apologising for what he had brought about. The round of goodbyes had been emotionally exhausting. And then there had been the packing. The final gathering of what was important: clothes and a few small treasures. Jean had even sneaked back to the flat she had shared with her father for so many years and taken the set of six teaspoons from her mother's drawer one morning when her father was at work. They had been promised to her and she had been determined not to leave without them. Aside from these small things, though, there was remarkably little to show for their toils in Clyde-bank.

The men went to the bedroom to put away the cases, and she heard Donald doing the protesting for both of them, but he was unsuccessful, and when he tried to bring it up with Hannah in the kitchen, Jean shook her head quickly. This was not the time.

Jean grasped the back of the nearest chair and steadied herself for a moment and then she went into the bathroom, grabbing the opportunity for two minutes alone for the first time that day. She wondered how many women were right now doing the same thing. Hiding briefly from their world as it pressed in around them and attempting to shut the door against it all. She washed her hands with the sliver of soap and wiped them dry on the thin towel that hung on the back of the door.

Back in the kitchen the bowls had been filled with broth, thick with potatoes and barley. A brown china teapot sat in the centre of the table with steam ribboning upwards from the spout.

'So we need to get on with finding you some work,' said Tom as he sliced the loaf of bread with a practised hand. 'I'll take you down to the dockside with me tomorrow.'

'Do you think there will be a problem, with what happened at Singer?' replied Donald.

'I don't know, to be honest, but there is one particular foreman we can speak to. He reads the newspapers and I remember him talking about it at the time. I think he might be sound.'

'It's a start,' said Jean.

Tom nodded. 'Mind you, it's likely he would deny it to his last breath, so we need to be careful.'

They sat around the table in the gas-lit flat, with the children being allowed to stay up for once, and they made plans until it was time to wash the soup pot and put the oatmeal in it to soak for the morning. The children needed to sleep and that meant that everyone had to do the same. Jean could see that this was not going to be sustainable for long.

In the bedroom, she laid out Donald's work clothes on the chair. His belt needed another new hole but it would do for now.

She hung her dress in the wardrobe, noticing the empty hangers which had been left for her, and then she lay beside Donald and listened to his quickly coming sleep and felt his breath as he turned to her in the bed. At the end of the street she could hear a tram bell ringing, and the whirr of its cables above the rails. And she wondered if these sounds would ever become as familiar as home, or if she would always feel like a stranger in this city.

Connie

'Don't say anything, Mother. I don't want you to jinx it!' Connie scrutinised herself in the hall mirror on the morning of the interview.

Her new skirt and blouse were comfortable and the winter coat fitted well. She was satisfied with how she looked – not overdressed, not ostentatious, but reliable, well turned out, neat and tidy – all the things she hoped the hospital would expect of a member of staff. As she examined her reflection for the final time it seemed as though her father were there with her, a sensation she hadn't expected at all.

'I won't say a word,' replied Kathleen, pretending to be offended.

'I'm taking my best shoes in a bag. There's snow forecast and I don't want to ruin them.'

'You'll be home at the usual time?'

'I expect so. I'm going straight to the office after I'm finished. I did ask, but they wouldn't give me the whole morning off, so I won't be able to come home and change before I go back.'

'I'll see you later. You can tell me all about it this evening.'

'Bye then.' Connie checked her watch for the hundredth time, and opened the front door. She was surprised how nervous she felt about the interview, but there was no need to rush; she was in plenty of time.

The three-storey red sandstone building stood at the western end of a long corridor leading to the Medical wards. Connie pushed aside her memories of the last time she had set foot in the hospital, and she braved the cold wind to stand outside for a few minutes and admire the grand turrets and the huge windows that marched diagonally up the front face of the building. Behind the glass she saw nurses in blue and grey hurrying up and down the staircase, their bright white aprons catching the light.

Working here, she thought, must feel like being part of a giant jigsaw puzzle, with everyone having their place in the finished picture. Her job at the council was similar, but this seemed so much more important. She climbed to the second floor and stopped to catch her breath and compose herself before the final flight to the top.

It was almost nine thirty. A row of seats was arranged along the wall next to the door marked 'Office' and a woman with her hair pulled back in a tight bun was already sitting waiting.

'Hello.' Connie sat down, leaving an empty seat between them. 'Are you here for the interview too?'

The woman gripped the handles of the handbag, which was resting on her knees, more tightly and gave her a look as though to insinuate she was a fool.

Connie gave her the benefit of the doubt and smiled back. 'Nine thirty? Mine is at ten.' There was no response.

The office door opened and a well-dressed young lady appeared, carrying an expensive-looking coat over her arm. She walked confidently past them, leaving a trail of Miss Dior in her wake, and pressed the button to call the lift.

The clatter of the concertina gates opening as it arrived brought a diminutive woman in a pewter-grey dress out into the corridor. She stood and watched in disbelief as her previous interviewee disappeared from view. She shook her head and made a mark with her pencil on her clipboard. 'Mrs Russell, you are next. Come this way, please.'

Connie took her gloves off and sniffed her wrists, hoping that her cologne had faded. She changed into her shoes and slid her boots under the chair. Surely no one in a hospital will steal boots, she thought.

She sat and watched the comings and goings while she waited for her turn. Porters carried bales of cloth wrapped in brown paper past her and into a room further along the corridor. There was a delivery of mail, and several parcels. She listened to see if any hints could be gleaned from her competitor's interview, which was taking place just a few feet away, but all she could hear were muffled voices.

At last it was her turn. 'Good morning, Miss Baxter.' The manager held out her hand. 'I am Miss Archer and I'll be conducting your interview this morning.' Her skin was cool and dry against Connie's anxious palm. 'Let's go into my office.'

The room was tiny, the cream walls looked as though it had been many years since they had seen a paintbrush and there was the faint sound of machinery somewhere nearby. A bowl of dried rose petals on the desk sat next to a framed photograph of a man in military uniform. Pale yellow petals, tinged with pink.

'Peace,' said Connie, speaking her thoughts unintentionally.
'Indeed.'

'I'm sorry, I didn't mean to say that out loud.' She stumbled with embarrassment.

'The Peace rose is my favourite. You are a gardener?'

'My father used to grow them. We have a rose bush beside the back door.'

'I see. Well, Miss Baxter, if you would like to take a seat, we can begin.' Miss Archer pressed her hands together, linking her fingers like a child praying in a school assembly. 'I should have mentioned in my letter that the interview will be in two parts, so we'll begin with the first and then conduct the second afterwards.'

This was an unwelcome deviation from any interview Connie had been to before and she tried not to panic.

'First, I need you to tell me more about your current position.'

'I'm a typist. I work in an office at the City Council. I've been there since 1945, so that's ten years.' Her mouth began to dry up and she could feel herself starting to gabble. 'It's a busy place and it's quite noisy. You have to be good at concentrating and being precise.' She took a breath and forced herself to slow down. 'I worked in a similar job during the war, dealing with the distribution of rations.'

'I won't ask you about that; not everyone is in a position to talk about their service.' Miss Archer glanced at Connie's hands. 'And you are single, Miss Baxter?'

'I am. I live with my mother. My father passed away last year. That's part of the reason I have applied for this job – he died in this hospital.'

'I'm sorry to hear that. It can't have been easy to come back.'

'You have to, don't you? You can't just stop doing things.' This woman had a knack for getting her to say things she normally kept to herself.

'Very true.' Miss Archer glanced momentarily at the photograph on her desk. 'I think that's all I need to know for now.' She leaned forward as though she was about to impart a great secret. 'The next thing I need you to do is a practical test, so I'll take you through to the heart of the operation, so to speak, and we'll see how you get on.'

When the connecting door between the office and the work-room was opened, Connie realised that this was where the hum of the machines was coming from. As she looked from table to table she realised with horror that all of them were powered by electricity. She suddenly felt like an idiot.

Miss Archer studied her reaction. 'Is there a problem? You *can* sew, Miss Baxter?'

'Oh yes, of course.' She decided that the only thing to do was to be completely honest. 'My mother taught me so I have sewn all my life. I even made the clothes I'm wearing today, in case you wanted some proof, but I'm afraid I have only ever used a hand-crank machine, not even a treadle.'

'I see.'

'So I think that perhaps I have been wasting your time.'

'I will be the judge of that, Miss Baxter. I think we should continue, if you don't mind.'

By the time Connie eventually got home it was almost six o'clock and she was a wreck.

'You're so late, I was worried,' fussed Kathleen.

'It's been quite a day.'

'What happened? Did it go well?'

Connie hung her coat up and took off her shoes. 'It was awful; you really won't believe how awful.'

'I think you'd better come through to the kitchen. You can tell me all about it while I heat up your soup.'

'Lentil?'

'Split pea and ham.'

'Lovely.'

'And jam roly poly and custard.'

'If I eat all that I won't fit into these clothes ever again.' Connie sat down at the table and lowered her head slowly onto the tablecloth. 'That was the most embarrassing interview ever, in the history of the world.'

'I think you are being a touch overdramatic.'

'I'm not. Wait until I tell you what happened and then you'll understand.'

Kathleen ladled out two bowls of pale-green soup, speckled with pink ham shreddings. 'It's very hot, so don't burn your mouth.'

'The first part was fine. It was very quick, just a few questions.' Connie made figure-of-eight swirls in the thick liquid.

'And then?'

'After that I had to do a sewing test.'

'I don't understand why that would be a problem. You've been using my sewing machine since you were in primary school.'

'The machines were electric, Mother. Every last one of them.'

'I see.' Kathleen waited for further explanation, but Connie ate the rest of her soup in silence, not speaking until she had finished the last drop and dabbed her mouth with a napkin.

'I don't know what I was thinking. I just assumed that maybe if I got the job I could go and try an electric machine in a shop before my first day to get a feel for it.'

'So what happened?' Kathleen picked up the bowls and took them to the sink. She lit the gas under a small saucepan and stirred the custard methodically with her wooden spoon.

'It all went wrong. I tried to sew a seam, and just let me tell you, those electric machines may look like yours but they aren't the same at all.'

'I didn't think they were very different. That does sound strange.'

'I sat there like a prize turnip and I couldn't make it stitch properly. It just galloped away from me like some sort of race horse. And it had a forward and a reverse stitch so I had to do some darning as well.'

'But you've done that at home.'

'Yes, but not with the needle bashing up and down at breakneck speed. It was a bedspread I was repairing. There were little holes in it like cigarette burns, and it was a proper mess by the time I'd finished.' She groaned, and put her head in her hands. 'And then they asked me to cut some green cotton into big squares with these massive shears, far bigger than the ones we have here, and I had to hem them. I'm not sure I made a very good job of that either.'

'Is that everything?'

'Isn't it enough? I must have spent twenty minutes trying to get the corners nicely mitred and then the woman in charge said that was all they had time for and thanks very much for coming and she ushered me out of the door.'

'Dear me. Well, I can see why you're upset.' Kathleen divided the suet pudding into even portions and slowly poured the custard around the edge of each bowl, leaving an island in the centre. 'This will make you feel better.' She spooned an extra dollop of jam on top of each slice of red-veined sponge.

'That's not everything. When I finally got back to work, I was an hour later than I had said I would be, so the supervisor gave me a warning and all the worst jobs for the afternoon – and that's why I'm late.'

'When will you hear from the hospital?'

'Probably never, based on my performance today.' Connie looked down at her bowl. 'But this looks really tasty and it's exactly what I need, so I'm just going to enjoy my pudding and try not to think about it anymore.

Fred

Blog: Mid-September 2016

Edinburgh

No luck on the job front yet.

Time to start selling things to pay the bills.

Fred has propped the front door open with the old sewing machine to help the flat to air, and is shoulder-deep in the hall cupboard when a voice calls out from the hall.

'Hello? It's Wendy.'

His next-door neighbour is flanked by two small boys, one clutching a scruffy blanket and the other keeping a firm grip on a toy car. She eyes his freshly shaved head but doesn't comment. 'I hope you don't mind. I know it's a bit early.'

He fights the urge to say that actually yes it is FAR too early because he hasn't had three cups of coffee and breakfast and maybe she could come back after eleven, but he has been dragged up properly and so he smiles at her, and at the boys.

'It's fine,' he lies. 'I've been up for a couple of hours.'

The older child can't take his eyes off Fred. 'What happened to your *head*?'

'Michael!' Wendy blushes. 'Sorry.'

'Doesn't matter. I'm just waiting for the explosion that is bound to happen when my mum sees it.'

'I can see why it might be a bit of a surprise.'

'She's not going to be happy.' He shrugs. 'Anyway, what can I do for you?'

'I just need to ask you something.' Wendy looks down at her sons. 'Or rather, Joe and Michael do. I hope this isn't a bad time – it must be a big job, sorting out a whole flat.'

'You wouldn't believe,' he says, realising too late that she might know exactly how it feels to be bereaved. She might even know what it is like to clear out a house of family stuff that is inconsequential and yet at the same time precious beyond words.

'Your grandfather was such a kind person. Nothing was too much trouble. He would take in parcels and even sit with the boys for ten minutes so I could nip to the shop for milk if it was pouring with rain.'

'I sometimes can't believe he isn't here now.'

The children are getting restive. 'Ask him, Mummy.' The younger child looks up at her.

'Ask me what?'

'It's about the cat,' she explains on their behalf.

'The cat?'

Michael scrutinises his newly bald neighbour. 'Yes. It's about the cat.'

Fred looks around for the animal under discussion. 'To be honest I didn't even know Granda had a cat until I came back in such a hurry when he…'

She nods, understanding. 'Of course it's your cat now but the boys were wondering if they could visit it.'

'I don't see why not.'

'They want to know if you'll be keeping it.' She pauses. 'I think they have designs on feline acquisition imminently.'

He blinks, and then realises that this is a sort of code. 'Right,' he replies. 'Well, obviously it would be expedient for a mutual meeting to assess the merchandise…'

She raises her eyebrows.

'The, erm, livestock?' He continues and her wince turns to a smile. 'In order to assess the habitat and visitations.' Oh heck, this is getting worse, he thinks. 'I'm not sure where she is at the moment actually.'

'She's in our flat,' Joe states, matter-of-factly. 'You can come and see her if you like.'

Fred realises that he should be inviting them in properly instead of having this conversation on the doorstep, but he is pre-empted by another offer.

'We have bubble juice,' says Joe.

'Bubble juice?'

'Yes. Brown bubble juice, white bubble juice, green bubble juice.' He is proud of the selection.

'I'm sure Fred is busy,' Wendy intervenes.

He looks around at the stacks of books awaiting new shelves and realises that he has had more than enough of the need to make a decision about each and every childhood paperback for one morning. 'Bubble juice sounds perfect.'

'Or coffee?' she suggests.

'Even better. I would offer but…'

'No milk?'

'Got it in one.'

A few minutes later Fred is standing in a flat that seems to be host to even more carefully labelled boxes than his own.

'It's temporary,' says Wendy. 'We're having a house built on a plot of land over in Fife, so we sold our flat around the corner from here and we're renting this one until the construction work is finished. It was the only way to avoid multiple school moves.'

'Sounds like a big project.'

'It's nearly finished, so I'm hoping we'll be in before Christmas. My husband is pretty much living there, trying to push things along as fast as possible before the darker evenings kick in again.'

'Well it sounds like something off a TV programme. It certainly makes my struggles over whether or not to rip out a piece of Formica worktop seem a bit pathetic.'

She weaves her way past a wall of cardboard and into the kitchen. 'It's not the same thing at all. What you are doing is much more difficult.' She smiles at him. 'Now, the boys are entertaining the cat with a toy mouse in the front room so, would you like bubble juice? Or coffee?'

'Coffee, please.'

'OK.'

'Are they serious about the cat?' He realises as he asks the question that he isn't sure he wants to know the answer.

'Deadly serious, but you don't need to worry. I have no intention of asking about adopting her or anything like that. I'm sure she's more than happy living the quiet life with you.'

He takes the hot mug from her. 'I never thought I'd say this, but I'm glad. I've become quite attached to having her around the place.'

The big task on Fred's list for the afternoon is to deal with the one remaining sewing machine. This would be a lot easier, he thinks, if it wasn't locked. He is quite sure the key for it must be somewhere in the flat but he hasn't found it yet, so he consults the all-knowing internet for advice. A particularly knowledgeable website instructs him to equip himself with a 'soft cloth such as an old T-shirt' and a screwdriver 'to be used with caution'.

Living alone has some advantages. There is no one to poke fun at his habits, and the airing cupboard, cleared of ancient towels and faded flannelette sheets, is now home to a neat pile of ironed T-shirts in colour order. He regards himself as organised, not obsessive. The T-shirts represent his running career, if it can be called that. He has done races all over the country including one marathon from his own wet and windy city. After that particular event he vowed never to run that far in one go ever again; too many miles and too many hills. On a lower shelf, in a less tidy heap, are the T-shirts that have migrated from New to Best, through Pub and Car Washing, before finally reaching Painting Walls.

He selects one of his earliest event tops, holding it up for inspection and realising just how thin and insubstantial it is. That's biological detergent for you, he thinks.

He clears the kitchen table, lifts the wooden case onto it and proceeds with care, as instructed, wiping away years of dust with the damp cloth. The wood is thirsty, and the old varnish is cracked and peeling. Along the front of the case, in faded gold capital letters, is the legendary name: SINGER.

The cat jumps up beside him, rubbing herself against his arm. 'Oh Crabbie, do stop it. Go and do something useful like catching a real mouse or something.' It's as though she has worked out that he no longer has any intention of getting rid of her. He walks over to click the switch beside the kettle and drops a teabag into the only clean mug in the kitchen. His standards are slipping.

Outside, the weather is drizzly and uninviting. He mentally crosses 'RUN' off his list of tasks.

'So, my feline friend. What do you think about this thing, then?' He points to the still locked sewing-machine case. 'Worth anything? eBay-able? What would someone pay for something like that? I suppose there must be collectors out there who would bite my hand off for it. Heavy, though. Not the sort of thing Postman Pat would love me for sending.'

The kettle clicks off and he pours water onto the teabag, rescuing it after half a minute and saving it for a second cup. 'It would be nice to have someone to share a teabag with. You're a handsome creature, but your conversation is a bit lacking.'

He ignores the cat's pleading for milk – mindful of Eva's instructions – and fills up the water dish. Crabbie looks up at him in disgust.

Back at the table he chooses a screwdriver from the toolbox and puts it into the keyhole. Too small. The next size up seems to fit and he turns it cautiously, not wanting to cause any damage. To his amazement the internet is right and the lock turns easily.

'Excellent, now let's see what's inside.'

After a bit of manoeuvring the lid lifts off without any problems.

'Oh, very nice. Very nice indeed.' He adjusts the spotlight beside him and leans forward to examine the ubiquitous black enamelled sewing machine more closely. 'I wonder how old you are, then? More research needed, I think.'

Blogs, forums and news-lists have created an encyclopaedia of collected insight and knowledge and he mines them for information. Hundreds and hundreds of images are presented to him on the screen. Thousands. He is like a small child with an I-Spy book as he tries to work out which model it is. It would be a lot easier if this was a bird or a bus, he thinks.

'There must be an easier way to get this information.'

He dampens the torn cloth again, wringing it out well, and wipes the brass plate on the front of the machine to reveal the serial number more clearly.

'F1567 something something something.' He turns back to the computer, scrolling down the list of dates. 'Wow. 1911.'

He runs a finger across the number, feeling the indentations. 'You are a very old lady indeed, but still a very pretty one.'

Like a man on a mission, he goes back to the auction site to search through the listings. When he finds what he's looking for, he cracks open the black notebook he uses for everything from shopping lists to sketches of room layouts, and starts to jot things down. 'So, what are these old machines worth then, Crabbie?'

Slowly the page fills with model numbers and dates. He follows a few of the auctions that are ending soon, and tracks the bidding patterns. It's a complicated business; some models are clearly more sought-after than others and the sellers who will post or ship by courier definitely have the edge.

He closes the browser tab and moves to the next open page to look at the local estate agents. Methodically he makes lists in the section of his book earmarked for property research and ticks off the ruled columns, one by one: date, price and result. It's far less interesting than the vintage auctions.

The flat is almost silent; the only sound is the buzz of the compressor on the old fridge as it clicks on and off. Occasionally there is the beep of a car horn from the street outside but it barely registers. He can hear the children next door, their games muffled.

A couple of hours later he is relaxing on the folded-up sofa bed and he logs back in to the auctions and checks the listings again, making more notes.

'The answer to what this thing may be worth, my dear Crabbie, is not much.' The cat jumps onto the seat beside him, and he tickles her behind the ears and across the back of her neck. 'If this thing was pristine, with the original receipt and manuals and no scratches and lots of feet, whatever they are, then maybe a hundred at the absolute most.' He sighs with resignation. 'It's probably not worth selling after all.'

The machine seems to exert a magnetic pull on him and he goes back to the table to look at it again. He tries to turn the handle for the third time since taking the cover off, and fails. It seems to be jammed and the needle won't go up and down.

'I'm not sure it's actually working, which means even a charity shop won't want it. Maybe if I can get it going it might be different.'

Another twenty minutes is lost down a rabbit hole of YouTube videos before he finds a basic 'How To Oil Your Machine' explanation. There are strict instructions to use only proper sewing machine oil and all he has is an almost empty can of spray lubricant, which is apparently strictly forbidden on pain of ruining the shiny black finish. Undaunted, he decides to explore further and he swings the machine backward out of the base to examine the mechanism underneath.

'Oh my goodness.'

He can see immediately why the wheel won't move. Under the machine, stuffed into the space where rods and cogs should be moving freely, and filling the base completely, is a brown paper package.

He lifts it out onto the table. 'This looks as though it's been done by an expert. I wonder how many people could wrap a parcel like that nowadays?' he says. 'I know I couldn't.' He briefly considers using the kitchen scissors, but then decides to do things properly and disentangles the string, one tightly tied knot at a time. He wonders what could be inside.

Money. Please let it be money, he thinks.

It isn't money.

Inside the brown wrapping are sixteen small notebooks. Some have homemade covers cut from scrap paper. Fred can see that one has been made from a road atlas, and another has a picture of sweet peas on a page from a seed catalogue. There is a school jotter and an old cash book. At the bottom of the pile, the final notebook is covered with a familiar wallpaper with cars on it. 'My bedroom,' he says softly.

He opens one of the books. Each page has a line of stitching running vertically near the outer edge. Yellow stitches on the first page, then white, blue, black. And caught in the seam every time is a scrap of cloth, maybe two inches by one. The pages have writing on them too and he catches his breath; it's the same as the handwriting on the first six of the birthday cards in his treasure box, and on the jam jars in the larder.

Inside another book he finds more stitches, and beside each line, a description in a different hand. The first page reads:

Dress. Bust 34.

Full skirt. White collar.

4 yards. 36 inch wide.

Supplied by customer G Hardwick.

Started 13 September 1949.

Finished 27 September 1949 (K).

He runs his fingers slowly along the apricot seam.

Trapped under the stitches is a rectangle of cotton fabric printed with tiny flowers and pastel green leaves.

Jean

April 1915

Leith

Every afternoon, at about the time Donald was due to come home from work, Jean looked down from the top floor window to watch for him turning the corner. It was her habit to put the kettle on as soon as he appeared and have it boiling before he came through the door. If she put the right amount of water in, and didn't overfill it, then the timing was perfect. It was a small thing, and she knew that he probably didn't notice, but she liked to do it for him anyway. A hot drink after a long day working outdoors was a kindness.

The men from the docks always came home together, walking up the street like the army they were not a part of. Sometimes she would hear them before she saw them, their deep voices shouting a greeting to their sons and daughters, and chivvying them to get home and help their mothers. There had been less of that recently. They were under pressure to get the warships built and they took the work seriously. Donald said the place was different now. There was less chat and the breaks were shorter. He and his workmates ate their sandwiches at lunchtime and got back to work at the first opportunity.

His footsteps thumped up the final flight of stairs just as the kettle began to rattle on the black hob. Jean took the thick checked cloth from its nail and wrapped it around her hand to protect her skin from the metal handle; a burn could be nasty. The teapot was on the table, already primed with tea leaves, all ready for the spitting liquid.

'Hello, my lovely,' he said as he came through the door, and Jean didn't mind at all that his words weren't directed at her, but at six-week-old Annie who was lying in her crib with a full tummy, which would hopefully keep her content for a couple of hours. They were lucky. The wee one was a good sleeper, and so far, in the weeks since she had been born, she had settled into a routine all three of them could manage.

'Sssssh!' Jean admonished. 'I've just put her down. You can have your play time after you've had your dinner.'

He put his arms around her and lifted her up so that her shoes barely touched the floor and twirled her around as he had once done in his flat in Clydebank. 'Well, in that case I'll just have to play with you instead.'

'Donald, stop it. She might be listening.' She wriggled away from him in mock irritation as he set her down, and then came quickly back for a kiss and a hug.

'Yes, Miss,' he replied. 'I'll be good.'

'Get your hands and face washed then, and I'll put your food on the table.'

He sniffed the air. 'I smell rabbit.'

'You do, but there will be no food on the plates until those hands are washed so if you've brought a hunger home with you, I suggest you get on and do as I ask.'

The smell of pink carbolic wafted across on the breeze that blew from the open window as Donald began to wash his hands and arms. He worked the soapy lather all the way up to his elbows before sloshing the suds down the drain hole. And then he washed his hands a second time, making sure all the tiny fibres of metal were gone. He dried himself carefully and walked back to the crib. While Jean had her back to him, serving up the steaming stew onto white plates, he leaned over his sleeping daughter. 'Do you hear that mother of yours, bossing me about? Maybe I'll have you for my dinner instead, my wee Annie-rabbit?'

The baby began to stir. Her fingers tightened into little fists and she turned her head towards him, her eyes screwed up against the late afternoon sunlight pouring across the room.

Jean reached up tall and tapped him on the shoulder. 'Just exactly what do you think you are doing?' She put her hands on her hips. It was a pointless exercise, trying to persuade him to leave Annie to sleep; he couldn't resist.

'I'm only saying hello.'

'On your own head be it. She'll need holding now while we eat our food and it'll not be me with that honour, Donald Cameron.'

'Ah, but I don't mind a bit.'

'You will when she possets all down your shirt.'

He scooped the baby up and arranged her so that she was resting against his shoulder.

Jean started to cut the meat and vegetables in the stew up into smaller pieces for him. 'Just don't think for a minute that I'll be doing this for you when you're an old man,' she said. 'I'll have better things to do with my time, that's for sure.'

Connie

Connie looked down from the top floor of the red sandstone Diamond Jubilee Pavilion. Below her, she could see the gardeners mowing the grass between the tall ward buildings. A green scent rose up to her; it felt as though the last essence of summer was making an effort before the leaves began to fall. It must be nice to work outside in the sunshine sometimes, she thought, instead of being indoors with the smell of hospital dinners slithering upwards through the floorboards from the ward kitchen below.

Only Connie and Miss Archer were left in the department at the end of the afternoon. It was past home-time, but there were a few uniforms that needed to be altered urgently and Connie had offered to stay back and do them.

The tap at the door was hesitant, but they both heard it.

Miss Archer looked at the clock and shook her head. 'You get away home. We've finished most of these and the rest can wait until the morning. We have made good progress.'

'Did you hear a knock?'

'I did, and I am ignoring it.'

'Would you like me to answer it?' Connie picked up her woollen coat – too warm for the final flush of September sunshine – and folded it into her basket.

'Tell whoever it is to come back tomorrow. The hours are clearly marked on the sign outside. There is no excuse.'

'See you tomorrow, then.'

'You will indeed. Thank you for your help this afternoon.'

Connie was fully expecting to find a delivery of sheets or doctors' coats lying on the trolley in the corridor. Instead she was greeted by a tall man who was vaguely familiar.

'Hello.' He looked down at her.

'Can I help you?'

'Um. I hope so,' he replied.

She could almost have sworn that there was a hint of a blush around his ears. 'Are you lost?'

'Is this the Sewing Room?'

She pointed to the sign. 'It is.'

'I was wondering if you might be able to help with my trousers.'

'Your trousers?'

'I need to get them repaired; the knees have gone.'

'And you are?'

'Alf Morrison.'

'Yes…' She was right, she had met him before; he played chess. That incident outside the library had been most embarrassing.

He held out a pair of brown corduroy trousers with rips across both knees. 'I was wondering if these can be mended.'

Behind her, Connie could hear Miss Archer's chair scraping across the floor and her footsteps approaching.

'You work here?'

'I'm a groundsman.'

'I'm afraid we don't do that sort of repairing here. We do nurses' uniforms, curtains for the wards, counterpanes. We don't do clothing repairs.'

The footsteps stopped.

'Oh well, I'm sorry to have troubled you. I thought it wouldn't hurt to ask.'

'I'll show you the way out,' she replied, realising as she said the words that this was ridiculous. He had found his way in, so he must know the way back. She pulled the door closed behind her and they headed towards the wide staircase that would take them down to the ground floor.

'Have we met before?' His question seemed quite innocent.

'At the library.' She avoided his eye. 'It was last year. I'm afraid I ran off without saying thank you for saving me from that bus. My father was furious with me when he found out how close I had come to being hurt.'

'Bruce Baxter, of course. The Baxter Chess Cup is named after him.' He paused. 'I was sorry to hear that he had passed away.'

'Thank you, it's been a difficult year. My mother is still rather lost, I think.'

'It must be hard when you have been with someone you love for a long time, and then suddenly they aren't there anymore.'

They walked side by side out of the hospital and on to Lauriston

Place. Connie expected him to make an excuse to leave and head off in some other direction, but he kept walking beside her.

'Are you going home now?' she said.

'Now that depends,' Alf replied. 'It's a nice sunny evening and perhaps I might go for a stroll instead.'

By now Connie knew exactly what he was doing, but was rather enjoying the attention so she played along. 'We can walk together then – I'm heading along to Shandon.'

They set off along pale tenement streets, and talked about Ian Fleming and chess and Miss Archer's Peace rose. Eventually, when they arrived outside the flat, she asked the question she had been planning for the last forty minutes. 'About these trousers?'

'Yes?'

'I could mend them for you if you like.'

'I'd be happy to pay. Getting clothes to fit me is difficult so I hold on to what I have for as long as possible...' His conversation, which had until now flowed easily, suddenly dried up.

'Don't be silly. I wouldn't dream of asking for money. Just give them to me now and come back in a couple of days. This is where I live, the one with Baxter on the bell. Shall we say Friday?'

'Thank you very much.'

'Thank me when it's done. I must go in now. Mother will be waiting for me.'

She watched him leave, his shadow long on the pavement, and she wondered how many other items of clothing from his wardrobe might need a stitch or a button. There was plenty of time to find out.

'Who was that you were speaking to in the street?' said Kathleen as soon as the front door was closed.

Connie sighed. 'Nothing gets past you, does it?'

'If you've nothing to hide, you'll tell me.'

'I couldn't have any secrets even if I wanted them, could I?' She raised her eyes upwards. 'His name is Alf Morrison. He works at the hospital as a groundsman. He seems nice. Will that do?'

'That name is familiar.' Kathleen screwed up her eyes. 'Let me think for a minute.'

'He plays chess.'

'That's it. I knew I'd heard the name before. I think he played in the competition for your father's cup.'

'Really?'

'Oh, he didn't win it or anything, but I remember someone on the committee mentioning the name when they came round to tell me the results. I think they were quite impressed with him.'

'Well, since you know as much about him as I do, you can mend these if you like?' Connie put her basket down and pulled out the pair of torn trousers.

Kathleen lifted them up and gave the thick corduroy a shake. 'Fixing his clothes now, are you?'

'It's just one repair, Mother.'

'That's where it starts. Are you going to do them right now?'

'Might as well. Come and talk to me while I do it.'

They went through to the sitting room. Ownership of the chair in front of the sewing machine had gradually transferred from mother to daughter. It had been several months since the blue handkerchief with the red pin-tucked edge had been entered into one of the notebooks.

Connie turned the trouser legs inside out and examined the tear more closely. 'This is such an odd place for the cloth to get ripped. It's not where you'd expect at all.' She rummaged in the box of cotton reels for the right shade of brown. 'And the fabric from the back pocket isn't heavy enough for a patch. Is it alright if I look in the scrap box for something of Dad's?'

'Go ahead. It might be a good omen.'

'Stop it, Mother. You are being impossible.'

'It was how I won your father's heart.'

'Mending?'

'I had just gone back to teaching after…'

'Mmmmm?' Connie was concentrating on finding the best piece of fabric for the job, and not really paying attention. 'I think I might use this cotton drill, doubled up. What do you think?'

'Yes, that'll work.'

'Sorry, I wasn't listening properly, keep going.'

'He was organising the Christmas play, and there weren't enough costumes.' Kathleen opened the nearest drawer in the writing desk beside her chair and took out a package, wrapped loosely in crimson silk cloth and tied with a coral ribbon. 'These are my old records,' she said. She undid the bow and searched through the contents of the parcel. 'Let me see now. It was Christmas 1918.' She held one of the books out for inspection.

Connie stopped what she was doing. She had never looked through these older notebooks, the ones that dated from before she was born. They weren't hidden away, but she always felt as though it would be prying, like reading someone else's correspondence. She leafed through the pages.

'Why do we still keep these records anyway? I mean, I do it because you do it, but you've never explained why.'

'It's a long story.'

'I've got all evening' – she smiled – 'and I love a good romance.'

'You're going to be disappointed, then, because it didn't start off like that.' Kathleen put the book back with the others. 'It was quite different.'

'I'm listening.'

'Well.' Kathleen paused. It was as though she was trying to decide what to say next. Eventually she took a deep breath and said the words that she might, had circumstances been different, have taken to her grave. 'I have been married twice. The first marriage was to a man called Philip Wright.' Kathleen rolled the ribbon up like a measuring tape between her fingers and then held it out in mid-air, allowing one end to waterfall down to the floor. She coiled it back up again. 'He was an accountant, and he dealt with all the financial matters for our family business. My father thought he was a wonderful man; polite, efficient, that sort of thing. And Philip Wright thought he was pretty special himself, although I didn't find that out until later.'

As she spoke she rolled the ribbon up slowly and methodically, making the edges match perfectly each time before it was unfurled.

'We got married in 1910 after what you might call a whirlwind courtship. My father was very pleased that I was settled, and of course I had to give up my teaching post but it didn't seem important because I was going to be a married woman with a husband to support me. In fact, Father was so pleased that he bought this flat for us to live in.' She looked around the room. 'It hasn't changed much: new curtains, brighter walls, a new cooker in the kitchen next to the old range, but really, it's much the same as the day I moved in.'

Connie didn't say a word. She pinned and unpinned the patch of cloth onto the trouser leg, adjusting it this way and that, but she didn't dare do anything to disturb the story that was unfolding.

'It was Philip Wright who wanted me to have a sewing machine. He told me it would be a gift for our first wedding anniversary. I can remember the day we went to the shop as though it were yesterday. He insisted that I have the biggest, most expensive treadle machine in the most ornate cabinet available. The salesman thought all his Christmases had come at once.'

'So how did you come to have this one instead?'

'I didn't want a grand monstrosity. I didn't actually want a machine at all.' Kathleen smiled at the memory. 'I told the salesman that I had been led to believe that treadle machines were not used by well-bred women.'

Connie couldn't restrain herself. 'You said *what?*'

'It was a rumour at the time. I've got no idea how it started but it was certainly much discussed. Some women thought that treadles were unladylike. Of course it was complete nonsense, but I used it to my advantage. I hoped we would manage to leave the shop without making a purchase at all, but Philip Wright' – she said his name with precision, and shuddered a little – 'Philip Wright insisted that I was looking pale and tired and made me sit down at the front of the shop while he went into the office at the back to conclude the sale.' Kathleen shrugged. 'I had no idea what he had ordered because he wouldn't tell me, but a month later, there was a knock on the door and that,' she pointed at the sewing machine in front of them, 'was delivered.'

'And then?'

'And then he disappeared.'

Connie had read the word in many novels and magazines, but she had never experienced it herself – she was dumbstruck.

Kathleen stopped playing with the ribbon and picked up the pile of notebooks in the same way as she would have held a pack of cards. They were odd sizes, no two the same. She turned them around and around, tapping them on one edge against her lap with each turn, but was not able to get them all to line up neatly.

At last Connie found her voice. 'He disappeared?'

'Vanished.' Kathleen held the books a little more tightly. 'And he took with him every penny from the bank accounts of our family business. I was the only child of a widower, and with the benefit of hindsight, I think that was part of his plan.' She sat up straight in the chair. 'My father died two months later.'

Connie felt quite sick.

Now that Kathleen had begun it was as though someone had lifted the lid on decades of secrets. 'I was told by our solicitor that the family house would need to be sold to cover the business debts, and the only saving grace in all of it was that the only name on the missives for this flat was mine. There was no mention of Philip Wright. When I think back now, I can remember going to the lawyer with Father. He watched me as I signed my name. I have always wondered if he had some inkling, some premonition that I might need it one day.'

'Mother, the light is starting to go. I can do these trousers tomorrow.' Connie got to her feet. 'Given what you've just told me, I'm surprised you can bear to sew on this machine at all.'

'I haven't thought about all that in a long time. And I'm tired now. I think I might just go to bed.'

'If you're sure?'

'I am. I promise I'll tell you the rest tomorrow. It's a relief to talk about it, to be honest. It's been so many years.'

Curtains for Mrs Sanderson in number 81. PAID

Repair to brown corduroy trousers. A Morrison. No charge. (C)

Shirt collar turned and replaced. (C)

Fred

Blog: Late September 2016

Edinburgh

I sent Sam an email yesterday saying I was sorry it hadn't worked out. Not sure why I did that, a week after the event. Good manners, I suppose.

Two letters came this morning. Final confirmation of my uselessness – my P45.

And notification of my last salary payment. I'm hoping to hold out for a few more weeks before I sign on for benefits. I don't need much at the moment. The light is pretty good until about eight so I can keep the lights off – the electricity meter spins round at a scary rate.

I've been wondering about the heating. It's fine at the moment but I should probably get the old boiler serviced. How low could I keep the bills, I wonder?

I need to make a list for the cold months, which are on the way.

Consider double glazing.
Draught excluders.
Live in one room? It's what people used to do and there's just me, so why not?
Paint the walls white to reflect light. (A bit extreme.)
Get low-energy bulbs.

Obsessed? Moi?

But it's all possible, and there are dozens of websites about how to live frugally. Sadly, most of them require that you live in the middle of nowhere, have a fully pro-

ductive mature vegetable garden and a complete set of fruit bushes. Oh yes, and the ability to burn wood, which I'm pretty sure is not allowed here.

I'm tinkering with the idea of selling stuff but I'm not sure it would be very lucrative. I mean, I could still try it, but suddenly I really, really don't want to. Granda said not to treat this place like a museum but I don't want to get rid of things and then find I need them again later.

I need to be tough about this and not sentimental though. I have to eat.

The champagne will stay in the larder for now.

Fred is just about to turn off the computer when an email arrives with its customary audible swoosh. It's from the agency.

You have been selected for a first round interview at 16:00 today for a position in sales support. Please confirm that you will attend.

He feels his mood lift a little. He replies immediately.

Yes, I confirm that I will attend today.
Fred Morrison.

He smiles at the prospect of a job, and goes through to the bedroom where he now sleeps, having abandoned the sofa-bed after Sam's visit. Crabbie is curled up in the centre of the bed, asleep. She is right on top of his best trousers, which he had left there for want of a coat hanger. He shoos her off and heads into the bathroom to shave. Perhaps things are looking up.

It's a longer task now he has his head to do as well, and he isn't yet confident enough to rush. By the time he has finished the cat has again taken possession of the bed and is unhappy about being moved a second time. She protests as he lifts her up, and digs her claws into his trousers. Too late he sees the fine loops of thread as the fabric is snagged. He drops her back down quickly, but the damage is done; his interview suit is ruined.

There is no time to get anything else washed and in a moment of desperation he flings open the doors of the wardrobe and takes out a pair of his grandfather's trousers. They are far too long. The old man had been a slim six foot five and Fred is barely five foot nine. He is by now in full panic mode and runs back along the hall to check the pulley in the kitchen and see if his black jeans are dry.

No such luck. They are still damp.

Next to the fireplace is Nana's sewing box. He wrenches the lid open and sees her dressmaking shears. Before he has time to think twice he has grabbed them. He lays his grandfather's trousers out on the kitchen table and then puts his damp jeans on top.

'Sorry, Granda,' he says, and chops off the bottom of the vintage trousers with their neat turn-ups.

There is no time to dig the ironing board out from behind the wall of boxes in the front room so he plugs the iron in, turns the trousers inside out and puts a towel down. He eyeballs the leg length, and hopes that they are both vaguely the same. The sewing machine is on the table beside him and for a mad moment he considers using it, but the idea is preposterous and instead he goes into the toolbox, pulls out a roll of silver duct tape, and tears off two long strips.

Ten minutes later he is ready. His shirt is clean, his tie is the wrong colour, his shoes are black, the only belt that fits the loops on the cannibalised trousers is brown and he rustles as he walks, but he is beyond caring. By tonight he should have a job and a salary and perhaps even a glass of champagne in his hand to celebrate.

Jean

November 1915

Leith

From her vantage point at the window, Jean saw the men walking back up the street in the late afternoon. They wore the grime like a uniform, the grey oiliness on their faces ending at the neck, or in the summer, at the waist. Donald wasn't with them.

Her mind began to work overtime. It couldn't be that there had been an incident; someone would have run all the way from the docks to tell her. They all looked out for one another, and the wives were part of that closeness.

She cradled her teething child in her arms, rocking from side to side in the way that countless mothers had done before her, the waddle of advanced pregnancy giving way to an instinctive see-sawing which was the same the world over. Annie was a miserable scrap at the moment: red-cheeked, sore-bottomed, fractious and feverish. There was no rest from it; her nappy would fill with stinking diarrhoea and she would wake again as the acid came into contact with her broken skin. The cream that everyone swore by had made no difference and Jean had gone back to basic petroleum jelly, slathering it on the angry craters because there seemed to be no other way of helping.

It was dark when Donald finally came home.

'Where have you been? I was so worried about you; I thought there must have been an accident on the docks.'

'No accident,' he replied. 'How is Annie?'

'Sleeping, but barely, so please just leave her. I couldn't face it if she woke again.'

'If she can get some rest that will help her. It will be good for you too. How much longer do you think this will go on for?'

'I have no idea, but never mind that for now. Why are you so late?'

'Let me get in and get washed and I'll explain,' he replied.

She was instantly uneasy but Donald wasn't someone who could be pushed into speaking before he was ready. The years after the strike had taught him to hold his own counsel for longer, to give words more consideration. He could still be spontaneous, but the fact that he wasn't rushing to tell her his news made her worry. She ran through the most likely possibilities in her head. Had he heard from Clydebank? Was he unwell?

He followed her instructions for once and didn't go next door to the bedroom to check on Annie. Instead, he went straight to the sink and began the ritual of washing the grime of the day away.

Jean found herself rattling off questions. 'You haven't lost your job?' She set a plate of mince and potatoes on the table in his place. 'What will we do if they don't have work for you anymore?'

'Sit down.' He ignored the steaming food, pushing it to one side. 'I have taken the King's shilling, Jean. I have signed my name and I'm going to war with the other men who want to fight.'

Any words she might have used were strangled at birth in her throat. She looked at him wide-eyed, and didn't move a muscle.

'Jean?'

Eventually, she spoke. 'But there is no reason. You are needed at the docks.'

'I want to do my part.'

'Have people been shouting at you in the street?'

He shook his head.

'But you were given a badge.' Jean searched her memory for when she had last seen it. 'That blue-edged badge that shows you are doing war work. No one should be saying wicked things to you about not being in uniform.' She got up and went to the coat hooks beside the door and felt the lapel of his jacket. 'It's not here.' She was desperate now. 'Did you lose it? I'm sure they will replace it for you if you ask.'

'I took it off today.'

'Why would you do that?' She was frantic. 'Why? I don't understand.'

'We were talking about it, me and the lads…'

'So the lads are going and you have decided to go along with them? This is madness.'

'No, Jean. They are staying. It's just me that's going.'

She sat down at last, gripping her apron tightly in order to have something – anything – to hold on to. 'I don't understand.'

'I know you don't. But I need to go. I need to be able to look at my Annie when she's grown up and say that I did my bit for my country.'

She felt it, before she realised what was happening. A deep rage beginning in her chest, a tightness, gripping her ribcage so firmly that she found it hard to breathe. It rose, up to her neck and along her jaw. Her whole head seemed to be on fire. She couldn't move.

Donald reached across the table to touch her arm. 'I need to be able to tell her that her daddy kept her safe.'

She stared at him. He really did believe what he was saying.

'There is a train leaving next week. I am one of the last to sign up for this group.'

Her body began to shake as though she had a fever. 'You didn't think to discuss this with me first?' she whispered, not trusting herself to speak more loudly.

'I thought you would understand. If I didn't do it today, then I would lose my chance.'

'What about your badge? Did the recruitment officer see it?' She couldn't believe what he was saying.

He shook his head and couldn't meet her eye any longer. 'No, he didn't.'

The penny dropped. 'He didn't see it because you had taken it off before you went in. That's why it's not on your jacket.'

'You don't understand. This is important.'

'So is the work on the ships,' she spat back. 'You know it is.'

'When I come back I will still have a job, I saw the yard owner, Mr James, on my way out of the gates today and I asked him.'

'You asked him what, exactly?'

'I'm not a fool. I know I'll need a job when it's all over.'

'You are telling me that you just *happened* to bump into the owner and spoke to him?' She couldn't hide the sarcasm from her tone. 'He won't know you from Adam so his promise is worthless.'

'He took my name, wrote it down in a book.'

'I don't believe you.'

'I have never lied to you in my life.'

She started to pace the floor. 'You need to go back to the recruitment centre and tell them you have made a mistake. Tell them you work at the docks. Take your badge and show them.'

'I can't.' He shook his head. 'It's done.'

'Tell them you have me and Annie and you need to be here to look after us.'

He looked down at his feet, weary now. 'I can't.'

'You can't? Or you won't?'

'I can't. I read the paper and I signed my name.'

For the briefest of moments Jean was on the edge of pointing out to him that he had never been top of the class for reading or for writing. But she stopped herself. Locked away the words. Hid them inside her. She was furious, but she would never be mean.

Tonight though, she didn't want him near her. Near them. She walked past his chair and paused at the bedroom door. 'I can hear Annie stirring. I will take her into the bed with me. I can comfort her more easily there. You can sleep in the chair beside the fire; I'll give you a blanket.'

Connie

Kathleen was sitting at the kitchen table, fully dressed, waiting for Connie when she got up.

'Good morning, Mother. You're up early.'

'I didn't sleep very well. I had a lot on my mind.' Beside her was a small pile of papers.

'You don't have to tell me, you know. I don't want you to think I'm going to pester you for information.'

'I know, but I've started now, so I may as well tell you the rest. It's much less bleak than what I spoke about yesterday. Where did I get to?'

Connie thought back to the previous evening's revelations. 'You were telling me about signing the missives for the flat.'

'Ah yes. The missives. Well, it was after that that the bills started to arrive. Nothing had been paid for weeks; some of the accounts were months overdue. Philip Wright had never let me open his correspondence. He always insinuated that it would mean I didn't trust him.' Kathleen fixed Connie with a firm stare. 'Promise me you won't ever marry a man who keeps his correspondence a secret, Constance. It's the most important piece of advice I will ever give you.'

'I promise.'

'Good.' Kathleen pulled her cardigan more closely around her shoulders. 'You asked me about the sewing machine. Well, one of the letters was from the Singer shop – there was a problem with the account.' She took a sheet of headed paper from the pile and set it down in front of Connie. 'Philip Wright had told me he had bought it outright and paid in full by cheque, so of course I went back to the shop to explain that there had been a mistake. It wasn't until the manager asked me to go into his office that I realised there was something badly wrong. And that was when he told me the cheque for the first payment had been returned by the bank.' She pointed to the red letters, which had been stamped onto a second piece of paper.

RETURNED PAYMENT.

'Goodness.'

'I know. My face was the same colour as that ink when I found out. I just wanted to be rid of the machine and everything it represented.' She stared down at her hands, lost in thought.

'What happened after that?'

'I think the manager could see how shocked I was. He offered me a glass of water, and he asked me if I had used the machine and I said no, and then he suggested that I wait for a week and think about things. If I wanted to keep it he would draw up a payment agreement, and if I decided to return it he would send someone to collect it.'

'But we never buy things on tick. Never ever. You've always taught me to save before spending.'

'I know.'

'So, you must have decided to keep it, in spite of that?'

'Not right away.'

'Why not?'

'You have to remember, I didn't want the machine in the first place. So much so that I hadn't even lifted the lid off to look at it.'

'But you love sewing.'

'I have come to enjoy it, yes. But in 1911, I didn't feel like that about it at all. I got home from my humiliating visit to the shop and there were two more bills behind the door and I just stood and looked at them lying there. I couldn't even pick them up off the mat because I had no idea what to do about anything anymore and I had no one to ask.'

Connie was seeing her mother in a new light. The woman in front of her, who in her eyes had always been so sure about things, seemed quite different now. 'What did you do?'

'I knew that there were too many decisions to make at once and I could only think about one thing at a time. I needed to pick one problem and sort that out and then move on to the next. The first one was the sewing machine. I did what the shop manager had suggested and I took the lid off and had a good look at it. You wouldn't think so now, when the gold decals have worn away around the front, and the case is a bit chipped, but it was quite a pretty little thing once.'

'I've seen the new ones. I can imagine.'

'I read the instruction book and threaded it up and tried to make some seams on an old table napkin. And that was when I realised.'

'Realised what?'

'That while I was concentrating on making the lines of stitching as straight as I could, I wasn't thinking about bloody Philip Wright.'

'Mother!'

Kathleen ignored the exclamation. 'I got an old sheet out of the linen cupboard and I cut it up and made the most wonderfully fancy dusters you can imagine, with tiny hems and perfect stitches. And I didn't think about him once.'

'Therapy.'

'Pardon?'

'They call it therapy. Something that makes you feel better.'

'Oh, it definitely did that.' Kathleen lifted up a piece of paper from the pile, all folded up neatly. 'But then the machine ran out of thread on the bobbin so I went back to the instruction book to find out what to do.' She started to unfold the paper. 'And that was when I found it.'

'Found what?'

'A secret message.'

Connie's eyes were like saucers. 'Quick, tell me everything, I can't wait any longer.'

'Steady, all in good time. Underneath the thread, which had been there since it left the factory, there was something wrapped around the centre of the bobbin. It took me ages to remove it because the thread had compressed it, but eventually I managed.' She finished unfolding the make-do envelope, took a slender strip of paper from it and laid it out on the table. 'This is it.'

Connie leaned forward. Her lips made the shape of the words as she read.

We have to leave. There is no work here for Donald. Wish us luck. Jean.

'What does it mean?'

'That's exactly what I wanted to know. I put it away safely and I went to the library the very next day and looked at the archive of newspapers until I found out.' She picked up the paper and refolded it, almost reverently. 'At about the same time Philip Wright was helping himself to our family money, there had been a strike at the factory where the sewing machines were made. The whole place closed down for several weeks and afterwards some people lost their jobs.'

'That sounds pretty serious.'

'It was' – she leaned forward, making sure she had Connie's full attention – 'and do you know what the most important thing was?'

'I'm sure you're going to tell me.'

'The strike was about women. Thousands of workers risked everything, to support fifteen women. It might not sound very significant now, when we have the vote and everything, but in 1911 the world was quite different, believe me.'

'Did you ever try to find her, this Jean?'

'No, there wouldn't be any point. All I had was those two names.' Kathleen's voice softened. 'But I owe her a debt, wherever she is.'

'A debt?'

'Because of her, I kept the machine, and I used it to help pay off all the bills. I put a notice on the window for a few weeks and work started to trickle in. Nothing complicated, but enough to pay for food and coal. Some people, like the grocer, let me pay in kind.'

'How did that work?'

'He was widowed. I did all his mending; made him new aprons, that sort of thing. In the end I had to insist on paying for my dried fruit and cake flour properly again.' She paused, lost in the past. 'Yes. It took me months, but I paid every single penny back. There isn't a bit of that sewing machine which was paid for by Philip Wright. If there was, I wouldn't have been able to bring myself to keep it.' She took out the Singer account book and opened the pages. 'All the payments in this book were made by me personally, to the manager of the shop, and when it was all cleared and the machine was mine, I'm not sure which one of us was the more pleased.'

'I had no idea. Why didn't you tell me?'

'In this life, some things are best kept private. I just got on with making a living so that I could pay my bills. You wouldn't believe it now, but for a long time I specialised in white goods; pillowcases, nightdresses, even a few christening gowns. It meant I only had to buy white thread and that kept my costs down.'

Connie thought about the reels of brightly coloured cotton that sat in their box next to the sewing machine.

'And then,' Kathleen continued, 'when I had settled all my financial obligations, I decided that if Jean was prepared to take a chance and try something new, then I could – and should – do that too, so I wrote to the Education Board and fought them to give me my job back, even though they tried to insist I was still married and couldn't work.' She stopped for a moment. 'And last of all, because I won that particular battle and went back into the classroom, I met a fine man who was a teacher in my new school, and married him.'

'Dad.'

'Yes. Your father.'

'So you write everything down in the notebooks to say thank you?'

'I don't know why I do it, to be entirely honest.'

'You don't?'

'It just feels as though it's important, somehow.'

Connie felt as though she had been flooded with information, but she had one more question. 'I need to ask... this Philip Wright, why do you use his full name all the time?'

'I haven't said his name for more than forty years. Not once. What else would I call him? If I just call him "Philip" it makes him sound like a friend I have lost touch with, and I'm certainly not going to call him "my husband".' Kathleen stood up and gathered all the papers together. 'And, before you ask, I don't know what happened to him and I don't care. For all I know, he was on the *Titanic* and ended up as fish food.' She laid the books and papers on the table and tied them back up with the coral ribbon. 'Now, what about some breakfast? I'm hungry.'

Fred

Blog: Late September

Edinburgh

I feel as though I am living through a succession of failed projects.

1. My failed relationship. I wasn't interesting enough to keep my girlfriend. In some ways it would be easier if she had dumped me for someone else. Then I would have someone to blame and be angry with, but she left me for nobody. I am so boring and pathetic that being on her own was better than being with me. You would think I would have seen it coming and been able to prevent it.

2. My failure to get another job. It seems that being a contractor isn't always seen as a positive thing. Instead, it produces raised eyebrows at interviews and a big fat 'LACKS STABILITY' written on the interviewer's metaphorical note pad. So far I've sent forty-three applications off and had four interviews. And one of those was in Aberdeen, which is hardly on the doorstep.

3. My failure to think of anything else to do that might bring in some income.

4. My failure to email my no-doubt-suntanned and happy mum, who is still away on her European Rail Adventure, and tell her that I am still unemployed. This is the one I feel worst about, oddly.

So today, in an effort to cheer myself up, I am going to abandon the endless job agency websites and do something completely different. I'm going to a car boot sale.

With my luck it will rain.

Heavily.

Fred knows it is Wendy-from-next-door who put the bright-green flyer about the car boot sale through his letter box. There's a guilt-inducing message on the back that reads: 'Hope you can come to this – it's for school funds!!!'

It has turned cooler in the last few weeks, but he's pleased to see that the promised downpour has stayed away. He shoves a hat into his jacket pocket before setting off on the familiar route to his old primary school.

It's busy. At a guess there are thirty cars in the playground, parked nose-to-the-wall with tailgates raised up into the air like a herd of hungry beasts, jaws open, calling for dinner. They temporarily obliterate the brightly painted hopscotch grid and the practice cycle roadway that are marked out on the tarmac.

All around him is bustle: parents snapping up the discarded home decor of others. Books, crockery and old toys are much in evidence. He is sure that everyone is secretly hoping to take home a valuable but overlooked treasure that will later be discussed on *Antiques Roadshow*, where an astonished expert will proclaim a huge value and the audience of onlookers will smile and wish it was they who had risked fifty pence on a nondescript vase the colour of lemon curd.

'You made it!' calls Wendy. She is in charge of a table that is laden with trays of cakes and cookies. He sees that she's also selling homemade bread, an obvious extension of the national baking obsession. As he looks around, he wonders how much his old school has changed in the last twenty-five years.

'I couldn't resist such a generous invitation.' He smiles, bowing in mock grandeur. 'What have you done with the kids?'

'They've been and gone. Their dad is taking them to see the latest Disney.'

'So you get to stand in the cold all afternoon without being interrupted.'

'Indeed. Are you going to have a look around or have you just come for the Empire Biscuits?'

'I suppose I should have a wander. Unfortunately, there is still no job' – he pulls an exaggerated miserable grimace – 'so I'm not planning to buy anything. I hope that doesn't matter.'

'Not at all, just enjoy the people-watching. You never know, you might go home with a bargain.'

She turns away to serve a customer and Fred starts to wander around the cars. People have brought folding DIY tables to arrange their goods on, some more artistically than others. It's surprisingly busy and many of the sellers have attracted a gaggle of potential purchasers who are inspecting and rejecting the goods on offer.

The ninth car on his circuit has just been abandoned by a large group of children and is momentarily quieter. In among the boxes under the wallpapering table is a tatty suitcase which has a large parcel label tied around the handle.

SEWING MACHINE. NOT WORKING. £10.

He bends down for a closer look.

'I can get it out for you if you like?' the seller offers. She is well prepared for the early autumn chill, dressed in a warm coat, a woolly hat and fingerless gloves – it looks to Fred as though she has done this car boot thing before.

'If you don't mind, that would be very kind.'

She manoeuvres the case onto the tarmac. It is covered with a fake crocodile-skin finish, part of which is torn away from the metal corners to reveal the boxy timber frame underneath.

'It doesn't have a key, I'm afraid. You can only keep it shut by snapping the locks over, so it's not very secure.'

He smiles. 'You're not really selling it to me, are you?'

'I really just want to be rid of it. My husband picked it out of a skip and brought it home. I don't know what possessed him. It's been cluttering the house up for years.'

She unclips the fastenings. Once the cover is off he can see that it's very similar to the machine he has at home, but it's in a much worse state. The black body is badly scraped, the gold decals are silvered and worn away almost completely in places, there is no cover on the bobbin race and the post on the top where the spool of thread should be placed is missing. He tries to work out how to back away gracefully.

'How much are you asking for it?' says a woman's voice behind him.

'Ten pounds,' comes the quick reply from the seller, cutting her losses with Fred.

He is still crouched down inspecting the locks but finds himself butting in. 'I'll give you fifteen.'

'Fifteen pounds?' His rival is scathing.

He stands up. 'Why not? It might just need some tender loving care to get it going again.'

'If I offered you sixteen pounds, could I have it?' The woman is speaking to the seller but looking very hard at Fred.

'You do both know that it doesn't work?'

Before he can reply, his competitor responds. 'That's fine. I'll be taking it apart anyway.'

'Hold on a minute, I was here first.' Fred feels in his pockets and remembers that he has limited funds. 'You win. Serves me right for forgetting to go to the bank. My fault.'

His competitor hands a ten-pound note and a pile of coins to the seller. 'You have to be quick when I'm around.' Despite her win, she is clearly cross.

'It's all yours.' The money is tucked away in a waist bag. 'Thanks very much.'

The buyer snaps the locks closed and picks up the case, cradling it awkwardly in her arms, clearly unwilling to trust the loose handle.

Fred is polite in defeat. 'It looks heavy. Would you like me to carry it to your car?'

'I can manage, thanks.'

'Are you really going to take it apart?'

'Oh yes, every last screw and cog.'

'I don't suppose you would sell me the bobbins? I mean, if you don't want to use it for sewing with?'

'Not sure it has any, but we can look.'

She heads off across the playground and sets her purchase down on one of the picnic benches in the corner. Before he can see how she has done it, the machine is out of the case, the compartment at the side has given up four bobbins and the race has yielded a fifth.

'Shall we say two pounds? I should really charge you ten, but I'm feeling generous.'

'Ten pounds seems a lot.'

'What do you expect when you pushed the price up without actually having the money to pay for it? I could have bought it for half what I ended up shelling out, maybe even less if I'd been able to haggle without you interrupting.' She looks at him suspiciously

'Who bids in five-pound increments, anyway? You're not in partnership with the seller, are you?'

Fred is taken aback. 'Of course I'm not. I don't know why you would think that.'

'Hmmmm, well, stranger things have happened at car boot sales before now.' She holds the bobbins out to him. 'So do you want them or not?'

He counts out a mixture of copper and silver coins. 'Sorry, it's a bit of a jumble but that should be right.'

'It's a pleasure doing business with you,' she says, handing over the steel spools. It's obvious that she doesn't mean it at all.

'I don't understand why you take them apart.'

'I use the components.'

'Ah, so you are doing repairs.'

'Oh God, no. I disassemble them and use the bits.' She hands him a business card. 'Here. In case you need more bobbins.'

He puts it in his pocket without looking at it. 'Why not mend them? It seems such a shame.'

'Not a shame at all.' She is abrupt now. 'Anyway, I must go. The wardens will be around any minute and I don't want to get a parking ticket.' She nods a goodbye and Fred is left standing in the playground, hands in pockets, as she walks off purposefully along the street.

'That's me told,' he says out loud, and heads back into the thinning gathering. The discovery of an unexpected five-pound note in his back pocket makes him look at the wares on display with a fresh eye. With the woman's words about haggling in his ears, he spends a pound on a red duvet cover with a thick black stripe in one corner, which he is warned is permanent ink. A sharp look from parent to teenager suggests that it may have been through the wash many times in an attempt to get rid of the mark. The same grumpy lad is selling an incoherent assortment of Lego bricks and wheels, which Fred pays over the odds for, remembering how his pocket money never stretched as far as he needed it to at the same age. He makes his way back to Wendy, who is now marking the last few muffins and bread rolls down to half price, and he spends the last of his change on a misshapen loaf of olive bread.

'Shall I give you a hand clearing up?' he offers.

'No, it's fine, I'll be here for another hour and someone is already on the chores list to help. You get away and enjoy the rest of your day.'

'If you're sure.'

'Did you find anything good?'

'Not much, just the beginnings of a present for two wee boys I know.'

'Awww, you mustn't.'

'Must go.' He leaves just as the stallholders and parents descend on the half-price baking.

Jean

September 1916

Leith

At the butcher's on Great Junction Street, Jean stood in the queue that formed every day, stringing along the counter and right out into the street. She adjusted the tight shawl wrapped around her body, into which she had tucked her wriggly daughter. In spite of Annie's increasing weight, it was far quicker to do this than to haul the borrowed pram up and down the tenement stairs.

She listened to the catalogue of orders taken and fulfilled: mince, sausage, ham bones, white pudding, black pudding, breast of mutton. It was a complete mystery who ate the sirloin and the leg of lamb, because there was little evidence that any of her fellow Leithers were buying them. Maybe the butcher himself took these treats home, she thought, and had a rare steak (whatever that looked like) each night with his family.

As the war had progressed she had noticed that the butcher's demeanour had changed. In the early months he had always asked his customers if there had been a letter from their sons or husbands, but little by little he had stopped enquiring. She got the feeling he was assessing each person individually and when a woman bought a more expensive cut, or increased the amount she purchased, an act usually accompanied by the diminishment of the black circles under her eyes, he was tempted to say more. He was careful never to ask a direct question but he might say, 'It's good to see you again, Mrs Smith', or, 'I hear the docks are working hard this week.' Many of the women had husbands who were riveters and stevedores, but their sons were soldiers or sailors. He had watched these boys grow up and didn't like to dwell on what news the postman might have brought.

On this particular day Jean was buying sausage meat. The butcher separated a handful off the pink lump on the slab. 'Annie is fair growing fast,' he said, remembering her name.

'She is that.'

'What age is she now, Mrs Cameron?' He made a ball of the meat between his cupped palms and weighed it on the balance scales before wrapping it in paper.

'She's almost a year and a half. I can hardly believe it.'

'Getting into everything then?' He accepted the sixpence she handed over and dropped the package into her basket.

She smiled at him. 'I need eyes in the back of my head, that's for sure. My friend has loaned me her big fireguard for the front of the range, but it's a huge cumbersome thing so I'm not sure how I'll get on with it. Seems to be more trouble than it's worth.'

The butcher saw the woman behind Jean in the queue sigh and shuffle her feet. 'I'm sure you'll come up with a way to make it work, Mrs Cameron. Thank you for your custom.'

As she left the shop Jean felt the beginnings of rain in the air, and saw the first splashes on the pavement. She wanted to buy potatoes but they were in short supply, and she didn't have the energy to traipse around four greengrocers to discover if there had been deliveries, so she bought a half loaf in the bakery at the end of her street instead. She would fry a couple of slices of it in the fat left over in the pan after she griddled the sausage, and give the crusts to Annie to chew on. She would like that.

Inside the tenement stair, Jean lifted the now sleeping toddler higher on her hip and wondered when she had got so heavy. She began to climb and to count the steps as she went. It was an ingrained habit of her childhood and it was how her mother had taught her about numbers, long before she stepped through the gates of the school. She had reached eighteen and was on the first landing when she heard a letter box slapping shut on the top floor and then the footsteps of the postman as he started his descent. She met him on the second landing. He moved to one side to let her go past with her basket of messages and didn't meet her eyes. He was gone before she uttered any words.

She stopped outside the flat with her key in her hand.

For as long as she didn't open the door, everything was alright.

Well, she reasoned, it wasn't alright in the sense that it had been a few years ago, when Donald used to come home every afternoon full of tales about dropped rivets and what might happen at the football on Saturday at Easter Road.

But that was then, and things were different now. She went to sleep alone in the wide bed and lay in the middle of it each night because she couldn't bear the vacant space on her left.

Annie, still asleep in her arms, began to squirm. Jean gathered her strength and put the key in the lock, opened the door quickly and looked down at the bare floorboards.

Nothing.

She wiped her feet on the doormat and went straight through to the kitchen, dumping the basket on the table. If she was careful, there might be the chance of a few more minutes of peace before Annie woke, so she slowly eased her daughter out of the shawl and set her down in the borrowed cot in the corner of the room. It was barely big enough, she had grown so much recently. Jean suddenly felt as though she had been suffocating and she rushed across to the open window to get a blast of fresh air. Outside the street was quiet: just a few women chatting at the stair doorways, and the coal merchant with his cart, doing deliveries. She stood there, looking at the normality of it all, and didn't move until she heard Annie begin to make her waking-up noises. As Jean turned to look at her daughter she saw the envelope, pushed to one side by the sweep of the door as she had come in.

The flat had lied to her.

Connie

'I've been thinking,' said Alf, looking over the top of his newspaper at his wife, 'that it's perhaps time you had a new sewing machine.' He had spent weeks trying to come up with a reason to do this.

'A new one?' Connie folded the last of the tea-towels and added it to the ironing pile.

'Yes, a brand-new one.'

The towels were stiff from hanging on the line in the back green for too long and getting wet several times over. She knew she should have brought them in and hung them on the pulley in the kitchen after the first downpour, but somehow it had seemed like too much effort at the time, and now her neglect meant they would be scratchy. Maybe it would be better to rinse them through with vinegar and start the drying process all over again, she thought.

The bedding was next. Alf abandoned the article he was reading about an American flight into space and got to his feet to help; they always did the sheets together, arms opening and closing, coming together and apart as though they were doing a slow jive. When their dance was over, he took the folded sheet from her, giving it one final flip before laying it on the table. 'Well, we can afford it since I got promoted and I'm sure I've seen you looking at them.'

'I'm not sure.' It was true, she wasn't at all sure.

He continued, pressing the point. 'I've heard you talking about the machines you had at the hospital. The electric ones are faster, aren't they?'

'Speed isn't everything, you know.'

He tried a different tack. 'When you were working there, what did your friends have?'

'Their own machines?'

He nodded.

'Oh, they all have electric now. I saw Pat a few weeks ago and she has just got herself a Featherweight. It's a nifty wee thing. It folds away into a black box, a bit like a vanity case.'

Alf had no idea what a vanity case might be but he ploughed on, regardless. 'What about one of those, then?'

'It doesn't do the new zigzag stitches,' she said, 'but I know there are attachments you can get for that sort of thing.'

He pressed on. 'So, what do you think?'

She thought about the old black machine, which Alf had put away at the back of the big hall cupboard out of sight, the last project unfinished. 'I could look for a second-hand one. I'm sure if I ask around I could find something suitable.'

'No, Connie.' He was not going to be put off. 'Almost every-thing in this place once belonged to other people before it was ours. I want you to have something which is yours and not a hand-me-down from your mother or mine, God rest their souls.'

It was true. The flat was full of furniture and crockery and pots and pans from earlier decades that were too good to get rid of.

'You aren't going to give up, are you?'

'I think you should have a brand-new one.' He looked out of the window at the last of the straggly daffodil leaves, and made a mental note to deal with them the next time he was outside. 'I would like to do that for you.'

'It needs to be investigated properly though, love.'

'Oh, I know, we don't have to do it in a rush. I'm sure there are catalogues we could look at first.'

'You don't know the first thing about them!' She laughed kindly. 'The only catalogues you've ever shown any interest in are full of car-rots and chrysanthemums.'

'Well, maybe it's time I broadened my reading. Anyway, I've been doing my own investigating.'

'Have you now?'

'I have. I took the trouble to walk past the shop last week on my way home from work and I saw that all the modern machines have a light built in. That's what made me think about it. This is the 1960s not the 1920s. If you had a proper light you could sew anywhere in the flat, not just in front of the window where you sat before. It would be a lot more practical.'

She looked around the kitchen. It would be good to be able to sit here in the winter with Alf at the other end of the table, reading his paper and relaying snippets of the news out to her as she worked.

'It wouldn't hurt to look, I suppose,' she conceded. 'We could go on Saturday, after you finish.'

'You're the expert. I'll be guided by you.'

'If it would cope with all your heavy gardening things, that would be a start.' Connie glanced at the pile of mending in her basket. 'I really must get that lot sorted out. It's mounting up all the time, and doing it by hand is so time-consuming.'

'Saturday, then. I'm serious. I don't want you trying to wriggle out of it.' He kissed her on the end of her nose. 'I have a new allotment, remember. I'm sure you don't want my fellow diggers thinking I look like I've been dressed from the rag bag.'

When Saturday came he held her to her promise and they walked in to the centre of the city. Connie didn't say much, but held Alf's hand tightly for most of the way. This was a big step, now there was only one wage coming in, despite Alf's promotion. But it wasn't just the money. Deep down, she knew it was time to put the past aside and make a new start

The shop was busy, and she left him standing near the door with another man who seemed to be on the same mission. Despite the offer, she was determined not to spend their hard-earned cash without a thorough exploration of the options and she wanted to do her research properly. She definitely wasn't in the mood for smooth-talking salesmen.

The staff were all busy with other customers so she was able to take her time, and easily managed to avoid their sales-talk. She had completed her first circuit of the store when she was suddenly faced with a machine that was little more than a shiny version of the one sitting in the cupboard at home.

Alf appeared at her side as though he had some sixth sense, and steered her back towards the newer models. 'Is there anything which takes your fancy?' he said.

'Maybe.' Her voice wobbled and she took a moment to gather herself. 'But these new machines look complicated. The ones at the hospital are different, big industrial things, not like these at all.' She pointed at a pale-cream example. 'I mean, look at all the switches and levers on this one. I don't think I'll be asking you to get your screwdrivers out for me. These will need proper looking after. They aren't going to be a job for an amateur and that will be an additional cost.'

'You let me worry about that,' he replied.

When she had seen all she needed to, they left the shop, but not until a salesman had pressed some promotional leaflets upon them.

'Do come back when you've had a good look at these,' he said. 'I'd be happy to arrange a demonstration for you.'

Connie smiled politely and tucked the brightly coloured papers into her handbag. She clipped it shut and put it back over her arm.

'Shall we continue?' Alf looked down at her; five foot nothing at all, in her summer coat and hat.

'Why not, it's a nice day.'

'We could walk along to the North British through the gardens.'

'Do you want to go and see the floral clock?'

'I could cast a professional eye over it.' He winked at her. 'Purely to assess the competition, you understand.'

They crossed the road, dodging cars and bicycles and went down the wide stone steps into Princes Street Gardens. Connie put her arm through his and as she curled her fingers over his sleeve she noticed that one of the buttons at the cuff was loose. How could she have missed it? She mentally moved it to the top of the mending pile. Her standards were slipping. She really had to get a grip on things. It wasn't fair on him; she was letting him down.

As they walked past the ice-cream stall, Alf's voice broke through her self-criticism. 'How about a cone?'

'That would be lovely, I haven't had one since…' Her voice dried up.

He took charge. 'Well, it's high time we put that right.'

They strolled along the footpath that ran along the top edge of the Gardens, below street level, until they reached the clock, and paused for a few minutes so that Alf could examine it.

'What do you think?' Connie asked. 'Is it an improvement on last year?'

'I think so.'

'Really?'

'Last year it was purple and acid green with a red centre. Something to do with heraldry.

'Oh yes. I liked the purple around the edges.'

'I know.' He glanced at her lilac dress. 'If it's purple it's always a winner for you. I think this is much nicer. And it's for the Lifeboats, so the Merchant Navy man in me approves.'

'Of course,' she smiled up at him, 'but given the choice, you would have planted it out with lettuces and radishes with a border of beetroot.'

'You know me too well. Perhaps it's a good thing I don't work for the council; I'm sure they wouldn't be happy with my two bobs' worth of opinion.'

At home Connie spread the leaflets out on the table and studied them for half an hour, completely engrossed. This was when Alf knew he had won this particular battle. He hadn't seen her concentrate on anything like this for months.

'Can you get me something to write on please, Alf?'

He fetched a used envelope from the drawer in the hall, took his pen knife from his trouser pocket, and carefully sliced open the folds to make a bigger sheet of paper. He set it down before her and laid a newly sharpened pencil beside it.

'Is it going to be very difficult to decide?' he asked.

'Not difficult, exactly, but there are so many possibilities.'

'I'll leave you to it, then. I'm off to cut the grass; it's our turn.' He smiled at her bowed head.

'Mmmmm,' she replied, not really listening.

Connie drew columns and rows to make a grid and wrote FEA-TURES at the top and MODEL at the side. She began to fill the chart in with ticks and question marks. It took some time. When she had finished with the leaflets from the shop she went over to the magazine rack and lifted out the latest copy of *Woman's Weekly*. She turned the pages, seeking out the advertisements for other sewing-machine manufacturers, and folding over the corner of each relevant page as she came to it. This new sewing machine would see her out, she thought, so it was all the more important to spend wisely and not fritter away the wages. There was no way of knowing what calls there might be on their income in the years ahead.

She went to the bureau in the front room and got out the blue correspondence case that had been a gift on her twenty-first birthday. She unzipped it and breathed in the leathery smell. On the right was the pad of writing paper: plain white Basildon Bond. On the left were pockets for envelopes and stamps. Her fountain pen was in the loop in the centre.

She wrote to three companies in her best handwriting, asking them for further information and then licked the stamps for each letter, grimacing at the taste. After she had put the envelopes out on the hall table ready for the post, she stood at the kitchen window for a few minutes. Alf – who was now in his shirt sleeves – was pushing the lawnmower from side to side across the grass. As she stood there, he paused and bent down to unhook the grass collector from the back of the mower, his shirt pulled tight over his back, his long legs and strong arms doing the work for both of them, and she had a rush of love for him, which she would never have been able to put into words.

He stood up again and turned towards the flat. His smile, meant for her alone, could have melted the heart of any woman watching.

Fred

Late September 2016

Edinburgh

There is a clattering on the front door just as Fred settles down to eat his lunch. The loudness of it makes him knock over his mug. Hot liquid puddles, perilously close to his laptop, and then meanders to the edge of the table and dribbles onto the floor.

'Hold on! I'll be there in a minute.'

He lifts the expensive electronics out of harm's way and is then frozen by indecision. Should he find out who's there, or mop up the mess? He grabs a tea towel from the pulley and stems the coffee-fall before heading into the hallway to answer the door, the computer balanced perilously on his arm. The mortice is still on; he is becoming a bit of a hermit.

'Hi, Wendy,' he says, peering through the security peephole his mother had insisted on installing several years earlier, much to his grandfather's disgust. 'Just give me a minute. I need to get my keys.' He heads back to the kitchen and dips his free hand into the bowl where the keys should be. They aren't there. 'Keys, keys, keys. Crabbie, have you moved my keys? This is ridiculous. They should be in the door or in the bowl.' He catches sight of them, next to the old key for the sewing machine case. He had been considering adding it to the ring. 'Found them,' he shouts.

When he finally gets the door open it's clear that his neighbour is frazzled. Behind her he can see a small boy with a toy car in each hand.

'Fred, I'm sorry to ask, but you couldn't look after Joe for me, could you? I have to take Michael up to the Sick Kids. He just fell off the top bunk and I think he might have broken something.'

'Of course.' He doesn't hesitate. 'I could come to the hospital with you, if you like?'

She shakes her head. 'Joe's been off nursery; he's got the tail end of a virus. He'll be fine with you but I don't think they would thank me for taking him up there.'

'No problem.'

'You really don't mind? My husband is away in London for a few days. I can't think who else to ask.'

'It's fine. My place or yours?'

Wendy looks apologetic. 'Yours?' I've got washing and stuff all over the place. I'd be embarrassed to let you in...'

'OK. He can come to me. I'm sure we can find something to watch on TV.'

Fred can see the relief on her face. She is close to tears but straightens up, having ticked one metaphorical box and now able to move purposefully onto the next problem.

He reads her mind. 'How will you get up there?'

'I'll have to get a taxi. I'll order one in a minute. Thank you so much. You have no idea how complicated things can get with two small boys around.'

He leaves his own door ajar and follows her back across the landing. Joe looks up at him, blond hair scrumpled as though he has just woken up. Fred kneels down. 'Want to hear a secret, Joe? We can't tell Michael.'

Joe nods.

Fred leans forward and whispers, 'I bought Crabbie a new toy, and she hasn't seen it yet. Shall we see if she wants to play?'

Five minutes later, he has been invaded. Joe has brought not only two cars, but a wheelie suitcase full of assorted vehicles, and his blanket and a scruffy teddy bear as well. Within half an hour the flat has been turned into a very complicated townscape with a car park, a motorway and a burger bar with a drive-through. Crabbie has gone to hide in the bedroom. Fred is bemused and impressed by his visitor in equal measure; it's been a long time since he played with toy cars but he enters into the game and follows Joe's instructions.

'Where are *your* cars?' Joe asks, looking at him with clear blue eyes.

For a moment Fred doesn't have an answer, and then he remembers. 'They are at my mum's house.' He hopes this is true. It would be a shame if his collection has been thrown out.

Joe compares notes. 'Do you have a police car?' He rummages in the suitcase. 'And an ambliance?'

'Definitely a police car, but I'm not sure about an ambulance.'

'My ambliance has broken down.' Joe holds out the offending vehicle. It's a sorry-looking object: the wheels are falling off, one of the axles has come adrift and it's clearly in need of repair.

Fred is suddenly four years old and sitting under Nana's table with cars arranged in lines along the floorboards. He can remember his chicken-pox itchiness as though it were yesterday.

'Hey, Joe, maybe you could take it to the garage to get it fixed?' Fred gets to his feet – carefully avoiding the lines of cars – and goes to the airing cupboard. The red duvet cover from the car boot sale is about to be pressed into service.

'What's that for?' asks Joe.

'I'm going to build a garage.'

Joe is immediately interested. 'Good idea.' He pushes the toy cars into an untidy heap. 'We really need one. Lots of the cars have crashed.'

'I can see that.'

'How are we going to build it?'

'Well, first of all we need to put all the cars back in your suitcase so that there is enough space to move the table.'

Joe isn't sure about this at all. He reluctantly does as he is asked and picks up the cars one at a time, in protest. Fred pulls the table out into the middle of the room and unfurls his scarlet bargain with a theatrical flourish, draping it over the surface and tucking the extra cloth under the legs to secure it.

'It doesn't look like a garage.' Joe folds his arms. He is not pleased. 'You *said* there would be a garage.'

'Ahhhh. We have to build it.' Fred hesitates for a moment. Perhaps this isn't the time to use Nana's best shears. He goes over to the pot of utensils next to the stove and holds the kitchen scissors aloft, snipping the air. 'Now, where shall we put the door?'

Joe's eyes are like saucers. He can't speak.

Fred takes matters into his own hands. 'First we need a window.' He eyes up the cloth on one side of the table and takes action, cutting three sides of a square in the sheet, halfway up, leaving the top edge as a hinge. He flips it upwards and pins it in place with clothes pegs.

'Wow. You made a hole!'

'I made a *window*.'

Joe is stunned and delighted at the naughtiness of it all. He starts to join in. 'There should be a door at the end.'

'Yes, sir.' Fred snips the air again, much to the delight of his four-year-old guest. 'One door coming up.' He slices two long cuts upwards from the floor, and rolls the fabric up, securing it at the top with more clothes pegs. 'Would you like to go inside, Mr Garage Man?'

'Yes *please*.' Joe crawls through the rolled-up doorway and looks out of the makeshift window. 'Hello', he says.

Fred sits cross-legged on the floor. 'Good afternoon, Mr Garage Man. I have a problem with my vehicle.'

'Is it the ambliance?'

'It is indeed. It has been making some very strange noises and I need a mechanic.'

'Right. Drive up to my door and I will have a look at it for you.' Joe pauses. 'You had better bring some paper with you so I can make you a bill when I'm finished.'

Two hours later, Joe will not be budged from his new workplace and also insists on eating his fish finger sandwich under the table at teatime. By the time Wendy eventually appears with Michael, who now has his arm encased in a bright-blue cast, the garage has been improved further by the addition of a swiftly improvised letter box and a cardboard sign saying JOE'S FIXING GARAGE. Michael is clearly torn between pride in his new cast and jealousy that his little brother has had all the fun.

After his young visitor has gone home, Fred lies on the floor looking upwards at the underside of the table and remembering another time.

Later, when he has finished eating his own fish finger sandwich, with the addition of a dollop of tartare sauce, and polished off with a glass of cold Vinho Verde, he takes the sewing notebooks down from the shelf where they have been stashed for safekeeping. He flips through them, checking the dates at the start of each one, and lays them out across the long table in chronological order. In the last book he finds what he is looking for.

Up the side of one page are three rows of stitches in red and green and orange.

February 1985

Table tent for Fred (chickenpox)

A great success!

Fred

Blog: Early October 2016

Edinburgh

Another two interviews last week, and for one of them I've been asked to go back to meet the rest of the team. I'm not holding out much hope though. Truth be told, I'm pretty fed up.

So far I've applied for sixty-three jobs and had nine interviews. Is that a good hit rate? I have absolutely no idea; it doesn't feel like it. I really, really need to get something soon. I'm definitely feeling the pinch now the weather is colder. How do people manage when this goes on for years?

Michael and Joe were over yesterday to visit Crabbie, and when Wendy came to get them she saw the old sewing machine. She's asked me if I could make bag for Michael's gym shoes for school. It will be a few weeks before the blue cast of doom is removed from his arm, but she doesn't want him to be different from the other kids.

Without thinking about it (because I'm nice like that, HAH!) I said yes. So now I have to make good my promise. I must be nuts. I have absolutely no idea how to thread the thing, let alone make it go.

Wendy wastes no time in giving Fred the instruction sheet. 'The class teacher thinks it would be a good project for parents to make with their child.'

'Really?' replies Fred, making no attempt to conceal his incredulity.

'I know. She clearly thinks we are all sewing experts with empty hours to fill.' She smiles hopefully at him. 'I understand if you can't manage it.'

'It can't be that complicated.' He looks through the instructions. 'You know, I wouldn't mind at all if you want to borrow the machine and do it yourself with Michael.'

She visibly shudders. 'I've got two left hands, Fred. There's no way I could do this.'

'OK. I'll give it a go. Any particular colour?' He thinks his way around the cupboards in the flat, one at a time. 'My Nana used to have a big box of cloth scraps but I haven't seen it since I moved back. I think Granda might have got rid of it.'

'Oh, I don't mind. The brighter the better.'

From across the stairwell they can both hear her phone ringing.

'You'd better answer that.' He smooths his hand across his still-shaven head. 'Leave it with me.'

'Thanks, Fred. You're a life-saver.'

He closes the front door and goes over to his laptop.

'Right, wibbly wobbly web, tell me what to do.' He clicks the trackpad and a message appears on the screen.

YOUR COMPUTER IS NOT CONNECTED TO THE INTERNET

'Yes it is.' He clicks again.

YOUR COMPUTER IS NOT CONNECTED TO THE INTERNET

He looks across to the router, which is plugged in next to Granda's emergency torch. The usual turquoise glow is absent. It looks dead.

'Brilliant, just brilliant.'

He flicks switches all around the room. Everything else is working, including the radio, which he has never found the need to use until now. A deep north-country voice blasts out at him: '… an ericaceous blend is essential for rhodedendr…' He turns off the assault as fast as possible. Even the normally untroubled Crabbie looks astonished.

'Granda's gardening programme.' He squints at the position of the needle on the analogue dial. 'Bloody hell. It's like it was waiting for me or something.'

He feels a sudden need to get away from the flat. The unasked-for link to the past has rattled him. He seizes his fleece jacket from the hook beside the door and steps out into the urban bustle of the afternoon. I'll go to the library, he thinks. There is bound to be a book on this sort of stuff.

Jean

November 1916

Leith

Jean saw the man as soon as she turned the corner. She stepped back into the shadow of the shop awning so as not to be seen. She had to be certain. He was standing outside their stair, looking upwards. Was it Donald?

Just as she had come to the marvellous conclusion that it really was him and was filling her lungs, ready to shout his name at the top of her voice, one of her neighbours came out and walked across the street to greet him. She watched as the two men stood for a couple of minutes, talking. When they had finished and he stood alone again, Donald – if it was him, she still wasn't completely sure – didn't move. What was he waiting for? She couldn't work it out. The figure looked up towards her flat a final time and then stepped, no, limped forward, and disappeared into the stair.

So he had injured his leg, she thought, and that was the reason why his letters had been so scant. It had been ten weeks since the first official envelope had arrived and turned her world upside down. The standard Army correspondence had said 'injured' and everyone knew that could mean anything at all. It had been some time before there had been any letters from Donald himself. After that, the post had arrived infrequently and provided her with little proper information, which had only intensified her worry. She knew in her heart that he was embarrassed about his poor spelling and grammar. News from the Front was everywhere and Jean had been to see the official film about the Somme. She knew that it was more than likely that he wanted to protect her from the reality of what had happened to him, but in her opinion, men were so stupid they didn't realise that this wasn't of the slightest help, and Donald was no different.

Her thoughts raced far ahead of her footsteps as she began to walk along the street. She didn't hurry. She needed to sort her head out before he saw her, or he would see straight into her mind and she wouldn't be able to hide her worries from him. She considered going to collect Annie from Hannah's so that she could be part of the homecoming. In the few letters that had arrived, he always wanted to know everything about her progress. It was just after four, and Hannah wasn't expecting her until five, so she had time to go home first, without Annie. Perhaps that would be best.

In the coolness of the stair Jean could feel her heart pounding, thumping so loud it must surely be heard on the top floor where he would be waiting.

Did he have his door key? She couldn't remember. As she walked up each flight of stairs she steeled herself for what was ahead, until the last few steps when she finally caught sight of his sandy hair, his head leaning against the wall, exhausted from the effort of climbing. There was a scar on his knee, just below his kilt. Whatever was making him limp would heal, it didn't matter. What worried her most was his oat-pale skin, the thinness of his cheeks and the looseness of his shirt collar where once there had been strong neck muscles.

It was only after she had drunk in her first look at him after so many months that she saw what he had refused to tell her in his letters.

The hand their neighbour had so readily shaken in the street a few minutes ago was the only hand he had. His left sleeve was empty and pinned out of the way. Before she could stop the thought, a memory from that very morning pressed into her head and she replayed the images of Tom reaching out to take Annie from her at the door of his flat, with his two good arms, and she almost fainted with the sudden fury and jealousy and sorrow all bound up in one invisible shudder that stole her breath and made her ashamed all at once. And then it was gone, and she hated herself.

'Jean.' Donald looked at her with those soft grey eyes of his, and reached out to her. 'My Wife.'

She remembered how he had addressed her in his letters. Not Dearest Jean, or Darling, but 'My Wife'.

My Wife, I have news…

My Wife, I wish…

And at last, *My Wife, I am safe…*

'Yes,' she replied. 'Your wife.' She moved onto her tiptoes to kiss him and found herself lifted clean off her feet and raised into the air until they were eye to eye.

He kissed her softly and put her down again, and wrapped her up close to him and whispered, 'I am sorry.'

'I know.'

'No, you don't understand. How can I ever…'

'I accept your apology.'

'You accept?'

'Yes, Donald.' Jean stroked the rough stubble on his face. 'I accept your apology, not because it is needed, but because you want to give it. You have been storing that up for weeks and now you have said it. And I don't want you to feel you have to say it more than once.'

He paused. The flood of words and explanation and regret was stemmed before it was uttered. At last he nodded his agreement, and bent down to pick up his pack, but she was too quick for him and had it over her shoulder before he realised what she was doing. 'I can carry that,' he protested.

'You could,' she replied, 'but if I carry it, you can hold my hand as we go inside and that would be much nicer, don't you think?'

In the few minutes it took to open the door and go inside, to lay down bag and basket, remove coats and finally to close the door again against the world, thoughts rushed around her head, tiny flashbacks of their years together. Donald vaulting onto the packing crates at the Singer factory. Carrying their bags off the train when they arrived in Edinburgh. Washing the grime off himself at the sink in the kitchen. Taking Annie from her when she was minutes old. But most of all she remembered her own hand, running her fingers down the page of her Bible to find the verse that had set them off on this journey: 'A time to rend, and a time to sew; a time to keep silence, and a time to speak.'

And she knew that it was time, once again, to speak. This time she would not speak with words, but with love and acceptance and hope, because she knew that, above all, he would need the last of these more than anything else she could offer.

Connie

February 1964

Edinburgh

It was as she was cooking breakfast that Connie told Alf about the vacancy. She was standing at the stove frying square sausage, wearing her new flowery wraparound apron edged with golden-yellow bias binding. It was the first thing she had sewed on her new machine.

A cooked breakfast was their Sunday morning treat.

'I met Miss Archer yesterday morning, in the Co-operative on Bread Street. She said that I am much missed in the Sewing Room and they still talk about me, even after nearly seven years of being away.'

'Oh yes?'

'She also told me that she is retiring soon.' She left the sizzling pan for a minute, took the warmed plates from under the grill and set them on the table before retrieving knives and forks from the drawer. She moved from cupboard to table fluently; everything was in the same place as it had been since her childhood. She could have done it with her eyes shut. There seemed no reason to reorganise it and move things around, despite the exhortations of the women's magazines she saw at the hair salon when she had her fortnightly shampoo and set. The constant push to re-do and change was overwhelming sometimes.

'Budge up, Alf. I need to lay the table and your paper is in the way.'

He obliged, shuffling his chair sideways, which wasn't what she meant him to do at all. 'She is retiring?'

Connie gave him a gentle shove to get him to move further up. 'I didn't think she was old enough but there you go – she's obviously very well preserved.'

He put the newspaper down to listen properly. 'And?'

Connie went back to her station at the cooker. She lifted the slabs of salmon-pink meat with her tongs and turned them over one by one, taking care that the fat didn't splash onto the enamel stove top. 'She said that I should apply for the job.'

'And what do you think?' He stood up to collect the teapot and carried it over to the table.

'Tea cosy, please,' she reminded him.

'I'm just getting to that. I was concentrating on what you were saying.' He snuggled a pleated hand-knit cover over the warm pot.

She spooned the melted fat from the sausage meat over the eggs and watched as the bright yolks faded and the membrane became opaque. 'I'm not sure what I think about it.'

'You don't see yourself sitting in that office dealing with the worksheets, interviewing new staff, you mean?'

'I think I could do it, but I'm not sure I would want to.' She brought the corner-bakery rolls out of the oven and put everything onto a big oval serving plate, the one with the willow pattern, which had been in the family since before she was born.

'Because?'

'Because I like being part of a team.' She spoke in the present tense without realising she was doing it. 'I like the sewing and I like all the problem solving. Taking a torn piece of cloth and making it serviceable again, trying to make things last as long as possible. It's like a series of little challenges.' She paused. 'It fits me, I suppose. It's how I am.'

'I thought Miss Archer did the sewing as well?'

'Well, she does, but not in the same way. It's really only when things are pushed and there's a deadline.' She smeared salty butter onto the rolls. 'There is always a separation between those of us at the machines in the sewing room and the manager in the office. I'm not sure I would want to cross over to the other side.'

'You could try it for a bit – go back and see how you get on.'

Connie picked up the serving spoon. 'It will all go cold if we don't make a start.'

'Yes, please.' Alf held out his plate for the eggs, crispy on the edge where the white had not quite stuck to the frying pan, and soft and wobbly in the centre, just how he liked them. He sliced the first one in half with his knife and watched the sea of yellow flow across the white china.

Connie didn't like eggs. In her opinion they were horrible slimy things, but she had mastered the cooking of them so that they were perfect for him. She had never told him how the smell of them made her feel as though she was going to be sick. There were some things it wasn't necessary for him to know. 'I don't think management is a job for me, that's all. I like being one of the girls.' She ignored the fact that the youngest woman in the department was thirty-eight years old.

He mopped up the yolk with the inside of his bread roll. 'I see.'

'I suppose if one of us went for the promotion, there might be a vacancy for a seamstress. They will always need people to do the repairs and hem the uniforms and make the theatre drapes.' She speared a rasher of bacon with her fork. 'The hospital doesn't want to throw things out when they can still be mended, and you can't speed that process up. It's not like being in a factory and making new things on a production line. I mean, there is no logic to where a hole will appear on a sheet. Smokers leave little scorched rings all over them – it shouldn't be allowed.'

She was about to set off on a personal hobby horse and he deflected her. 'Will anyone else apply for the position?'

'I don't know. Pat might; she's younger than the rest of us.' In her head she had made the transition from them to us. 'She has a way with figures. I think she even enjoys it.'

'It won't go to an outsider?'

'Not very likely.'

'Do you want to try for it?' Alf tried to make the question sound casual, as though it wasn't important at all.

'The supervisor job? No.'

Connie ate the rest of her breakfast, lost in thought, and he went back to his reading and said no more about it, allowing the possibilities to marinade and improve. After they were both finished he cleared the plates and stacked them in the sink. It was the same every Sunday. She cooked, and then he cleared up to the sounds of the Home Service on the radiogram.

Connie reached over for the newspaper and leafed through it to find the page with the crossword. 'Have you got a pencil?'

Alf rummaged in his cardigan pocket with wet, soapy hands and found the stub he had been using. She examined the point of the lead and handed it back. 'This is blunt.'

'Sorry, give me a minute.' He dried his hands, took his penknife out and opened the blade.

'Alf!' She shook her head at him. 'Not at the table. Outside!'

He walked over to the back door, and then paused before beginning the sharpening ritual. 'So if Pat was the new supervisor, would she be the one who would choose her replacement?'

'I expect so.'

'Well, I'm sure she would make the right choice.'

Going back to work was exactly what Connie needed to do, but it had to be she who made that decision. By the time he turned back to the room, her head was bent over the crossword.

'Hurry up with that pencil, love. I've got four clues worked out already.'

Fred

Early October 2016

Edinburgh

Fred is none the wiser about sewing techniques, despite finding no fewer than five books on quilting and tailoring in the library. He hasn't got the required personal identification with him that would allow him to join and take books out, so he returns to his flat empty handed. The corner shop is open, as always, and he steps inside. Perhaps chocolate will be a suitable analgesic for the fresh feeling of loss that has lodged itself deep inside him, courtesy of some specialist compost advice on a radio programme.

'Afternoon, Fred,' says Eva, as she unpacks a box of chewing gum and slots the small boxes into the dispenser on the counter.

He nods but doesn't reply.

'You OK? You look as though you've lost something.'

'I have.' Someone, not something, he thinks.

'You've lost it in here? Nothing's been handed in.'

'No, not here. It doesn't matter.' He stops in front of the confectionery. 'I need chocolate.'

'Aaaah. That sort of a day, is it?'

He runs his fingers along the enticing packets. 'They should call this stuff Mischief,' he announces. 'It would be an excellent name for it.' He picks up three family-sized purple blocks and plonks them down on the glass counter.

'Is that everything?'

'Yes.' He stops. 'Actually, you might be able to help me with something?'

'I will if I can,' replies Eva, ringing the bars of wickedness through the till, one at a time.

'Did you do sewing at school?'

She frowns. 'It's a long time ago, but yes, of course. All the girls did. The boys did woodwork and metalwork and we did sewing and cooking. I make a very good apple crumble, I'll have you know, all thanks to Miss Young.'

He perks up. 'So, if I were to – hypothetically speaking – want to sew something, how would I do it?'

'On a machine, you mean?'

'Yes.'

'Did your Nana not show you?'

'It's an awful thing to say, but I can't remember.'

'Well, I can tell you how we did it in class. I'm not much of a dressmaker though.'

'Go on.'

She picks up two pink-and-white candy-striped paper bags and puts them in front of her. 'We took the cloth and pinned it together along the seam.' She writes with the ballpoint that always sits on the counter next to the lottery tickets. 'Here, and here.'

'I see.'

'And then we tacked the seam line with a different colour of thread, so we could see it easily.' She pauses, transported back to a teenage classroom. 'Long stitches, like this.' She draws neat dashes, exactly along the pink stripe.

The bell jangles above the door, announcing the arrival of a portly man, who walks straight up to the counter.

'Excuse me,' he says.

Eva continues with her explanation, 'And then we stitched on top of the tacking…'

'Excuse *me*.' The man interrupts. 'There's a traffic warden outside and I need change for the parking meter.' He clearly isn't going to let Eva continue until he has what he wants.

'It's alright.' Fred moves out of the way and picks up his chocolate. 'You've told me what I need to know. Thanks very much.'

She shakes her head. 'No, Fred…' but he is halfway to the door and doesn't hear her.

The man holds out his ten-pound note. 'Coins please.'

'I'm afraid the till is locked unless there is a sale,' Eva lies. And then she slices open the cellophane on a second box of peppermint chewing gum and begins to fill the other dispenser, one packet at a time.

Blog: October

Edinburgh

The router is borked.

I'm blogging this from my phone while keeping my eye on the data usage bar chart. It never rains but it pours it seems. It's less than six months old so I'm not very happy.

I complained, LOUDLY, to the phone company. After going through a call centre and then technical support and then eventually speaking to a supervisor with some powers, they are going to replace it.

There must be an up-side to this state of affairs, but I'm not sure I can see one at the moment.

Negatives

Email – until now I have refused to set up email on any phone I have owned. I suppose I'm going to have to do it, though. I will just turn all the notifications off or it's more than likely all the pings and buzzes will make me want to throw it into the canal within hours.

Replacement – it's the usual get-out clause of 'within 28 days', so I may need to take up residence in a coffee shop and make a black Americano last a whole after-noon like the rest of the world.

The new model they are now supplying is out of stock.

Positives

I can't see any positives.

Really, I can't.

Fred plans Project Shoe Bag methodically. He sets out the equipment he thinks he will need for getting started on the kitchen table.

Rucksack.

Pattern instructions.

Tape measure.

Scissors.

On reflection, he decides that the eleven-inch tailor's shears from the sewing box are perhaps a little large and might be construed as an offensive weapon, so he puts them back.

In all of his thirty-five years, Fred has never set foot in a charity shop. The first not-new purchases of his entire life were the things from the car boot sale a few weeks earlier, and based on his bobbin-buying success, he fully expects to be home in half an hour with a neatly folded piece of child-friendly fabric. Patience is not a virtue he possesses and the excitement of finding a sought-after title in a second-hand bookshop, and coming home with three other books because they look interesting, is a delight that he has yet to discover.

The nearest charity shop to the flat appears to be deserted, reinforcing his prejudices about such places being full of stuff nobody wants. He wanders about, unsure what to do. Should he wait for an assistant?

He browses the rack of men's shirts and jackets. There are a couple of thick wool coats that look interesting, and one still has the original shop tag stitched to the sleeve, but they are the wrong size. He leafs through shirts and sweaters and ends up at the rack of ties. Every decade of fashionable neckwear is represented in all possible widths from barely bootlace to full kipper. He pulls a few out for a closer look; if he ever gets back into tie-wearing employment, this place looks as though it could provide a useful supply. Just as he begins to think the shop has no staff at all, a voice comes from the back of the premises.

'Morning! Lovely day, isn't it?'

He can't see who is speaking until she stands up; a tall woman with a very long grey braid of hair, which flows all the way past her waist. It makes her look a bit like that TV presenter on the gardening programme, he thinks, the one Granda liked. In her hand is a sunflower-yellow teapot.

'Yes.' He is useless at small talk.

She tries to find the best position for the teapot on an already crowded shelf. 'This is nice. Just came in yesterday. If you're interested in having it, I'd buy it now. It'll be gone by lunchtime.'

'I wasn't really looking for that sort of thing,' he replies. 'Although it's a great colour.' He wonders if this is what his social life has come to: discussions with women the same age as his mother about crockery.

'Cheerful,' she agrees.

'I was looking for some fabric.'

She moves a few bowls and a flowery jug out of the way and puts the teapot down on the shelf. 'I might put it in the window, you know. Someone will be sure to snap it up.' She picks it back up again and walks to the cash desk.

Fred follows her. 'Ummm. Fabric? For sewing with?'

'We don't have any fabric *as such.*'

'Ah.'

'There are things you could cut up. Is it for patchwork?'

'I need to make a bag.' He rummages in his jacket pocket for the instructions. 'Like this...'

The woman moves to the left so that she is standing in a better light, and reaches for the glasses that are hanging around her neck on a luminous green cord. She takes the paper from him.

'My granddaughter goes to that school.'

He reassesses her. She is older than she looks, not that it's important. 'So, what do you think?'

'It won't take long to make. An hour at the most.'

'Yes, but first I need something to make it *from.*' This is quite different from his usual, very specific, in-and-out-as-fast-as-possible type of shopping.

'You need something that will be different from all the other kids.'

Fred hasn't thought about this until now, but it's true. He remembers all too well the chaos of getting changed at the school gym hall in Primary One, and how he went home more than once wearing someone else's shirt. Michael will need to be able to find his bag easily in a jumble of thirty others. 'Good point. What have you got?'

She walks over to the racks of clothes. 'Boy or girl?' She fixes him with a challenging stare. 'Or doesn't that matter?'

'I don't know, to be honest.' He isn't sure what she means. 'It's for a little boy who lives next door to me. His mum asked me if I could make it for him because I have a sewing machine and I was stupid enough to say I would try.'

'You have a sewing machine?'

'My grandmother's. It's an old one.'

It's as though this stranger has put him under some sort of spell; he is never normally this talkative.

'Well, we haven't got much that is going to be hardwearing. There are some dresses but it seems a bit of a shame to cut them into bits, just to make a bag.' She selects a clothes hanger and extracts a mustard-coloured skirt with black stripes. 'This has been here for a while.'

Fred shakes his head. 'Not really what I am looking for.'

'I thought you wanted something different...' She puts it back on the rack. 'And that one is definitely different.'

He feels as though he is being told off. There appear to be rules about this sort of shopping, and number one is not to tell the person who is serving you about your plans for their treasure.

'What about curtains?' he says. 'Have you got any of those?'

'All the soft furnishings go to our shop in Stockbridge.'

'That's fine. I can walk over there and take a look.' He picks his rucksack back up.

'Hold on. I'll just check if they are open for you.' She heads back to the counter, opens a tatty-looking ring binder and runs her finger, tipped with white sparkly nail polish, down the page. 'They are closed until lunchtime today.'

'Ah.' He watches as she spins the teapot around slowly by its handle on the countertop, just as Nana used to, and for a few moments he is transported back to after-school tea (for her) and juice (for him).

She stops the twirling.

'How much is the teapot?'

'Three pounds. There was a jug as well but that's gone already.'

He digs in his pocket for some change and hands over the money. 'I'll take it.'

This project is proving to be more expensive than he anticipated.

Fred

Blog: Early October 2016

Edinburgh

Instead of staying at home and wasting time on the internet, I decided to go out into the great metropolis and do something different for a change. I went shopping.

Shopping, for me, has always been on a need-to-buy basis. I've never seen the enjoyment in trawling around town going in and out of shops, especially in the winter. Being alternately in an Arctic blast and then on a tropical island is not my idea of a fun experience. I used to go with Sam in London occasionally but I think she gave up on me and went with her girlfriends instead (one of the many nails in that particular coffin, now I come to think of it).

So I'm surprised to report that yesterday I went out to get something to make Michael's bag with, and I came back six hours later having quite enjoyed myself.

One of the advantages – there had to be one – of blogging from my phone is that it's easy to upload photos, so for the first time, there are some pictures on this diary/ blog/journal.

1. A yellow teapot. £3. I don't need a teapot. Granda had a perfectly good enamel pot that used to be in the shed at the allotment, and Nana's blue-and-white striped one is sitting on the shelf above the kettle. Either of them would make a perfectly good brew and since I usually just chuck a teabag in a mug anyway, buying a teapot was definitely not on my list for yesterday. Why did I buy it? I just felt I ought to make a purchase, you know – for

charity. And yellow is a happy sort of colour and I need a bit of that.

2. Gloves. £1.50. I have got used to stuffing a hat in every coat pocket now, but I completely underestimated how cold it was yesterday. There I was, heading up to Morningside and before I got half way up Lothian Road the wind was howling. One pair of gloves. Red wool. They look as though they might have been knitted by hand.

3. One cotton apron. £2.50. This is what I am going to use for Michael's bag. It's got thick green and red and white stripes like an Italian flag and I don't think it's ever been used. There's an embroidered green badge across the chest, which says 'Pizza Perfection'. I might take that off and sew it in a different place. Little boys like pizza, don't they?

4. Five reels of cotton. 30p each. Not sure how good the colours will be in the photos, so… Bracken (the colour of honeycomb), Fiesta Pink (pink, very), Mid Gobelin (blue/ green), Banana (like a very, very milky cup of tea – it definitely doesn't resemble any banana I've ever seen) and Dark Navy (what it says).

5. A fairly tatty paperback copy of 'How to Make Toffee and Confectionery for the Family'. 40p.

6. Two white cotton pillowcases. £1. I still felt I should buy something in every shop, even though it was getting a bit silly by then – I hope the Guide Dogs get extra-fluffy blankets in their kennels or something for that pound.

I make that £9.90.

The apron is for the bag.

The thread will be useful.

The gloves are because I am an idiot.

The teapot and the pillowcases because I am a soft touch.

And the toffee-making book because, well, I have a sweet tooth, what can I say?

At this rate, if I keep buying something in every charity shop I set foot in, I'll be bankrupt by Christmas.

So, do I sew first?

Or make tea in the new teapot?

Or investigate the location of the nearest dentist?

Outside the kitchen window a blue tit is hanging from the bird feeder, and three chaffinches are pecking at stray barley kernels that have fallen onto the ground beneath it. A tree planted as a sapling more than a hundred years before stretches upwards and marks the corner of the boundary wall between Fred's tenement and the one next door. The back green, shared by eleven flats, is filled with bird-song from early morning until dusk. Its original purpose as an area to dry laundry, with a weekly rota for each household, has been super-seded by near-universal ownership of tumble dryers and the people who live there seem to use their shared garden very little. Only the occupants of the two bottom flats use the space for drying washing now. The original cast-iron poles are still there, seven feet tall with one set of cross posts at the top and another halfway down. Fred has glimpsed Wendy teaching Joe and Michael to peg out their clothes, just as his mum taught him when he was their age.

He sits in front of the sewing machine and tries to remember how to thread it, eventually consulting the downloaded instructions on his phone. It takes several attempts to get it right, teasing the old levers into play and making tiny adjustments to the bobbin tension with a small screwdriver. He makes test seams on an old tea towel until he's happy with the look of the stitches.

The fabric has been measured four times and marked with a pen-cil before cutting. Nana's shears are fearsome things, much sharper than Fred anticipates, but eventually he is all ready to sew. He tries to remember Eva's instructions.

Pin.

Tack.

Stitch.

How hard can it be?

He makes a cup of tea in the new teapot before he starts. The woman in the first of the charity shops told him she thought it would take about an hour to make the bag. He is sure it is all quite straight-forward.

Fred

Blog: Early October 2016

Edinburgh

Eva was wrong.

Completely and utterly wrong.

I did exactly as she said.

I measured and cut, as she told me to, and I put the pins in.

And then I tacked the pieces together. I now know, because I Googled it on my phone after the bag came out like a dog's breakfast, that Americans call it BAST-ING. This is, of course, what we do to a roast chicken – no wonder people say we are divided by a common language.

I followed Eva's instructions to the letter and used contrasting thread for the tacking, an orangey colour called Red Salmon, easy to see against the stripes of the apron. I haven't done any hand sewing – apart from the occasional trouser button – since I was about eight years old, and I've certainly never tried to do it in anything approximating a straight line.

To make sure the line was perfect, I used a ruler and a pencil, and then I tacked exactly on top of it. Looked pretty good, though I say it myself.

And then I threaded the machine up with Gay Kingfisher, top and bottom, and I sewed on top of the tacking stitches.

I don't know why, now I come to think of it, that it never occurred to me that this was a monumentally idiotic thing to do, but it didn't. I sewed all around the bag, very carefully.

And then I tried to pull the tacking thread out.

I failed.

And after that I got the seam ripper from Nana's sewing box and – there is no other word for it – I EXCAVATED the Salmon in tiny shreds, one fibre at a time, from the stitching line where it had become welded beneath the Kingfisher.

Three hours, it took me. I was SO close to getting the shears back out and chopping the whole thing into tiny pieces. I'm not sure if kingfishers prey upon salmon, but this morning, after a hard fought battle, they won.

Lesson learned.

The bag is made, and I managed to salvage the Pizza badge, as planned. I'm off to show it to Eva and to tell her that I managed to do it in spite of her. She'll love that!

The shop is busy. It's lunchtime and there is a smattering of workmen queuing up for their Scotch pies and bottles of juice. Fred hovers at the back of the aisles, paying great attention to the display of toothpaste and baby shampoo. By the time the men have climbed into the fleet of white vans outside, he is feeling rather silly.

'Hello, Fred. What can I get you today?'

'You know I asked you about how to sew something?'

'Oh goodness, yes, and you rushed off before I could finish what I was saying.'

'Ah.'

'You were gone before I had a chance to tell you the rest of the story.'

'Right.'

She looks at him. The beginning of a smile appears at the sides of her mouth. 'You did what I said, didn't you?' She blushes, like a young girl who has been found kissing a boy behind the school bike shed.

'Well, yes. I did.'

'I am so sorry.'

'I did exactly what you told me to. I followed the instructions precisely.'

'Oh dear.'

He beams at her. 'And now I have come to show you what I made, in spite of your *deliberate* attempt to sabotage it.' He takes the project out from under his arm with a flourish and lays it out for her to examine, proudly covering the glass counter and the fizzy snakes and flying saucers with the new bag.

She lifts it up to examine it. 'This is pretty good, Fred. I'm impressed. How long did it take you?'

'Half an hour to cut it out properly, an hour to tack it together by hand with nice orange thread, twenty minutes to machine it and three hours to *remove* the thread I put in so carefully as per your advice.'

'Three hours.' Her always expressive face is a study in deadpan, but her voice gives her away as it ripples with barely contained laughter.

'Yes. Is that really how you were taught to do it?'

'In secondary school, yes. My sewing teacher was obsessed with everything being perfect – so perfect that I never sewed another thing after I left.'

'I can see why.'

Eva reaches under the glass and puts some sweets into a paper bag. 'I think I owe you these by way of an apology.'

'The air was blue.' He accepts the her peace offering. 'And several times I was just this far' – he pinches the air – 'from reaching for the scissors.'

'But you didn't. Well done.'

He smooths out the fabric and folds his creation back up. 'My first real project. I'm quite proud of it actually.'

'Your Nana would be pleased.'

'Do you think so?'

'Oh yes. Without a doubt.'

Fred doesn't trust himself to speak. He nods, and waves a goodbye as he leaves. And then he walks home along familiar pavements – because suddenly it *is* home, although if anyone asked him later, he wouldn't have been able to pinpoint the moment that it began to feel that way.

Bag for gym shoes for Michael. (F)

Cost – Fabric £2.50 (old apron)

Threads – Gay Kingfisher, Red Salmon

Five hours!

The notebooks are spread out on the kitchen table. No two are the same. He divides them first into separate groups, one with Nana's handwriting, and the other with the rather more elegant script belonging to his great-grandmother.

After that it's simply a matter of finding the dates and putting them into chronological order in one long line from one end of the table to the other, but it takes far longer than he expects because he keeps getting distracted.

1918. Alterations to waistcoat. Mr Walker. PAID.

1919. Grey wool coat for Mrs Hardiman. Buttons to be self-covered. PAID.

1919. Peacock silk dress, hand-finished hem. Matching scarf. Mrs Jones. PAID.

1919. Crimson and pink dress for self. Crimson tie for B.

1920. Sheets for nursery. White.

1920. Swaddling wraps (20).

1921. Pinafore overdress. Lilac.

1921. Repair to overcoat. (Bruce).

Every book is like a glimpse into the lives, not just of his family, but hundreds of other people as well, and although he is fascinated, he feels slightly uncomfortable. It's as though he is snooping.

Jean

August 1917

Leith

'I'm off then,' Jean called from the kitchen.

She could hear Donald getting Annie dressed in the bedroom, doing up the white buttons on her dress.

'Ready?' he said.

'Yes, Daddy.'

'I want you to see how many moons you can catch this morning.' There was a pause. 'One moon, through the clouds and...'

'I got it!'

'And the next moon through the clouds...'

'I got it!'

Jean stopped for long enough to hear the end of the game.

'Five moons! Annie Cameron, you are the best moon-catcher in the street.'

'Five moons,' she squealed.

'And now your hair...'

'Nooooooo! Not hair, not hair.'

At this point Jean pulled the door closed behind her and set off. The Edinburgh Rubber Company did not tolerate lateness, not with thousands of boots on order for the Front, and she needed to clock in on time.

She would never tell Donald how much she hated it. She had put up with enough of the sulphurous stench to last her a lifetime, but it was work and they needed the security, so she kept it hidden from him and forced herself to be cheerful. It made testing sewing machines seem like a piece of cake. At times she felt almost nostalgic.

It would have been so easy for Jean to get on a tram and save herself an hour's walk home, but she always resisted the temptation unless it was pouring with rain, and kept the hard-earned coins in her purse. Her feet smarted as she walked the last few yards – she needed to take her shoes to the cobblers; they were well beyond anything they could repair at home with hammer and tacks – but she put a smile on her face as she walked up the stairs to the flat. Donald was safe now and even though a part of her was still furious about what the war had done to him, she hid it well.

He opened the door with a flourish, just as she reached the landing, and Annie pushed between his legs and ran towards her. In an instant the anger was gone as she lifted her daughter up and planted kisses all over her face. 'Have you been a good girl for Daddy?'

Annie nodded vigorously. 'Good and secret.'

'Secret?'

Donald shook his head in mock despair. 'You will never be a spy, Annie, my girl.'

Jean raised her eyebrows and gave him a firm stare. 'There is a secret?'

'Come in and get your tea. I'll tell you when you have sat down and taken the weight off your feet.'

'What's for eating?' She took her coat off and hung it on the hook in the hallway, brushing a few long hairs off the collar as she did so.

'Stew and carrots and big fat dumplings.'

She didn't believe what she was hearing. 'I beg your pardon?'

'You heard. Now sit down and do as I tell you.'

'Is this to do with your secret?'

'It might be.' He wasn't giving anything away.

'Oh, Donald, you haven't been playing at cards? You'll lose more than you ever win.' Her father had been a gambler and she couldn't forget the all too frequent weeks when it was only her own wage that had kept the rent paid.

'I have not.' He was clearly offended. 'The very idea.'

She went over to the stove and lifted the lid off the saucepan. A wonderful smell escaped into the room, with tendrils of flavour curling into every bit of her.

'Alright, I'll stop asking and you can tell me when you're ready.' She watched as Donald doled out a portion of gravy and mashed carrots into a small bowl and blew on it until it was cool.

While Annie ate, Jean told her stories about the barges on the canal that ran alongside the factory, and the seagull that had tried to steal her lunch, and she waved her arms to show how fast the bird had swooped down with its yellow beak snapping for the sandwich. Donald listened but didn't say anything. This was their time.

When Annie had been put into her nightclothes and had finally fallen asleep, they sat back down at the table to eat their own meal.

'So, you have a secret from me?' Jean asked.

Donald spooned the meat and thick gravy onto their blue-rimmed plates. 'It's a good secret. Well, I hope you think so.'

'Mmmm. Has someone been teaching you how to cook when I'm out working all day?' She bit the words back as soon as they had been uttered. 'You know I didn't mean that.'

'I know. Don't worry.'

'This is really very tasty.'

'So, do you want me to tell you?'

'Enough with your secrets! Just get on with it.'

He smiled. It was a real smile, not a stuck-on grin, and she realised it was a long time since he had looked so cheerful.

'I went to the docks.'

'You took Annie to the docks?'

'Not today. I went to the docks at the turn of the year.'

'You went to the docks eight months ago and took Annie with you?'

'Don't fret. I left Annie with Hannah,' replied Donald. He picked up his knife and sliced into one of the three large dumplings on his plate. The gravy flooded into the holes and runnels in the dough while he swapped the knife for a fork. 'I went to the docks to tell Mr James that I wasn't going to be able to work.'

'Work?'

'Remember? He said my job would be waiting for me when I came back?'

'Heavens, I had forgotten all about that.'

'I hadn't.' He patted all that remained of his left arm, a stump just long enough to fix a prosthetic to. 'Well, I thought I should go and explain why I didn't expect him to keep his promise.'

'So if you did this in January, why am I only hearing about it today?'

'I didn't want you to be upset about the news I discovered.' He stood up and went to the sink to get a glass of water.

Jean knew what was coming. 'Oh no. Not his son?'

'Yes.'

'But wasn't he at university?'

'He was, and then he got called up, just after he finished his studies. He was going to be an engineer.'

'You just said "was".'

'He was killed eight days after he went to the Front.' Donald came back to the table.

'So many young men.'

'It happened in August last year. Mr James has hardly been at work since; the place is being run by managers and he only comes in when there are papers to be signed.'

'I don't understand why you are telling me this now?'

'I've told you, I went in January, and I found out about his son.'

'And that's your secret?'

'I'm not explaining this very well, am I?' He took another sip of water. 'I left a note for him a few weeks later. It took me ages to get it all written out properly. I said I was sorry to hear of the news, and that I couldn't return to work doing the same job as before. And I said if there was anything I could do to help instead, that he could let me know. I didn't think I would get a reply but I needed to write it down.' He paused. 'To say I understood.'

Since Donald had come back from France, Jean had realised that there were gaps between them. There were things he would not speak of, and which she had learned not to ask about. At other times he did surprising things that were unasked for, and it took her breath away.

Donald turned the last of his dumplings over and mashed it into the carrots. He had become adept at one-handed eating.

'Do you think he got your note?' There was simply no point in rushing him, Jean concluded, so she ate the last piece of meat on her plate and waited.

'I supposed he did, but I didn't know for sure until I got a letter last week. He asked me to go and meet him so I went this morning.' He put his fork down. 'I took Annie with me because he wanted to meet her too.'

'Go on…'

'There is a man, I have forgotten his name…' He frowned. 'No, I can't remember it. Anyway, this man saw that there would be a lot of sol-diers coming back from the trenches who were damaged. Men like me.' He looked at her. 'And he knew that these men and their families would need somewhere to live, so he has built houses for them, out near North Berwick. They are like farm cottages with pigs and chickens.' He leaned forward, across the table. 'Mr James wants to copy him, and he wants to do something for us.'

She shook her head. 'Life isn't like that.'

'You're usually right about things, but not this time. He wants to do something for you and me. And for Annie.'

'Pigs and chickens? I don't know anything about chickens apart from how to boil their eggs.'

Donald ignored her. 'So today, Annie and I went to meet him and, Jean, I swear I didn't know what it was about or I would have told you.' He rushed on, the words finally tumbling out on top of each other. 'But I wanted to see if it was good news before I said anything.'

'I don't know what to say.'

'He met us near the university and took us to a flat in March-mont. It used to belong to his son; it was where he lived when he was a student.' Donald took a deep breath. 'He is offering it to us. We can live there, for as long as we want to.'

Jean was incredulous. 'Why would he do that? He doesn't know anything about us.'

'He remembered me, and the note I left him. He said he had showed it to his wife and his daughter and it was their idea. They have no use for the flat. They don't want to sell it, because it's a place with a lot of good memories for them.'

'But…'

'It's not free, so it's not charity. We will have to pay rent.'

'How much will that be?' She refused to believe that any of it was possible until she had all the facts.

'Mr James asked me how much we paid for this place and I told him. He said it would be two thirds of that. He doesn't want to rent it to a stranger.'

'I see.'

He took her left hand, the one with her mother's ring around one finger. 'What do you think? There are no pigs and no chickens, but we can live there for the rest of our lives if we want. It will be written into the lease.'

'Donald Cameron, be honest now. Is this some fairy story you are telling me to cheer me up after a long day at the factory?'

'It's all true.'

'Right.' She pushed her chair back. 'I have one question.'

'Just the one?' He smiled at her. 'That doesn't sound like you.'

'How big is this flat? Is it a room and kitchen, like this one?'

'Three bedrooms, parlour, kitchen. Does it matter?'

'It does.' She walked around the table to stand beside him and took his hand and rested it on her belly. 'It matters, Donald, because soon there are going to be four of us.'

Ruth

Late June 1980

Edinburgh

Ruth stomped out of the flat. She hated night duty.

After only a short wait, the red-and-white double decker appeared in the distance and grumbled up the hill towards the bus stop. She paid her fare and sat down at the back of the lower deck, glad to get a pair of seats to herself. The bus climbed from Canonmills to George Street grinding every gear. In the row in front of her, a middle-aged man with neatly clipped greying hair stuck his little finger into his ear and began an excavation. She wondered briefly if people would still do these things if there were cameras trained on them, monitoring their every move. He got off at the foot of the Mound, waving cheerfully to a woman in a cerise-pink jacket. They hugged. Perhaps there was now a smear of yellow earwax down the woman's sleeve, Ruth thought.

The bus moved off again, heaving itself up the steep twist of the Mound, past the bank and the library, and onto Lauriston Place and the Royal Infirmary. She looked up at the wards with their not-quite pulled down blinds and her heart sank even more. The driver brought his vehicle to a halt at the top of Archibald Place to allow Ruth and half a dozen similarly night-duty-weary passengers to disembark.

The tiny locker-crammed changing room with its single bare light bulb was in the basement of the old nurses' home and it smelled strongly of foot deodorant and starched laundry. Ruth wrestled with the padlock on her locker, jiggling the thin key into just the right position to release the shackle, and opened the door. The pile of grey dresses on the top shelf looked for all the world like faded denim, but any idea that these were carefree pieces of clothing with echoes of music and sun-lightened hair was lost as soon as she touched them. Much bashing and thwacking in the hospital laundry had battered the life out of them over the last three years, but although the fabric was softer now, they could hardly be called comfortable. On top of the dresses were the aprons, starched so heavily they crunched. The cuffs for the sleeves weren't any better, and the stiff white collars had a bread-slicing capability that would have done a cutler proud.

Third year. Nearly finished.

She assembled the uniform in stages, fixing the collar on to the dress with three studs, and attaching the cuffs with buttons. Once this was done, she slipped the whole thing on and attached the apron with safety pins from the inside outwards so they didn't show, before adding the belt. Her black leather shoes were well worn and soft now, but she would never forget the horrendous blisters of her first few weeks on the wards.

She accessorised. Fob watch, scissors, paper, pens, antacid tablets. Finally, she folded the starched hat and buttoned it at the back before pinning it in place with obligatory white hairgrips. It was impossible to keep it looking smart, especially on orthopaedics where the bed frames knocked it off her head twenty times a shift. In her opinion the disposable paper hats that the newer student nurses wore were far more sensible, along with their zip fronted, apron-free dresses; tradition was all very well, but it was time-consuming. She gathered her red woollen cloak around her and set off, past the discreetly signed mortuary and up the steps to the long surgical corridor. This was the last fresh air she would breathe for the next twelve hours.

Orthopaedics was on the ground floor, the same level as A & E. Ruth wasn't sure if this was by accident or design, but was grateful not to be trudging up numerous flights of stairs to the very top of the hospital; one was quite enough at the moment. Just the tall double doors of the ward remained, and she remembered how she used to see them as the last barrier between peace and panic. It felt like a long time ago.

She hung up her cloak, and headed towards the nurses' station, past the kitchen, the dressings store and the room that, to the uninitiated, looked as though it contained miscellaneous scaffolding poles and weightlifting equipment. It was truly like a boys' best Christmas; nuts, bolts, spanners and drills all bundled up into one specialty.

This was probably her last ever set of nights – that was quite a thought – and then she would be back on days. She only had tonight and tomorrow to do, and she was here now, so that meant there was only one night left.

Not that she was counting.

After the handover at the end of the shift, Ruth took a different route, carefully avoiding the main kitchens with their nauseating smells of boiled cabbage and gravy. She walked past the huge black panels in the grand hospital entrance, where the names of past donors were inscribed in copperplate and gold paint; grand city merchants, lords and ladies, and Writers to the Signet. Two hundred pounds here, fifty pounds there, a thousand recorded on another; vast sums in 1862 or 1846. Scattered across the wards, small brass plaques hung above many of the beds, proclaiming: 'This bed was endowed by Lady Such and Such' or even 'In Memory of Miss Someone-or-Other'. Ruth thought that these public statements of generosity which pre-dated the start of the NHS were an interesting link to the past, but at the same time, she felt some of these must be a bit unnerving for the patients.

She nipped down the stairs beside the dining room and walked out into the sunshine. Her destination was the sewing room; she hadn't been back there since she had collected her uniforms on her first day at the Infirmary. As she approached the wide staircase she could see that the lift was empty, and force of habit made her touch the button, calling it back to the main corridor in case it was needed for the cardiac arrest trolley. The porters delivering breakfast in the wards above wouldn't thank her for doing it.

Wearily she climbed the stairs to the second floor and then ascended the last flight to the very top of the building.

According to the notice on the wall, she was too early.

She crossed her fingers, and knocked.

A few seconds later the door was flung open by a small grey-haired woman who clearly hadn't heard the noise and was astonished to see her there. A tape measure hung around her neck and she had a pencil tucked behind her ear. 'We haven't started yet,' she said. 'Not until half past eight.'

'Oh.' Exhaustion was starting to take over. 'Should I come back then?'

The woman peered at her over half-rimmed glasses. 'You look about ready for your bed. Night duty?'

She nodded.

'Come in and sit down. What is it you're needing? Are you here to be measured for blues? I bet you can't wait to get rid of those grey dresses.'

'Not exactly. I need these to be altered.'

'Altered? When do you finish?'

'In six weeks' time.'

'And can you not wait six weeks?'

'I'm afraid not.' Ruth bit her lip, her eyes filling with tears of fatigue and desperation. 'These will be even tighter by then.' Until now she had never said the words out loud, not once. 'I'm pregnant.'

'I see.' The woman glanced down at the tautness of the apron, and at the ringless left hand. 'Does your tutor know?'

Ruth shook her head.

'And you'll not be wanting her to find out?'

More head shaking.

The woman sat down at her table, an open ledger in front of her. 'The girls will be here in a minute, and you'll be measured, and everything will be written in the alterations book. And then we have to let the college know because they will get an invoice for the work.'

As she finished speaking, the door opened and another woman came in. 'Morning, Connie,' she said. 'You're in early; making the rest of us look like slackers as usual.'

'Morning, Pat.' Connie closed the ledger. 'Do me a favour and pop the kettle on while I give this nurse a new apron.' She disappeared into another room and came back holding a carrier bag, which she handed to Ruth. 'I've put two in there, nurse. I hope that's enough.'

'Thank you.' Aprons really weren't going to solve the problem, but the transaction was over. Ruth headed back down the stairs and across to the basement of the West Home. The bustle of the early shift had passed and the stragglers from night duty had already left. She sat down in the silence, next to her locker. No alarms, no clatter of curtains being pulled around bed spaces.

She felt her head begin to nod and stood up quickly. There was no point in falling asleep here. She took an aerosol can from the locker, held her breath as she slipped off her shoes without undoing the laces, and sprayed the lily-of-the-valley mist thoroughly into the smelly leather crevices.

She exhaled.

In the corridor outside she could hear the laundry trolley. 'Any uniforms to be sent away?' called the housekeeper as she put her head around the door.

Ruth kept her back to the woman. 'Nothing this time.'

'OK, nurse. Sleep well.'

'I will. Thank you.'

She didn't bother to get completely changed, just removed her apron, collar and cuffs, and then, breaking all the rules about travelling in uniform, she put her coat on over the grey dress and set off. It was a thirty-minute walk, downhill all the way, and she was going to need every penny for the baby.

Fred

Blog: Early November 2016

Leith

The sewing machine is misbehaving.

I've oiled it and adjusted it but I think it might be something inside that needs attention and for that I need an expert.

I've found someone who might be able to help so I'm off to visit today, after I've applied for another job.

Even encased in a sturdy blue IKEA bag, the 99K is unwieldy and bangs against his legs as Fred walks along the busy main road to the bus stop. There will be bruises tomorrow, he thinks. He resolves to take the bus one way and walk home afterwards even though this means a lost opportunity to sit on the top deck and spy into the tenement windows of his fellow city dwellers.

Forty minutes later, he is in Leith and walking along unfamiliar streets. After missing his turning because he stubbornly refuses to take out his phone and use Google Maps, he ends up outside an old primary school that has been converted to workshops. Above the entrance, carved into the stonework, is one word: GIRLS.

It is at once a familiar and yet a strange environment. High ceilings and a glazed cupola allow light to pour into a communal area in the centre of the building, and the corridors are edged with rows of child-height coat-hooks. Generations of blazers and duffle coats have been replaced by loops of colourful bunting, skeins of fat yarn and a horticultural explosion of wanton spider plants in hanging baskets. The open doors of former classrooms reveal tantalising glimpses of paint and machinery. He takes a circuitous route to the back of the building past Mozart and hip hop, and on to the Afternoon Drama on Radio 4.

The lime-green studio door of 18B is closed, so he knocks. A voice shouts something incomprehensible in reply.

When the door eventually opens, he finds himself looking at the face of Car Boot Woman.

'Yes?' There is a glimmer of recognition.

'Hello.' He points at the blue bag, which is now at his feet. 'I was told that you might be able to help me with some advice.'

'You're the person who got in touch yesterday?'

'Probably. I phoned and spoke to a man and he gave me the address.'

'My dad. He told me.' She steps to one side. 'You'd better come in.'

The room is divided in half by a tall shelving system. The square holes are empty, and beside the unit is a large box, overflowing with polystyrene peanuts and bubble-wrapped unknowns.

'Can you tell me what you want while I work?' she says, leaning over the crate. 'I was at a design show and I've got to get all this back on display by this evening. I have a buyer coming.'

'I just want a bit of advice really. I'm not sure I've come to the right place.'

She straightens up, holding a perspex stand. 'It depends on what it is you want to know.'

'Are you a sewing-machine mechanic?' He can see from the look on her face that this is a very poor question; her expression changes from busy-but-listening to my-God-another-idiot in a flash.

'I think I explained when we met before?'

'At the car boot sale, yes. You gave me a card.' He knows he is rambling. 'And then I lost it…'

'I take old machines apart, so I have a good idea how they work, but no, I'm not an actual mechanic.' Her tone borders on condescension. 'If you want one of those, you need the yellow pages.'

'Perhaps I should explain?'

She turns her back on him and goes back to the unpacking, taking each parcel out of the crate and putting it on a long table which appears to double as a workbench. 'I'm listening, but I really do have to get this done.'

'Right.' It is disconcerting talking to someone who seems determined to ignore him, but Fred presses on. 'I have this old sewing machine – a 99K handcrank.' There is no response, so he continues. 'And I've decided I need some feet, I've been looking on the internet'

– he definitely hears a sigh at this point, but presses on — 'and I'm thinking I want a wide hemmer and maybe a felling foot.'

She is starting to unwrap the packages and arrange the contents on the table. A vintage dressmaker's dummy stands beside the window and he watches as she drapes a silver chain around the neck. Fanning out from it, like the rays of a child's drawing of the sun, are long bobbins enamelled in red and black and purple. She lays out a dozen brooches on the bench, adorned with parts he recognises from the winding mechanism. This is followed by a striking necklace which has the circular cover plate from the back of a bigger machine dangling from a thick silver loop.

'Those are interesting.' He means it.

'Glad you think so.'

'You use all of the parts?'

'That's the plan. I'm firing screws and washers in the kiln tomorrow.'

'Maybe I should come back when you aren't so busy.'

'I'm nearly finished.'

'Right.' He feels rather inadequate in the overwhelming evidence of her creativity.

'What is it you need, exactly?' She turns to look at him. 'I mean, apart from the feet.'

'Well, I've been using the machine quite a lot and I think it needs more than just a drop of oil here and there. The crank part is a bit stiff and I'm wondering if it needs greasing inside where I can't reach.' He is decidedly flustered. 'I know you're saying you aren't a mechanic but do you think you'd have time to look at it for me?'

'If it's old, I could take it off your hands?'

'No. I definitely don't want to sell it. It's a historical object. I like using it.'

She shrugs. 'I really don't get the whole vintage thing. Personally, I'd buy a new one.'

He feels cornered. 'So you can't help?'

'I'm an enameller and a jeweller, not a mechanic.'

'Oh.'

'I suppose I could have a look at it,' she relents. 'I can't promise anything, though. It might have something inside that's broken and that can't be fixed.'

'But you are bound to have spare parts, yes?'

'I do, but I use them for all this' – she draws her arm across the table and points at the dress form – 'so I might not have the bit that's needed.'

'So, if I leave it here, could you look at it for me?' He is convinced she is trying to put him off, and tries one last time. 'Please?'

She goes over to the door and returns with a broom, sweeping up the scattered packing peanuts as she walks.

'Oh, I suppose so, but I can't do it tomorrow or anything like that. This is my busiest time; the last six weeks before Christmas.'

'Thank you, I really appreciate it.' He realises he is grovelling.

'You can leave it in the corner over there.' Her phone trills and she peers at the screen. 'I must take this. It's important. Leave your number on the blackboard; there's chalk in the tray on the left-hand side. I'll ring once I've had a look at it and I'll let you know what I think.' She presses the Answer Call icon on the screen. 'Hello, this is Ellen, how can I help?' and she turns away from him to face the window.

He is dismissed.

Jean

Jean didn't like to be first to arrive, but it was her habit to be at Fountainbridge Library by ten each morning so she could spend an hour with the broadsheets. The newspaper room was quieter than usual, she thought, as she nodded a greeting to the regulars who raised their heads as she came in. It was good to be informed. First she read the *Scotsman*, and then the *Glasgow Herald*, and then after she had finished with those, if there was time, and if it was available, she liked the *Manchester Guardian*. The newspapers were arranged on angled reading panels, which could be raised and lowered to suit the height of the reader, and she appreciated the assistance. It was the reason she still came here and didn't go to the library nearer to her home. She liked the exercise, and although he had been gone for many years, she knew Donald would have approved of her getting out of the flat every day – he had never been one to stay at home and look at the four walls.

As the years had passed, he had ceased to worry about whether anyone looked at his empty sleeve and he had only worn the uncomfortable prosthetic arm when absolutely necessary. Together, with the children in tow, he and Jean had walked all over Edinburgh, taking greaseproof-wrapped sandwiches to the Botanical Gardens, the Blackford Hills and beyond. There had been frequent bus trips to Portobello where they got sand between their toes and ate fish and chips as they watched the lights of the ships coming up the Forth at dusk and tried to guess which port they had come from.

Even when Donald had become frail and the children were adults with families of their own, they had still come home every Sunday. They walked with him in an untidy gaggle around the Meadows and along the path at the back of the Royal Infirmary, and he smiled as his grandchildren crisscrossed in front of him and raced to be the first to bring him a conker or a sprig of cherry blossom. The mile-long circuit had become more and more truncated in his last year, and the routes less well trodden, but they all walked beside him until he couldn't manage the short distance from the flat to the park any longer. After that it was just a few weeks until he died, leaving behind a legacy and expectation of muddy wellingtons and woolly hats in the home of each of them.

On this particular day, Jean went to the *Herald* first. The latest news from Clydebank, which she had heard on the radio the night before, was that the Singer factory was going to close on the 27th of June. She leaned forward and smoothed the page with the flat of her hand, forgetting about the charcoal-grey newsprint, which transferred itself to her fingers. Over the decades since she had left, she had remained quietly up to date with goings on in her hometown, never mentioning her research to Donald or to anyone else. It was her private obsession. And now the factory was definitely closing. After being bombed in the war, and modernised and even visited by the Queen, production was coming to an end. There had been rumours for months, and no doubt if she had been still living there, the possibility would have been talked about in the nooks and crannies of the place for years. These things were never a surprise to the people they most concerned. Jean knew what she had to do now. It would take her half an hour to walk to Haymarket Station through the subway. She wasn't in any hurry to get the timetable information she needed; she had been waiting for sixty-nine years, and a few more days wouldn't make any difference.

Jean

Late June 1980

Clydebank

Jean waited on the platform until the train pulled away. She was smaller in stature now, a full two inches had been lost from her height as calcium had leached gradually from old bones and her vertebrae became compressed. Inside, though, she was ten times stronger than the girl of eighteen she had once been could ever have imagined, and a hundred times more determined. She breathed in the familiar smell of iron and steel rising from the railway track. She had known that the station, with its six bay-ended platforms and thousands of workers, would have changed, but she was completely unprepared for the lack of people.

The last time Jean had stood in this place it had been with Donald beside her. The weather had been the same; history was repeating itself in warm light and blue sky.

What she remembered most was the fear and the shame.

Her fear had been well wrapped up and concealed in the necessary façade of certainty. She had been the driver and the decision-maker but for the rest of their time together she never, ever told him how worried she had been that it would all go dreadfully wrong. She had never forgotten Donald's shame at having – in his eyes – let her down. His courage had ebbed away until, much later, he had rediscovered it in a foreign place without her.

Jean looked at the factory from the vantage point of the platform. The jumble of old buildings and new boxy additions was at the same time familiar and alien. She had wondered about returning last Friday, on the final day of operations, and deliberately witnessing the end of it all – but she hadn't been able to bring herself to make the journey. It would have been mean; waiting for a few days had been the right thing to do. She knew what it was like to lose a job, to be forced out against your will. It had destroyed Donald and she did not want to see that emptiness on the faces of other men and women, almost seventy years later.

She searched inside her handbag for the envelope she had

brought from home, and as she touched it, she formulated a new plan. She was going to walk to the gates, if they still existed, the same gates on which they had posted the result of the strike ballot. She was going to cross their threshold and enter the lair of the dragons and stand there in defiance of them all.

After that she was going to walk into the town, along the Blitz-ravaged, tenement-lined streets, right up to the door of her old stair, just to look at it. And then she was going to buy an ice cream, to help her remember that there had been good times too.

But in the end she did none of these things. There was no joy in any of it. She realised now that anything which she needed to prove had been done in another lifetime when she had stood on this plat-form in the sunshine and held the hand of the man she loved, and set out on an adventure with him, in spite of all of them.

Jean caught the next train back to Glasgow Central.

From there, she chose a non-smoking carriage on the slow train to Edinburgh. In the seat opposite her a young man in a grey suit was leafing through his Filofax. He wrote appointments into the diary and opened and closed the rings with a snap as he organised his life in front of her. She watched him make a list in bold black ink and capital letters:

BIRTHDAY CARD

SHOELACES

M.O.T

BABY LOTION

After this last item he flipped to the middle of the leather folder and found a hole-punched photograph of a woman and a small baby. He stroked it with his finger and smiled to himself briefly before shutting the binder and pressing the snap fastener securely closed. He opened his briefcase and took out some papers.

'Such a shame you have to work on the train,' Jean said, 'when there is beautiful countryside to look at.'

He looked up, surprised by her voice. 'Any other day I would join you, but I have an interview I need to prepare for, I'm afraid.'

She nodded. 'Needs must. I'll not disturb you.'

The scenery was far more engaging than the magazine she had bought at the station and, after looking at the first few pages, abandoned. For the rest of the journey she sat with her hands in her lap, looking out of the window at the countryside changing as she was taken from west to east. An hour and a half later the train pulled into Haymarket. One more stop.

She started to gather up her belongings, putting her reading glasses into the case embroidered in blue cross-stitch by one of her granddaughters.

GRANNY X

She stroked the stitches, feeling the uneven threads and loving it all the more for the childish imperfection.

The guard's whistle blew and she felt the train begin to move again. Almost immediately the daylight was gone and they were engulfed by the tunnel, emerging minutes later into Waverley; huge, grimy and smelling of diesel. Her fellow traveller got off the train first and then turned to offer her his arm as she stepped down onto the platform.

'Thank you,' she said.

She patted her bag and checked her pockets for her ticket.

'Have you forgotten something?'

'Just my magazine.'

'Would you like me to go back for it?'

'Not at all, but thank you for the offer. I'll leave it for the next person.'

'Do you know where you're headed to?'

'Oh yes, this is home for me, I know where I'm going now.'

'Well, if you are sure?' He was uncertain. Now that she stood next to him on the platform he thought she looked quite frail.

'I'll be fine,' she asserted. 'I have my stick.'

'Take care, then.'

'I will, and good luck in your interview.'

He half smiled and then walked away from her, turning at the end of the platform to wave as though they were friends of long standing instead of strangers glancing off one another before moving on to the next fraction of their lives.

Jean stopped to catch her breath and as she stood there another train pulled in on the opposite side of the platform and opened its doors, disgorging dozens of besuited businessmen with leather briefcases, aimless backpackers and women with children in tow. She stood beside a pillar, out of everyone's way and then, thankful she only had her handbag to worry about, she made her way onto the concourse.

She turned left, and remembering the steep steps up beside the hotel, elected to walk slowly up the long ramp and onto the street, with her stick for assistance. The smell of the city was unmistakeable. No coal dust from the steam engines anymore, but the flavour of the wind blowing early summer flowers along the gardens and the hint of money in the air. As she walked up to Princes Street she realised that it had been a long time since breakfast, and she decided that maybe a cup of tea was in order.

She would go to Jenners.

Ten minutes later she was standing in the cosmetics department of Edinburgh's grandest store. All around the world, she thought, women were at this moment inhaling a hundred different expensive perfumes in stores like this one, their brains overloaded with a million messages all at once. She made her way through, declining the offers of sprayed samples, and climbed the stairs into the galleried atrium of the shop. The lift was tiny; just enough room for four people and a chair, which was placed in the corner, serving no purpose that younger legs would understand. She would never reduce herself to sitting down in a lift, however, and she gripped the brass handrail tightly instead and felt the cage lurch upwards.

The restaurant was at the front of the building. Jean chose a seat beside the window and waited for someone to come and take her order. From her vantage point she could see almost from one end of Princes Street to the other. Buses, taxis and cars were nose to tail, and over it all, the castle presided.

Her tea arrived, and a warm scone with raspberry jam and unsalted butter. She studied the baking with professional interest. Not too bad, perhaps a little dense, the fat rubbed into the flour with a machine, not cut with a knife, but quite acceptable. And the jam was certainly not homemade, with no whole fruit in evidence at all. Jean smiled to herself; it was hard to change the prejudices of a lifetime.

She reached under her chair for her handbag, stowed out of tripping distance. The scent of face powder rose up. The loose clip on her compact had sprung open again – maybe it was time to go back to the heavily scented cosmetics department and choose a new one. Donald would have wanted her to do that. He had always wanted her to have the best.

She took the precious envelope out of her bag and dusted the powder off it before setting it to one side on the table. It held scraps of a life past. The pot of tea was brewed enough now, and peering inside, she saw that it was proper leaf tea requiring a tea strainer. While she drank her tea and ate the scone, she kept an eye on the street below. Her tip was generous.

Back in the cosmetics department Jean headed for her favourite brand and looked at the display. Loose powder was best, but only suitable for the dressing table and useless for carrying in a handbag where it would be a recipe for disaster, like carrying a box of pink icing sugar around.

'Can I help you, madam?' The immaculate young assistant tilted her head to one side, assessing this new potential customer.

'I need a new compact. Mine has broken after many years' service.'

'And powder as well?'

'Yes, powder too.'

'Right, the compacts are here. Stratton are the most popular, as I'm sure you know.'

The girl was barely twenty, Jean thought. 'I'm not sure what to choose, really. What would you recommend?' It had been a long time since anyone had paid her this much attention as a customer; mostly the make-up girls sold her what she asked for with barely disguised disinterest and moved on to younger and, they assumed, wealthier clients as fast as was decently possible.

'Would you like to try a couple of the powders?'

'Try them?'

'Yes, I have a chair here, and if you aren't in too much of a hurry, I could give you a bit of a facial and then you can see how they look.'

She seemed genuinely willing to help and so Jean sat in the chair behind the counter and leaned her head on the neck rest. First there was cleanser, a cool creamy liquid, which was followed by a cotton-wool ball soaked with something like rosewater, and finally the moisturiser: light, and not draggy.

'This is very kind of you.'

'It's my job,' said the girl. 'My supervisor expects me to sell something to every customer who walks past the display, which is impossible, so I pass the time by doing this for people who might enjoy it. Now, perhaps some foundation and then a little cheek colour, and then we can look at the powder.' When she was finished she held up the mirror. Jean fumbled for her glasses and looked at her reflection.'You've worked magic, my dear. I look almost elegant.'

The girl helped her off the chair and then took her to the counter where the compacts were displayed. Jean felt as though she had acquired a temporary granddaughter. She chose a simple gold-coloured design; nothing would really replace the one she had been given by Donald.

'Would you like me to put the powder into the compact?'

'Yes, please. My fingers don't work as well as they once did with fiddly things.'

'I can dispose of the broken one for you?' An upturn in her voice marked the question.

'Oh no, definitely not. It was a gift from my husband many years ago.'

'OK, I'll take you over to the till to pay.'

'That's kind. Thank you very much.' Jean gripped her stick to steady herself. By the time she had completed the transaction and her items had been placed in a special carrier bag, the attention of the sales girl had been taken up by three expensively dressed women who were dabbing at the testers and smearing lines of lipstick across the backs of their hands. Jean gave a little wave of appreciation and headed back out towards the street and the sunshine.

She paused in front of the heavy glass door and took a breath, gathering her strength to push it open. She was through the door and standing on the top step when she became aware of a commotion in the shop and she turned back to find a thin man running towards her.

'Stop!' the doorman shouted. 'Shoplifter!'

The thief pushed past before Jean could get out of the way. She felt herself being dragged forward as the culprit grabbed wildly at anything and anyone to stop himself tumbling over his own feet. She felt her handbag being tugged from her fingers as he bowled past and she instinctively gripped the handles more tightly. The unexpected entanglement pulled her towards the steps but she was determined not to let go.

She held on.

She won.

She put her hand out, instinctively, as she fell.

She heard a crisp, defined sound as her arm broke, just above the wrist. And then there was a brief silence before customers and passers-by let out a collective, synchronised, 'Oh.'

Ruth

Late June 1980

Edinburgh

Ruth hung her red cape in the ward cloakroom and peered at her reflection in the mirror above the sink. She hadn't slept well and tomorrow morning couldn't come quickly enough.

She unzipped her make-up bag and searched for a restorative lipstick. 'I don't know why I'm bothering,' she said to the empty room, but applied the colour anyway. She added an extra couple of white kirby grips to her starched hat as protection against the destructive attentions of the Balkan beam frames that made every bed look like a high-tech four-poster. Then she took a deep breath and fixed a smile on her face before opening the door.

At the nurses' station, the late-shift staff nurse was adding up a fluid-balance chart. 'You look tired, nurse. Are you not sleeping?'

'They are digging up the road outside the flat,' replied Ruth, getting all the confirmation she needed that the lipstick had been a complete waste of time.

'Earplugs, but I expect you know that already.'

'Tried them; they fall out.'

'Oh well, it's your last night, so you've only got a few more hours to do.' She unpinned the drug keys from beneath her apron and held them out. 'The other nurse is running late, but she'll be in before I leave. Is it OK if I give you these now? I don't want to take them home by mistake.'

Ruth took the keys, participating in a small ceremony that was taking place all over the hospital. 'It's fine.' She folded an observation chart in half and wrote the date on the back of it. 'I'll do a handover. It helps me to sort everything out in my head anyway.'

'How long is it until you finish?'

'I've just got a few weeks left.'

'Got a job yet?'

'Not yet. Something will turn up, I expect.'

The staff nurse balanced the metal Kardex on her knee and flipped it open.

The new patient was wheeled into the ward on a trolley just as the day to night report was coming to an end. The porter and the nurses did their best to move the woman onto the bed without causing any pain but it wasn't easy. Ruth consulted the Accident and Emergency admission sheet and bent down to speak to her patient.

'Can you tell me your name and your date of birth? I know you'll have been asked before but I need to check again.'

'Jean Cameron. The twenty-first of May, 1893.' She paused for a moment. 'I am eighty-seven years old.'

Ruth looked down at the blue sheet of paper. 'Jean Cameron?'

'Yes, nurse.'

'That's not what I have here, but your date of birth is correct. Did you give a different name to the receptionist when you came in?'

'I don't know. I answered the questions they asked me.' She winced as she tried to move her head to look at Ruth.

'I'm sorry. I know you must be sore.' Ruth knew there had to be a logical reason for this. 'What did they ask you, exactly?'

'My date of birth. And then whether I am married. And after that, my name.' She fiddled with the simple wedding ring on her left hand.

'I think someone has misheard you. This says you are unmarried, and it says your surname is Ferrier.'

'Ah. That might be my fault, nurse.'

'Oh, I'm sure it's not. We can easily fix it.' She took the black pen from her breast pocket.

'Ferrier is the name I was born with. The person who asked for my details wanted the name on my birth certificate...' she whispered, '... after I told her I wasn't married.'

Ruth still wasn't sure she completely understood. She tried again. 'What does your GP call you at the surgery?'

'Oh, he calls me Mrs Cameron, of course.' Jean looked hard at Ruth. 'Cameron was my Donald's name. You won't tell the doctor that we were living over the brush, will you? I wouldn't want him to know that.'

'I'm sure your GP wouldn't mind, but no, I won't say a word.'

'Thank you.' Jean seemed to relax a little. 'Could you get in touch with my son and tell him what's happened? They said they would do it when I arrived in the hospital but they were very busy so I don't know if they had time.'

'Of course.' Ruth pulled back the bed curtains.

'You won't forget?'

'I promise.'

Jean's voice tightened; she was clearly trying to keep tears at bay. 'He'll be very worried if I'm not at home; he telephones me every night.'

'I'll be back in a minute. I just need to check something.'

The late-shift staff nurse was still at the desk in the centre of the ward, finishing off paperwork in the spotlight of an anglepoise lamp.

'I have a problem.'

'Go on…'

'Miss Ferrier is actually Mrs Cameron, but she gave her maiden name in A&E so that's what is on her name band.'

'Why did she do that? Is she confused?'

'Not as far as I can tell. I think it was just crossed wires.'

'Well, she can't be written up for analgesia until the details match, and I suppose medical records will look for her under the wrong name.'

'And there's the theatre list as well,' Ruth said, unsure how this additional complication would be received, even though it wasn't her fault.

The staff nurse stood up and adjusted her hat. 'I *knew* I wouldn't get away on time tonight. If you get started on her observations, I'll ring the receptionist. You can do her admission papers once it's been sorted out.'

Ruth went back to Jean's bedside. 'Mrs Cameron, how are you feeling? I just need to take your blood pressure, if that's OK?' She wrapped the grey fabric carefully around Jean's uninjured arm, taking care not to damage the papery skin, pumped up the cuff and adjusted the valve. The silver liquid bobbed as it slipped down the thin tube, nudging a little lower with each heartbeat.

The woman opened her eyes. 'Call me Jean,' she said quietly.

As Ruth leaned over the bed to adjust the pillows she was aware of the snugness of her uniform and felt a seam start to give way. She breathed in. The dress just had to last a few more weeks.

Night duty was always ghastly; that sick feeling at about four o'clock. Ruth started writing the Kardex an hour later, with a welcome cup of tea beside her and a couple of slices of hot buttered toast. When she was finished, she did a last walk around to check all the charts before the onslaught of the morning routine began.

Jean was already awake. 'Morning, nurse,' she whispered.

'Hello, how are you feeling?'

'Not too bad. I had a sleep earlier.'

'Are you sore?'

'I'll be alright. That injection helped a bit.'

'Anything I can do for you right now?'

'Well, if you have a minute, could you pass me my handbag please?'

Ruth looked down at her fob watch. She didn't really have time. 'Of course,' she said, lifting the bag from the back of the locker onto the bed. 'Do you need something in particular?'

'I just want to make sure everything is there.' Jean fumbled with the clasp with her uninjured hand. 'Could you help me please, nurse?'

'Tell me what I'm looking for?'

'There should be a letter; an important letter.'

Ruth lifted out a brown envelope. A light dusting of face powder was released into the air. 'This one?'

'That's it.'

'It's in a bit of a state.'

'It's very important,' Jean whispered.

'Well, maybe I could have it locked up for you if you like?'

'It's not valuable to anyone but me; it's just a few papers.' She looked hard at Ruth. 'I can see you're busy, nurse. It doesn't matter.'

'I have a few minutes. What do you want me to do with it?'

'It needs to be sent to my flat.'

The paper was tatty and thin from being handled many times. 'I'm not sure this will survive being posted, to be honest. Hold on for a minute.' She went to the stationery cupboard, came back with a new envelope and put the dusty, fragile one inside it. 'That's better, I think.'

Jean nodded. 'Now, one last favour, nurse. Would you write my address on the front and put a stamp on it?'

Ruth didn't understand, but did as she was asked. 'Won't your family come in and take it home for you?'

'Ah,' Jean whispered, 'but you see, they don't know I have it.'

'I'll put it through the hospital mail for you. That'll take care of it.'

'Absolutely not!'

Ruth was surprised by the determination in the old woman's voice. 'It's no trouble; the mail room won't notice an extra envelope.'

'The National Health is doing quite enough for me as it is. There will be a stamp in the pocket at the front of my bag.' Jean watched as Ruth searched. 'No, not that pocket, the one with the zip.'

Ruth found what she was looking for and stuck the stamp onto the envelope. 'I'm afraid I need to go now, Mrs Cameron, but I'll pop back when I've finished giving report and I'll post it for you on my way home.'

Jean wriggled her head into a more comfortable position on the pillow. 'Thank you, nurse. I'm tired now. I think I'll try to sleep.'

Fred

Blog: Mid-November 2016

Leith

Rushing.

Just got a text to say the machine is ready.

I hope it's not going to be too expensive.

Still no job.

Ellen is taking photographs when Fred arrives. She waves him in. 'Just a few more to do,' she says.

He watches as she arranges a brooch on a swathe of tweed draped on the dressmaker's dummy and adjusts the angle of the floodlighting.

'I'm not in a hurry.'

'Just as well. I had to finish a big Christmas order. I wasn't able to look at your machine until the weekend.'

She looks comfortable with the camera and takes photos from a distance as well as close up, checking the images on her computer between each frame. She seems to be happy with the results.

'Thank you.' He hopes that weekend work doesn't come at a premium price.

'It's on the bench, at the far end. Go ahead and have a look.'

Fred goes past three other black carcasses in varying states of distress and lifts the bentwood cover off his 99K. She has done far more than fix the mechanical problems.

The old machine gleams in the sunlight that bounces down from the tall windows. 'It looks great,' he says, inadequately. 'The metalwork is definitely brighter than it was last week.'

'It's quite a nice example,' she says grudgingly. 'Not too battered about. If you ever want to get rid of it, let me know.'

'It's not for sale, I'm afraid, but thank you very much for doing the dirty work. I wouldn't have had a clue where to start.'

Above the long table is a piece of hardboard screwed to the

wall, and on it is an impressive array of pliers and hammers, carefully sequenced from large to small. Each one is surrounded by a dead-body outline, like a crime scene. At one end is an old square tin containing a ferocious-looking blowtorch and half a dozen gas canisters. Jam jars of screwdrivers are arranged on a shelf with their business ends pointing upwards to the ceiling.

Fred points at the blowtorch. 'That looks like a serious bit of kit; a bit more than you'd need for finishing off a crème brûlée.'

Ellen pulls a face. 'Oh, that's nothing. You should see the new equipment I've just ordered.'

'I still don't understand why you ruin them.'

'And I don't understand why you want to preserve them, so we'll just have to differ on that particular topic.'

He changes the subject. 'You said you'd have a look for some feet for me?'

She opens a cupboard and slides a catering tray off one of the shelves.

'I haven't seen one of those since I was having school dinners.'

'Shepherd's pie and pasta bake?'

He nods, remembering.

She pushes the tray across the table until it comes to rest in front of him. 'Sounds like my school, too.'

'We'll be saying "when I was young" next.'

'Tell me about it. My nephew goes to the same school that I went to and it's very weird going back to nativity plays and things as an adult.'

'A bit like working here?'

'I guess. Anyway, feel free to have a look at the current selection. I'm not sure what some of these are, to be honest. I just take them apart. You probably know more than me, being an antiques expert.'

Fred ignores the dig and starts to extract small pieces from the mechanical jumble. 'I have a reasonable idea. Some of these look familiar.' He tries to find the best examples and arranges them in a line. 'Is it alright if I have these?'

'Sure.' Ellen up-ends a chipped pottery mug and five bobbins roll out across the table. 'I found these lying around. The surface of the metal is a bit damaged so they're no use to me, but I think they'll work. You can have them if they'll be useful?'

'That would be great – it'll save a lot of time.'

'How come?'

'Well, I use a lot of black and white and grey, and more bobbins means I'm not putting layers of other colours on top of each other.'

Curiosity gets the better of her. 'What are you actually making with all this stuff?'

'Long story, but the short version is that I lost my job and I'm filling in my time while I hunt down a new one.'

'Bad luck.'

'I've applied for everything going in my field, and for all sorts of other jobs, too. I think I'm not being taken on because I used to be a contractor and regular employers think I'll dump them as soon as something more interesting comes along. The sewing is just a temporary distraction.'

She looks over at the classroom clock that still hangs above the blackboard. 'Look at the time!'

'Sorry, I'm holding you back.'

'No, that's not what I meant. I'm hungry, that's all.' She hesitates. 'Would you like a sandwich? My dad dropped my lunch off just before you arrived and he always gives me too much.'

'Are you sure? I mean, if you have enough, that would be good.'

'You'll be helping me out. So, what have you been making on this sewing machine of yours, then?'

'All sorts of things; whatever seems interesting at the time, to be honest. There isn't a plan or anything. My Nana used to sew a lot, and I've got nothing else to do at the moment.'

'You're making it up as you go along?'

'Pretty much.' He wonders if she will think he has lost the plot but ploughs on. 'For example, there are two wee boys who live next door, and I can hear them when they play outside. They argue all the time about who owns which toy car.'

'That sounds horribly familiar.'

'And then the other day I was in a charity shop and there was a single curtain in the cheap-box with vehicles all over it so I bought it.'

'And?'

'I'm going to cut it up and make them a car bag each. They'll be moving to Fife soon, so it's like a going-away present.'

'My brothers could definitely have done with something like that.' Ellen flips open the plastic sandwich box. 'Dad is a bit of a foodie. Hummus and rocket, or gorgonzola and walnut?'

'It smells fantastic. Does he do this every day?'

'He does.' She walks over to the old Belfast sink in the corner of the classroom and fills two glasses with water from the tap. 'He has that enviable combination of early retirement and a flat that is a stone's throw from Valvona and Crolla. I want to be him when I grow up.'

Fred takes the glass from her and eyes up the sandwiches.

'I'm serious, help yourself. Tell me more about your Nana.'

'She was lovely, but she died when I was eight.'

'That's hard.'

'It was a heart attack. I had never seen my Granda cry before, and I think that was almost as shocking as the fact that she was gone.' He takes a sip of water. 'When I was little she made me a play tent for using indoors. It was like a big tablecloth with windows and you sat under the table in a kind of house.'

'Sounds cool.'

'I can remember having my breakfast in there every morning, sitting cross-legged under the table. Nana couldn't get me out of it.'

'Maybe she didn't try that hard?'

'You might be right.' He points at the sewing machine. 'That was hers.'

'Aaaah.' The penny drops. 'Now I get why you don't want to sell it.'

He takes a bite of sandwich. 'Mmmmmm. This is incredibly good. I'll need to call in at that shop on my way home, I think.'

'Good luck with getting out of there without spending anything.'

'Thanks for the warning. I need to pay you first, though, before I go buying hand-picked olives. You haven't told me how much I owe you for the repairs.'

She undercuts herself – 'Twenty will be fine' – and then compounds it by telling a lie: 'It didn't take long.'

'If you're sure?' He hands her a purple note. 'Thanks very much.'

It's not until he is on the bus home that Fred realises Ellen hasn't charged him for the accessories. He searches for EC Vintage in the contacts list on his phone and starts to tap out a text.

    IOU for the feet. Sorry.

A few minutes later, she replies:

    Don't worry. You can pay me if you use
    them and bring them back if you don't.

He continues:

> And thanks again for lunch.

The phone beeps.

> You're welcome.

He taps out his thoughts and hits Send before realising what he's done.

> Next time I'll bring biscuits.

There is no reply.

He berates himself silently for being an idiot. And then the screen comes to life again.

> I prefer carrot cake.

Granda's overcoat. Undo sleeve lining, shorten sleeves, restitch. Charcoal.

Roman blind for bathroom. Grey striped cotton. Never again.

Ruth

Ruth slept until four in the afternoon and woke up when her alarm clock – deliberately set for late afternoon – screamed at her from the opposite side of the room. She groaned and pulled the sheet over her head, knowing that this was a short-term solution. If she didn't get up now she'd never get back into day-mode. The pneumatic drills outside in the street seemed to have stopped at last, so that was something positive, at least. She was stiff and her bladder felt as though it were about to burst.

'Food,' she said to the empty flat as she made her way from bathroom to kitchen, picking up the post beneath the letter box on her way past. One bill and a postcard of Ibiza showing a beach stretching out below stunning blue sky. She turned it over. It was for the absent Ursula.

> *Having a splendid time with lots of S, S and S.*
>
> *Wish you were here, sis.*
>
> *Yvette xxxxx*

'Still nothing.' Ruth propped the card and the unopened bill against the tea caddy. 'Nobody loves me, everybody hates me, I think I'll go and eat worms… or maybe cornflakes.'

The university term was finished, and now that her party-animal flatmate had graduated and moved out, there was no one to steal the milk from the fridge. Even better, if she went out to work and left the immersion heater turned off, she didn't have to worry about whether the little red light above the switch would be blazing away when she got home again. The rent was paid for two more months, and then… well, who knew what would happen after that?

The carrier bag from the woman in the Sewing Room was still lying on the table. Ruth had left it untouched in the vain hope that the aprons would somehow be bigger, longer or miraculously all-concealing. Two bowls of cornflakes later she couldn't put it off any longer and she took them out of the bag. She shook the first one out and measured it up against herself. Too short. The second one looked the same but as Ruth held it up to her chest, a slip of paper fell out of the folds of cloth and onto the floor. She bent down to pick it up.

Connie Morrison. 496 0243. Phone me.

The handwriting was neat, with a funny old-fashioned loop on the capital M at the start of Morrison. And written in pencil.

She thought back to the woman in the uniform room. Was that Connie Morrison? She couldn't remember seeing a name badge, but wasn't that what the other woman had called her?

Her stomach rumbled, and, knowing that breakfast cereal was about the only thing edible in the flat, she began to get ready to go out. There was a phone box at the end of the street. It wouldn't be hard to find out what the message meant.

Two days later, the sun was shining as Ruth walked slowly up to the centre of the city from the Botanics, a plastic bag of clean uniforms in her hand. She had spent an hour there, listening to the birdsong, eating her lunch in the open air and enjoying the feeling of being outside again after a week of night-duty hibernation. The Festival Fringe was yet to start but the influx of summertime tourists was in full swing. They gathered every day at the foot of Castle Street and pointed their cameras at the great lump of rock that loomed over Princes Street and the castle on top of it. Ruth apologised her way around the lenses and headed towards the Mound. If she was lucky, there might be an empty bench in the Gardens, beside the National Gallery, and, if not, she would sit on the grass and watch the ice-cream sellers doing a roaring trade from candy-coloured vans. How different it was from the winter, when the wind screamed up the green corridor between dolerite and Dolcis.

After an hour in the sunshine, the hands on the North British Hotel clock moved round to five thirty and she started to make a move; she had an appointment to keep. The tourists were thinning back to their hotels before they headed out in search of cafés and restaurants. Ruth had heard that the Indian place at Haymarket was good but the thought of spiced curry at the moment was enough to induce instant heartburn and she pushed on past the restaurant and up Dalry Road, under the subway to Fountainbridge and further out to the west in search of the address she had been given.

The tenement was the last one in the street. Ruth hesitated outside. The heavy stair door wasn't locked and she pushed it open and stepped into the coolness. The cupola above the third–floor landing cast dusty sunlight downwards onto the bannister, polished smooth by generations of occupants. To her right was the front door she was looking for, lacquered with black gloss a Prime Minister would be proud of and without a speck of dust on the panelling, in contrast to her own. The faint smell of dinner crept through the doorframe and her courage evaporated. She hadn't yet pulled the bell, so no one would know she was there. She turned to leave just as the door opened.

A tall slender man with salt-and-pepper hair and half-rimmed glasses looked down at her. 'You must be Ruth.'

She nodded, hit by a sudden shyness.

'Well, you must come away in then. My wife is waiting for you and the tatties will be smoorach if they boil for a minute longer.' He stepped aside and showed her into the kitchen.

'That's very kind. I wasn't sure I was in the right place.'

'Is that her arrived?' Connie's voice, more friendly than her efficient work manner, came from somewhere else in the flat.

'It is.' The man smiled at Ruth. 'Have a seat at the table while we get organised.'

Connie appeared in the doorway. 'Well, why didn't you say so?' She sighed, hands on hips. 'I expect you are hungry. I know you girls all survive night duty on toast and not much else.'

Ruth did as she was asked. She felt as though she had stepped into a time warp. Spider plants drooped down from the mantelpiece above an old black range that dominated the room and had been completely taken over by houseplants of every description. Below the window a heavy china sink was skirted with a bright, spotted curtain on a spring cord, and beside it was a front-loading washing machine, its shop-display label proudly proclaiming 'Super Fast 800rpm spin'. The gas cooker, flanked by two short pieces of red Formica worktop, seemed to have been placed in the room as an afterthought.

'Cornflakes and chocolate, actually,' she replied.

'Alf Morrison.' The man stuck out his hand. 'We haven't been properly introduced.'

'Ruth Watkins. I work at the hospital.'

'So I gathered.'

'Of course.' She felt like a fool, but he didn't notice her embarrassment.

He moved the vase of flowers, which had been in the centre of the table, to one side.

'Are those snapdragons?' she asked.

'They are.'

'I thought so. We used to have them at home, but I wasn't allowed to touch them.'

He frowned momentarily, and changed the subject. 'Are you hungry? There is chicken pie for tea. We always have pie on a Thursday.'

'Always?' She hoped it didn't sound like a rude question.

'Oh yes, ever since we got married. Mondays are leftovers, Tuesdays are my chess night so we just have cold meat sandwiches, Wednesdays are mince and tatties...' Alf reeled off the routine, deadpan.

Connie opened the oven door and brought out an enamel pie dish crowned with golden-brown shortcrust pastry. 'Come on now, Alf. I'm sure this young lady doesn't want to know what we have for dinner every night.'

Ruth thought his name suited him perfectly. 'You really have the same every week?'

Connie hung the oven gloves back on the hook next to the stove. 'We have been married for a long time. It's nice to have a routine. It keeps things right.'

'Long enough to get told off and not fuss about it,' said Alf.

Ruth began to relax. She was hungry and the smell of home-cooked food was providing an emotional warmth she hadn't felt for months.

After dinner, and ice cream and tinned peaches, Alf waved aside all offers to help and started to clear the table. 'I believe you ladies have things to do,' he said.

Connie ushered her visitor to the small room at the other end of the hall where she kept her sewing machine. In the middle of the room was a dressmaker's dummy, draped in a soft pink satin.

'It's a bridesmaid's dress for my neighbour's daughter.'

'Very pretty.'

'Yes, but terrible fabric. You can't make any mistakes with it at all.' Connie pushed the figure back against the wall. 'Right, let me shut the door now and we'll have a look at these dresses.'

'Thank you. They are clean. I wasn't sure if you needed them to be pressed so I did it anyway, I hope that was the right thing to do.' Ruth handed Connie the plastic bag. 'You don't know how much this means.'

Connie took two more dresses from her basket and laid them on the table. 'Well, it's not the easiest thing to smuggle out uniforms, but I have managed to pauchle two old torn ones, so with any luck we can add a few panels to the front and hide them under your aprons.'

'Thank you.'

'You need to stop saying that. I'm doing what anyone would.'

'Th…'

'How far on are you?'

'About three months. But all those grateful chocolates at the nurses' station means they were a bit tight anyway.'

Connie nodded. 'And how much more have you to do?'

The coolness of the measuring tape slipping around her warm belly made Ruth gasp. 'Oooooh, that's cold!'

'Sorry.'

'Six weeks, and one of those is annual leave.'

'At the end?'

'Yes, so five more weeks of wearing these grey things.'

'Well, I should be able to alter them enough to let you get through five weeks without splitting the seams.' Connie made notes on a piece of paper. 'You're not staying on to get your Pelican badge, then?'

'I guess not. I was going to – I always wanted my hospital badge – but I don't think me and the tin budgie are intended to be friends now.'

Connie slipped a clean uniform over Ruth's head, muffling the words. She pulled the dress closed. Although the buttons met the buttonholes, it was clear there was no spare room in the garment to move or lift, or bend. 'Do your aprons hang below the hem of your dress?

'I think so.'

'I'm going to cut this now.'

'While I'm still in it?'

'I'll be careful, don't worry.' She took her shears and cut the dress up the front from hem to waist, and then she began to pin a new wedge of fabric into the gap. 'It's not exactly the same colour as your dress, but under the apron, no one will know.' She worked quickly with pins squeezed between her lips.

Ruth stood silently, not wanting to interrupt the process.

When she had finished the skirt, Connie stabbed the remaining pins back in the strawberry pincushion on the table. 'Right, now let me look at the bust. You need more room there too but I don't want to put panels in at the sides because it will mean taking the sleeves off – and changing the neckline means your collars won't fit.' She was talking as much to herself as to Ruth. 'Maybe another wedge will sort the problem out. I'll try that anyway.'

Ruth wrapped herself in the dressing gown Connie provided and sat down while the adjustments were made.

'I'll be done in a minute and you can try it on before I sew it properly.' Connie added her next question without pausing. 'So are you getting married, then?'

'No.' Ruth's voice was barely a whisper; she breathed the word instead of speaking it out loud. 'He's American, works on one of the North Sea rigs. I met him up in Aberdeen last year when I was visiting a friend and he swept me off my feet at a disco. We went out for seven months but between his offshore rota and my shifts, we only met up half a dozen times. And then he told me he had to go home for a few weeks.' Her voice dropped still further. 'I haven't heard from him since.'

Connie looked up. 'Not at all?'

'Nothing, not a word.' Her voice broke. 'I am so stupid. How could I have been such an idiot?'

'That seems very strange.'

'I sent a letter to the only address I have and he hasn't replied. That was before I knew about the baby, so it's been ages. Plenty of time for him to write back.' Great tears began to roll down her cheeks. 'I'm not even sure it's the right address. He might be married, for all I know.'

'What about your parents? Will they help?'

'I haven't told them.' Ruth took the cotton hankie that appeared in front of her. 'They will be furious.'

'In my experience, people surprise you when the chips are down. I'm sure they will help when they know what's happened.'

'I wish I had your confidence.'

Connie put the sewing aside and rested her hand on Ruth's arm. 'Come on, there is always hope.'

'If you say so.'

'I do.' She changed the subject. 'I think I've pinned enough for now. I'll alter this dress first and check the measurements.

'How long do you think it will take to do them?'

'Well, this is Thursday, and Alf always goes to the allotment after he finishes work on a Friday, so I'll do the first one tomorrow. And if I'm happy with it then I can get the others sorted out over the weekend.'

'Thank you.'

'I don't want you getting any daft ideas either.'

'How do you mean?'

'If it wasn't for the fact that the Infirmary insisted on all that paperwork, you could have had this done at the hospital.' She stared at Ruth, making sure she had her attention. 'I want you to know that I'll be very, very offended if you try to pay for these alterations.'

'But it's a lot of work.'

'It's not. I spend a good part of my week doing this sort of thing so I can almost do it in my sleep.' She paused. 'And Alf would be most upset, so please don't try.'

'That's me told.'

'Just as long as we're clear.' Connie smiled. 'Now, if you're on an early shift on Monday, you can have your tea with us, if you like?'

Ruth wiped her eyes. 'Leftovers.'

'Indeed. The best meals are made that way.'

Connie

Alf arrived back home at dusk, smelling of clean sweat and raw earth after a long evening of essential weeding in the late summer sunshine. The flat was in darkness. Even the window above the front door, which would normally have given out a warm glow into the stair, was unlit.

'Connie?' he called, as he put down the bag of carefully chosen lettuce and early beetroot, and felt in the pocket of his old conker-brown corduroys for his keys. In his haste, he dropped them and had to waste precious seconds guddling about in cool leaves and feathery carrot tops to find them. By the time he was able to put the key in the lock and open the door, his heart was racing.

'Connie?' he shouted again, as he stepped into the hall.

There was no reply.

He tried again, feeling the beginning of panic rising inside him. 'Connie! Where are you?'

'I'm here,' she replied at last. 'I'm in the kitchen.'

It didn't sound like his Connie at all. Just a couple of strides of his long legs and he was beside her in the gloom. The last of the day's light struggled into the room from the tall sash window above the sink.

'What happened? Why are all the lights off?'

She was sitting at the table, with the grey denim uniforms strewn in front of her. 'I blew the fuse.'

'You daft scone. How did you manage that?'

'I plugged the machine in and there was a pop and every light in the house went off. All the sockets, the fridge, everything.'

'And you have been sitting here since then?'

'I couldn't think what to do; it only happened ten minutes ago.'

'But it's dark in here, love. Why didn't you go and sit in the back green or something?'

'It's not dark, Alf. Not properly.'

'I'm sure there are candles in the drawer, or you could have gone next door until I got home?'

'I didn't know what to do.' Her throat was all clogged up, as though she had been crying. 'I couldn't think straight.'

'But you are alright? You're not hurt?'

'Well, I got a fright, but I'll live.' She sighed. 'Not so sure about the sewing machine, though. There was a flash over there, at the plug.'

He picked up one of the kitchen chairs, the old one with the scrape on the seat which wouldn't come to any further harm from his gardening shoes. 'Let's worry about one thing at a time. I'll check the fuse box first and see about getting the lights back on.'

'Yes, but I promised.'

'Later, love. We'll deal with all that later.' He went to the hall cupboard, lifted the emergency torch from its customary home and shone a beam of light upwards towards the electric meter box beside the front door. 'It's likely just a bit of wire. Easily fixed.'

A few minutes later the lights were back on and the fridge was purring. Alf took her in his arms and hugged her close.

'What am I going to do about all this?' Connie pointed at the table, which was covered in grey uniforms in various stages of deconstruction.

He leaned over the machine and sniffed at the acrid melted plastic. 'I think the motor is burned out.'

'Can you fix it?'

'I'm afraid that's beyond me. I can take it into the shop tomorrow, but it's the weekend – I doubt anyone will look at it before Monday, and then if it needs parts, they'll have to be ordered, I expect.' He filled the kettle and plugged it in. Now that he was home, he could look after her.

'That long?'

'It might even need a whole new motor.'

She stroked the pieces of cloth. 'But I have to do these dresses for Ruth.'

'Surely the lass will understand. It won't hurt to wait for a couple of weeks.'

Her voice dropped to barely a whisper. 'It will.'

'Is she in that much of a rush?'

She looked at him. 'You mustn't tell her that you know, Alf.'

'Know what?'

Connie picked up the tape measure and began to wind it into

a coil, inch by inch. She didn't answer until she was finished. 'You mustn't tell her that you know about her baby.'

It was his turn to sit down. The kettle clicked loudly in the silent room as it turned itself off and it was Connie and not Alf who poured boiling water onto the tea leaves and swished the liquid around to hasten the brew.

He didn't say anything for a long time.

She waited, hoping that he was trying to think of someone who could fix the machine more quickly; maybe one of his friends might know how to do it. She poured the tea into their usual mugs.

When he eventually spoke, it wasn't what she wanted to hear at all. 'You can use the old machine.'

She looked at him in disbelief. 'No.'

'You can use the old machine,' he repeated.

'I can't.'

'You must.'

She shook her head. 'It's impossible. I just can't.'

He took her hands and held them, and stroked the gold ring he had put on her finger so many years before. And then he spoke softly. 'I can go to the shop tomorrow for you, and we will see what they say, but I think the old machine is the only solution.'

'I can hand sew them,' she protested. 'With a needle and thread.'

'You could, I suppose, but from what you say, don't they need to be ready quite soon?' He didn't wait for an answer this time. 'I'll move this useless lump of metal into the hall for now, and I promise you I'll get up early tomorrow and deal with it first thing in the morning. I expect it needs a completely new motor.'

It was Connie's turn to take his hands, still dusty with earth from the plot. She lifted them up to her face and breathed him in. 'I'm not sure.'

'You will be,' he replied, 'when you have had a chance to sleep on it.'

Ruth

Early July 1980

Edinburgh

It was bad luck for Ruth to be on an early shift on the Monday after nights. Most ward sisters tried to give their staff a late at the very least, but the rota hadn't worked out that way. She sat on a hard plastic chair beside the nurse's station at the top end of the ward, pen and paper ready, and waited for the report to begin.

The night staff nurse was apologetic. 'Jean Cameron died this morning. It wasn't expected. This place has been non-stop all night and we had moved her into the side room to try to give her a decent sleep. She was gone when we went in to turn her just after five. She was seen by the Resident and I rang her family. They came in, but didn't stay long. I'm really sorry, we couldn't make a start on last offices until they had gone. They'll be back later for her things.'

Sister nodded. 'Don't worry. These things happen.' She looked around the circle of day staff. 'The auxiliaries can do breakfast. And we have Nurse Smith here from Ward Nine for a little while to help.'

Ruth knew what was about to happen. Sister pointed at her. 'You, Nurse Watkins, take Nurse Smith and look after Mrs Cameron.'

'Yes, Sister.'

Everyone stood up and began to move away to their assigned tasks.

'You'll have done this before?' asked Ruth.

The girl, wearing the now ubiquitous apronless blue uniform, shook her head. 'I was just sent to cover for the start of the shift because you're so busy.'

'Sister should have checked.' Ruth looked up the ward. The drug round was already in progress; it would be hard to interrupt.

'I'm sorry.' The student's paper hat with its single stripe seemed to broadcast inexperience.

'It's not so bad.' Ruth tried to be reassuring. 'I'll explain as we go along – just follow me.' They headed up to the laundry cupboard to collect the last offices box. She was struck by the incongruousness of the box every time there was a death. It was the same as those owned by almost every mother in the country, bought from Mothercare and filled with cotton wool, baby lotion and nappies. In the hospital it contained mortuary labels, soap, name bands and paperwork. It was the bookending of a life.

In the side room, only the bed light was on. Ruth reached beneath the still-drawn blind and lifted the sash window a couple of inches.

'Why do you do that?'

'Some people believe it lets the soul out.'

'Really?' The student nurse sounded sceptical.

'No idea if it does anything, but it can't do any harm.' Ruth wheeled the bedside locker to one side to get more room at the head of the bed. 'This is just like doing a bed bath; everything you've been taught in class. I usually end up talking to them, though. Force of habit, I suppose.'

'I'll be fine. Just tell me what to do.'

'OK. First we check the medical notes and her name bands and make sure they match. See? Jean Cameron. Jean Cameron. And we fill out two new ones with extra information on them for the mortuary.'

'And then?'

'We look after her.' Ruth paused. 'We give her a full bed bath, just as if she were still with us.' She filled a basin with warm water at the sink, and moved over to the figure lying in the bed. 'Jean,' she said, 'my name is Ruth, and I'm going to give you a wash now.'

'What about her wedding ring?' asked the student when they had finished.

'We leave it on unless the family have asked us to take it off. It's not right to remove something like that without permission.' Ruth lifted Jean's hand and checked the ring. 'It's a bit loose on her finger, so if you pass me the zinc oxide tape I'll put some round it.'

'Just like when someone goes to the operating theatre.'

'Exactly the same. I'll brush her hair and then we're almost done.'

They rolled Jean from side to side to change the sheet and tucked the white shroud under her shoulders and hips to hold her limbs firmly in place. And then they covered her face and wrapped her up tightly in the sheet and secured it with Sellotape. Ruth filled out a black-edged square of paper and stuck it onto the sheet-wrapping, upside down.

'That wasn't as bad as I thought it would be,' said the student.

'Good. It's important that it's done with respect. You did well.'

'What else is there? Is that it?'

'Belongings. We need to list her things and get them ready for her family to collect.' Ruth didn't want to kneel down and strain the seams on her uniform. 'You empty the locker and I'll write it all down on the form.'

'OK. Are you ready?'

'Yes. Just start.'

'One pair of pants, one vest, one dress, one pair of brown sandals, one cardigan, two scarves, three nightdresses, one pair of slippers.'

Her family must have come in, thought Ruth. She could see over the student's shoulder that the clothes were all clean and ironed, neatly stacked on the shelf. 'You don't need to list toiletries separately. Just leave them in her wash bag.'

'And her handbag?'

'We need to check inside.'

'Handbag, containing one handkerchief, one purse with' – she counted out the coins and notes – 'three pounds and forty-seven pence. And there's something else.'

'Can you hand it to me?'

The new compact and powder were still in their box, and at the bottom of the bag was another one, lying in a haze of pale-peach dust. 'Two powder compacts, yellow metal, one broken.' Ruth suddenly felt a bit lightheaded and leaned on the bed-table for support. 'Right, we can clean the locker when she's gone, but if you could put all this into a bag and leave it in Sister's office that would be great. I'll deal with the trolley while you do that. I won't be long.'

On her way back from the sluice, Ruth ducked into the changing room and washed her face with cool water before returning to Jean. The student was holding an envelope. 'This was at the back of her locker; we missed it.'

'Oh.' Ruth recognised it and immediately felt a wave of guilt. She had made a promise and broken it. 'Well, never mind. If you give it to me, I'll add it to the rest of her things in Sister's office.' She leaned against the wall to steady herself. Her head was swimming. 'The last thing we do is ring the head porter. You can do that, if you like.'

'What do I say?'

'I'll show you.'

They went together to the phone booth beside the housekeeper's desk. 'See, there's a list of numbers. All we do is ring the Porter's Lodge, give them the ward number and say that there is a card to collect.'

'A card?' The student looked puzzled.

'It's the mortuary card with all her details on it. The porters need it before they can take her away.'

'Right.'

'The thing is that you never know who is standing outside the phone cupboard, even with the door shut. The Nursing Officer might be there, or even worse, it could be a relative. You would never say that there was a body to be picked up; it wouldn't be right.'

Sister strode towards them. 'I think we can manage now, Nurse Smith. You can go back to your own ward. Nurse Watkins can finish things off. Be sure to thank Sister for sending you to help me out this morning.'

'Yes, Sister.'

'Thank you,' said Ruth to the student after the frilly-hatted figure had gone back to the main ward. 'I'm not sure if I can sign your record book for doing last offices, but I'll be qualified in a few weeks, so it might be OK. If you see a clinical teacher, you could ask them.'

'OK. I'd better go.'

Ruth stepped inside the phone cupboard with its tiny glass window, and pulled the door tightly shut behind her. She dialled the number and cupped the phone between her head and her shoulder. As she waited for the call to be answered she toyed with the envelope, sliding it backward and forward along the edge of the shelf where it met the wall.

Without warning, the door opened behind her, and she turned her head quickly to see who was there. Suddenly dizzy, she gripped the shelf, pulling it slightly away from the wall. The envelope slipped from her fingers.

'Sorry, nurse.' The housekeeper peered over her half-moon spectacles. 'I didn't see you there. Will you be long?'

'I'll be finished in a… Oh, hello. Porter's Lodge?' The door closed at her back. 'There is a card to collect in Ward Four. Thank you very much.'

As Ruth replaced the receiver she saw that only a small brown triangle of paper was still showing above the shelf. She tried to retrieve it, but as she tugged at the ledge in an effort to gain a grip on the remaining corner, it slipped further. In less than a second it had vanished behind the panelling and was gone.

The booth door opened again. 'Are you finished now, nurse? I need to speak to the main kitchen about the lunch numbers.'

'Ummm.' She blushed. 'Yes, I am. It's just…'

'Right, well, if you don't mind, I'll take your place so we can both get on with the things we have to do.'

It was twenty minutes before the porters arrived outside the ward, their mortuary trolley covered with a pink cotton cellular blanket. They collected the card and Ruth pulled the wheeled portable screens across the ward entrance. Every patient knew what was happening, but the auxiliaries continued to clear away the breakfast plates and the nurses checked the fluid balance charts in readiness for the doctor's round.

Later, Ruth sat at the desk in the middle of the ward and found Jean's paperwork in the Kardex. She wrote the last entry.

Died at 05:25. Family informed. Belongings listed. RIP.

Fred

Blog: Mid-November 2016

Edinburgh

I had a phone call today.

I had completely forgotten about the man I met at Granda's funeral. I thought I recognised him at the time but it was a difficult day and I wasn't taking that much notice of exactly who people were. He came up to me at the end to shake hands, in that way people do when they are expressing condolences. I never quite know how that works: it's like the opposite of a wedding break- fast when everyone is so happy and the in-laws and out- laws are trying to pretend that they haven't fallen out over the choice of wine. On this occasion, of course, everyone was sad, which was a bit surreal because Granda wanted the walk-out music to be that mad song from Life of Brian.

The man said he had to rush off but that he had some- thing for me from Granda's allotment. At the time, I assumed it was a trowel or a spade or something, but he seemed to think it was important so I gave him my num- ber... and yesterday he rang me.

His name is Stan.

This afternoon he came round to the flat, straight from his plot. He even brought me some curly kale. He had been working the ground next to Granda for more than fifty years!!! He is seventy-two (and quite proud of the fact). Anyway, when Granda got older and couldn't man- age the heavy digging anymore, the other folk on the allotment came up with a sort of unofficial arrangement among themselves and they took over part of Granda's plot without telling the council so he didn't have to give it up. I don't know how they got away with it, but they managed to keep it under the radar somehow.

I can remember going down there when I was little – I suppose Stan would have been in his forties then, but I don't really remember him.

So we sat in the kitchen and I made him a cup of coffee and we talked about allotments and how they used to be when so many of the men used them as an escape from work and home.

I thought he was going to have the whatever-it-is with him, but he says it's at home for safekeeping and he'll bring it another day.

He has also invited me down to meet everyone, so I'm going to take him up on the offer.

On the sewing front, I had a good look at the extra bobbins I got from Ellen. Each one has layer after layer of different coloured threads. It's like a geology of dressmaking. One of them was all greens: bottle green to pea soup. I wonder if it was all for a school uniform or something like that? The second was plain white with a few sections of cream. And the other two were a sort of rainbow mish-mash – everything from fuchsia pink to peacock blue.

I am starting to see colours everywhere I go, especially in unexpected places like brick walls and manhole covers. It's all very interesting.

I've had an email from Mum and she'll be back next week. She apologised for the radio silence!

The machine is now set up permanently next to the window of the front room overlooking the street. Without Fred being aware of it, he is slowly being integrated into the community. He has become very useful to delivery drivers, who call on him to take temporary custody of all manner of things from parcels of books to wine crates, and this, in turn, means there is a stream of grateful visitors ringing his doorbell when they get home from work. It's a source of some astonishment to him that his neighbours are buying Christmas gifts already; he has inadvertently become the keeper of many secrets.

Children on their way home from school pause outside the window and watch him sewing. He recognises all his neighbours now, and they, in turn, know him. A lifetime's embarrassment at being unable to remember people's names is banished because they are all written on the parcels and it's now impossible to walk to Eva's to buy a pint of milk without being greeted with a smile at least once.

Stitching has become his default decompression system; challenging enough that it occupies his thoughts, but not so complicated that it's stressful in itself. Today he is mending a blue-and-white striped shirt that he picked up at the weekend at a jumble sale. The cloth has been softened by detergent, and years of washing machine thwacking has done the collar no favours. Fred takes a spool of vintage white cotton thread from his growing stash of reels and places it on the spool pin. He wraps a few windings onto the bobbin by hand and then adds a tiny mark with a felt pen dabbed onto a single strand so that he'll know when it's almost empty just by looking at the underside of the seam. He is quite proud of this idea and assumes that he's the first person in the world to think of it. With the full bobbin in the race, he returns to the wooden reel on the spool pin and takes the smooth fibre on a route past the spring and lever; a meandering path, which he now plots several times a day. It has a pleasing familiarity and is a skill that has arrived unannounced. The vibration of the cogs and crankshafts hidden within the black casing as each stitch is formed soothes his worries with every loop and lock.

He spreads the old shirt out on the table, takes a few photos and gets down to work with the stitch ripper – his new favourite tool. There is no joy in rushing to snip stitches and tug away at the old threads so he takes his time and smiles to himself at the first glimpse of the inside of the collar stand, hidden from the world since the day the shirt was made. It's a much brighter blue – untouched by the bleaching effect of decades of washing-line sunshine. He imagines the owner choosing the shirt from Forsyth's tailoring department (the label is still inside) and wearing it for the first time to a dance, or a wedding, or perhaps on the first day in a new job. He sets the collar aside for his next project, and ever mindful of his experience with the shoe bag, inserts the pins at right angles to the new seam.

The old sewing machine has no reverse stitch so there is more backward and forward fiddling to be done before he is ready to make the first slow turn of the hand crank. As the seam begins to form beneath his guiding fingertips he eases the cloth under the needle and makes micro adjustments to the position of every stitch. At last he is finished and he takes the newly grandad-collared shirt closer to the window to examine it.

'Not bad,' he says to the empty room, and he slips it on over his T-shirt.

His reflection in the long mirror stares back and he rolls the sleeves up a couple of turns to hide the frayed edges. Cuffs look much more complicated, he thinks, so this will do for now.

Shirt, upcycled.

Granda's brown tweed waistcoat, unpicked side seams, restitched.

Fleece hat – fluorescent orange (running).

Ruth

Alf was uprooting tiny weeds from between the bedding plants in the small patch of garden at the front of the flat when Ruth arrived to collect her uniforms.

'Just go in. She's waiting for you,' he said.

She stepped into the cool stair and tapped on the front door. It was half open, and it moved under her fingers but she waited politely and didn't cross the threshold. 'Hello?'

Connie emerged from the workroom. 'Come in, come in.'

'These are for you.' Ruth held out a bunch of freesias. 'I thought you might like them – they have such a fabulous scent.'

'You didn't need to do that, but yes, they do.' Connie breathed in the perfume. 'My vases are on that high shelf in the kitchen.'

'I can use a chair to reach one for you.'

'Oh no you don't!' Connie was horrified. 'They can go in a jam jar until Alf comes in. What are you trying to do to me? Give me heart failure?'

'Sorry.'

'Right, I want you to try these dresses on and then, if they fit, we can have our tea.' The smell of some sort of pie was filling every corner of the kitchen.

The dresses, with their newly created central panels, were hanging on clothes hangers on the back of the workroom door.

'I know they look strange,' said Connie, 'but this is what we do to the staff nurse's dresses when the girls are expecting and it works out perfectly.'

Ruth pulled her summer dress off over her head and slipped on the first of the uniforms. 'You are sure they will be alright?'

'No reason to think they won't be. I'm very glad you aren't in the new blue dresses with the zips up the front.'

'For once, so am I.'

'Yes, I have no idea how we would have managed if you had those. In fact, we probably couldn't have done it at all. The girls who are pregnant are going to get tabards to go over the top of them, apparently.' It was clear from her face that she was unimpressed by this plan. She motioned to Ruth to turn around so she could check the back view. 'Right, that looks fine. Now just hold on a moment.' She took a starched white apron from her basket and handed it over.

'A new pinny? How did you get that?'

'Ways and means, don't ask.'

Ruth wrapped the apron around herself and pinned it on the breast of the dress.

'Make one more turn around slowly so I can see the sides and the back.' Connie scrutinised her work. 'It looks good to me. In case this extra room isn't enough, I've put a long dart in the middle of each section, so if they feel as though they are getting snug, just take your scissors and snip the stitches out, and that should give you another two inches. You may not need it, but it's there if you do.'

'Thank you so much for this.'

Connie shook her head and put her finger to her lips. 'Shhh.'

'I know you said I mustn't, but I really feel I need to need to pay you for the alterations.'

'I told you last time, I won't hear of it. Many people have been good to me and mine, and this didn't take long at all.' She didn't mention the blown-up motor on the electric machine or the decision she had needed to make over the weekend.

While Ruth got dressed again, Connie took a small notebook from her workbox, peeled the price sticker off the back cover and cracked the spine before opening it up at the first page. She slid the paper under the needle and turned the handcrank very slowly. A line of grey stitches began to appear, parallel to the edge of the page. After an inch or two, she lifted the presser foot briefly and tucked a small square of the soft grey denim beneath it, and then she completed the seam.

Ruth watched, fascinated, as Connie clipped the threads and then wrote something next to the stitches.

'Do you mind if I ask what you are doing?'

Connie passed her the book.

Alterations to uniforms. Five dresses.

'Why do you do that?'

'It's an old habit. I keep a note of what I sew on this machine. My mother did the same before me when it was hers. There's a shoebox of little books on the shelf over there. Alf thinks it's funny but he does the same with his seeds in the garden so we are equally obsessed.'

'Didn't I see another machine when I was here last week? Do you do the same with that one?'

'Oh no, that one isn't the same at all – it's just a workhorse that is away getting serviced at the moment. This is a longstanding obligation really. Something we've always done.'

Ruth looked around the room taking in more detail. The door to the cupboard was open, and inside were shelves bearing neatly labelled boxes of patterns: Vogue Designer. Simplicity. Butterick. There were other boxes marked Ribbon, Petersham, Ric Rac and Bias Binding. It all looked very organised. She could see fabrics, folded loosely and piled up according to colour; a silky print with pink flowers on top of a thick, tweedy cloth, which was the colour of raspberry jam. More than two dozen potential garments lay side by side on the shelf, waiting for their moment.

'You sew a lot then,' she said, stating the obvious.

'Yes, I learned from my mother. This was her machine.'

'It's a family heirloom?'

'I suppose so. I've never thought of it that way. There were thousands of them made, perhaps millions. They are quite common – not the sort of thing you see in an antique shop.'

'She must have been a good teacher.'

Connie shrugged. 'I picked it up from watching her. I've sewed all my life.'

'So, how did you end up in the Uniform Room?'

'I've worked there, on and off, for twenty-five years, but it almost didn't happen at all.'

'Really?'

'I went for the job and I didn't think I had done very well at the interview.' Connie began to coil up the tape measure, turning it round and round in her fingers.

'I know what that feels like.'

'There was an ordinary interview, and then there was a practical test.' Connie smiled, remembering the event as though it was yesterday. 'I didn't discover until much later that the manager wanted to see if I would give up on a difficult task, or keep going.'

'Wasn't that a bit sneaky?'

'I suppose it was. But they offered me the job so I must have passed muster, I suppose.'

'Do you just do uniforms now?'

'No, we make linen for the theatres as well; the green-and-blue drapes, you know?'

Ruth nodded.

'And we still do repairs on bedspreads and sheets, and there are sometimes grander things, like curtains for the Board Room. A lot of the work is the nurses' uniforms, though. Turning up hems, making them fit, but not too well.' Connie smiled. 'I know what young nurses *think* they want, but they soon realise that bending and stretching all day means they can't be fashion plates.'

'I remember thinking that mine were awful, all baggy and frumpy, and being very put out when we were told by the college that they couldn't be altered.'

'It's always been that way. If I had a penny for every time there has been a request to take a dress in or turn it up, I would be a rich woman.'

'I won't have to think about any of that for much longer – I have a finishing date now. It came through last week.'

'Are you staying on the same ward until the end?'

'Yes. It's good in a way. Orthopaedics is quite heavy, lots of lifting, but no one will look very closely at me. I was a bit worried that a fresh set of eyes would see this.' She rubbed her bump. 'We should be fine.'

Ruth had been right about smelling pastry. The evening meal was cold meat sandwiches and apple pie. Afterwards Connie refused their help with tidying up and insisted that Alf took Ruth outside. The back green was part of a connected network of shared gardens with dividing walls marking the boundary for each tenement. Some of the walls were ten feet high, others were low and still embossed with the telltale wartime stubble of chopped-off railings.

Connie stood at the kitchen sink and washed the dishes. She could see Ruth asking questions and Alf explaining as he worked his way along the flowerbeds, deadheading faded blooms as he went.

They stopped at the spot where the Anderson shelter had once been, and Connie watched the wartime story unfold, Alf's gestures showing how deep the holes had been as he told Ruth about the time the men from the flats had dug out deep channels in the ground after they finished their work for the day, and how, many years later, he had helped to fill in the four connecting chambers to make the gardens safe again for the children in the tenements.

At the back of their own flat was the space he had claimed for them, thronged with climbing roses and sweet-smelling honeysuckle and snapdragons. There had been no complaints from the other owners about the unofficial takeover; it meant a bit less grass to cut for everyone and who would object to that?

Eventually, the walk came to an end and Ruth and Alf sat together on the bench beside the window, still talking as the warmth of the day gave way to dusk. Connie knew that he would be telling her that he knew about the baby, and suggesting that she should write to her parents. Perhaps he was even giving her the words to use.

Fred

Blog: Mid-November 2016

Edinburgh

I went to the allotment to meet Stan today. I thought it would be quiet, but it seems it's where everyone goes to escape the Christmas adverts on the TV, which have been going on for weeks.

When I was little it seemed to be quite a daunting place. It was full of old men who talked about earthing up and chitting and dibbers – a foreign language to a five-year-old whose main passion was Teenage Mutant Ninja Turtles. After Nana died, Granda would sometimes collect me from school and take me there until Mum got home from work. If it was raining I would sit in the shed doing my word tin while he was outside getting wet, and if it was dry I was sometimes given the responsibility of watering things. I do remember the most fabulous strawberries, far better than anything you can buy in the supermarkets now. When I ate them, there were splashes of sweetness, dancing across my tongue.

I took biscuits – Jammie Dodgers – and Stan introduced me to everyone. There was Andy – he's quite new and is clearing the ground on a rather overgrown plot. He joked about needing a flamethrower. Maybe I should introduce him to Ellen – or, on second thoughts, perhaps not.

A man called Zac has the plot on the other side of Granda's. He's into organics and something called heritage seeds, which means he grows old varieties that you can't buy anymore.

Granda's plot looks different from how I remember. I

know it's November, but there don't seem to be any flowers for a start. His shed has been painted dark green by the family who have taken over. The new owner (do you own a plot?) is Olivia, and she is very appreciative of all the raised beds that he built over the years.

After I was shown around, we went to Stan's shed for a cup of tea. He has a little gas stove; all mod cons! And suddenly – maybe it was something about the fresh air, or the smells – it was as though I was back there, six years old on a Saturday morning, sitting on the bench outside with my feet swinging because my legs were too short to touch the ground. Granda always brought a vacuum flask of cocoa to the allotment. He made it up at home and put it into the canvas bag he used, and then we walked to the bus stop and waited for the bus. Even though it was smoky upstairs he took me onto the top deck so I could look into the windows of the houses as we went past.

And then, after a bit of weeding or some spelling practice, he would bring out his old flask and uncork it – I still have it in the larder – and he would pour out the cocoa. I remember he used to bring a small bottle the same shape as a Marmite jar but in clear glass. He would put the cream from the top of the milk bottle in it as a treat for me and then he added a little bit of brown water into his own. I now know that this was rum but of course I had no clue at the time. And then he would open the biscuit tin and get out the packet of chocolate fingers that was always there and which never ran out because it was a magic tin.

While I was at the site I asked Stan about how to go about getting an allotment. The tenement back green is shared among all the flats, so while I might be able to get away with a few exotic cauliflowers and some herbs, I can't see the rest of the stair residents going a bundle on swathes of earthed-up potatoes and a fruit cage.

Unfortunately, it looks like I'm out of luck. Stan says the waiting list is YEARS. Until he said that I didn't even know I wanted one, but now I think I do, so I'm putting my name down on the council list as soon as I've finished writing this. In the meantime, he said that any time I fancy getting some exercise I can go and get a full workout with his spade, and you know, I might just take him up on the offer.

The tea was stewed, and black – 'nuff said.

It was a good afternoon. Over the years, Granda shared the plants he grew from cuttings and there are little pockets of him all over the plots, a few raspberry canes here and a rhubarb crown there. I think he would like that.

It's as though he isn't gone at all.

Ruth

Late July 1980

Edinburgh

The early weeks of being desperate to wee at ungodly hours in the morning had passed, and it was almost ten o'clock when Ruth woke. Sunlight was struggling through the sliver of a gap between the heavy curtains. She stayed in bed, unwilling to move until the last possible minute. The ward rota had given her a nine-day stretch of shifts and she felt no guilt at all for having a lie-in. Eventually she couldn't wait any longer and she threw the floral covers back and began the process of getting up. The pastel pinks had not been her choice, but it was one of her last connections to home. Her mother had packed everything into the car when they had brought her to Edinburgh, saying that it would be a waste of money to go and buy new bedding when it would all just sit in the airing cupboard, unused. It felt odd to have something she so disliked as a memento of her adolescence, but frugality was in her DNA and she hadn't been able to bring herself to get rid of the unwanted linens. The same family parsimony meant that it had been the only trip north her parents made; although Ruth had endured the long coach journey home on several occasions, they had never visited again.

She put these thoughts aside; it didn't do to dwell and she had plans for the day. Necessary ones. Her jeans were too tight and last year's summer frock – bought in the sale in September when she had someone to impress – was distinctly snug across the bust. She raked through the wardrobe and picked out the only thing that was still comfortable: a soft lawn Laura Ashley dress with deep frills down to her calves. Her appetite was back with a vengeance and this meant a trip to the bakery on the other side of the street. She pulled the dress on and tied her espadrilles and headed out across the cobbles to the bakery on the other side of the street.

A large apron did nothing to disguise the baker's expanding waistline, and the usual dusting of flour was speckled across his black hair. Ruth had heard him tell wide-eyed small children, visiting the shop with their mothers, that it was a protective powder and was responsible for the fact that he would never go bald.

'Morning.' She opened her purse to check the coins before ordering.

'Day off today?'

She nodded. 'Not one day, but two. Aren't I the lucky one?'

He picked up a croissant from the large tray beside him before she had finished speaking. 'Your usual?'

'I think I might have two of those, actually.' The shop was casting its customary spell on her. 'And a wheaten loaf as well, please.'

She walked back across the road to the empty flat. The grey-haired postman, crooked from decades of carrying his delivery bag, was coming out of the stair but she couldn't face asking him if there had been any post for her – she would know soon enough. Her heart began to beat a little faster, and not only from the exertion of two flights of stairs – but when she unlocked the door there were no letters lying on the rug. She let out a small sigh of relief, knowing that she could continue with her day-off ritual without it being spoiled by bills, or worse.

She ate the first croissant straight from the bag, leaning forward to allow the crumbs to fall on the table. She had to prevent herself from immediately reaching for the second one.

Her list for the day wasn't very long but it was all essential:

1. *Make list*

2. *Buy T-shirts, baggy*

3. *Buy skirt (maybe Cottonfield?)*

4. *Toothpaste*

5. *Brie*

6. *Potatoes*

7. *Shave legs*

8. *Laund…*

List-making was interrupted by the clatter of the letterbox and when she went into the hall, there it was. The larger than average stationery was familiar from ten paces away. It must have been put through next door's letter box by mistake and they had redelivered it to be helpful. Ruth stood and looked at it. From this safe distance it seemed quite innocuous and she decided to leave it lying there for the moment. She waited until she had drunk her tea and finished the second croissant before picking it up. The bread knife made short work of opening it.

Inside was a single sheet of matching watermarked notepaper.

Dear Ruth,

We have done our best to bring you up to be a responsible and respectable citizen.

Clearly you have failed.

Do not contact us again.

We will not reply.

Nicholas Watkins

He hadn't even been able to bring himself to write 'Dad'.

She read it a second time and then folded it carefully. And then she went back to bed, fully dressed, and pulled the duvet up over her head to block out the words, which swam in front of her eyes.

She could imagine him sitting at his desk, fountain pen in hand, forming the letters carefully with his big swirls and elaborate capital letters. Everyone always commented on his handwriting and he was vain enough to make sure he got his splendid pen out in public at every opportunity, signing cheques, filling in the permission slips for school and Guides, writing the Christmas cards on behalf of the three of them, and then the envelopes – especially the envelopes – as he imagined people smiling and taking pleasure in a well-spaced address and carefully-positioned postage stamp.

Seven months of promises and a split condom had wiped out twenty-one years of family, and it was all her fault.

Ruth

Late July 1980

Edinburgh

Ruth waited until Friday before going to the flat to see Connie. She had been desperate enough to consider visiting the Sewing Room at the Infirmary, but decided that this would probably embarrass both of them.

'I hope you don't mind, I just wanted to tell you that I have had a reply from my parents,' she said when the front door was opened.

'I'm pleased to hear it. Come inside. I'm just getting the dinner on. You'll have something to eat with us?'

'I'm not very hungry, to be honest.'

'Nonsense. You must have something to eat, and I can easily peel a few more potatoes. There'll easily be enough for all three of us.' Connie held up wet hands. 'Just give me a minute to finish up and you can tell me all about it.'

Ruth sat herself down at the table in the warm kitchen and took the luxurious envelope with its flamboyant script in blue-black permanent ink from her bag. She held it out to Connie, who was about to go back to stripping carrots of their skin with a paring knife.

'I wasn't sure what to say, so I asked Alf and he told me what to write.'

'And they have replied.'

'Yes, or rather my father has.'

'Excellent. What did they say?'

'I think you should read it, really.'

Connie sliced the carrots against her palm – which made Ruth wince with every cut – and then dropped the orange discs into a pan of boiling water one at a time. 'You see, I knew things would work out for you.' She pulled the loop of roller towel, which hung beside the sink towards her and wiped her hands dry. There wasn't a speck of blood to be seen.

Ruth waited.

'Now, where are my glasses? I can peel vegetables by the feel of them, but I need my glasses for reading. Alf is always saying I should put them on a cord and hang them around my neck, but that just makes me feel so old.'

'Do you need me to help you with finding them?'

'No, no, they are here somewhere.' She patted her apron. 'Here they are, in my pocket all the time. Right, let me have a look.'

'It won't take you long.'

Connie took the envelope and sat down in her usual place at the table. She felt the weight and texture of what was obviously expensive stationery and noted the tissue paper lining where the flap had been sliced open.

'What lovely handwriting. I do like a nice script. It's a sign of a good education, I always think.'

The pot on the stove began to spit boiling water and splashes hissed as they vaporised on the cream enamel.

'I'll get that, while you read.' Ruth went over to the cooker and peered at the control knobs to work out which one was too high, so she didn't see a horrified Connie cover her mouth to prevent her disgust erupting into the room. By the time Ruth had found a lid for the pot and turned the gas down, the sheet of paper had been refolded and was back in the envelope.

'My father never was one to mince his words.'

'So I can see.' Connie slipped the letter into her apron pocket and glanced up at the clock. 'My goodness, Alf will be home soon and I forgot to buy any milk.' She opened her handbag and took out her purse. 'If I gave you some money, you could go and get a bottle from Eva in the corner shop. Would you mind doing that for me?'

'Of course I wouldn't. Is it just milk you need?'

'I need some bacon as well.' She opened the door of the well-stocked fridge and looked inside, lost in thought for a moment. 'But you'll need to go to the Co-op to buy that; the butcher will be closed by now.'

'Streaky or back?' said Ruth, desperately trying to cling on to the normality of buying groceries.

'Ayrshire Middle, please.' She handed over a five pound note. 'That will be more than enough.'

It took twenty minutes to buy both items because the shops were in opposite directions, but it gave Ruth the opportunity to escape from the sudden coolness of the atmosphere in the flat. She resolved to hand over the groceries and make an excuse to leave as fast as humanly possible, without being rude.

Ruth walked up the path to the tenement. As she approached the heavy main door there was no mistaking the sound of Alf's voice coming from the open window. It was raised and angry. He was clearly not a happy man. Her heart sank still further as she went inside the stair and waited next to the now familiar black front door. For several minutes she stood there before deciding that the best thing to do was simply to leave the milk and the bacon on the doorstep and hope that Connie remembered the errand at some point in the evening. As she put the items down, the door to the flat opened and she found herself facing the tall figure of Alf.

'I'm sorry, I can't stop. Please tell Connie that I forgot I have to finish doing my leaving papers and I have to hand them in at work tomorrow, so I have to go.' Her words came out in a deluge.

'Tomorrow is Saturday. There will be no one in any office in the entire hospital until Monday morning.' He opened the door wide, inviting her in. 'And, anyway, you'll not have had a meal since lunchtime so it's about time you had something to eat, or that baby won't be happy.'

Ruth did as he asked, and made her way to the kitchen, still uncertain of her reception. 'Has Connie shown you the letter?'

He seemed to grow even taller before her eyes, his shoulders squared and his back straight. 'She has indeed.' And for the first time in almost a quarter of a century, he made a major decision without consulting his wife. 'It seems to me that you are in need of a proper family, and I think we can help you with that.'

Connie didn't mind in the slightest.

Annie

October 1980

Edinburgh

The flat in Marchmont was silent until they invaded.

Annie was first through the door, followed by her husband, her brother and his wife, their collected children – all but one – and two grandchildren in prams. In all there were thirteen of them. They gathered in the kitchen and went through the family ritual of pulling out the leaves on the long table so it was stretched out to its full length and then they went in search of all the chairs and stools that were scattered around the flat. Everyone sat in their usual places. The seat at the end, nearest the cooker, was left empty.

Annie looked across at Jim. At almost six feet tall, he towered over her, but in her eyes he would always be her little brother. She raised her eyebrows to offer him the role, but he shook his head.

'You speak. You're the one who has dealt with all the paperwork and everything.'

'Well, if you are sure.'

The front door banged as Annie's son arrived, bearing dinner in the form of a dozen fish suppers from the chip shop on the corner. He dumped the bags on the table. 'I just got salt and sauce for everyone – it was easier that way. I hope someone else got the drinks?' He had barely finished speaking before the packages were being shared out and a vinegary smell filled the room.

Jim stood up. 'I'm going to let my sister talk us through what happens next' – he pulled the ring from a can of lemonade – 'but I'd like to raise a toast to my parents, Jean and Donald Cameron, without whom none of us would be where we are now.'

Around the table, cans fizzed as they were opened, and the toast was repeated.

'No business until everyone has eaten,' announced Annie, pushing her steel-grey bob behind her ears. 'I don't want to eat cold chips, thank you very much.'

'First of all, I want to say thank you to all of you for coming. I know some of you have travelled a long way to be here.' Annie looked at the faces around her, all of them tied together into one family. 'I asked everyone to come here for a very good reason. As you know, this flat, which so many of us regard as home, is not ours. That has never been a secret. It was provided to Mum and Dad in 1917 by the trust set up by the James family, and the conditions of the lease were that they could live here as long as they wanted.'

Heads nodded in agreement.

'What you younger folk may not know is that when Dad died in 1952, things got a bit complicated for a while. Mum got herself into a terrible state because she thought she was going to have to leave. The thing she was more worried about than anything else, and which only the oldest of us here know, is that she and Dad were never married.'

At this there was a collective gasp from the younger members of the family.

Annie held her hand up. 'Questions after I've finished, please.' She took a sip of ginger beer before continuing. 'That's right, all those years when she was coming to our weddings and getting soppy over the flower arrangements, she and Dad had never actually tied the knot themselves. And the reason she was so worried was because she thought the Trust would discover the truth and put her out in the street. She was her own worst enemy. She didn't tell any of us until she was just about demented with worry because she couldn't find the lease after Dad died.' Annie looked around the table at the younger members of the family. 'Let this be a lesson, by the way. It never does to keep things to yourselves.'

Jim tapped his fingers on the table. 'Annie is absolutely right. You must always tell someone if there is something wrong. Sorry,' he deferred to his sister, 'I interrupted. You keep going.'

She picked up where she had left off. 'When she finally *did* tell us, all we had to do was go back to the Trust and get a copy, but we didn't know what the paperwork said until we read it. As with many of these things, in the end it had been a lot of stress for nothing – the lease had always been set up to continue until either of them wanted to leave or they both died.' She paused. 'Jim and I always made it clear to Mum that she could move in with one of us if she wanted to. We asked her many, many times and she always said no.' She smiled. 'Being stubborn is a family trait, but the reason I'm telling you all this now is because everyone needs to understand what happens next.'

A hand went up at the far end of the table. Annie shook her head.

'I'm sure you have lots of questions and I know I'm hogging the conversation here but if you'll just bear with me for a bit longer that would be helpful. This part is more complicated.' She took a deep breath. 'Jim and I have had several meetings with the Trust. It's a much bigger concern now. The flat originally belonged to a young man who was killed on the Somme in 1916. His family never needed the rent that Mum and Dad paid, so they used that income, along with some other funds, as seed capital to buy another flat. And then they repeated the process, over and over again. All these flats are now being leased to veterans at low rents on the same terms as Mum and Dad. It's not a well-known organisation, and the properties are scattered all over the country: in Glasgow and Stirling and even in Aberdeen, where they could probably be sold for a fortune at the moment because of North Sea oil.'

'Does everyone understand so far?' said Jim.

There were nods around the table.

Annie took another drink from her can. 'Right, this is the big part of it all. Mum's solicitor has suggested that we might like to try to buy the flat. There isn't anything in law that says we have the right to do that, but she thinks we should ask the Trust if we can.'

She looked from face to face. 'Jim and I have discussed it, and the reason we have asked you here today is to tell you that it might have been a possibility, but we have decided we don't want to do it. We don't even want to approach the Trust to ask the question and we *definitely* don't want there to be any family rumours or secret conversations going on about it.'

She half laughed to herself. 'I have to tell you that the solicitor thinks we are mad, because this place is now worth quite a lot of money. But we, that's Jim and I, think that part of the reason Mum and Dad were so happy here is because they knew they had it for life – even though they were living in sin under our noses. We think that the flat should pass to another veteran, just like Dad, and maybe his or her family will make it their home for another sixty years. Every single one of us in this room has benefited from the fact that Mum and Dad lived here. We went to school up the road, and we didn't have to move five times in five years because some landlord was putting the rent up all the time. I went to college from here, and Jim went to university. We all have our own homes and although most of you still have mortgages, we are ten times better off just because we were able to stay in one place when we were growing up and know it was secure.

'Technically, this is our decision alone, because Jim and I are Mum's executors, but that's not how our parents did things. They included everyone in their big decisions, so' – she took another deep breath – 'we have asked you to come here to vote on it.'

There was near silence in the room.

'This is very important. If anyone has any questions, now is the time to ask them.'

No one spoke.

'No questions at all?' Still, there was silence. 'So, a show of hands, then. Are we going to please the solicitor, or pass the flat back to the Trust as soon as possible? All those for making the solicitor happy?'

Every hand stayed down.

'And for handing it back?'

It was unanimous.

'Good.' There was a sense of relief in the room. 'We do need to do some final paper clearing and chucking out. The Trust would like the place to be emptied so it's ready for the next family. Jim and I have gone through almost everything already and taken away a lot of paperwork and family stuff, but the bigger pieces of furniture will be collected next week and taken away to go to a charity shop on Gorgie Road.'

Annie's daughter rubbed her pregnant belly thoughtfully. 'If no one minds, I would quite like to have this table; ours is a horrible plastic-covered thing and I quite like the idea of all of you coming to me for Christmas this year.' She looked around to see if there were any objections. 'OK, thank you very much. And can I just say, Granny keeping it a secret from everyone is just incredible.' She grinned. 'After the hard time she gave me and Callum for living together before we got married, I'm not going to forget that in a hurry.'

Jim cleared his throat. 'Thanks, everyone. We thought you would agree with us, but we had to ask you to make sure.' He stood up. 'There is one final thing. There is an envelope missing. Mum kept it in her bedside chest. We don't know what was in it, but years ago she made us promise to keep it safe... and it's gone. So, over the years, if any small fingers' – he looked around the table – 'have accidentally picked it up, or if one of you finds it tucked away in a book or something, I'd be very grateful if you let me know. I don't think it's Premium Bonds, but she obviously thought it was important, so it's a great shame that it's gone missing.'

As they were about to leave the flat, Annie claimed to have forgotten something and she went back inside for a final look. She walked from room to room, taking in the nicks and scratches. The marks behind the door in the kitchen where they had all been measured every year on their birthdays were still there, along with the vacant pale rectangles on the walls where their photographs had hung.

She closed the red front door for the last time. 'Goodbye, number nine. Look after the new folk for me, won't you?' she whispered, before walking down the path to her family.

Connie

October 1986

Edinburgh

The clocks changed the weekend before Halloween. This made the evenings even darker and spookier to Fred and he became even more obsessed, if that was possible, by the impending weekend adventures. The playground was full of excitement about it all, and Nana had sent him to school with a surprise in his packed lunch; between the slices of ham in his sandwich, she had spread a sticky layer of tomato ketchup. As planned, it had oozed satisfyingly from the side of his mouth with every bite, to the delight of the boys in his class.

By Monday afternoon, when Connie collected him from his classroom, the cloakroom was full of excited children. She could hear the buzz: ghosts, treats, turnips, and candles featured heavily in the chatter.

'I need a costume for Halloween, Nana.'

She bent down to do up the horn toggles on his black duffle coat. 'And what would you like this costume to be, Fred?'

'I have to be scary.' He pulled a face, revealing three missing teeth, which added to the effect. 'Really, really scary. With blood and black stuff.'

Connie took his small hand as they waited at the zebra crossing outside the school for the traffic to pass.

'Is this for guising on Friday?'

'It's for school *and* for guising. My-teacher-Mrs-Brown is having a special story time and we can dress up if we want.' He paused as his hand was gripped firmly and he was marched across the striped road. 'And I DO want.'

'Have you asked Mummy about going out guising?'

'I won't be on my own,' he replied, anticipating the objection.

'Tell me who else will be there?'

'There are four of us and two of them have some big brothers, so that's...' He counted on his fingers. '... Quite a lot.'

'I think Mummy will be working on Friday night, so we might need to ask Granda if he can help a bit.'

'OK. Have you got anything we can make a cape from?'

'You want a cape as well?'

'Yes. A cape that is long and thick and swoops out behind me when I run along the road. It needs to be red, to match the blood.'

'Would you like to look in my cupboard when we get home?'

Fred's eyes lit up. 'Yes! After I have had my snack.' Post-school hunger ruled everything. 'Are we going to see your mummy and daddy, Nana?'

'I thought we might. It's the quickest way home and your tummy is rumbling, I can hear it.'

His slightly sticky fingers held on to her cool papery ones, and they dissected the events of the day until they arrived at the arched gates of the cemetery. Connie took her usual route along the pebble-strewn path, and when they arrived at their destination, Fred chose one of the graves, which had a rectangular marble edge framing the plot, and he sat down. They came here once a week, on a Monday afternoon, just the two of them. It was their secret, and they had been doing it for as long as Fred could remember.

Connie touched the top of the headstone, smoothing it with her fingertips, and dusting off a few twigs that had fallen from the leafy canopy above. A blackbird and his drab wife had built their temporary nursery in the branches and gone on to raise two broods of the next generation; she found this a comforting thought. In the last few weeks the nest had been abandoned and the sycamore leaves had turned yellow and tumbled onto the grave.

'Help me sort things out a bit, Fred,' she said, and he got to his feet and began to move the black-spotted leaves to one side, until the grass-covered mound was cleared. It was the only tidy grave in the whole row.

'I wonder where *my* daddy is?'

'Mmmmm?' she replied, engrossed in moving the last few leaves.

'I said, I wonder where *my* daddy is?'

'Why do you wonder that?'

'I just do, and the boys in my class said I should ask Mummy.'

'Well,' Connie said carefully. 'You could ask her, I suppose, but I know it makes her feel sad to talk about it.'

'I don't want her to be sad.'

'Neither do I, Fred. Maybe it would be better not to ask her until you are all grown up.'

He picked up one of the sycamore keys and rolled the stalk between his fingers. 'OK.' He threw the distinctive seed upwards into the air and watched it twirl back down to the ground. 'Look, Nana, I have been practising helicopters with Mummy. There is a tree near her work.'

'You are definitely getting better at it.'

'My-teacher-Mrs-Brown says that the biggest helicopter tree in the whole of Scotland is in Edinburgh. Did you know that, Nana?'

'I did not know that.'

He was getting bored now and took her hand. 'Nana, I need the toilet,' he lied. 'Can we go now?'

'Alright.'

She bent down beside the grave before they left, as she always did. He watched her close her eyes and touch the words chiselled into the headstone, one word at a time, all the way to the bottom where the letters were a different shape and not as moss-infested.

'And can I have crisps?'

'Please,' she said automatically.

'Crisps, *please*, Nana.' He chanced his luck. 'Monster Munch are even better. The blue packet with all the arms.'

'Oh, I expect we can manage that, but don't tell Mummy. She doesn't like you having crisps; she says they get stuck in your teeth.'

'I promise I won't say anything,' he replied, including his weekly visit to the cemetery and the questions about his father in the vow.

Cape. Halloween.

Black with red satin lining.

Fred

For Fred, hearing his mum's voice on the phone is no substitute for seeing her in person.

'Long time, no see, stranger. I wasn't sure you were going to come back before Christmas!' he says as he opens the door.

Her expression changes from happiness to horror in an instant. 'Oh my God. What have you done to your hair?' She gives him a professional once-over. 'Are you sick? Is everything OK?' She steps forward into the hallway and examines him even more closely.

'Everything is fine. I just had to face up to the fact that I'm going bald, that's all.' Fred wraps her up in his arms. 'Welcome home.'

She pulls back from his embrace. 'Honestly? You would tell me if there was something wrong, wouldn't you?'

'Of course I would. I'm not a complete fool.'

She still isn't sure. 'Hmmm. Well, just as long as you do.' She pokes him in the stomach. 'And you might have warned me.'

'I missed you too, Mum.'

She shrugs her shoulders. 'You really did give me a fright there.'

'Sorry,' he replies.

'I see next door is up for sale.'

'Yes, the family who were living there have been building a house in Fife. They moved out at the weekend and it looks as though the landlord wants to get rid of the place.' He shoos Crabbie off a chair.

'You've still got the cat then?'

'I know. I never got around to taking her to be rehomed. She's good company.'

'Listens well and doesn't answer back?'

'Something like that.' He folds his arms in mock annoyance. 'Anyway, I thought you were coming back tomorrow? I was all set to come and meet you off the train and everything.'

'It's fine – my plans changed at the last minute. The old friend

I was going to stay with in London had some domestic crisis and I didn't want to impose.'

'So? How was it, then?'

'It was amazing.' Her smile says everything. 'I never want to go back to work.'

'I was afraid of that.'

'Well, not for a bit anyway.'

'I want to hear all about it.'

'Really?' She looks around the room, taking in the new domesticity, clothes hanging on the pulley, a bright-yellow teapot on the table and a cushion for the cat on top of the old black range in the chimney breast. 'If I start talking I may not stop for a week.'

'Do you need food? I haven't got much in – I was going to go shopping tomorrow in your honour.'

'Takeaway?' she says hopefully. 'I could murder a Rogan Josh.'

'Sounds good to me.'

Two hours later, after she has told him everything he might ever want to know about the workings of Swedish railways and the tram system in Helsinki, both of which seem to be heavily punctuated by the name Lucas, she starts to ask him about the last four months at home.

'You said in your last email that you haven't found a job yet.'

He groans. 'I knew you were going to ask about that.'

'No luck at all?'

'I've decided I don't want to do any more contracting, so I'm looking at other things.'

'Go on…'

'Well, I know you wanted me to go to university instead of going straight into the bank when I left school' – he doodles on the table with his fingertip, following the grain of the wood – 'but I'll be thirty-six in a few weeks, and maybe I should try it.'

'About time too.'

'Pardon?'

'I said, it's about time too.'

'You think it's a good idea?'

She nods. 'What do you want to study?'

'I'm thinking it might be history.' Fred opens the drawer in the table, takes out his black notebook and releases the elastic that holds it closed. 'I've been talking to a friend about it, and taking notes. She says she'll help me with the application form if I need a hand. I would have to go to college first to do an access course because my Highers were taken in the last century.'

'A friend?'

'Her name is Ellen.'

'What happened to Samantha?'

He thinks back to the summer. 'It turned out that I wasn't Samantha's sort of bloke.' It feels like a lifetime ago. 'Or maybe she wasn't my sort of woman… which is probably a good thing.'

'And Ellen is…?'

'Ellen is a friend, Mother,' he says firmly. 'Just a friend, that's all.'

She changes the subject. 'Right. So that's your future plans sorted out. Now, tell me about the flat. I see you've been getting things organised. How many skips did it take?'

He laughs. 'Just two small ones.'

'You've been very restrained, then. I thought I would come back to acres of white walls and simplicity.'

'Am I so predictable?'

'I see you've got nice new curtains in the front room. I wouldn't have marked you down as a soft furnishings sort of man.'

'Hey!' He puffs out his chest. 'No scoffing. I'll have you know that those curtains are all my own work. I made those, and the ones in my bedroom and the blind in the bathroom. And if you care to look in the kitchen drawers, you'll find a set of new table napkins and two aprons.'

'I'm impressed.'

'I'm not finished.' He unwinds the cord for the pulley, one figure-of-eight loop at a time and lowers it gently to eye level. 'One bathrobe, one vintage shirt, six pillowcases and' – he pulls on the cord to raise the pulley back up and locks it off on the hook – 'two waistcoats I found in the wardrobe that belonged to Granda and now fit me.'

'You've been busy. Did you trade in Nana's sewing machines for a new one?'

'One of them went in the skip,' he confesses. 'I was going to put the other one out there as well, but I was short of cash before my back pay arrived so I decided to sell it instead.'

'You sold it?'

'No, not in the end. I kept it because it was full of secret history.'

'I don't understand.'

'Let me show you. Hold on a minute.' He disappears into the

front room and retrieves the notebooks from their home beside the sewing machine. 'See?' He puts them on the table in front of her.

'Oh my goodness.' She lifts up one of the books.

'Hold on a minute, Mum. Don't say anything yet.' He starts to put them in order, fanning them out across the table like a croupier with a deck of cards at a casino. 'Right, that's all of them apart from mine.' He adds his own notebook to the spread.

'Where did you find these?'

'In the base of Nana's machine.'

'I had no idea there were so many.'

'You've seen them before?'

'A long time ago. I thought they would have been thrown out.' She picks up the first book and examines the copperplate school-teacher hand.

'This is Nana's mother. She was called Kathleen.'

He thinks back to the cemetery he last visited as a child and tries to remember the names on the headstone, but it's too long ago. 'My great-grandmother, then. You might be right. Look, there is a K beside every project. Do you know anything else about her?'

'Not that much.' She holds the book in both hands. 'She was married twice and Nana was born during her second marriage. I think she was a school teacher, but that's about it really.'

'Well, I've been doing some research, so let's see if we can fill in the gaps.'

She leans forward in her seat and concentrates.

'The machine was bought on a payment plan; see, here's the record book. There's something funny about the first few payments and I can't work out what it is, but they are made every week. If we look at the sewing notebook there are lots and lots of white things sewn. Nightdresses – far, far more than one person could ever use. And petticoats and even Christening gowns. And if Nana was born in 1920, all this was made long before then, so they weren't for her.'

'So she was sewing to make ends meet?'

'It looks like it.'

'And then what?'

'There are gaps when not much was made – a few dresses, little girls' pinafores and that sort of thing. But not much sewing for adults, so I think that there was more money in the household than there was at the beginning and by the 1920s most of the sewing was for Nana.' He picks up another book. 'And then there are more dresses and other clothes and Nana's writing starts appearing. Some of the pages have a pattern number, and you can look those up online. This is one of them and it matches up… here and here.' He passes over the sheet of paper he has printed off.

'I'm no dressmaker, but that looks really quite complicated.' His mother peers more closely at the fabric and the pattern. 'She told me once that she started working at the Sewing Room in the Royal Infirmary in the 1950s, and she made new clothes for the interview.'

'That explains it, then. I suppose she would have wanted to make a good impression if sewing was going to be her job, wouldn't she?'

'What's in the books after that?'

'Quite a lot of basic sewing. Repairs, alterations, curtains, more pinafore dresses.' Fred closes the book. 'And then it stops.'

'Completely?'

'Yes. Nothing at all from 1963 until 1980. Do you remember her making things for you?'

She folds her arms. 'I can't say that I do, Fred, but she had a new machine as well, an electric one – probably the one you threw out.'

He doesn't notice that her voice is wobbling a little. 'Hmmm. Maybe that's it.'

'And what happens in 1980?'

'It says: "Alterations to Uniforms. Five dresses." And then there are measurements and numbers. I wondered if these were yours?'

'Is there anything else? Written in the books?'

'Just baby things. See?'

She takes the book and reads:

November 1980

Cut up cellular blanket into four, hemmed.

Cot sheets – six.

Cot bumper

Hooded towels – 3

'Could you give me a glass of water please, Fred.'

'Of course.'

'And a couple of paracetamol, if you've got any.' She stifles a yawn. 'And then, I'm sorry, the food was great and it's lovely to see you after all these months, but I really need to get back home. Maybe we can look at these another time?'

'Of course. You look shattered.'
'I am. I think I'll phone for a taxi.'

Fred

Blog: Early December 2016

Edinburgh

Mum is back, which is great. She looks really happy, but she's going to have a couple of days by herself to get her laundry and stuff sorted out before she goes back to the solicitor's to see how things are progressing. I'll probably see her at the weekend.

Stan came round yesterday. He brought me the thing he's been keeping safe for me. I had no idea what to expect, but it's an old cash box.

It's locked. He thought I might have the key, but unfortunately I don't.

And then he told me this really odd story about it. He said Granda gave it to him for safekeeping in the 1960's. He said it was the year after Sean Connery played James Bond in Dr No – Stan had been to see it three times – and he said that Granda was behaving like 007!!!

Apparently Granda was new on the plots then. He had moved from a different site and no one really knew anything about him. Stan told me that he was there early one Sunday morning, having a smoke and a brew, and up the path came this tall stranger with a box under his arm. They sort of nodded at one another and shook hands and then Granda went into his shed and shut the door. He was in there for more than an hour.

When he came out, Stan said it looked as though he'd been rubbing his face in nettle leaves, it was so red.

A few months later, just before the wet autumn weather started to come in, Granda appeared on Stan's plot one day and asked him if he would take the box home for him and keep it safe. Apparently he was worried about the dampness in the shed damaging what was inside.

I asked him what happened next... and he said that the two of them had talked about how Granda's leek seedlings were coming on, because the parent plants had been transplanted from his old plot. He remembered that bit particularly, because they saved some seed from the crop and Stan still grows them today.

Of course, that wasn't what I meant at all – what I wanted to know was whether he had ever asked Granda what was inside the box – and when I asked him the question again, he looked at me as though I was some sort of alien and said, 'Why would I want to do that, son?'

He kept it safe all this time; he even took it with him when he moved to a new house.

The whole thing is simply bizarre.

So now I have this locked box. There is definitely something inside it. I can hear it moving about when I give it a shake. No idea what it is, though.

Fred

Blog: Early December 2016

Leith

This week has been quite crazy. The day after Mum came back, the ancient fridge finally broke down and the freezer section at the top of it defrosted. There was a puddle of melted ice cream all over the floor. Lovely.

So one way and another (cleaning floors, buying a new fridge-freezer) I've been a bit busy, and the mystery of the box got pushed down my To Do list of things, but this evening I thought I'd get it open and see what's inside. Granda had a few screwdrivers in his toolbox and there's a hammer with a wooden handle and a wobbly head but not much else, so unfortunately, despite my best efforts, it has proved to be an impossible task.

I'm going to jump on a bus in the morning and go down to the workshops to see if Ellen can help. She has this wall of tools with saws and pliers and metal files – pretty much every tool you can think of. I'm sure she must have lock-picking equipment tucked away in there too.

Fred arrives at the old school before eleven, bearing a sticky toffee doughnut from the bakery over the road. The door to Ellen's studio is ajar and he knocks loudly.

'Anyone home?'

'Fred, you should have rung me – I'm about to go out.' She looks different. The T-shirt and the tradesman's jeans with their multiple loops and pockets have been replaced by a chilli-red dress and Doc Martens to match. Her wavy hair has been straightened into a smooth bob and one brightly-enamelled bobbin hangs from each ear lobe.

He tries not to stare and holds out the paper bag from the baker's.

'Sorry, I forgot to charge my phone last night and I needed to come down to ask you a favour.'

'I've got a meeting at a gallery.'

'Ah.'

'Is it something quick?'

'Not sure.' He empties the contents of his small rucksack onto the workbench. His dead phone and its charger, and the essential black notebook and pen, all tumble out. At the bottom is the cashbox, and he takes it out of the bag more carefully and sets it down in front of her.

Ellen glances up at the wall clock. 'My dad is going to be outside with the engine running in eleven minutes, Fred.'

'Sorry,' he says for the second time. 'It's just that I need to break into this box. It's locked and I don't have the key.'

'And it's so important it needs to be done today?'

'I didn't know you were going out.'

'You didn't ask.'

He points at his phone. 'I did try.' He realises this is a very lame excuse. 'Yes, you're right. I could have waited.'

She shakes her head in the same way a parent would when their small child has just announced that they have been invited to a birth-day party that starts in an hour but they forgot to bring home the invitation. 'Never mind. You're here now.' Ellen picks up the box and shakes it. 'What's inside?'

'That's the point. I have no idea.'

'None at all?'

'It belonged to my Granda. Could be the title deeds to a castle or half a dozen old seed packets.'

'Intriguing.'

'Very.'

She peers at the lock. 'I don't think I've got a key that will fit this. You'll have to drill it out.' She looks back up at the clock. 'I really do have to go.'

'I can come back another time. It's fine.'

'I must be mad, but,' she pauses, 'if you promise not to touch any of my other tools, and I do mean *any* of them...'

'I promise,' he says quickly.

'... then you can use my old mini-drill to bore out the lock mechanism. It's the red one in the crate under the bench. Don't be tempted to use the new blue one, on pain of death.'

'Thank you.'

'You can repay me by waiting until I get back and telling me the secret.' She picks up a hard black briefcase with EC DESIGNS tooled onto the front in silver. 'I'll be back by two o'clock.'

'I really do appreciate it.'

She gives him a final stern look as she leaves the room. 'I hope that bag has something tasty in it; I didn't have time for breakfast.'

After Fred has plugged in his phone to charge it and made a return trip to the bakery to buy carrot cake, he attacks the cashbox. The mini-drill is small but powerful and the screaming smell of pulverised metal reminds him of the childhood visits to the dentist that were more than enough to turn him into an obsessive tooth-brusher for life.

The lock is drilled out surprisingly quickly and he sweeps the metal filings and dust up carefully, reasoning that if the box has been locked for more than half a century, a few more minutes won't matter.

Fred sets it down, squaring it against the edge of the table and tries to lift the lid, but it's firmly jammed onto the base and it takes considerable pressure from both thumbs to push it open. When he finally gets it to budge it's all rather an anticlimax. All that is inside the box is a sealed envelope, and across the seal is his grandfather's signature as a defence against tampering.

'OK, then. I said I liked a mystery and that's what I've got.' He looks for something to open it with, unwilling to just slide his finger under the edge and rip it apart. Next to Ellen's computer is a big flowerpot of pencils and pens, and he rummages in among the sticks of colour for something small enough and sharp enough to do the job. His fingers find a six-inch black plastic ruler emblazoned with the words ROBOT WARS. 'Perfect,' he says.

He slides it under the flap and starts to slice the paper slowly and carefully. All sorts of possibilities run through his head. Some money, perhaps, stashed away for a rainy day. Or maybe a love letter.

But it isn't anything like that at all.

He reads the words at the top out loud: 'Extract of an Entry from the Register of Deaths in Scotland.'

He studies the document closely, puts it down and goes back to the mini drill. Very slowly and precisely, he starts to wind up the cable, wrapping it around the handle so that each loop is perfectly nested against the one before it, leaving no gaps. He resists the impulse to indulge in distraction therapy by emptying the whole box and meticulously re-organising all the drill bits and screwdriver heads into size order. Only when he has tidied everything away under the bench does he go back and pick the paper up for a second time. His hands are shaking.

Lilian Jean Morrison.

Born. 3 July 1957.

Died. 18 January 1963.

Father. Alfred Morrison. Gardener.

Mother. Constance Morrison.

Cause of death. Measles.

Informant. Father.

Fred can hardly get the words out.

'Five years old.'

He paces around the workroom with the certificate still in his hand. Nothing makes any sense.

Eventually, he puts it back into the envelope and unplugs his phone from the charger to make a call. There is no answer and voice-mail kicks in. 'Mum? I need to talk to you, I'll be over this evening.' And then he waits for Ellen.

He is sitting at her desk when she walks through the door a few minutes after one thirty.

'I'm back.'

'So I see.'

'I brought sandwiches. Is there any cake left?'

He doesn't reply.

'Fred? Is everything OK?'

'I need to talk to someone.'

'To someone in particular, or am I the only someone available?'

'I'm sorry, that was rude.'

'Apology accepted.' Ellen waits for him to continue and when he doesn't say anything, she prods gently. 'Is this to do with what you found in the box?'

Fred shudders. 'Something terrible has happened and I don't know what to do about it.'

'That doesn't sound good.'

'Well, it happened a long time ago, but… it's complicated.' He gets to his feet and starts to pace up and down the classroom. 'I'm not sure where to start. There seems to be a family secret and I didn't know anything about it until today.'

'Go on.'

'My mum was born in 1959 so she must have known.'

'Must have known what?' Ellen grabs his sleeve as he walks past her. 'Sit down, Fred, you aren't making any sense.'

'She must have known that she had a sister.' He has tears in his eyes and a catch in his throat. 'She had a sister who died.'

'Jeez Louise.' It's her turn to be shocked. 'Sorry. I mean, keep going…'

'She died from measles. I'm not sure how infectious measles is. I mean, I don't have any children, but I can't get my head around having a child and then seeing it, no, seeing HER die.' He rushes on. 'And measles is one of the things we don't worry about now. I'm sure I got immunised against it when I was a baby; my mum still has my record card.' He looks at her for confirmation. 'You must be about the same age as me so you'll have had it too.'

'I've never asked, to be honest, but I suppose so.'

He picks the envelope back up and removes the certificate. 'This is what was in the box. I don't understand it; the whole thing is so bloody weird.'

Ellen reads the stark details on the paper and shakes her head. 'I am so sorry, Fred. I have no idea.'

'It's a standing joke between me and Mum about the fact that we are both only children, that there is only one of each of us because we are so special – in an "Oh my God, we must have been so awful they never had any more" way. Me, Mum, Nana and my great-grandmother, all singletons.' He stops. 'Only now we aren't. And not one of them ever, *ever*, said anything to me.'

'What are you going to do?'

'I rang Mum and left a message on her phone to say that I'll be round to see her this evening, but I haven't said what it's about. And now I have all these questions.'

'Such as?'

'Well, if Lilian Morrison is buried somewhere in Edinburgh, where is her grave? And should I try to find it and pay my respects, whatever that means?' He can feel his throat getting tight and his voice beginning to sound thick and he can tell that any minute now, he is going to cry, so he pushes on before it happens. 'Because the thing is, Ellen, I need to know what happened, and it doesn't look like anyone else has been interested for a very long time, does it?'

And he stands there with this woman he barely knows, and his tears make channels down his cheeks and he can't move, and he waits for her to come over and hold on to him before he can begin to make sense of it all.

Fred

Early December 2016

Edinburgh

Fred doesn't wait for the evening. As soon as he has managed to start being coherent, and with a carb load of iced fudge doughnut as fuel, he leaves the studio and goes straight round to see Ruth. When he arrives, she is unloading the shopping from the car.

'Hello there. I was driving when the phone rang, sorry.' She reaches for a box of milk and bleach and red wine in the back of the car. 'Your timing is excellent.'

'Move out of the way then and I'll take that one; it looks the heaviest.' He is short with her, not trusting his voice.

'Thanks. I've just listened to your message. What's so urgent?'

Fred starts to walk up the driveway towards the house. 'There's something I need to ask you.'

'Sounds mysterious.'

'It is.'

After the groceries are unpacked and put away, he takes the envelope from his pocket and puts it down in front of her. 'I want you to tell me about this.'

Ruth picks it up. 'What is it?'

'Open it.'

She adjusts her glasses, takes the certificate from the envelope, and reads.

'Well?'

She shakes her head, going back over the words again and again.

Fred folds his arms across his chest, 'Why didn't you tell me?'

After what seems like several minutes, she replies. 'Because I didn't know.' Her voice is barely audible.

'That's nonsense.'

'I didn't know,' she repeats.

'You must have known. I may not be the brightest spark in the box but I can do basic arithmetic.'

'I'm telling you the truth.'

He tries to stay calm, but can feel his temper rising. 'You were three years old when your sister died. You must have played with her, watched her go to school.'

'No, Fred. I'm telling you, I had no idea. This is the first time I've seen this.'

'So you have a diabolical memory? I don't think so, Mum.'

'I need to think for a minute.'

He starts to pace around the room, silently counting his steps.

At last she is ready. 'I suppose I should tell you. They are both gone now and no one will be hurt.'

'Tell me what?'

'Don't rush me.' She rests back in the chair, working out what to say and which words to use. 'OK, I want you to listen carefully.'

He can hardly keep the sarcasm from his voice. 'I'm all ears.'

She points at the paper which is lying, unfolded, between them. 'I need to explain some other things first, before we talk about that.'

'If you must.'

'You've seen your birth certificate.'

'Of course. I've got two copies.'

'This isn't easy for me to talk about.' She puts her hands in her lap in an effort to keep them still. 'If you don't mind, I'd prefer you to sit down. I'm finding all the marching about you're doing quite difficult.'

He scrapes a chair back from the table, not caring about the noise. He doesn't look at her.

'In 1979 I was going out with an American.'

'An American? You've never told me that before.'

She ploughs on. 'We were madly in love. We even talked about getting married.'

'And that was my father?'

'Yes.'

'I always thought he was English and he came from York, not from America.'

She looks puzzled. 'Where did you hear that?'

"I'm not sure. It must have been from Nana.' He tries to think back. 'I must have been about six or seven. We were doing something at school about the Viking invasion and she told me not to tell you, because York made you sad.'

'Goodness, talk about getting your wires crossed. Your father's name is Harry York,' she smiles fleetingly, 'or rather Harry S. York if we are being precise about details.'

'That's quite a name.' He tries it out. 'Harry S. York.'

'I suppose it is. He was named after one of the Presidents of the United States, but he never used the S. To me, he was just Harry.'

'Were Nana and Granda pleased?'

'It's more complicated than that.' She stops again in search of the right words. 'They asked me not to tell you, so I didn't.'

'I don't understand.'

'Oh, Fred.'

'Oh Fred, *what?*' He is exasperated. 'This whole thing is beyond ridiculous. You aren't telling me anything which makes any sense. Stop dressing all this up to try to make it look pretty and just *get on with it.*'

'OK.' She says the words, slowly and clearly, so there can be no misunderstanding. 'Nana and Granda are not your grandparents.'

He doesn't answer.

'I told you it was complicated.' Her voice is quiet and he strains to hear some of the words. 'I was doing my nurse training, and I was in my final year. Harry came to meet me from work one day, out of the blue, and said that he had to go back to Chicago because his mother was ill and that he would write.' She scratches at the patch of eczema on her arm. 'And I trusted him, so I believed him.'

'And did he write?'

'He did not.'

Fred didn't know what to say.

'And then I found out I was pregnant. I wrote to him, several times and I waited to get a letter or a card or just *something*. I even thought he might fly back and turn up on the doorstep.' She doesn't wait for him to react, but presses on. 'I had no idea what to do. My uniforms were getting tighter and I had six weeks to work before I qualified. I was sure that if the College of Nursing found out, there would have been an almighty fuss. All I wanted to do was to finish the course, and then find a job so I could look after both of us without having to answer any awkward questions.' She looks across at him. 'I was trying to do my best for you.'

He doesn't speak.

'So, I made a plan. I went to the Sewing Room on my way off night duty. I was hoping they could give me a couple of new dresses if I told them I had put on a bit of weight by eating too much chocolate.' She laughs without smiling. 'I was desperate.'

Fred listens, harder than he has ever listened before, collecting her words and trying to make sense of them.

She fiddles with the silver ring she has always worn on her right hand, twisting it round and round in the groove on her finger. 'Connie – I mean Nana – was early for work that day. It was pure chance. She was the only person there when I arrived and she told me all about the forms that needed to be filled in and signed off, the measurements, the reasons.' She stops, remembering that morning. 'And then some other people came in to start work and she went away into a cupboard and came out with a plastic bag and she told me she was giving me new aprons.'

'How did that help?'

'It didn't, but by that time I was too tired to think straight so I just said thank you and left. It wasn't until a couple of days later that I realised she had put her phone number in the bag as well.'

'And then what?'

'I rang the number and I went round to the flat. Your flat, it is now. And she altered my dresses.'

'And you finished the course?'

'I did.'

'And…' He isn't sure how to ask the next question.

'Granda said I should write and tell my parents, even though I didn't want to. He told me that they would understand and that everything would be alright. So I wrote.'

He waits.

'It wasn't alright.' She stops again. 'The thing you've always known about me being an only child, well, that's true. My parents were never really happy with anything I did. I was the only one, so I had to be the best. It didn't matter whether it was a race at sports day or ninety-one per cent in an exam, they always wanted to know why I hadn't run faster or why it wasn't ninety-three per cent.'

'So when you told them, what did they say?'

'My father wrote back and said that they never wanted to see me again and that I was not to contact them under any circumstances.'

'Wow.'

'Indeed.'

'And your mother?'

'It would definitely have been a joint effort; she was even worse than he was.' She folds her glasses up and puts them on the table. 'I felt as though I was totally on my own.'

'And what happened after that?' He needs to know everything.

'Granda was out when I showed Nana the letter. She read it and then she sent me off to the supermarket to buy cheese or something. I forget what. You know, Fred, I actually thought she was trying to get rid of me. By the time I got back to the flat I knew she had told Granda because I could hear him shouting.' She smiled for the first time since he had arrived. 'It's the only time I ever heard him swear.'

'Granda never swore.'

'Well, he did that time. It was so loud I could hear him from outside the front door. He was yelling at the top of his voice. It was quite funny in hindsight, but it didn't feel like that at the time. He was absolutely furious.' Her voice softens. 'And then, when he realised I was at the door, he came to get me and he took me into the kitchen and sat me down at the table, the same table that's there now' – she is crying now, tears falling, her voice all tight and high and strangled – 'and he said that they would be my family if I wanted, and then later on, when things had calmed down a bit, he said that they had a spare room and would I like it?'

'What did you say?'

'I didn't have any energy for words so I just nodded. And that was it really.' She points at the book in front of her. 'All the things Nana made after that were for me and you. Maternity dresses, cot sheets and blankets – including that one you carted around everywhere until it fell apart – and shirts and little dungarees, I don't think I bought any clothes for either of us for years.'

'But' – Fred folds his arms – 'why have you never told me I had other relatives?'

'You called them Nana and Granda, and they *were* your grandparents, so what would have been the point? You never seemed to notice that I sometimes called them Connie and Alf.' She sighs and scratches her arm again. 'I suppose I didn't want to rock the boat. Nana retired when she was sixty, just a week before you were born, and she started to look after you so I could go back to work. Everything seemed to be working out.' She looked at him. 'It wasn't done out of badness, I promise you.'

Fred scrabbles to tie up the ends. 'What about your parents?'

'I have absolutely no idea.'

'No idea at all?'

'They were completely disgusted by me.'

'You've never been tempted to get in touch?'

'No. Never. I discovered recently that they had told the neighbours I had died from leukaemia – the things you discover on social media, eh?' She shakes her head firmly. 'I had nothing to say to them, and I certainly didn't want them to get anywhere near you.'

'But you are a Morrison. We are both called Morrison, like Granda.'

'You really do want every scrap of information, don't you?'

'I need to understand.'

'I suppose that's fair.' She closes her eyes, remembering a conversation that had taken place many years earlier. 'At about the time all this was going on, there was a patient I looked after, a very old lady, and she told me she and her husband had never married, she just changed her name. I didn't even know it was possible before she said it, but the more I thought about it the more I knew I couldn't bear to be a Watkins anymore, so I asked Nana and Granda what they thought. And Granda said – I can hear him now – "I would be honoured if you would be a Morrison", so that's what I did, a few weeks before you were born. That's why you are a Morrison too.'

'So really, I'm a Watkins.' He looks at her. 'Or maybe a York.'

'No, Fred. You are a Morrison.'

He tries to take it all in. Everyone had always said how alike he and his grandfather were. He is named after him, for heaven's sake. He is hit by sudden rage against he knows not what.

'So you have lied to me for my entire life. You have all lied. Every single one of you.'

'I did what seemed best.'

'Why didn't you tell me? Why not?' He goes back to pacing around the kitchen in fury until another thought comes to him. 'If you lied about that, what else have you not told me?'

'What do you mean?'

'My father. What about him?' He folds his arms again, challenging her. 'For years I've thought he left us and ran off to live in the north of England. It would be funny if it wasn't a massive lie.'

'I'm sorry.'

'You are sorry?' He can feel himself starting to unravel. 'How do I know he's dead? How do I know that's the truth?'

'I told you, I wrote to him in America.'

'And?'

'And I didn't get a reply.'

'So he might still be alive?'

'No, Fred. He's dead. Granda wrote a letter as well. It came back with "DECEASED" written on it in blue pencil.'

'What if that's wrong?'

'I wondered if that was the case too, so a few years ago I decided to find out, and I looked him up on the internet. He died in a car accident in Chicago, not long after he flew home. There was a notice in the newspaper. He would never have got my letters.'

'What happened to the one with the blue writing on it?' Fred is clutching at straws, trying to poke around all the nooks and crannies of what he has been told to see if there are any more secrets.

'Granda burned it at the allotment, just like he burned the one from my father. He said if I kept it, it would be like having a scab that you keep picking so it never gets better. I think he was probably right about that.'

'And that's it? That's absolutely everything?'

'I think so, except…'

'Except what?'

'I really didn't know they had a daughter. They never spoke about her.'

'You never suspected anything?'

There are tears in her eyes. 'Never.'

He picks up his waterproof jacket from the back of the chair. 'In that case, if there's nothing else, I'm going to go home now. I'm tired and I have a lot to think about.'

She gets up to give him a hug and a goodbye kiss but he has already gone, banging the front door behind him. The vibration of the bookcase next to her in the hall is all that remains as evidence of his visit.

Fred

Early December 2016

Leith

The corridors of the former primary school have been decorated with tinsel and paper-chains, but Fred can't remember a time when he has felt less like celebrating Christmas.

The studio door is open and lined up on the workbench is a parade of gleaming silver machine heads, stripped of their black paint. They have lost their vintage appearance completely.

'It's me again,' he says to the familiar figure who is wielding a camera.

Ellen keeps taking photographs. 'Hello, you. I'm nearly finished.'

'Those look as though they've just come off the production line.'

She puts the camera down and turns to face him. 'I know,' she replies theatrically. 'Aren't they *fabulous*?'

'Not sure I'd go that far, but it's quite an impressive sight.'

'They haven't been in this state since they left the foundry.' She is clearly delighted. 'I'm so pleased with them.'

He reaches out to touch the metal surface. 'What are you going to do with them?'

'Naked sewing.'

'Pardon?'

She laughs. 'I'm winding you up. It's the last bit of the puzzle. I can use everything else: enamel it, bend it and make doorknobs from the flywheels. The cases go to a woodworker and what he can't use gets chopped up for kindling. But I always had to send the machine heads for scrap, until now.'

He smiles at her enthusiasm. 'Is this something to do with the new equipment you mentioned?'

'You remembered! Yes, there's a new artist who has taken over one of the studios and she's offered to buy them from me for twenty quid each if I get them stripped down like this.'

'It looks like a lot of work.'

She smiles. 'It's not me that's doing it though. My cousin has a garage so I shelled out for a sandblaster. He's doing them for me and we're splitting the profit.'

Fred is hit by a sudden wave of envy as he wonders what it must be like to have brothers and cousins and aunts. He pulls himself back to the conversation, annoyed at feeling so needy. 'And what is this artist going to do with them in all their nude splendour?'

'She's going to hand-paint them and turn them into things of beauty.'

'And she thinks she can sell them?'

'She does it with other things like old bicycles and garden tools so she's already got a following for her work. That's half the battle when you're making a living from your art.'

'It's weird to think it hasn't looked like this since it was in the factory.'

'I know. And these are the only parts I hadn't found a use for, so it seems like the perfect solution.'

'So everything is used apart from the squeak, like a pig on a smallholding.'

'Hey.' Ellen screws up her face. 'Watch out for my vegetarian sensibilities, why don't you? But yes, everything. For me, doing the machine heads is' – she pauses – ''it's necessary.'

'You would win the recycling badge at Brownies.'

'You aren't the first person to point that out. How's the dress-making?'

'Don't scoff. You're the second person to poke fun at my stitch-ing.'

'I'm not scoffing, I'm serious.'

'You really want to know?'

'I do.'

'Well, in that case, it's going quite well. I've graduated from making alterations to Granda's old clothes' – he points to his waistcoat and does an exaggerated twirl – 'and now I'm considering buying a pattern and making something from scratch.'

'What sort of something?'

'Not sure. I'm wondering about a nightshirt.'

She splutters. 'I think this vintage thing has gone to your head.'

'I'm just carrying on a family tradition.'

'All you'll need is a nightcap to finish the ensemble and it'll be like the movie version of *A Christmas Carol*.'

'My great-grandmother used to make them on my machine, a hundred years ago. She wrote down everything she sewed in a notebook; that's where I got the idea. I hope she would have been proud of me.'

Ellen smiles. 'Funny you should say that. I feel the same about mine.'

He sighs. 'Except that she's not my great-grandmother.'

'What?'

'She's not my great-grandmother, and Nana isn't my Nana and Granda isn't my Granda.'

'This all to do with that certificate, isn't it?'

He nods. 'Yes.'

'I think you'd better explain.'

'Well, the short version is that my father disappeared while my mum was pregnant with me. She found out later that he had died, but at the time she thought he'd just abandoned her.'

'That's terrible.'

'I know. I spent years not asking about him because I was told it would upset her if I did.' Fred picks up a screw which is lying on the bench in front of him and rolls it between his fingers. 'She got in touch with her parents and they basically disowned her, and after that my Nana and Granda offered her a room in their flat.'

'Why did they do that?'

'I don't think she ever asked them; she was just so grateful to have someone looking after her – and looking after me as well, I guess. When I saw the death certificate I assumed it was some massive family secret she'd been keeping from me for some reason. But it turned out that she didn't know about Lilian either.' He shrugs. 'I think that maybe Nana and Granda treated her as the daughter they never saw grow up.'

'That's a bit creepy.'

'I suppose it looks that way from the outside, and I've thought about it a lot since last week, but honestly, Ellen, I've come to the conclusion that they were just ordinary people who did something extraordinary. I was so angry when Mum told me, but afterwards, when I had time to process everything, I realised that she was as shocked as I was.'

'It's still pretty huge.'

'I know, but the more I think about it, the more I ask myself why *would* they have told her about Lilian? They wanted to help Mum, not make her think she was part of some weird daughter replacement scheme.'

'I guess.'

'And of course, all the things I just accepted as a child now have more complicated explanations, like the fact that there were no photographs of Mum growing up – Granda said they had been burgled and the thief stole the photo albums – which is ludicrous, but you just accept the stories you are told, don't you?'

'How are you feeling about it all now?'

He gathers his thoughts before replying. 'Granda wrote me a letter, which was given to me after he died, and I read it again last night. It says something like: "The flat is somewhere your mother always called home" – and of course she *did* call it home, but that doesn't mean it was *her* childhood home. It feels as though all these clues were right in front of my face and I didn't see them.'

'I think your brain just fills in the spaces sometimes.'

'Absolutely. I mean, there are all these notebooks as well.'

'I was going to ask you about that.'

'They're a record of everything made on the machine, from the first stitch. There are a few gaps, but now I know the other pieces of the puzzle, I can see how it fits together. There are about twenty years missing and I thought some of the books had been lost.'

'That's a pity.'

'No, you don't understand, the bit that's missing is between Lilian's death, and Nana sewing Mum's uniforms. She didn't use the machine for nearly twenty years.'

'She just stopped sewing?'

'I don't think so. There were two machines in the flat when I was doing the clear out. There's the one you've seen, and a 1960s one with a burned-out motor, which didn't look safe, so I threw it in the skip. I think the notebooks belong to the machine, not to the person, if that makes sense.'

'I'd love to see them, if that would be alright?'

'Of course. I'll bring them next time I come over. Better watch out, though; you might get all soppy and sentimental.'

'What about your "real grandparents"?' She brackets the words in the air with her fingers. 'Are they still alive? They would be quite old now.'

'I don't know.'

'Your mum has no idea?'

'None, and she definitely doesn't want to find out or get in touch. I asked.'

'Maybe if you went with her?'

'She isn't interested. She found out recently that they told everyone, even her old school friends, that she had cancer and died.'

'Bloody hell.' Ellen can't keep the disgust from her face. 'And no one thought to check?'

'She never went back, and she had changed her name by then. Who would challenge grieving parents about whether it was true?'

'What about you? Do you want to trace them?'

'I don't know. She said I could if I wanted to, but that she definitely doesn't want to be part of it and that makes it kind of difficult. I don't want to go behind her back.'

'And what about your father's family?'

He shrugs. 'I don't know. I feel as though everything I took for granted is upside down and back to front.'

'You'll get there in the end. It'll just take a bit of time.'

'You're probably right. Anyway, I want to think about something else for a bit. Take me to see this person making the painted art things. I have Christmas presents to buy and my mum likes supporting people who make unusual stuff.' He opens the studio door. 'What the...'

An enormous marmalade-coloured pile of fur is lying on the floor, exactly where his foot would have landed. It stretches, slowly.

'Ah.' Ellen sees what the problem is. 'I'd like you to meet Dundee, our resident mouser. Mind you, I think everyone feeds him so he's not very motivated.' She bends down and tickles the cat, and when it doesn't move, she steps over it. 'There is no point in expecting him to get out of the way; he thinks he owns the place.'

Fred follows her into the corridor and pulls the door closed behind him. 'I think that's not unusual at all,' he says.

Fred

Blog: Mid–December 2016

Edinburgh

We have found another piece of the Morrison jigsaw puzzle. Or rather Mum has.

She came round yesterday with a parcel that looked just like the one the notebooks were in. After she saw them, she remembered that last year Granda had given her a box of things to look after. It was about the time when she was getting all the quotes for the double glazing so she had put it away in the hall cupboard where it wouldn't get tripped over. And then with everything else that happened, and the train adventures – and meeting Lucas, who is apparently coming to visit soon (!!!) – she forgot all about it.

Inside the box were two brown paper parcels. The first one was an album of black-and-white family photographs. One picture is of an old lady holding a baby in her arms, with a much younger Nana sitting next to her. On the back, in Granda's writing, it says 'Kathleen, Connie and Lilian, September 1957'.

There's a photo of a toddler wearing a pinafore dress, sitting on the grass in my back green, dated 1958. And there is one of the same girl, a few years older, holding up a turnip by the leaves – I can see an allotment shed in the background, but it isn't the one I remember. Our plot was square and open; this one is long and skinny with an embankment at the end. I remember Stan saying Granda was new to the site when he met him so he must have left the plot in the picture and started over *again, perhaps where no one would ask him any questions.*

The last photo was taken outside my old school. Lilian is standing there in her uniform with a big smile on her face and a front tooth missing, holding Granda's hand.

The second parcel was soft and floppy. Inside was a little girl's dress. It's the colour of sweet potatoes and ginger, like autumn leaves, with tiny cherry-red petals all over it, and there are two long sashes that come out from the waist to be tied at the back in a bow. The pattern was there too. Age 5–6.

The hem is raw. It was never finished.

As Fred and Ruth get closer to the school they can hear that it's break time. There is the sing-song rhythm of a skipping game and the slap of a rope on the tarmac: 'Forty-ONE, forty-TWO, forty-THREE and OUT.'

A stream of children are racing from one end of the playground to the other at full pelt and there is a yell as one of them falls flat on his face, but as they watch, he gets to his feet again and limps to catch up.

The gates of the cemetery look smaller than Fred remembers and the trees are bigger. A light breeze makes the unswept fallen leaves scatter before them as they make their way up the path.

'You are sure it's here?' says Ruth.

'It's up at the top, near the back wall,' he replies. 'I didn't realise you'd never been here.'

'Nana was cremated, like Granda, and Kathleen died long before I knew them. If what you say is true, then Nana wouldn't have brought me here anyway. It would have meant too many questions.'

Fred slows his pace and searches for a landmark that is familiar. 'Helicopters,' he says, picking up one of the Sycamore keys and spinning it into the air. 'It's around here somewhere.'

His mother points at a headstone. 'Isn't this it?'

The slab of granite is being taken over by lichen, and tiny tufts of moss have made a home in the inscription.

Fred takes his gloves off and runs his fingers around the letters.

Bruce Baxter

1887–1954

Loving husband of

Kathleen Baxter

1886–1958

And below it, at the bottom of the stone, almost hidden by the foliage of a Christmas rose, there is more:

Lillian Jean Morrison

Their granddaughter

1957–1963

Fred and Ruth look at one another and eventually it's Fred who breaks the silence.

'Nana used to bring me here every week, on the way home from school.'

'Every week? When you told me about this yesterday, I thought you meant you'd been here once or twice.'

'It was every week, on a Monday.'

'Why didn't you say anything?'

'She said it was our secret, so I didn't. Thinking back, I probably thought it was just a different way to walk home. She used to tell me that we were visiting her mummy and daddy.' He smiles. 'Anyway, I was far more interested in the crisps she was going to buy me from Eva's afterwards.'

Ruth wipes a tear away from her eye. 'They must have wanted Lilian to be with someone she would have known.'

'It looks that way. I imagine Granda came here too, but we just never knew about it.' He looks up and down the row of graves. 'If you compare our plot to all these others, it's not overgrown at all. He was probably still visiting right up until he died.'

The clouds overhead have darkened since they left the flat and rain begins to spatter the gravestones and the gravel path.

As they turn to leave, Ruth puts her arm through her son's and pulls him close. 'We can come back another day and tidy things up a bit,' she says. 'But right now all I want to do is get home. I'm going to make us two big mugs of cocoa, and we can have a really good look at that photograph album.'

Fred

When Fred arrives, the studio door is open and Ellen is at the work bench, unscrewing the tension assembly from the front of a particularly sad-looking sewing machine. Billie Holiday is pouring from the speakers, and Ellen moves from side to side with the music as she works. Fred pauses before going in. Clearly there are no gallery visits today and no clients coming to the workshop either because she has reverted to her working clothes. Her hair is stuffed under a headscarf tied in a knot at the front, above her forehead. If this was a black-and-white movie, he thinks, with her dungarees and that concentration on the task in front of her, she might be working in a wartime factory. As he looks at her, he realises that if anyone saw him sewing and cutting and pressing, they would see the same focus. They are two ends of one continuum, with the old sewing machines at the centre. He knocks loudly on the door and goes in.

Ellen looks up and smiles but keeps working. Unwilling to interrupt the song, he walks over to stand in front of her and makes a C shape with his hand and mouths, 'Coffee?'

'You can speak, you know. Billie won't mind.'

'I didn't want to interrupt the flow. You finish what you're doing, I'll make the drinks.'

By the time the water has boiled, the task is finished. She eases backward slightly to stretch out the stiffness in her spine.

'I'm sure that's bad for your back.'

'Good morning to you, too.'

He shrugs. 'Don't blame me when you are stiff and achey. Old age doesn't come by itself, you know.'

She ignores his teasing. 'What baking delight have you brought for me today?'

'Two mince pies and slice of Christmas cake.'

Her face is a picture. 'You didn't?'

'If you could just see yourself.' He laughs and puts the bag from the bakery on the table, just out of reach. 'No, it's just one of your five-a-day, as usual.'

'Oooooh, carrot cake. You know me so well.'

She leans over to pull the bag towards her, tears it open and arranges the square of cake and the lumpy cheese scone he has bought for himself at opposite ends of the paper before leaning over so she is at eye level to the icing. 'Not bad. Seven out of ten, I think.'

'You do know that the woman in the baker's doesn't even ask me which one I want anymore, don't you? She just gives me the piece with the most walnuts.'

Ellen ignores the dig and picks up the thickly frosted cube, cupping one hand beneath it to catch any crumbs. 'Quite right too.'

'You are impossible.'

'I know. And since I don't have any china plates or fancy cake forks I'm going to eat this right now,' she says, and takes a bite.

Fred realises that this is another tick on the list of 'things I like about Ellen' and tries to find something else to think about in case she read minds as well as everything else she seems capable of.

'I brought the notebooks for you to look at,' he says, 'but I'm not getting them out until you've finished eating and washed your hands again.'

She finishes the mouthful of cake. 'You sound like my mum.'

'I probably sound like everyone's mum.'

'Speaking of your mum, who I'm sure is awesome, by the way, how are things?'

'I forgot, I told her about you helping with the university stuff. She's pretty happy about the plans.'

'That's not what I meant, and you know it.'

'Ah, I see. She's fine.' He screws his face up. 'Me, I'm not so sure about yet.'

'Understandable.'

'I'm getting there, but it was such a lot to absorb. Everything I took for granted about who I am has changed.'

She reaches across the table and squeezes his arm gently. 'It will take time, that's all.'

He nods and pushes the untouched scone to one side. 'Right, I wasn't kidding. Get those hands washed.'

While she is at the sink, he takes the parcel of notebooks out of his bag and lays it on the table.

She comes back and holds her hands out, palms up and then palms down, like a small child.

He leans forward to inspect them, carrying on the game. 'You'll do.'

She reaches out to touch the parcel.

'Hold on a minute, let me set the scene. You have to go back a bit, to a few weeks before I made an idiot of myself at that car boot sale. I had lost my job, and I was thinking of selling Nana's old sewing machine because I was really short of cash. Everything and anything in the flat was fair game at the time, but the machine didn't seem to be working. When I investigated, this parcel was hidden in the wooden base, and it was stopping the driveshaft – or whatever you call those long rods – from moving.'

'So you really *didn't* have the money for the machine that woman was selling?'

'On that particular day I was down to less than ten pounds, so I was telling you the truth. The back pay from my last job was taking forever to come through and I was too proud to go and sign on. I was almost completely broke.' Fred points at the package. 'This is pretty much how I found it, same string, same brown paper.'

'How exciting.'

He starts to untie the fraying twine. 'I'm ashamed to admit that I was hoping it was a stash of bank notes, but instead, I found these. I've added one of my own since I discovered them.' He arranges the books on the table in a long line. 'They go right back to the first time the machine was used by Kathleen, my now-great-grandmother. As far as I can tell, it's a full chronological history of everything that was made on it.'

'Wow. When you said there were notebooks, I thought you meant two or three. I had no idea there were so many.'

He picks up a blue cash book from the 1930s and offers it to her. 'Have a look.'

'Are you sure?'

'Go on. They are like little time capsules.'

She opens it, and her eyes widen when she sees page after page of stitched lines and scraps of cloth. 'These are amazing, Fred.'

'That's pretty much what I said. There are hundreds of projects, more than thirty in each book. I've been through all of them. There are a couple of wedding dresses and a waistcoat for a groom and all sorts of other stuff as well. From what I can see, both Kathleen and Nana used the machine to earn a living, or at the very least to supplement their wages.'

Ellen is engrossed in the book she's holding and doesn't look up. 'I think that wasn't uncommon.'

He picks up a school jotter. 'Granda's allotment trousers get several mentions; clearly he wasn't one for throwing things away. One of the last things in Nana's handwriting is the cape she made for me when I was five. It was for Halloween. She didn't sew much after that.'

'What's the first thing?'

'Dusters, made by my great grandmother in 1911.'

'Dusters?' Ellen starts to laugh. 'Honestly?'

'I suppose it made sense to start with something simple.'

'Can I see the first book?'

'Sure.' He hands it over. Twenty-four pages, roughly cut and folded.

She opens it and runs her fingertips slowly along the seam on the first page. 'So this was stitched more than a hundred years ago.'

'I know. It gives me the shivers sometimes. It's like touching history.'

'What's this?'

Tucked into the back of the booklet is the homemade envelope, fragile from being opened many times.

'Have a look.'

She takes the fold of paper out carefully and opens it up. Inside is a thin strip of paper, folded into four along its length like a joiner's wooden rule. She stares at the words.

We have to leave. There is no work here for Donald. Wish us luck. Jean

Ellen drops it onto the table as though it is on fire. 'Good grief. Oh my God. This...'

'What's the matter?' He doesn't understand her reaction. 'It was...'

She completes his sentence: '... wrapped around the bobbin.'

'Yes.' He frowns. 'But how did you know that?'

She stares at the paper.

Fred opens up the envelope and flattens it so the words hidden on the inside of it can be read. 'Look, this is Kathleen's writing; it's quite different from the writing on that message.' He reads the words out loud. 'Found on the bobbin, September 1911.' And then he realises that she has started to cry and he has absolutely no idea why. 'Ellen?' he says, as gently as he can. 'What's the matter?'

Eventually she manages to get the words out. 'That piece of paper.'

'What about it?'

'It was *my* great-grandmother who wrote that message.' She wipes her face on her T-shirt. 'I must remember to buy some tissues. This is getting to be a habit in here.'

'So that means...' He tries to get his head around what she is saying and gives up.

'It's an old family story, one of those tales passed down where there's no actual proof, you know? The piece of paper was taken from a Bible. My auntie still has it and there's part of one page missing.' She takes a deep breath and looks around her at the tools and partly dismantled machines and the camera equipment. 'It's the reason I do all this.' She sweeps her arm around, encompassing everything in the studio.

'I don't understand.'

'Jean, the person who wrote the message, was my great-grandmother and she worked at the Singer factory. And Donald, who was my great-grandfather, worked there too, in the foundry. In 1911 there was a massive strike and almost everyone stopped work and walked out of the gates. About twelve thousand folk. You can't imagine that happening today, but it did. It was before many people were in unions and it was one of the first big strikes anywhere.'

'Singer must have wondered what had hit them.'

'I imagine so. They responded by locking the gates to keep everyone out.'

'Big business taking charge?'

'I think so. After two weeks, the strike was still holding, so the company sent out postcards to all the workers, saying that if six thousand men and women said they wanted to return then the gates would be unlocked. By that time people were hungry, and they had rent to pay. So after three weeks on strike, they went back to work.'

'And then?'

'Some activists found that they were no longer needed. Their departments were restructured or there was some other imaginary reason for getting rid of those people who were identified as troublemakers. My great-grandfather was one of the strike organisers. So there they were, Jean and Donald, not even married yet and with only one job between them, and quite possibly with that one hanging on a shoogly peg as well.'

'What did they do?'

'Jean left her job and they moved through to Leith to find work. They lived a few streets away from here, actually.'

'A happy ending then?'

'I wish. Jean's father never spoke to her again and died a few years later. And then Donald volunteered in 1915 and was badly injured in France. He lost an arm.'

Fred doesn't know what to say.

Ellen leaned forward to look again at the thin strip of paper. 'He survived but times were hard, and from what my parents tell me, he probably had shell shock as well. Jean was working in the rubber company making Wellington boots by then but when the war was over and the men came home, they wanted their jobs back, and she was laid off.'

'I think that happened a lot. What did she do?'

'They had moved by then. She went to work in a bakery and Donald stayed at home and looked after their children.' Ellen stands up and walks across the studio, and takes four small frames down from the wall behind her desk. 'You probably haven't noticed these.' She sets them down on the table one on top of another in front of him, in a stack. 'The first two are their strike postcards from the factory. There was a part that had to be returned to say you wanted to come back to work.'

He lifts up the first two frames one at a time, and studies them, reading the words on the card.

'It's still there on this one.'

'Donald never sent it back. We don't know why it's missing from Jean's. In fact, we didn't even know these existed until after she died.'

'So how come you have them now?'

'Ah, that's a story in itself. You're not alone in the family mystery department. They lived in a flat in Marchmont that was owned by a Trust, and that Trust provided, no, still provides, tenancies for ex-servicemen and women. Once people move in, they stay a long time. Great-Granny Jean lived there from 1917 until she died in 1980.'

'That's a long time to live in one place... sixty-three years?'

'Isn't it?' Ellen looks down at the framed postcards. 'And, then, about six years ago, a letter arrived at the flat completely out of the blue. There was an old stamp on it and, thankfully, some kind soul in Royal Mail delivered it. The present tenant recognised who it was for and sent it on to the head office of the Trust, and then they tracked us down and returned it.'

'Serendipity.'

'You could say that, yes. The postcards were inside a really battered old envelope, and someone had put everything inside another one to keep them safe. If that hadn't been done, I doubt we would have them now.' She reaches up to untie her headscarf, and runs her hands through her hair. 'It arrived just after I was made redundant from my boring office job. I started to read up about the strike, and I plotted out the family tree. And then one day I was going down Leith Walk and there was an old sewing machine lying on the pavement with some household clearance rubbish, waiting to be picked up by the bin men. I lugged it home and borrowed my dad's screwdrivers and I took it apart. Every last screw and nut.'

He looks around the room at the displays of jewellery. 'And the rest is history.'

'Sort of. I went to an evening class in basic silversmithing and well... that took me to here.'

'So your work is some sort of political statement, then?'

'Yes and no. I'm often asked if I'm settling a score and it's not that at all. Even though I never met them, what my great-grandparents went through – the strike, the new start, the war injury – well, it inspires me to make the best of everything and take chances. I'm sure they would be horrified if they thought I was doing this because of a grudge.'

'I still don't really understand.'

'You want me to do the Creative Arts Funding pitch?'

'If it'll help.'

'The one-line version is: "I make art that represents the waveform of worked experience using old sewing machines as my source material."'

'You lost me at waveform.'

'Unfortunately, if you want funding, you need to have a one-line pitch, and that one seems to work. Do you want to hear the expanded version?'

'Go on then.'

She picks up a bobbin from the bench, holds it out between finger and thumb, and hands it to him. 'The sewing machine has provided work in manufacture, eased work in the home and facilitated work when there was none to be had. By designing with the individual components of a discarded machine, I connect with the hands of the workers who built it in the factory, and with the people who used it in the home. In doing this I acknowledge those whose experience and determination paved the way for the working lives we have now.'

Fred looks at the bobbin lying in the palm of his hand for a moment. 'You know, that's very impressive.'

'Thank you.' She bows.

'So, if we go back to the notebooks for a minute. You and me, we are sort of related.'

'Not related, exactly, but certainly connected.'

'Families are strange, aren't they?'

'Tell me about it. You haven't met my brothers yet.'

He looks back at the two remaining frames. 'And these?'

'Those are the envelopes. If I took the one with Jean's writing on it out of the frame, you'd find it smells of old-lady make-up.'

Fred studies these scraps of her family history, feeling rather honoured to be trusted with them. The old envelope looks quite battered, with faded writing and scuffed corners. He puts it aside and lifts the fourth frame, which is lying upside down on the bench.

'I kept that too, because it's part of the story. It's the one that was delivered by the postman. It arrived with everything inside it.'

He turns it over, expecting something quite ordinary. His mother's unmistakeable bold script and quirky capital letters leap off the paper at him.

Ellen is folding the headscarf up into a neat square and doesn't see the confusion on his face. 'So, Fred, have you decided?'

He is lost in a swirl of unspoken questions and only half hears her. 'Sorry, what did you say?'

'I asked if you have decided? About your other family, I mean?'

'I think so,' he replies, thankful for the distraction.

'What are you going to do?'

He sets the frame back down on the bench.

'It feels as though every time I think I have it all worked out, something else happens,' he pauses for a moment, 'but I'm sure about that particular decision, at least.' He starts to organise the notebooks, checking the dates inside each one. 'I'm not going to do anything.'

She watches him become engrossed in the task and doesn't interrupt. When he is finished, and the colourful fan of papers is arranged to his satisfaction, he looks up at her. 'Those other people aren't important to me at all because I *have* grandparents. Their names are Alfred and Constance Morrison. I don't need any others.'

Ellen walks around the workbench and gives him a hug. 'I think you're right.'

As he leans down to kiss her for the first time, there is a loud knock at the door and a broad-shouldered man with sandy-salt hair walks into the workshop without waiting for an answer.

'You forgot your lunch, Ellen, so I thought I'd bring—' He breaks off.

'Dad!'

'Sorry, I didn't know you had a visitor.'

'I've told you before, I might be with a client, you can't just walk in.'

The two men look at each other.

It's Fred who breaks the awkward silence. 'We haven't been introduced, but I've had the pleasure of enjoying your sandwiches with Ellen.' He holds out his hand. 'Fred Morrison.'

The man doesn't hesitate. 'Ellen has mentioned your name a few times.' He shakes Fred's hand with a confidence inherited from his father, and his grandfather. 'I'm Don Cameron, and I'm very pleased to meet you.'

Acknowledgements

Many people have helped to move this project from the first half-idea to the finished novel you have in your hands.

I have made numerous phone calls to all sorts of organisations, and sent countless emails to others. Without exception, the people I have contacted have been enthusiastic and offered a great deal of historical and technical advice.

Thank you to the staff at Clydebank Library and the Singer Museum, who allowed me to look at their public archive of photographs and documents. There is also an excellent film of the Singer factory on the National Library of Scotland website, entitled *Birth of a Sewing Machine*. It can be found here: http://movingimage.nls.uk/film/1592

Thank you to the staff at Lothian Health Service Archive and, in particular, to Alice Doyle, who looked up all sorts of obscure facts for me.

The Scottish Veterans Garden City Association offer housing to injured veterans, and they have a small row of houses in a village near to my home. I would like to thank Ann Hamilton from the SVGCA, who provided lots of information about the work of the association, which has found its way into the nooks and crannies of my story.

Jessica Howarth, a designer in Leith, who uses both textiles and enamel in her jewellery creations, generously offered to show me around her studio and explain the processes to me.

I would like to thank Lesley Scott, from the Royal Botanic Gardens, Edinburgh, who provided information on the long-term storage of seeds and papers.

Thank you to the staff of Fountainbridge Library in Edinburgh, who showed me archive material about the area, and also about the library itself – it's a marvellous building.

Thank you to Scott Pack, from Unbound, who said 'Yes' to my pitch, and to Xander Cansell, who has guided me through the publishing labyrinth. I have benefited from the editing expertise of Celine Kelly, Leena Lane and Annabel Wright, as well as the patient assistance of Molly Powell.

No book is complete without a cover, and Mark Ecob has produced an amazing design and included me at every stage of it. Thank you, Mark.

I would like to thank Ann Carrier, Mary Whitehouse and Debbie Tomkies, who read the manuscript in the early stages and again when it was almost finished. Their input was invaluable.

I want to offer my thanks to Claire Askew and the team behind the women's writing courses known as 'Write Like a Grrrl', who gave me the confidence to keep going.

Thank you to everyone who has supported me by pledging, listening, providing information and being enthusiastic. I couldn't have done it without you.

Thank you to my mum, Sarah Sandow, who has sewed far more exotic garments than I will ever make.

Last, but by no means least, thank you to my husband, Gavin, who told me all this was possible, and made me believe it.

Patrons

Kersti Anear-Sämann
Tim Atkinson
John Auckland
Brian Bilston
Dianne Blackett
Ray Blake
Kayleigh Bohan
Mandy Brimble
Anne Brooker
Caroline Brown
Ruth Butterworth
Ruth Churchman
Freyalyn Close-Hainsworth
Jacky Cooper
Becci Davis
Will Dean
sharon Dennett
Mary Donaldson
Jackie Donovan
Julia Duffield
Susan Eiseman Levitin
Sharon Etheridge
SJ Farrell
Fubsy
Nan Gibbons
Rachel Gibbs
Alison Gibson
Sandra Grimes
Julie Hall
Susan Hanlon
Claire Hardie
Lucy Harkins
Maddie Harvey
Katherine Hegarty
Cecilia Hewett
Pamela Hilton
Kaye Hudson

Ollie Hulme
Claire Jaffe-Beer
Sam Johnstone
Dorothy Jones
Lazy Katy
Jonatha Kottler
Sarah Lambert
Joshua LaPorte
Marie Leadbetter
Janet Lees
Elizabeth Lloyd
Ruth Macfarlane
Denise Macfarlane
Sue Margolis
Helen Matthews
SarahLouise McDonald
Stephen McGowan
Karyn McMurray
Virginia Moffatt
John Munro
Aimée Nicholson
Julie Odell
Debbie Orr
Vicky Osborne
Fleur Parker
Marie Philip
Rebecca Prentice
Katherine Pungitore
Lucy Ribchester
Christelle Riguer
Amy Roberts
Lindsay Roberts
Janey Robinson
Riccardo Sartori
Cathy Scott
Anne Scott
Jill Shaw
Sarah Shaw
Kirstyn Smith
Dori Smith
Clare Stevens

Janet Taylor
Terri Tester
H A Topping
Andrea Topping
Solitaire Townsend
Julia Tratt
Ruth Turner
Val
Anna Louise Walker
Margaret Walker
Louise Walters
Karen Wanke
Annabel Wardrop
Rose Marie Weerdenburg
Fiona Whiteside
Cat Widdowson
Maureen Wilkins
Richard Williams
Judy Wilmot
Alexandra Wingate
Rebecca Wright